LONGARM AMBUSHED!

He was cutting back across that same weed-grown lot when a voice behind him yelled, "Longarm! Hit the dirt!"

So he did, and not too soon, judging from all the gunshots he could hear as he rolled sideways, crushing green tumbleweeds as he got out his own gun and put some space between where he'd landed and where he wanted to be when and if someone tried to send a bullet up his ass through the hardly bullet-proof screen of knee-high greenery. . . .

TABOR EVANS

LONGARM

AND THE
LONE STAR CAPTIVE

JOVE BOOKS, NEW YORK

LONGARM AND THE LONE STAR CAPTIVE

A Jove Book / published by arrangement with
the author

PRINTING HISTORY
Jove edition / August 1991

ISBN: 0-515-10646-1

Jove Books are published by The Berkley Publishing Group,
200 Madison Avenue, New York, New York 10016.
The name "JOVE" and the "J" logo
are trademarks belonging to Jove Publications, Inc.

PRINTED IN THE UNITED STATES OF AMERICA

10 9 8 7 6 5 4 3 2 1

★

Chapter 1

The night train down from London Town had been delayed by an awesome summer fog. But time nor tide wait for no man, and the tides of Southampton were awesome in their own right. So the *Royal Mail* bound for the States had already cast off, and the Steam Schooner *Travis* of the Starbuck Line was fixing to follow suit when it was hailed from the pea soup ashore by one of those prissy dudes they manufactured in fancy British boarding schools.

He came up the gangway wearing an Inverness cape, a deerstalker cap, and a worried expression. When the ship's purser barred further progress, he explained he was Sir Cecil from the Foreign Office, and that the bloody bastards aboard the ruddy *Royal Mail* had lit out for the City of Washington without the state present Her Majesty had commissioned as a special gesture of friendship. It had to be in Washington in time for the Fourth of July. He added, "They just told us at the Crown and Anchor you lot would be putting in just downstream from Washington, eh, what?"

The American purser answered, "No seagoing vessels put in within miles of Washington Town itself. We might have been able to work something out with a steam lighter for you, had you got here more sensible. But we're fixing to cast off the moment one of your steam tugs gets here to carry us over the bar in this infernal fog. So, if you'd be kind enough to clear that gangway . . ."

1

Then a somewhat older voice of far more authority cut in to ask just where, and how big, this present from Queen Victoria might be. The crusty American skipper added, "My grandaddy fit 'em at Saratoga and my daddy fit 'em at New Orleans, but I was brung up to admire a good loser."

Before anyone could answer, the fog was rent by the shrill penny whistle of their steam tug, coming alongside starboard. The purser knew it was not his place to warn the skipper how wildly the tides might ebb and flow in these waters. The skipper was supposed to know. He did. When the Englishman assured them they were talking about an oaken office desk, well crated and properly tagged, the skipper told the purser, "Swing her aboard and we'll carry her as deck cargo with them other last-minute crates the boss lady ordered off that fancy china shop in London Town."

Then he was gone, to see about making fast on the far side to that tooting tug. So the purser bawled for some deckhands and then, turning back to Sir Cedric, said, "Be best if we had someone waiting on your queen's fool present once we get there. Things are ever sort of confusing on the docks and seeing they was expecting to meet your *Royal Mail* . . ."

Sir Cedric brightened and said, "We can alert our own lot in your Washington by way of that new transatlantic cable. Save us all the bother of filling out bills of lading."

The deck shuddered under them as the tug thudded snugly against the far side of the hull. The purser nodded curtly, and ordered his visitor and a couple of deckhands ashore to sling the damned desk and swing it on board while there was still time. That was how Queen Victoria's presentation desk, addressed to President Rutherford B. Hayes of Washington, D.C., wound up on its way to Washington on the Brazos, Texas, lashed to ringbolts on the forward deck.

Things got even sillier when the *Travis* hit heavy weather off the Florida Keys. The ringbolts held, but the address tags and chalk marks were all washed away, and it was a good thing the purser knew the Lime Juicers wanted that crate delivered to somebody important up the Brazos in old Washington Town.

And so it came to pass that a good week or more after the Glorious Fourth, Deputy U.S. Marshal Custis Long of the Denver District Court was inhaling deviled eggs and needled beer at the Parthenon Saloon when a runner came in from the nearby Federal Building to tell the tall tanned

2

lawman, "Longarm, they want you at your office, *poco tiempo* or sooner!"

To which Longarm could only reply with an innocent glance at the wall clock above the free lunch counter, "I ain't overstayed my damn lunch hour. I got ten minutes and a dozen eggs to go after a mighty tedious morning in court."

The runner insisted, "You're off that murder trial. Your boss says Deputy Guilfoyle can guard a murderer good as anyone else and that this one's right up your alley. So I ain't supposed to come back without you if I value my life, hear?"

Longarm glanced at the clock again, washed down that last mouthful with the last of the beer, and reluctantly placed the empty schooner on the bar to amble out into the clear thin sunshine of the Mile High City after Billy Vail's desperate messenger. Most any chore had to be more interesting than riding herd on a poor asshole who shot Indian agents in the back in front of white witnesses. But Longarm hoped his boss wasn't planning on sending him out of town, with that Sunday-go-to-Meeting-on-the-green coming up. For he'd been invited by a mighty buxom alto of the First Congregational Choir, and the prairie was just getting right for romantic reclinings that didn't leave grass stains on a sweet little thing's unmentionables.

They passed other sweet young things in the marble hallways of the Denver Federal Building, and some of them smiled at Longarm before he'd made it to the oaken door with UNITED STATES MARSHAL, FIRST DISTRICT COURT OF COLORADO inscribed across it in gold leaf. But once you got inside you found yourself in a reception room inhabited by no more than a tall skinny kid and his typewriter. Longarm nodded and asked, "What's up, Henry?" only to be told, in a breathless tone, "Trouble so deep they won't even tell *me*. Go right on in!"

Longarm did, to find Marshal Billy Vail's oak-paneled inner office filled floor to ceiling with pungent blue cigar smoke, through which his older, shorter, and stubbier boss was pacing back and forth instead of lurking, as usual, behind his big desk by the window. When he spied Longarm looming nearby in the blue mist, Vail pointed a cigar stub at him accusingly. "They asked for you by name, dad blast your roving eyes! I thought I warned you and that sassy Jessica Starbuck to be discreet. So how come even the fucking State Department knows you two have been—"

"Watch it, Billy Vail!" Longarm told him. Billy Vail stopped speaking. When Longarm saw he wasn't going to have to throw his badge in the older man's red face after all, he reached for a three-for-a-nickel cheroot to smoke in self-defense as he suggested, more mildly, "Why don't you take a deep breath and try to tell me, decently, what they think me and the boss lady of Starbuck Enterprises may have been up to. Might she and that half-breed *segundo* of hers been at any of that Lone Star bullshit we've both warned her about, Boss? I confess I ain't seen neither of 'em for a wistful time."

Vail moved around to the back of his desk to rummage atop it for something. So Longarm sank easily into a leather-covered chair on his side of the desk, figuring he was in for a considerable story.

He was. Vail gave up searching for the exact figures on paper as he asked, impatiently, "Did you ever hear tell of the ill-fated Franklin Expedition back around '45?"

Longarm nodded. "I was just fixing to get born in West-by-God-Virginia when them poor Lime Juicers all got froze to death up near the North Pole. We got taught about the famous Franklin Expedition in grammar school, though. Seems everyone kept looking for 'em, all over the Arctic, for a coon's age. Wasn't it some Americans as found what was left of Sir John Franklin and his boys in the end?"

Vail nodded grimly and growled, "No. Back in '71 our Charles Hall aboard the U.S.S. *Polaris* found some odds and ends of the Franklin Expedition near Thank God Bay before he froze to death himself, or got poisoned by his crew, take your pick."

Longarm grimaced impatiently. "It's starting to come back to me. I read the *National Geographic* now and again in waiting rooms. But what in thunder could ill-fated Arctic expeditions have to do with ladies running cattle and business empires in the warmer parts of today's world, Boss?"

"I'd get to it more sudden if you'd shut up and listen tight," Vail grumbled. "The problem ain't that simple, even before one gets to crazy young gals who ride all over creation with Japanese throwing-stars and even crazier sammy-boys!"

Longarm chuckled fondly. "Her *segundo*, Ki, is only half Jap, and I think they call gents of his mother's class *samurai*."

Vail grimaced. "Whatever. I ain't got to *them* yet. First you got to grasp how Sir John Franklin led two ships and close to a hundred

4

and thirty men to their frozen doom. Like I said, bits and pieces and educated guesses lead one to conclude they got froze in solid, tried to march out across the pack ice, and that was that, with no survivors. I told you how Hall found scraps of evidence showing Franklin and his men made a run for it and never made it. Before that a British rescue operation led by an asshole called Belcher set out with five steam-sailers, among which was the sturdy H.M.S. *Resolute*."

Longarm brightened. "Oh, I remember the loss of the *Resolute*. It was in the papers just before the war."

"More like five years before, you mean. Edward Belcher was court-martialed and barely managed to stay outta prison for losing four outta five ships when *they* got iced in. He ordered all his men aboard one vessel and abandoned the others in the mistaken notion they'd be going down any minute. The ships were sound and the spring thaw was near. Sixteen months later some Yankee whalers found H.M.S. *Resolute* floating free, far from where Belcher had abandoned her. They put a salvage crew aboard and sailed her back to Connecticut around Christmas '55."

Longarm nodded and asked about the other three abandoned vessels. Vail shrugged. "They were never seen again. Maybe Belcher was right about 'em. The point is that H.M.S. *Resolute* was bought off them whalers by our federal government for a considerable prize award, refitted, and returned to the Royal Navy. She continued in service up to just last winter, when they decided further repairs were just throwing good money after shipworms and busted her up for salvage. Her hardware and even some of her timbers were still sound."

"Billy, you said all this had something to do with friends of mine, down Texas way," Longarm protested, only to be told to just hush. Vail went on. "Queen Victoria's not only fat as your average elephant, she prides herself on the same powers of memory. So as soon as she heard they were scrapping a gift from the American government, she ordered 'em to make something nice for the Americans out of the old ship's well-seasoned oak. They came up with a big Presidential desk, six feet long by four feet wide, all fancy-carved with Presidential seals and such. British spies must have told 'em President Hayes has grown displeased with the gloomy office Lincoln, Johnson, and Grant were using before him. His Lemonade Lucy picked out an oval guest room with more windows just down the hall, and that big oak desk from

5

Queen Victoria was designed with the dimensions of the new oval office in mind, see?"

Longarm frowned sincerely. "Nope. I'm sure the President will be mighty pleased with his new desk in a new office, but what in thunder could all that diplomatic crap have to do with me or anyone I know well enough to howdy?"

Vail said, "Queen Victoria's gift to President Hayes was put aboard one of Jessie Starbuck's trading vessels by a lame-brained British official who likely got his job through family influence and now wishes he hadn't. He cabled the British Embassy in Washington, the one in the District of Columbia, and they naturally had another sissy waiting on the docks of Alexandria, Virginia—for what I understand to have been a desperately long time before they decided the steam schooner bringing their queen's gift must have sunk. Take my word on the paper-flapping that followed, and suffice it to say, we just found out what happened. The asshole in England sent the crate to Washington on the Brazos, the original capital of the Republic of Texas."

Longarm had to laugh. "Since they moved the state capital to Austin, Washington on the Brazos has reverted to a dinky settlement of, say, three hundred souls tops, on a Saturday night!"

"I just said that," Vail told him. "In its day, as *you* just said, Washington on the Brazos was more important, and they got a plaque on the 'dobe where the first Texas Legislature used to meet. One of its members being Jessie Starbuck's father, and with her still owning the cotton gin and feed store there, the damn fools aboard her schooner sent that crate on up the Brazos, care of *her*. Seems they recalled chalk marks addressed, sort of vaguely, to something like a capitol building in Washington Town, in care of whoever might be in charge."

"But Jessie don't own that old 'dobe capitol building in that dinky town, Boss."

To which Vail replied, with a weary sigh, "I'm sure somebody told 'em, after they'd pounded on the padlocked door a spell. You can't even enjoy a look-see inside without a permit from the State Historic Society. In the end they got someone spitting and whittling near the landing to sign for the damned old crate in Jessie Starbuck's name, since everyone agreed nobody *else* in town was important enough to be getting gifts from Queen Victoria."

Longarm smiled thinly and glanced about for some evidence of an ashtray. "I'm surprised neither Jessie nor her *segundo*, Ki, wired the British Consulate in Galveston for further instructions as soon as such unrequested merchandise got delivered out to her Circle Star."

Vail grimaced. "It was never delivered, and even if it had been, neither Jessie nor Ki would have been yonder to notice. I told you things were confused as well as delicate. The waterfront loafer who signed for the delivery in Jessica Starbuck's name seems to be a total stranger to anyone we can get in touch with on the payroll of Starbuck Enterprises. Nobody in Washington on the Brazos can say who he might have been, or where he went with that big crate once he'd had some Mex kids load it aboard a dray for him later that evening."

Longarm whistled softly. "Jessie or Ki would know for sure."

To which Billy Vail replied, friendly as a snapping turtle with a bellyache, "That's where *you* come in. They want you to find the lady known as Lone Star and just ask her whether a new hand or a brass-balled sneak thief signed for a gift nobody ever intended for her. Then either way, they want you to get the damned desk back and see it's delivered intact to the President's new oval office."

Longarm had often remarked on the lack of ashtrays or even spittoons on his side of the desk. But since nobody seemed to listen, he just flicked ash on the rug, as usual, and calmly inquired, "Wouldn't Jessie be close to home at her Circle Star this time of the year? With the winter grazing done and high summer coming on, she'll want to make sure they shift her herd to higher range and shorter grass while there's still some green to it."

His superior glowered at the fresh tobacco ash near Longarm's big old stovepipe boots, but stuck to more important matters. "If Jessica Starbuck or anyone else we could ask was anywhere near her usual haunts, we wouldn't be having this dumb conversation. She's got her mostly Mex or Oriental help too well trained to gossip about her comings and goings, but as well as us feds and the Texas Rangers can put things together, our Jessie's at it again with steel stars in her hatband and that crazy Jap sammy-boy tagging along after her on the trail of some mighty unfortunate cow thieves. Seems the Circle Star herd tallied short in the recent spring roundup and so, the price of beef being higher than usual this year . . ."

"I wish Jessie wouldn't do that," Longarm said with a sigh and some more ash on the rug. "It was one thing after some crooks had murdered her father and set out to wrest his business holdings from

7

his only child and sole heir. But dammit, betwixt me and her and that lethal *samurai* she inherited from old Alex Starbuck, half the crooks out our way and every damn one of her original enemies wound up dead or doing hard time for the foreseeable future."

"Mayhaps she considers anyone who'd steal her stock with the market rising a *new* enemy," Vail suggested. "At any rate, as seems to be her usual wont, she lit out from the Circle Star all gussied up in her Lone Star outfit, and as you must have noticed by now, neither she nor her sammy-boy go in for making human contact or even leaving an easy trail for anyone else to follow when they're on the trail of outlaws. So what are you waiting for, a kiss good-bye?"

Longarm scowled. "You ain't my type. Wouldn't it make more sense for me to start by trying to cut the trail of that heavy dray out of Washington on the Brazos? To begin with, the hombre who left town with it has to be closer to that missing furniture."

"We got the Texas Rangers working on that," Vail answered. "They were starting closer to begin with. They're working with the name the rascal gave as well as a good description of him, the crate, and even the mules hauling it outta town in the general direction of the Circle Star. They lost his trail on the well-traveled wagon trace to the west. Asking nesters along the trail whether or not they recall a wagon rolling by any number of days ago is like asking one of the gals at the Silver Dollar how many times they got whistled at the last time the herd was in town."

Longarm said he still wanted a handle on any names the cuss might answer to, as well as what he looked like. So Vail said, "I got young Henry typing as total a dossier as we got, along with your travel orders and such. Pick 'em up on your way out, and for Pete's sake don't go charging any more honeymoon suites to the federal government if and when you catch up with the pretty little thing."

"God damn it, Billy . . ." Longarm began, as he rose to his sometimes ominous height.

Vail quickly smiled. "Just joshing, old son. I'd as soon not know just what you and little Jessie get into when you're out back with the corn-silk cigarettes and French postcards. Seems like only yesterday I was young as you and bouncing that adorable baby on my knee, and now she's taken to killing other naughty kids with a man-sized double-action or them shitty-kids from far-off Japan."

Longarm soberly explained, "I think they call those throwing-stars *shurikens*. She says Jap hired guns called *ninjas* invented 'em to kill silently, and sometimes she likes to do that when she's in one of her Lone Star moods. You're right about the tricks she knows to throw folks off her trail. She told me one time that, growing up, her daddy let her play with Comanche when she wasn't playing with his *ninja* help. So rather than try to cut our Jessie's trail, I'd best see if I can get on the trail of the jaspers that stole her beef. If they're lucky, I'll catch up with 'em first and then, when Jessie and Ki come along—"

"It won't work." Vail said, interrupting. "Her vaqueros had no notion which way her cows had been driven when they reported 'em missing. Some Rangers I regard as fair trackers tell me they were unable to cut the trail of either Jessie's stock or Jessie. Texas gets that way, once the range bakes firm and the grass sun-cures springy as broom straw."

Longarm snorted in disgust, and rose to leave the inner office. "Jesus H. Christ, I just said Jessie learned tracking tricks off Comanche!"

Soon after, he left the outer office with a springy step, as well as the typed notes he'd grabbed from Henry. It wouldn't be *his* fault if he busted hell out of some sensible resolutions he and the lady known as Lone Star had agreed to the last time they'd parted. For the shapely honey blonde they had him tracking in the line of duty made that buxom little thing he'd been planning to grass-stain look like a sack of potatoes as soon as a man compared the two of 'em in his dirty mind.

And so it came to pass that less than an hour later, in another part of Denver, a sneak who'd been posted near the Union Depot was whispering in a gloomy hotel room to an even gloomier older man, "You was right, Boss. Longarm just left for Texas on the afternoon southbound. That pesky Lone Star must have sent for him again, as we feared she might!"

To which the older and wiser one replied, "There was never any doubt in *this* child's mind. But don't worry. With any luck he'll never make it past Pueblo alive."

★

Chapter 2

Despite what anyone else might think, the lady known as Lone Star had no idea Longarm was headed in her general direction as she dismounted out front to stride toward a side entrance of the sprawling state capitol complex in Austin. Despite the way Billy Vail and even Longarm might have pictured her that afternoon, such weaponry as she was packing was concealed by the fashionable whipcord riding habit she had on, suitable for the sidesaddle on the Tennessee Walker she'd just tethered behind her.

She'd left the Stetson she wore out on the range with her six-gun rig at the hotel, and had her long gold locks pinned up fashionably for a straw summer boater to perch atop, partly secured from sudden gusts by the veil of silk Chantilly lace covering her face as far down as the tip of her pert nose.

To say Jessica Starbuck was traveling in disguise might have been overstating the case. Anyone who knew her well would have had no trouble recognizing her up close. On the other hand, she didn't want to advertise this visit to the state brand inspector's office, and even if she had, Austin was getting so sissified that most folks stared and some even gasped at a grown gal riding astride as well as mannishly dressed in a Stetson, work shirt, split skirts, and such. She suspected the crusty old gent she was calling on might be one of those spoilsports who'd voted for womenkind to ride sidesaddle as soon as he'd noticed how many young gals liked to ride astride at a trot. She and her *segundo* hadn't come in to

10

Austin to shock anyone needlessly. They just needed information that ought to be on paper in one infernal file or another. For as Longarm had observed that very day, Jessica Starbuck had been trained to track by Comanche and Caddo, and the first thing her Indian teachers had taught her was that hound dogs followed a trail by sniffing the dust like some old piss-ant moving along a kitchen baseboard, while human trackers, having duller noses and smarter heads, tracked by paying more attention to where their quarry might be *headed* than where it might have *been*.

But finding the office she was searching for amid the dark dusty corridors soon became a chore. Texas kept jawing about the fine granite statehouse they were fixing to put up any day now. They kept talking about damming the brawling Texas Colorado out front as well. Meanwhile the centrally located but otherwise makeshift sprawl got sun-dried and flooded, monotonously, year after Texas year. The corridors were dry, but smelled of mildew left over from the usual spring flooding as her heels clicked along the Spanish tiles, her spurs ringing just a bit more vaquero than one might have expected under such ladylike riding skirts. She finally found the door she'd been searching for and went in. She knew the old cuss seated at a rolltop desk near a far window. His drab though shapely enough receptionist, seated just inside the door, asked who Lone Star was and what she might want, in a voice just a hair to the polite side of venomous.

Lone Star was used to having that effect on plainer women of the Texican persuasion. Plain or fancy, Texas gals were raised to be as truthful as common sense and personal safety warranted. Lone Star hadn't ridden all this way for a hair-pulling contest with a poor little drab who'd obviously been behind the door when the looks had been passed out. So she simply smiled sweetly, identified herself as Jessica Starbuck of the Circle Star spread, and asked if by any chance her "Uncle Caleb" might be about.

Now as everyone there knew, unless they were blind, Caleb Krinke was the burly old Dutchman staring her way from that rolltop by the window. He still stared thunderstruck as he rose to his feet, declaring, "Great balls of fire, could that really be little Jessie Starbuck standing yonder on my very doorsill, a woman growed even grander than that there Princess of Wales from Copenhagen Town?"

"I ate my vegetables and drank my milk, Uncle Caleb," his visitor replied with a gracious smile as the receptionist sniffed and

11

muttered, half to herself, "Princess Alexandra may think she's the bee's knees too, but they say she's over thirty and owes all that red hair to modern chemistry."

"Takes one to know one," murmured Lone Star, sweetly, before she swept by the receptionist's desk, rather grandly, to let old Caleb bestow a gallant kiss on the back of one gloved hand. Then, since the shapely snip behind her no doubt deserved it, Lone Star flustered all concerned by planting a daughterly kiss smack on the old man's cheek and hanging on to both his big rawboned hands as she confided, "I need help with a road brand, and my late father always said that if you didn't have a brand in your amazing head it has never been recorded on paper west of the Big Muddy, Uncle Caleb."

To which Caleb Krinke could only modestly reply, being Texas-bred despite his Dutch ancestry, "I've been known to show confusion about herds grazing north of the Arkansas Divide or west of Apache Pass. I heard what happened to your pa, girl. Heard you was running things about as good and . . . Trail brand, you say?"

Lone Star nodded. "My tally riders figure someone throwing a community loop made off with at least a thousand head of mine just before the spring roundup. That's *beef* we're talking. We could be talking half again as much *veal*. A lot of brood stock that was branded Circle Star last fall doesn't seem to be with us as of this spring."

The snippy receptionist, as if to prove she worked there and didn't like to be ignored, piped up. "How do you know your stock wasn't stolen—or maybe it strayed—anytime since late last fall? That's the last time anyone would have made a serious tally."

Lone Star and the crusty old brand inspector exchanged knowing glances. Lone Star said nothing. Since he was supposed to be teaching the fool child, Caleb Krinke explained. "Nobody herds a thousand cows and Lord knows how many calves far enough to notice off their winter range. Not unless somebody *wants* to be noticed. The best time to run stock past honest folk without attracting notice is just about the time they'd be expecting to see stock being moved. Cow thieves like to ride in bold and cut out as much beef as they can manage just before the regular riders gather for more honest dealings."

The receptionist sniffed. "If you say so, sir. If you ask me, it sounds like an awful chance to be taking just for a few scrawny beef critters."

Nobody had asked her. Lone Star still took pity on her and said, "They know they're taking a chance. I've told my own hands not to string cow thieves up without a trial, but I can't speak for all my neighbors, and on this occasion the rascals were almost caught in the act."

Turning back to Caleb Krinke she explained, "None of my own line riders spotted the thieves or their branding fire. If they had, we might not be having this conversation. The thieves must have heard what you said about riding in and out bold. They never tried to run my Circle Star brand."

"Hard brand to run," the brand inspector observed.

To which the only child of the man who'd designed the famous brand said, "My father *wanted* a hard brand to run. It's almost impossible to think up a pattern that would hide a star inside a circle. So what they did was simply slap their own road brand next to mine, as if to show they'd paid for Circle Star beef and were herding them to market."

The plainer lady present brightened and said, "We keep separate files on trail brands. We *are* talking about those bigger and easier reading brands like those dreadful Thompson brothers use to mark the consolidated market herds they run north as contract drovers, aren't we?"

Lone Star smiled crookedly and pointed out a cow thief would have to be *loco en la cabeza* to copy the trail brands of Ben or Billy Thompson. "The rascals who helped themselves to my beef, and no doubt some other stock sharing the same open range, trail-marked with a big lazy V, open end aimed at my Circle Star as if it was meant to lead my brand away. Which it was doing, in considerable numbers, when my cows were spied a county away by young Tom Gomez, hunting strays in the chaparral for the Slash Double S."

Caleb Krinke pursed his lips thoughtfully. "That'd be the Slade spread. Ewen Slade married the daughter of Hernan Sanchez back in '43, and they lost their oldest boy in the war at Chickamauga. They're all right. Did this vaquero as rides for 'em say which way they was being druv, Miss Jessie?"

Lone Star shook her head. "He didn't loiter about long enough to notice. They were being moved up a draw, and so Tom was regarding the whole scene from higher ground when one of the Anglo flank riders waved a six-gun at him with a remark about showing him the way greaser graveyards got started. So Tom contented himself with a rude reply, and proceeded to search elsewhere for longhorns he'd been hired to worry about. You were right about all this taking place a few short days before my own riders were sent out into the mesquite to gather and tally my winter's increase. So Tom assumed the uncouth riders down in that draw were putting in an honest day's work and feeling unhappy about it. He only read things a mite more sinister after Freddy Vasquez, riding for me and asking questions in many a cantina, told him we were missing all that stock. Tom had naturally noticed my late father's famous brand, and said some of the other cows moving along that draw had worn others less familiar. So far, knock wood, we seem to be the only ones missing that much stock in our neck of the chaparral."

Old Caleb Krinke had been thinking as well as listening. Rubbing his jaw as if to determine whether he needed a shave or not, the brand inspector said, cautiously, "I only know of one outfit as uses anything like a single lazy V with no trimmings, and they don't quite work, praise the Lord. The three Grayson brother, Rafe, Jake, and Alvin, recorded their brand as Lazy Triangle. It's supposed to be a symbolic jest. The Grayson brothers pride themselves on their sense of humor. Poured coal oil all over this goat one time and set it afire on the dance floor over in Wheatsville whilst the darkies was having a big shindig."

Lone Star frowned thoughtfully and asked just where one might find such humorous gents with such a remarkable brand. Caleb Krinke looked dubious. "I told you Lazy Triangle don't work as Lazy V until and unless you run that last line, and the Graysons don't drive beef to market branded any which way. I just told you they brag on being lazy. Like most of the hardscrabble outfits over to the Hill Country west of town, they let contract drovers enjoy the long dusty chore of getting their beef up to the Kansas yards, or mayhaps Nebraska this year. The boys tell me beef's selling for two or three dollars more a head in Ogallala than Dodge."

Lone Star insisted, firmly, "I know where to get the best price for my beef, Uncle Caleb. It's other folk getting any price for it I can't abide. You say these Grayson brothers may be found in or about those limestone hills near here?"

The old man answered, grudgingly, "The Lazy Triangle's up near the headwaters of the Pedernales, just this side of Cain City. Ever'one up yonder seems to think sardonic. The Grayson home spread lies in a limestone canyon, controlling one of the bigger springs as feeds the Pedernales. Don't go up there accusing folk

14

of stock stealing unless you're certain you can prove it, Miss Jessie."

The girl who worked there chimed in. "Those hills are the haunts of trash whites, uppity nigras, and worse Indians. My parents told me, ages ago, all the Texas families of quality settled sensible on the rich flat land betwixt the Brazos and Colorado. Them as pushed on into the Hill County were, well, you know."

Lone Star smiled down sweetly and replied, "Cow folk. I'm sure your parents never would have approved of mine. They didn't have any slaves with them. And those chalky hills just across the river are only the kicked-up edge of the big rocky rug running west under that higher half of Texas. So they decided to raise beef instead of cotton. Now I'd best go see if any of my beef is sipping springwater up around a town named after Cain."

She couldn't resist adding, grimly, "That's what I'll be raising if I spy a single head of Circle Star stock up yonder." Then she started to turn for the door. But she had an even grander notion and asked the old brand inspector, "Might anyone raising beef the hard way in that Hill Country have recorded a brand that looks anything like a wagon wheel, Uncle Caleb?"

Krinke shook his head. "I was already a length ahead of you there, Miss Jessie. Your daddy must have told you about the unfortunate sharper who tried to run his Circle Star to Penny Farthing."

Lone Star nodded soberly. "I was too young to ride with my father and the boys. But they said it was a grand funeral in Fort Stockton once the gunsmoke cleared."

The drab who looked down on folks from the Hill Country looked confounded and murmured, "Penny Farthing?"

So Lone Star explained. "One of those high-stepping English bicycles with a big wheel up front and a much smaller one behind. The cow thieves Uncle Caleb just recalled registered a rather fancy brand consisting of a simple rendering of a penny farthing bicycle. By adding a hub and spokes to the simpler star enclosed by a circle—"

"I see what you mean," the other girl said, trying to remember that she disliked the more attractive and fancier-dressed Jessica Starbuck with her high-toned airs despite her West Texas address and cowgirl lore.

It got harder to dislike her as much when Caleb Krinke told his feminine helper to start going through the files for any mention of wheels on bicycles, wagons, or anything else, and Lone Star said no. "A fair hunter I know likes to say one should eat one's apples a bite at a time, Uncle Caleb. I'll take your word there's nothing like that up around the headwaters of the Pedernales. After that, neither your doubtless underpaid assistant nor I have time to consider every infernal brand betwixt here and the Eastern meat packers. The thieves have such a lead on us they could be hiding my poor cows most anywhere. But starting with what you've given me on that Lazy Triangle, and seeing it's not too far . . ."

"It's a hard overnight ride, and Miss Violet here is right about the sort of trash whites they got infesting both banks of the Pedernales, Miss Jessie."

When that didn't seem to work he tried, "You just said your ownself the cow thieves had druv your cows Lord knows where afore you missed 'em. So who's to say they ain't already been druv clean to market? You don't want to go messing with them Grayson boys over cows that could be as easily be bully beef and sausages right now, do you?"

Lone Star shook her head and said, "They haven't left cow country yet. They only had a few days' lead on us, and naturally my *segundo* wired business contacts in every sensible direction before he got around to telling me I was missing some stock."

The brand inspector started to ask a dumb question. Before he could Lone Star continued. "Friends who knew my brand were watching for it along all the usual trails and a few used more by unusual travelers. Mexican gun runners I met through a deputy marshal who ought to be ashamed of himself assure me nothing wearing my brand has been seen along the Laredo Loop down Mexico way for some time."

"We heard about what you and Longarm done to them Mex cow thieves that time," Caleb Krinke said wistfully.

But Lone Star just went on. "Indians I'm on good terms with have assured me about the Staked Plains. Nobody could have slipped that many head east across the San Antone Flats in the time they had to work with. But a sneaky series of moonlit drives, avoiding the small scattered settlements between my range north of the Big Bend and the mostly unsettled Hill Country north of San Antone and west of here, just might work. There must be hundreds of unmapped canyons with enough water and summer grazing to last 'em until they figure my boys and I have lost interest."

She wrinkled her nose under her veil and added, "They don't know the daughter of Alex Starbuck at all if they think they'll be

16

able to drive *her* stock to market, unscathed, in the foreseeable future!"

As she was leaving, she overheard the other girl remarking on the high value certain people seemed to place on scruffy calico longhorns. She couldn't have improved on old Caleb's explanation that cow folks didn't shoot thieves because they stole stock as much as to assure themselves their stock would *not* be stolen. Her *segundo* and mentor, the mysterious breed called Ki, had already warned her she could be taking the loss of her stock more seriously than the actual losses called for. The Circle Star herd, now scattered on more than one spread she'd inherited from her father, were only the foundation of the vast business empire Alex Starbuck had amassed during an ambitious but never foolish lifetime. Since his murder at the hands of business rivals, his lovely but sometimes lethal daughter had added to Starbuck Enterprises, and so she supposed that, thinking only of profit and loss, she *could* be just a tad overwrought about those fool cows.

"You can take the cowgirl away from her cows," she murmured self-mockingly as she threaded her way out of the maze of corridors, "but just don't you go taking any cows away from the cowgirl, hear?"

Then it got worse. Standing in what she felt sure was the same side entrance, blinking against the dazzling Texas sunlight, Lone Star saw neither hide nor hair of the damned horse she'd left tied to that very damned hitching post over yonder!

Stepping back into the shade, Lone Star hoisted her whipcord skirts to get at the little Harrington Richardson sixgun, chambered for .32 shorts and packed in a garter holster with its black hard-rubber grips nestled against an inner thigh as pale as sugar-pine and not much softer. For Lone Star rode sidesaddle only when she needed to seem sedate.

Holding the drawn .32 discreetly down to her side with a fold of skirt concealing it to the casual eye, Lone Star stepped out into the bright light for a more serious stare up and down the damned street. The Tennessee walker was not to be seen in any direction. She wasn't too surprised by this. It was mid-afternoon, and so nobody was lounging about to be questioned about missing horseflesh. The Texas sun was inclined to glare down at Austin even during the cooler hours of the day. It was glaring like hell at Lone Star as she crossed the street to catch such shade as there might be between there and her hotel on Congress Avenue. There

17

wasn't all that much shade on either side. Her only consolation was that the hotel was less than a quarter mile off and that she was so worked up right now, she felt she could have flapped her arms and flown after the freak of nature who'd just stolen her horse, if she'd had any notion which way to fly!

As she strode the dusty flagstone walk in the bone-dry sunlight, mad as a wet hen, Lone Star couldn't decide whether she'd just been the victim of an opportunistic horse thief or if the same villains who'd run off her beef were adding insult to injury. She knew it was just as likely some saddle tramp with an eye for horseflesh and no shame about riding sidesaddle had simply followed the natural inclinations of his kind. Thieves stole what could be stolen, and a lady who owned a heap of valuable assets just had to keep an eye on everything she damned well owned. It was getting to be quite a chore at the rate Starbuck Enterprises kept growing.

As she'd tried to explain to that stubborn Custis Long more than once, a girl hardly needed to think money-grubby once she'd been left a certain amount of money. In a world where only a few half-cracked Utopians jawed about trust-busting or extending that dumb British income tax to the citizens of a free country, it was only the first million a body had to worry about.

As her moody protector and occasional lover liked to point out, while drawing less than a thousand a year as a senior U.S. deputy, getting that first million could be a bitch, and that had no doubt been the reason those other rogues had murdered her dad and tried to rob her of her birthright. But once one *had* one's first million—and her dad had left her far more than that—the money just tended to increase like rabbits were said to in Australia, where they had no natural enemies.

A lazy heiress, just leaving a million or so in the bank at three percent interest, would be hard put to spend more than her money earned just sitting there, in a world where folks could live high on the hog on three-figure yearly incomes. As soon as one paid the least attention to investing extra *dinero*, the profits seemed to roll in faster than a body could spend them, or even give them away, without hurting herself. Lone Star gave more to worthy charities than she let on, and still had enough left over to indulge her notions of simple justice, as the rascals who'd stolen first her cows and then her horse were surely going to discover as soon as she caught up with them!

Meanwhile, as she strode along a dusty cactus fence between

the walk and the dusty peach trees of a backyard orchard, some folks seemed to be catching up to *her*, at a full gallop, whooping like drunken hands in town on a payday night.

Which was sort of odd as soon as one studied on it. So Lone Star broke stride to stand with her bustle to the cactus hedge as they tore down the street in broad daylight, nowhere near any sensible outfit's payday—and how come they were in town on a Thursday afternoon to begin with?

Thus it came to pass that as two of the three riders threw down on the lonely female figure by the roadside, Lone Star was crawfishing backwards through the cactus pads, replying in kind to their wild fusillade with her own bitty six-gun, and from the way one of them yipped as he loped on past, her aim was better!

Then she was sprawled in the backyard dust with her straw boater blown off and shredded peach leaves floating down on her like green snowflakes. They'd been lobbing more serious bullets her way, and darn it, a man could ride quite a ways with a .32 or more in him no matter where.

The back screen door of the 'dobe that went with all those peach trees opened, and a fat Mexican lady peered out with a worried expression. "For why are you sitting in our garden, señorita?"

Her own gun being on the far side of her, Lone Star felt no call to display it as she sweetly but vaguely replied she'd been thrust through the hedge by "*vaqueros rudo.*" The older woman told her to get out of her backyard anyway. So she picked up her straw boater, then herself, to do so.

Back out on the walk, she saw the dust was still settling and that all those gunshots had attracted a modest crowd of mostly kids with a few curious adults. As she sedately moved on toward her hotel, letting them figure things out for their fool selves, a more familiar figure strode up the walk to meet her.

Like his boss and erstwhile pupil in the martial arts, the tall and rather catlike Ki could appear on the scene wild or sedate as the scene called for. As *segundo* or foreman of the Circle Star, as well as bodyguard and confidant to Jessica Starbuck in or out of her Lone Star mode, Ki dressed for visits to the state capital more like an American in the cattle business than a man of action trained in the martial arts of his mother's people.

Ki's father, a friend of Alex Starbuck whom he'd never really known, had been an American adventurer in Dai Nippon just after the Black Ships of Admiral Perry had forced the Shogun to open the ports of Shimoda and Hakodate to such unwelcome visitors.

Ki's mother had been the highborn if somewhat naive daughter of a noble house, and while Ki had heard more than one version of their ill-fated elopement, he knew all too well how rough the results had been on them as well as on himself—one of the more obvious results.

He'd been considered, and treated, as a freak of nature in his mother's country. People here in his father's land seemed to take him for some sort of breed when they looked twice at his curious blend of Oriental and Anglo-Saxon features. After growing up tough, from pillar to post and for richer and poorer in his mother's class-conscious country, Ki had found Americans both more tolerant and more ignorant than his mother's people. For he'd yet to meet Nihongo who didn't identify him at a glance as an alien Gaikokujin. Dressed as he was now in Stetson and Justin boots, with a business suit between and a .45 riding under his frock coat, Ki could be accepted as a good old boy with mayhaps a tad of Caddo or Mex he might not want to talk about.

As he and Lone Star met in the shade of a cottonwood near the corner, Ki could see by the way she was packing her hat in one hand and a fistful of skirt in the other that he'd been right to worry about those recent gunshots. He nodded down at her and said, "I knew you'd ridden up this way. When I returned to the hotel from Western Union to find your Tennessee walker out front and your room key still at the front desk—"

"They stole my horse and then left it at our hotel?" Lone Star said with a puzzled frown. Then, because she was starting to think more calmly as the ringing in her ears cleared up, she made a wry face. "Right. They wanted a less shifty target than I might have presented posting sidesaddle. Lucky for me they chose the wrong wall to spatter me all over!"

As Ki spun to fall in beside her, Lone Star filled him in on the gunplay without breaking stride. He agreed someone just didn't want her on their trail, cold as it seemed to be. She said, "I may have hit one of the dastardly cow thieves. I'd know for certain had I been blazing away with that Colt Special my dear old dad gave me for my eighteenth birthday. But you know how silly a girl walks with that much gun between her legs."

Ki didn't answer. Having come of age in a land where Victorian restrictions against mentioning anything as intimate as one's legs hardly applied, he was used to Jessie's tomboy talk around a man she thought of as a rough-and-tumble older brother. They'd established, long before the budding Jessica Starbuck had been old enough to be treated as a woman, that to Ki she'd always be a genderless *damio* or feudal leader. But that was because that was the way things had to be, not because Ki was stupid or devoid of feelings. Forcing himself not to picture the phallic grips of a six-gun protruding from between naked thighs he knew all too well, although chastely, Ki softly murmured, "I'd let them have the cows if they want them that badly, Jessie. Cow thieves have a way of getting themselves hung by one outfit or another as they follow the owlhoot trail, and this bunch seems determined to get gunned or strung up sooner than usual."

Lone Star nodded grimly. "That's for sure. They had no call to threaten Tom Gomez and make certain he'd remember 'em, and that foolishness just now got at least one of 'em pinked by little old me. Now if only we can find the doc I just sent one of the rascals to . . ."

"Jessie," Ki said. "An outlaw with a flesh wound has less trouble finding a discreet sawbones than an unwed schoolmarm might have getting rid of an unwanted indiscretion. Even if we could track down some back-alley quack who'd admit he took a .32 slug out of some cowboy, we'd still be wasting a lot of valuable time. There's more to Starbuck Enterprises than a few longhorns."

"You call a thousand head or more a *few*?" she asked. "At today's beef prices we're talking *mucho dinero, segundo mio*!"

Ki answered, wearily, "Whatever. Meanwhile, that bone china you ordered from England is awaiting your pleasure in your Galveston warehouse, and I couldn't tell them whether you want the stuff out at your home spread or marked for resale, and if so, at which of the Starbuck stores."

She dimpled and replied, "Good heavens, I want it sold at a profit, of course. What on earth would I do with a ton and a half of bone china personally?"

Ki nodded. "*Hai*. I'll tell them to move those goods to your *zakka-ya*—I mean general store in Houston. That's the best chance at the most profit without having to haul the fragile load a dangerous and expensive distance. Now, about that furniture you had made for us in England . . ."

"I never did," she said with a puzzled frown. "Nobody beats our own Grand Rapids on price when it comes to cheap furniture and you know I prefer Oriental cabinetwork for joinery, or French if we're talking fancy."

Ki shrugged. "Must have been a mistake then. You'd know whether you'd ordered a heavy oak desk from London. It's just as well if you didn't. Our shipping agents in Galveston tell me there's some sort of fuss over the dumb creation. It seems it was taken aboard one of your trading vessels in Southampton at the last minute, with no proper bill of lading and some confusion as to where it was bound."

Lone Star, thinking as Jessica Starbuck, frowned indeed as that sank in. She said, "That's not the way the Starbuck Line is supposed to handle cargo. Who's the fool purser who made me look so foolish, and what are we going to do about it, Ki?"

Her saturnine *segundo* smiled thinly and replied, "He doesn't work for you anymore. You've always told me to use my own judgment, and I thought he made us look bad too. In fairness, he was expecting someone to be waiting on the Galveston docks for the crated desk when it arrived. Nobody was. So he said something about getting it up to Washington on the Brazos before he headed home to see if his sweetheart in that port still loved him. He'll find out he's been fired if and when he ever comes back. Meanwhile, it seems the crate was last seen headed for the Circle Star. A lighter took it up to Washington on the Brazos, and someone there signed for it in your name."

Lone Star insisted, "Ki, I never ordered any fool desk, oaken or pine, from any English furniture maker!"

To which he agreeably replied, "You just said that, Jessie. Meanwhile, the Rangers have been out to the Circle Star, pestering your housekeeper to no avail, because that desk has yet to arrive. And meanwhile, everyone seems to be in a big uproar over it all. Nobody working for us seems to know just what could be going on. I wired I'd check things out with you and get back to them. I got the impression it was important, Jessie."

But Lone Star just kept striding, jaw set and spur rowels ringing. "Forget that fool furniture. I said I never sent for it. So it's not my worry. My worry right now is a thousand head or more of stolen beef stock. It could be over in the Hill Country around the headwaters of the Pedernales. So that's where we're going, *poco tiempo* if not sooner, hear?"

★

Chapter 3

Longarm had boarded the southbound D&RG Limited in the full knowledge he'd be getting off all gummy-eyed at El Paso in the wee small hours of a Friday dawn. He'd nevertheless resisted the temptations of a private compartment or even a Pullman bunk. The Justice Department allowed a deputy on the move far more a mile than a coach car seat cost a thrifty traveler. Longarm's railroading pals didn't expect a friendly gunhand to buy a railroad ticket, as long as he didn't ask for trimmings. But a body asking for a rolling flop was supposed to at least *offer* the going Pullman rates, and if some spoilsport conductor took him up on it, there would go all the fun and profit of cross-country travel by rail.

They'd charged him scandalously for buffalo tongue and taters, along with rabbit grub he'd never ordered, in the dining car. As he sat out on the observation platform of the club car, smoking a cheroot and nursing a beer they'd had the nerve to charge a nickel a bitty glass for, Longarm reflected pensively on the tedious hours yet to be killed aboard this pokey passenger train. The infernal sky was still dusky rose and lavender above the inky Front Range to his left. Now and again they'd pass a High Plains' soddy with its small windows glowing a jack-o'-lantern welcome, and it was odd how all such windows made a passing stranger feel left out and homesick no matter how many times he told himself, as an experienced lawman, how many nesters beat their wives and knocked up their daughters.

There was simply something about soft window lights in the first cool shades of evening that made a body with a tumbleweed job wonder what he was doing out here in the dark when the rest of the world seemed to be nestled in snugly for the night.

It got worse when the train stopped somewhere between Pueblo and Trinidad to jerk water. Longarm knew he could have gone forward to ask where in thunder they were, if it had really mattered. Instead he sipped the last of his skimpy beer while they filled the tender tanks with boiler water from the trackside tower. Then he heard the distant tinkle of a piano and, somewhere else in the night, the laughter of some gal who just had to be young and pretty.

Then they were rolling on and he wondered, staring wistfully back at the few receding pinpoints of light, where the party had been taking place in that small prairie town, and what that gal with the pretty laugh might have thought had he joined her uninvited.

Meanwhile, the reading matter he'd picked up back at the Denver Union Depot was awaiting his perusal, unless someone had gotten into the possibles stowed under his seat in the smoking coach. So he rose and headed forward for a crack at the latest *Scientific American*. It said on the cover that Linde's compressed-ammonia refrigerator cars were likely to change the beef industry beyond human understanding, and some of it was confusing enough already.

He placed his empty glass on the bar running up one side of the overpriced club car as a woman gussied up in black lace and maroon satin shot him an odd look from her seat behind a writing table by a window. Longarm liked statuesque honey blondes no matter what color hair they might have. But he saw no way to break stride and hail her as another vessel on the sea of life without getting laughed at in the crowded club car. So he just kept going, neither slow nor fast, and she caught up with him as he was out on the dark platform between the next coach forward and the one beyond. He stopped and she sort of sobbed, "Please don't think me forward, kind sir, but I can see you are a gentleman of the old school and . . . Oh, this is all so embarrassing, unaccustomed as I am to accosting strange men on railroad trains!"

Longarm ticked the brim of his Stetson politely as he sedately assured her, "Accosting strange men at a circus must feel even more awkward, ma'am. But now that we're past that part, what can I do for you?"

She fluttered her lashes and looked shyly away as she demurely replied, "I've locked my silly self out of my compartment. I went back there to the club car in hopes they might have some lemonade, and it was only just now I realized I'd left my key in the lock on the inside of the door."

Longarm started to ask why in thunder she didn't consult the conductor or, better yet, any of the Pullman porters. Then he wondered why any man who liked gals at all would want to ask a fool question like that. So he assured her he was tolerable at opening doors, and by the time she'd led him two thirds of the way toward the baggage car, and indicated the door she wanted opened in the gloom of a forward Pullman, they'd established she was on her way to Brownsville by way of El Paso and that, while her given name was Messalina Graves, her friends all called her Messy.

He'd given her his own handle without going into what he did for a living. So as he proceeded to pick the lock of her compartment with one of the trickier blades of his pocketknife, she was inspired to ask him how often he was called upon to be so, ah, clever.

He said not often, and offered to just forget the whole deal if he was offending her. She told him not to be silly, and after a million years of wiggles and jiggles he got the confounded key out of the door inside. After that it was easy. Old George Pullman was more interested in building cushy railroad cars than bank vaults, and only used about a dozen basic key screens in his simple locks. As Longarm slid Messy's door open and spied her key on the carpeting inside by the dim light spilling in from the corridor lamps, he hunkered down gallantly to get it for her, adding something about how anxious he was to read up on railroad refrigeration. She said the least she could do, after all he'd done for her, involved the pouring of a nightcap. So that was how they wound up inside, and try as he might, he just couldn't get the wall lamp to stay lit in there.

She said she'd noticed before there was something wrong with the lamp's wick, mantle, or both, as she slid the compartment door shut, plunging them in deeper but not too depressing darkness. He wasted another waterproof Mex match in determining her lamp wick was indeed not there. She said there was moonlight enough to see by, and so he quit messing with Messy's lamp when he saw that, sure enough, she seemed able to manage two tumblers,

25

a bottle, and the tap of a built-in corner sink by the wan silver light through the soot-grimed compartment windows.

She told him to take off his hat and coat if he meant to sit a spell. He did so, hanging both on a brass hook near the window seats that turned into a bottom bunk. He adjusted his sixgun, but left it on as he sat down on the green plush by the window. Messy handed him a thick glass tumbler filled with a heroic dose of bourbon and branch water, judging by the smell, and lowered her own broader bottom to face him, riding more backwards as she raised the tumbler. "I don't like to sip anything this strong when I'm alone. They say it can lead to bad habits."

He felt for what he hoped they'd have built in if this was a standard compartment, and murmured something about hard liquor leading to all sorts of habits, good or bad, in mixed company or riding alone. Sure enough, he found the tricky fold-out table built in under the windows, and folded it out between them.

She declared she'd never. He placed his heavy tumbler on the polished hardwood and suggested, "Why don't we put the bottle and mayhaps some water on this, so we can drink more handy, Miss Messy? I'm sure you'll find a metal ewer with a pitcher spout behind that mirror over the sink. It swings open to let you at the handy shelves old George built in behind it."

She put her own tumbler next to his and jumped up to find out whether he knew what he was talking about. When she found the ewer right where he'd said it would be, she said she'd never, again, and filled it with tap water. She brought it back to the small table, along with a big square bottle of odorous bourbon, and confided, as she resumed her own seat across from him, "I knew you were a man of the world, Custis. But you know your way around this wicked world so well a girl might not be safe with you! Just what do you do when you're not picking locks and teaching me how to tend bar in the dark, you wicked thing?"

He smiled thinly. "I'm neither a burglar nor a bartender, Miss Messy, and no offense, I suspect you gals are as safe with me as you aim to be. I wish I could say I'd be riding all the way to the Gulf port of Brownsville, but as I told you earlier, I'll be getting off somewhere betwixt four and five in the cold gray dawn when this old train rumbles in to El Paso."

She didn't answer right off as they both sipped at their big drinks. Then she softly said, "That's liable to be an awkward time for us to part, no matter what we've been up to in the meanwhile."

He nodded soberly. "It might make more sense if I was to just finish this swell nightcap and leave a lady to her own devices. If you were to turn in, drunk or sober, this side of midnight, you'd likely never notice when they swap engines and such in El Paso."

She softly asked, "What about you, Custis?"

To which he could only reply, wistfully, "I have to get off there in any case. It's likely to hurt less if I've been sitting up, bored and raring to go with my boots on."

She sipped thoughtfully at her drink, and took her time before she softly asked whether he might not feel even friskier in El Paso if he got off after a few hours' sleep and, say, a washup with that running water.

He finished his drink, put the tumbler down, and covered it with his hand as she started to pour another, saying, "I'd best not, Miss Messy. I know you pretty little things enjoy killing time aboard a tedious train with harmless teasings. I can go along with the fun as long as I'm sober, but . . ."

"What made you think I was only teasing?" she said, purring deep in her throat. "If we set my alarm clock we may have time for some really fond farewells in those cool silent hours stolen from a sleeping world of less romantic souls."

He couldn't come up with any answers that might not have sounded as mushy. So he just moved the bottle, ewer, and tumblers to one side and got that small table out of the way so he could reel her in for a howdy kiss. She kissed him back with a passionate French accent, but when he started to fumble with the buttons up and down the back of her bodice she protested, "We don't have enough time for that! Don't tease me, Custis. *Do* it! Do it while we still *can*!"

So he just did it, although he insisted on getting his gun rig as well as his tweed pants half out of the way while she lay back and hoisted her fashionable skirts.

She hadn't been wearing pantaloons, and her black mesh stockings were gartered less than a third of the way up each moonlit thigh. Yet even so, she came close to missing out on the joyous occasion entirely. She managed a soft moan of pleasure as he wedged his bared hips between her soft welcoming thighs to enter her pulsating velvet gates of desire. But by the time he was coming

27

in her, as any man in his position would have soon or later, she was snoring sweet and soft. It was sort of insulting. So he never even kissed her as he milked the last of his ejaculation out in her with his last morose thrusts and then withdrew to sit up and mutter, wiping his insulted member clean with the hem of her petticoat, "I was hoping I was wrong, but I *thought* that was chloral hydrate I smelled in spite of the pungent bourbon you'd mixed it with."

Messy didn't answer. She'd served him enough knockout drops to put a man his size or more on the floor for quite some time. So he'd really knocked her galley west by switching their glasses while she'd been puttering at the sink with her back to him.

He hauled his pants back up and buckled his gun back on before he hauled her carpetbag up on the plush between them to see what other surprises she might have been planning to spring on the less wary.

By match and moonlight Longarm determined the mysterious Miss Messy packed a nickel-plated whore pistol chambered for nine rounds of .25 Hollow Point. Women didn't get asked for voters' registration cards like vagabonds in pants. But Messy had been smart enough to outfit herself with library cards from a half-dozen towns and membership in three branches of the Women's Christian Temperance Union. He chuckled fondly at the unconscious temptress as he put her papers and whore pistol, minus those mean little bullets, back where he'd found them. "I'm glad you only serve hard liquor in a good cause, little darling. I'd sure like to hear your reasons for what just transpired. But as you doubtless know, lawyers can make such a bodacious deal out of the arresting officer fornicating with a lady just before he slaps the cuffs on her."

Messy didn't answer. Longarm got to his feet, slipping on his hat and coat as he gazed wistfully down at the undignified pose she lay snoring in. Then, being a good sport as well as the winner, Longarm straightened her legs more sedately to leave her stretched out with her ankles crossed. Then he pulled her skirts down to leave her in an even more dignified state as he murmured, "You might not follow my drift if I was to leave two silver dollars on this shelf, and I'd rather spend it drinking to your memory than insulting you crude or subtle. I'm sure you'll figure what happened, once you come out of that coma meant for me."

He found her coin purse and the bottle of knockout drops in her smaller handbag by the door. He left her her money, but put the vial of chloral hydrate in his own coat pocket for the same reasons he'd emptied her whore pistol. Then he went back to his own coach seat to finish his overnight train ride in a far more tedious fashion.

It was a caution what they could do with compressed ammonia these days, according to the magazine he could barely read by the sickly oil lamp a couple of seats off. The Western beef industry, as Longarm and other Anglo-Saxons now knew it, was less than half a century old, and changing by leaps and bounds as the century progressed. Lots of folks held the buckaroo, or vaquero, was an old-time rustic chasing scrub cows hither and yon just for fun. But it was the technology of the late Victorian era that made Western beef a serious investment worth the time and considera-tion of serious business combines East as well as West. Without the railroads pushing out across the Great American Desert after the War Between the States, the state of the buckaroo's art would have progressed no further than that of ragged-ass vaquero gath-ering hides here and tallow there for marginal rancheros. Shipping whole cows—hide, tallow, and fresh juicy beef—from the West to the hungry East and beyond made the whole game worth the candle.

Given plenty of water, a little fodder, and halfway decent ship-ping weather, a cow poked aboard a railcar out this way could expect to arrive in Chicago or Cincinnati alive and well enough to slaughter and sell as fresh meat. If they got that Linde process to where a beef critter could be slaughtered in its prime, smack on its own range, and shipped any time of the year as Grade A beef . . .

"I can't let it go," Longarm decided, noticing he'd just read the same paragraph three times and didn't really give a shit about dead cows.

That gal he'd just brushed with was dangerous. There was no use telling himself a man who picked up strange women aboard the D&RG had it coming to him if she rolled him for all his *dinero* or worse. Those had been hollow points in that whore pistol, and the whore had loaded that tumbler with a mighty lethal dose as well. He'd gotten rid of some of her original serving, pretending to drink some of it before he'd been able to make the switch, and what had been left had still poleaxed a fair-sized adult in the middle of the sex act.

"What was she going to do with our mortal remains after-wards?" Longarm asked himself, half aloud, as he put his copy of *Scientific American* away and rose in the gloom to peer each way, in vain, for another figure of authority. The train was slowing. Longarm hauled out his pocket watch, consulted it, and muttered, "Right. They'll be wanting to replace the water we boiled away getting over Raton Pass back yonder."

Having his bearings, and knowing the conductor would be busy a spell with pilgrims getting on or off at the next stop, Longarm ambled on back to the club car. It was about time he had another beer in any case. As the colored barkeep served him, Longarm introduced himself and explained, "I'd like a word with your boss or, even better, any railroad dicks you might have aboard. It don't seem to be federal, but I do have some suspicions to pass on about another passenger."

The barkeep said he'd already known Longarm was the law, and added, "We got us two Pinkerton men aboard, suh. But they'll both be riding forward in the express car, with a shipment from the Denver Mint, unless Mister Abe, our train master, asks for some backing back this way."

Longarm sipped some of the cold beer, grimaced, and declared, "I'd best just pass it on and let Abe decide. I know him of old, and he likes to think it's his train."

The barkeep didn't argue. Longarm lit a cheroot to go with his beer as he stood at the bar, keeping one eye on the forward doorway.

They stopped about where Longarm had expected, on the trestle, where the crew could literally jerk water from the Ocate with buckets lowered from the tender, while mail and a handful of red-eyed passengers got on or off. Then they were on their way again, and before Longarm had to order another beer or light another smoke, the portly conductor called Abe came back to the club car to wet his own whistle after a job well done.

Longarm didn't offer to buy. He knew Abe got a better rate than himself from the D&RG. As the train rumbled south through the night Longarm said, "It's your train and your business, Abe. But I couldn't help noticing, just now, you got a lady on board in the habit of inviting young boys to her compartment and then slipping them an indecent amount of chloral hydrate."

The conductor didn't seem to get as upset as he might have. He smiled thinly and asked if they could be talking about a lady in maroon and black with honey-blond hair.

When Longarm confided they sure were, Abe nodded and said, "I was wondering about her earlier. She was ghosting up and down

30

my train like she was hoping to pick up a young boy. Only she turned down the first half-dozen offers, as if she was picky about who she might try to sting for her supper and cider sippings on her way to Texas."

Longarm frowned thoughtfully. "It's nice to feel special. She told me she was booked on through to Brownsville, on the Gulf."

Abe shook his head. "Not hardly. El Paso. I punched her ticket personal, and wondered why she'd booked a sleeping compartment, seeing she didn't figure to spend the whole night with us. I thought it even odder when she got off just now, back in Colmor on the Ocate."

Longarm blinked. "That big sneaky blonde got off at that last stop?"

To which the conductor could only reply he'd just said that. "How was I to know the law was after her, Longarm? It's a free country, and does a lady want to book a compartment to El Paso and get off less'n halfways there . . ."

Longarm ignored the burning sensation in his earlobes as he growled, "You say she turned down other offers earlier, as if she had me or someone just as nice in mind all the time?"

When Abe confirmed this Longarm grimaced. "Her intent was more serious than I first figured. Had I rolled out her compartment window in the dark, Lord knows where or when in the Sangre de Cristos I'd be found. By the buzzards in a day or more, if at all."

"She'd have got off at El Paso with a hell of a lead and none of us the wiser," Abe added. "We can wire the sheriff of Colfax County when we stop at Las Vegas, you poor half-murdered cuss."

So that was what they did, after midnight, in the vain hope Colfax County would be able to apprehend a strange female who'd left the train in pitch darkness, changed into any sort of costume, and either holed up or lit out in any direction, aboard any means of transportation. Longarm naturally requested they keep him abreast of their efforts by wire as he rode ever further from the scene of Messy's crime, or attempted crime. But when his train pulled into Albuquerque he found a message of despair waiting for him there, and when he got to Las Cruces, the night about shot, they'd informed him once again that they'd been unable to cut the trail of the mysterious Miss Messy.

So a little over an hour later, when the D&RG Limited rolled into El Paso by the oyster-gray sky-glow of a West Texas dawn,

Longarm was still working on who Messy had been, and why she'd been out to do him so dirty if it was neither his *dinero* nor his fair white body she'd been after.

Meanwhile, she'd wired down the line from Colmor—in code, of course. So a couple of far uglier figures were eagerly awaiting Longarm's arrival in El Paso. Knowing the ways of the D&RG and folks getting off half asleep in such tricky light, they'd stationed themselves near a baggage cart under the corrugated iron canopy running the length of the rear side of the depot. They were almost invisible there, as well as forted in behind that baggage cart. The younger of the two hired guns was still whining as he peered out at the passengers coming their way alongside the train, fully exposed to such light as there was from the sky. "I don't see him! Messy said he'd stood aboard that there train and that we couldn't miss him walking taller than everyone else with his Stetson crushed Colorado-style. So where could he be, and what if we miss him? They say he's good, Quirt!"

His somewhat more experienced sidekick growled, "Blow your nose and try to act full-growed, Elroy. If he got off that train as well we got nothing to worry about. The boss can't hardly chide us for not getting someone as ain't there, can he?"

The last of the passengers, an elderly couple walking arm in arm, came toward the two gunslicks through a cloud of swirling mist from the Baldwin locomotive's steam box. The one called Elroy said, "There ain't no more getting off, Quirt. What do we do now?"

Quirt shrugged and said, "Stay put a few minutes. That lawman's said to be smart, for one of *them*. He might have got off further up the line to hunt for Messy. Maybe he caught on to her usual methods. On the other hand, he could decide to get off here at the last minute. It's tough to ambush bastards as refuse to act predictable, and he might have noticed that in his time with Uncle Sam."

Longarm had. So he said from the shadows to their rear, in a surprisingly conversational tone, "I hope you boys both understand I have the drop on you. Figuring Miss Messy might have set up further surprises for me, I just rolled off the rear platform and made my way up the far side of yonder train. So now you're both going to unbuckle your gun rigs, with no sudden moves and— God damn it, that was *dumb*!"

The one called Quirt never heard those last words as he went down with a six-gun in one hand and a round of .44-40 in his brain. Longarm shouted, "Don't you dare!" as he threw down on the one called Elroy with his still-smoking double-action. But Elroy just kept running up that empty platform as if he meant to board the train, and though Longarm aimed to lame him with a round in one buttock, he could tell by the way the rascal's hat went flying that he'd nailed him through the lower spine.

By the time Longarm could get to him, Elroy had crapped and likely come in his pants. He'd bit his own tongue half off as well when Longarm rolled him over. It sure beat all how hard some men could grin and glare in the first few moments after death. But by the time a couple of uniformed roundsmen from the El Paso P.D. could join him on the platform, neither of the young owlhoot riders wore any expression on their dead faces. Their personal identification left a lot to be desired as well. But El Paso accepted Longarm's credentials as well as his story.

By this time it had dawned bright enough to make out colors. The younger one, who'd been spine-shot on the fly, was dressed cow in faded blue denim. The older one, who'd slapped leather on Longarm and died quicker, lay half on and half off the railroad platform in a dark gray shirt and pants made of shoddy and meant to be black.

Longarm and both copper badges recognized the cheap black suit of clothes they issued a gent getting out of prison after a long stint at hard. It faded to just that shade of black-eyed purple in less than six months. One of the El Paso lawmen nudged the dead man's left leg with a boot tip and opined, "He's done him some riding whilst sun-fading his start-over duds. See how much darker and shiny them pants are down the inside seams, from gripping sweaty leather where the sun don't shine?"

His partner agreed. "Shoddy wears slick and shiny like so, just before it wears through entire."

Longarm didn't say anything. But he nodded. Hardly anyone bought duds made of shoddy with his own money. Shoddy was old wool pulled apart by ragpickers to be respun and rewoven into a product that resembled virgin wool to the extent newsprint resembled bond paper, for about the same reasons.

If the man called Quirt had been sent out the gates of a state or federal prison with a new suit, a five-dollar bill, and instructions to sin no more within the last year or more, there'd be some record of it. But after that it got harder, given the number of sons of bitches getting out of prison in a given year.

By this time others who'd been attracted to the early morning gunplay were drifting out back of the depot. When Longarm spied the tin star winking at him from a fresh white shirt, he loudly announced he meant to sashay on over to Western Union and make a full report of what had just transpired to Uncle Sam. He got on better with some Texas Rangers than others. Most seemed good old boys, but others were still nursing grudges left over from Reconstruction. The proud and proddy Texas Rangers had been disbanded by the victorious army of occupation right after the war. But President Hayes had more recently rid Texas of her hated carpetbag state police and restored the Rangers to their former glory.

The one bearing down on Longarm and the other strangers he'd just shot must have been feeling glorious. He growled, "I know who you are and how important you think that makes you, Denver boy. We're still going over to Ranger headquarters and fill out a total report on this bullshit, ain't we?"

Longarm sighed and said, "Well, I was planning on heading out to Fort Bliss and borrowing me a pony and mayhaps an army mule. But I reckon I got time to admire the stock your own captain might have on hand. I can see right off he's got one swell jackass braying loud as any rooster at yonder sunrise."

★

Chapter 4

Far closer to that same sunrise than Longarm might have guessed, the man called Ki was scouting the surrounding skyline from the brushy crest of a limestone outcrop in the rugged Hill Country of Central Texas. Down below, only half hidden by dusty cottonwoods, the lady known as Lone Star was bathing her nude flesh in the tepid depths of what a geologist might have called a karst sinkhole, although the lady bathing in it, like other Texicans, would have called it a tank.

Ki had been up and about, bathed and cold-shaved, for some time. Part *samurai* caste by birth and *ninja* by early training, Ki was no more able than the mockingbirds in the surrounding chaparral to lay slugabed as even the first stars surrendered to a coming dawn. If he seemed unaware of the lovely blonde splashing about in the morning light down yonder naked as a jay, it was without any conscious desire to spare either of them an iota of embarrassment. They'd both seen one another naked more than once, and even though neither had been blind to the other's physical charms, neither had given in to either awkwardness or desire.

In Ki's case, this was simply the result of the culture he'd been raised to puberty in. The sometimes passionate people of Dai Nippon knew why boys and girls were different. That was why there were so many boys and girls in his old country. But unlike the Victorians of his father's country, Japanese were simply not as astounded nor even aroused by the mere sight of one another's genitalia. Pornographic Japanese books, and they printed a lot of them, tended to show folks in mighty odd positions, fully dressed in ceremonial robes. They knew a gent's hard-on, like a lady's old love-gash, tended to be far uglier to look at than it felt, once you could get at it. On the other hand, the notion of actually sticking it to a lady dressed formally, with her hair and rice powder just so, struck most Japanese as wild and wicked, like farting at a funeral or telling dirty jokes in church. Tearing off a piece in private with an old pal stripped of her kimono and hair lacquer seemed no big deal to a healthy young Nihon-jin who'd never been taught that anything that felt so good could be sinful. So Victorian notions of virtue would have been lost on Ki and his generation back in Dai Nippon.

He still had trouble grasping those notions after all this time in the States. Yet neither he nor his mother's people were without morals, and a Japanese who'd throw a casual screw to a willing waitress on a sudden whim would never dream of carrying on the way the current Prince of Wales was said to, behind the backs of gentlemen he played cards with.

To Ki and his kind it was less important what one did to a woman who was at all desirable than which women one was allowed to desire. Jessica Starbuck was the daughter of Ki's dead *damio* or feudal lord, the late Alex Starbuck of West Texas and the Nagasaki tea and silk docks. He'd given an outcast half-breed, denied by his American kin as well, the chance to earn his own way in this sometimes bewildering Amerika Gasshukoku. Hence the little Kojo, Jessica-San, had been as forbidden as any other princess to her father's ferocious young retainer before she'd been old enough for the matter to come to the surface.

Since she herself was in fact a proper Victorian—and a little country, before her dad had sent her East to that finishing school just in time—Jessica Starbuck's moral views, advanced for her time, would have called for more explanation had not they taught her at that finishing school to keep such advanced views to herself. They'd never found those books by Virginia Woodhull under Jessica Starbuck's mattress. She'd also been smart enough to hide her tobacco and tequila from home under the floorboards as well.

But there was more to Jessica Starbuck's sophistication than the sometimes sniggering Miss Woodhull wrote in her forbidden tomes on forbidden subjects, such as birth control and women voting.

The late Alex Starbuck had been willing to take on a half-wild kid who barely spoke English because, aside from being a decent man who'd known Ki's American father in a younger world, the Texas cattle baron and international trader had spoken fair Japanese in his own right, and already had a few Orientals on his payroll out at his Circle Star home spread.

Not unlike Ki's American father, Starbuck had seen the golden chances Admiral Perry had offered a savvy businessman by forcing the boy Shogun to open the forbidden ports of Dai Nippon to Yankee, or better yet Texas, trading vessels. Starbuck Enterprises had struck paydirt swapping Texas hides, tallow, cotton, and such for Oriental goods manufactured in or transshipped by way of Nagasaki at the southern tip of Japan, handy to Chinese and Korean ports as well. Starbuck had traded fair and treated folks decent in sunshine or in shadow, and so, unlike some other traders, he'd come through the overthrow of the shogunate and restoration of the Meiji Mikatos smelling like roses. He'd been smart enough to hire old boys, even earlier than he'd hired Ki, who'd told him the new emperor preferred to be called "The Personage Who Signs with the Chrysanthemum Seal." Those old boys could surely be proddy about such delicate details, he knew, for gents who bathed bare-ass in front of womenkind.

Gut feelings for such distinctions had been imparted to Jessica in her childhood by Japanese house servants, including a shy feminine shadow who'd never let on how she might or might not comfort the master of the house after Jessica's mother had died young, never to be replaced, officially, by the heartsick Alex Starbuck.

Like the soft-spoken Oriental governess who'd taught the daughter of the house perhaps more facts of life than her father might have approved of, Ki had taught the tomboy martial arts her father *had* approved of, situated as they were in Comanche country and not all that far from Chihuahua.

There was simply no way a man could grab a budding young girl by the crotch and throw her across the mat without noticing she had a crotch. More than one *jujutsu* or *jiujitsu* hold involved a hardly delicate grasp of a man's crotch as well. And without a basic knowledge of *jujutsu*, it was dangerous to even attempt the more subtle styles of unarmed combat. And so, in sum, Ki barely glanced Lone Star's way when she waded out of the tank in the bright morning sunlight, not unlike Botticelli's Venus rising naked from the sea. Nor did she even consider the virile youth on

37

the rocks above as, well, a virile youth, though she knew, when and if she thought about it, he was hung like a horse.

They both knew she wasn't a mare. She was Lone Star, getting dressed by the side of the tank to ride on after cow thieves in her serious hunting costume.

Knowing how hot the Texas sun could get, even up there in the Hill Country, she began by donning a mannishly cut work shirt of fine gray Nagasaki silk. That was not as contradictory as some might have taken it, given the practical as well as luxurious qualities of silk. Until such time as mankind came up with an even tougher fabric, silk had all others beat when it came to cool and tough. *Samurai* in old Dai Nippon had worn silk of the same weight and weave under their armor, knowing they'd not only ride as coolly as possible under all that hardware, but that should an arrow actually punch through the steel slats, the silk would refuse to give and simply follow the arrowhead in as deep as it might want to go—making it easier to extract the arrow later just by gathering the silk bunched about the wound and giving a good sharp tug.

Jessica Starbuck wasn't expecting to take any arrows through her silk shirt. Chief Quanah called her Little Sister, and she'd taught less friendly Comanche and Kiowa-Apache not to mess with her by counting coup on some misguided raiders in her girlhood. They said the Comanche medicine man Isatai called her "Man-Too-Big-to-Fight-Who-Squats-to-Piss." It sounded dreadfully rude, and she'd sent a message to the old troublemaker that she'd piss in his face, standing up, if he ever messed with her stock or her riders again.

Silk-clad from the crotch up, Lone Star slipped on her split skirts of *charro*-tanned buckskin, which could double as chaps in stickerbush, and buckled on her birthday gun before sitting down on a boulder to haul on her spurred Justins. She'd paid for both the boots and spurs. She felt more sentiment for the last birthday present her father had bestowed upon her before his untimely death at the hands of hired killers. He'd had it made special for her by Colt Arms of Hartford, Connecticut, lest she brush up against John Wesley Hardin, The Kid, or some other such pest packing the new double-action.

Her birthday gun bore a family resemblance to the Colt Model '78 packed by Hardin and her better friend, Deputy Custis Long, save for being chambered to fire the same .38 rounds as the somewhat weaker-framed Lightning favored by the petite Henry McCarthy, William Bonney, or whoever Billy the Kid might really be. All Colt double-actions were notorious for their heavy trigger pulls, next to the perhaps slower but hair-triggered Peacemaker. So Alex Starbuck had asked them at the Hartford plant to see what they could do about the sears with the fine feminine paws of his birthday girl in mind.

They'd done wonders. Anything was possible when one took the time and trouble a rich client could demand and get. In her Lone Star role, or just looking out for herself, Jessica could get off all six shots, with deadly accuracy, faster than most gunhands could fire twice.

After that, aside from all the bare-handed killing tricks she'd been taught as a child by the deadly Ki, Lone Star could fall back on the blade in one boot and the *shurikens* or Ninja throwing-stars she'd gotten at a discount from a certain weapon smith in a distant seaport.

She usually carried one pinned to the crown of her gray felt Stetson as if it was a lady's fancy, or some sort of badge. Others could be hidden in plain sight as perhaps fancy conchos attached to her tooled-leather gunbelt and roping saddle. Putting her Stetson on that morning, she tested a point of the *shuriken* attached to her hat with a finger, gingerly. Every point was needle-sharp, while the edges of the star-shaped little weapon had been honed razor-sharp. Should she need to, or want to, the lady known as Lone Star could send one of her *shurikens* spinning halfway through a pine plank, or a human skull, at fifty feet.

Adjusting the brim of her Stetson, she glanced up at the sky-line, and wasn't surprised when she failed to spy Ki atop that out-cropping. Breaking camp went smoother when one camped with a *segundo* who rose before dawn full of ginger. Jessica Starbuck was perfectly capable of rolling her own bedding and saddling her own bronc. But when she got to the brush-filled gap in the rocks they'd tethered their mounts in the night before, she found Ki and their four ponies waiting for her, ready to go. Ki hadn't even asked which of her two matched bay barbs she might find most *nozumo* this morning. They both knew she'd ridden the one with the larger white blaze out of Austin. She nodded as she noticed that that one now packed her lighter trail supplies, and that Ki had cinched her Muller Brothers roping saddle to the fresher gelded barb. As she forked herself aboard, Ki followed suit, mounting a buckskin about a hand too tall to be pure Andalusian, pretty as it pranced. The more sedate mounts that they'd brought by rail to Austin, like their fancier duds, had been left back there in the care of Missouri Pacific. So Ki's half-cowhand, half-*ninja* trail garb inspired her to laugh lightly and trill, "*Iko, Ki San! Omachido sama, shikashi atsui no de oyogi ni yukimashita.*"

Ki seldom answered in Japanese when he was really pissed off. He knew without being told in any tongue that they were getting off to a late start because she'd been unable to resist that swimming hole since she knew the day was going to be a real scorcher. Ki took the lead along the narrow game trail through the house-sized limestone boulders, calling back, "I don't think anyone could have trailed us this far if they noticed us slipping out of Austin at all."

She replied she assumed he'd had a good tough look at the lay of the land ahead. To which he replied, even gruffer, "*Hai. Shikashi*, who could be expecting us? I don't know where we're going, or why, myself!"

Lone Star sighed and called back, "I told you back in town. My stolen stock has to be somewhere, and that trashy Grayson clan squats on about the right amount of grass, water, and reputation."

Ki protested, "A good two days' ride away from anyone or anything *I* can connect to a cow chip dropped by a single head of Circle-Star stock, Jessie! I told you back there, and I'm telling you now, that this has all the earmarks of a snipe hunt! Trash nesters steal stock all the time. That's why their neighbors refer to them as trash. But we're after a gang dealing in serious numbers, capable of moving stock a good many miles, if we assume that purloined beef of yours made it half this far from the Circle Star."

She insisted, "We've had oodles of friendly eyes reading brands of passing beef all over Texas, and so far to no avail. That means we can forget all the market trails and a heap of open range as well. How many times do I have to explain my notions about these low-slung but mighty jagged limestone ridges?"

She waved her free arm expansively at the rocky, tree-punctuated ridge to their near right. "Consider how many cows a body could be grazing a quarter mile north, invisible as if they were on the moon. We're no more than a month's drive from the last place my poor little cows were seen."

40

"Jessie," Ki said firmly, "we're talking more like six weeks on the trail, if there *was* any sensible cattle trail between our usual range and this torn-up country."

To which she replied, as certainly, "They've had *more* than six weeks to work with, counting the time it took us to notice a single head was missing. You just made my very point about the trail, or make that the *route*, they might have chosen."

"Jessie, there isn't any damned cattle trail running east from the Circle Star to this Hill Country. There'd have been no point to blazing one for any honest or, hell, sensible cattle drover!"

"I just said that," she sweetly replied. "That's why we rode to Austin by rail well south of the cross-country drive I have pictured in my head. Since nobody on our side saw as much as an interesting dust cloud, the rascals must have run my stock up through the Glass Mountains, beyond Fort Stockton, by way of any number of canyons cutting through the Stockton Plateau, and then—"

"What's wrong with the canyonlands of the Big Bend, even closer?" Ki asked, picturing lots of Texas range as rugged as these limestone central hills. They weren't nearly as dramatic to look at as the red-walled canyons of the Upper Rio Grande, or even as confounding to ride through as the drab but steep-walled gulches of the Staked Plains.

When he tossed *them* in, Lone Star shot back in a tone of matching annoyance, "I keep telling you. Do you have *ro no mitsubachi* in your ears this morning? We have friends in the bandit country along the Big Bend, the Staked Plains, and Glass Mountains. We *don't* have friends in this unfriendly Hill Country, and some sticky-fingered cow thieves are hiding my poor cows in *some* damned kind of country!"

Ki didn't answer as they rode on. He was still alive that sunny morning because he'd outguessed other men a time or more. But he'd never claimed feminine intuition, so farther along, as that *baku* Longarm liked to sing, he figured they'd know more about it.

Ki repressed a shudder as the words of that old American hymn popped into his head unbidden. Then he chuckled wryly and began to hum the tune to himself aloud, thinking, "Well, you wanted to be a half-assed *amerika-jin* instead of a lowly *yaban-jin* back in Dai Nippon, didn't you?"

Behind him, Lone Star was regarding their surroundings with less distaste and more interest. The Texas Hill Country was more forbidding to the plow than to grazing, and her experienced eye told her the grass sprouting from the rocky slopes where it could was as nutritious, in its browner Texican way, as the famous blue grass of the Kentucky horse country.

Grass-eating critters grew faster, on stronger leg bones, where the grass had plenty of lime in it. Most she saw seemed to be gramma, the best kind of shortgrass anywhere west of, say, Longitude 100°, and even better growing on limestone soil. In low spots, where rainwater took longer to soak in, she spotted greener sedge the cows just loved, and even a few tufts of that love grass they'd fight one another to get at. Custis Long said love grass likely reminded cows of vanilla ice cream because that was what it smelled like to him, fresh-sprouted after a rain. Lone Star idly wondered where that handsome galoot might be right now, and then, because a woman riding a horse astride got enough stimulation down yonder, forced herself to think of uglier men, such as those who'd stolen her poor cows.

The deeper they rode into the Hill Country, the more it struck her as a natural range to hold cows off the market and out of the sight of their proper owners.

The poorly mapped and uncertainly defined Hill Country comprised about thirty thousand square miles. Where good grass didn't grow, the rocky outcroppings were garnished with wind-tortured live oaks, reclining scrub cedar, and the pesky but useful mesquite. The whole awesome mess, almost the size of all Ireland, must have discouraged the hell out of the first settlers forging west across the flat blackland farming country of East Texas. As a cattle baron's daughter with friends from all over, Jessica Starbuck knew how all farm folks and even some cow folks felt about mesquite. She'd been raised in West Texas to face marginal range as the Good Lord had chosen to serve it up. Mesquite was an invasive weed tree that would bull its way into your back garden and uproot all your rose bushes if you let it. The twisted trunks and branches weren't worth warm spit as lumber, but burned mighty hot and made barbecued goat taste fit for human consumption. Mesquite hid stock at roundup time, and made it harder to chase any stock one could see as it tried to trip one's pony and rip one's legs to ribbons with its wicked thorns. But after that, mesquite could feed stock through a bad drought, sucking water from sixty feet down and staying green of leaf and sweet of pod after even prickly pear had commenced to lie down and die in a serious Southwestern summer. So Jessica Starbuck sort of cottoned to the stuff.

Over here, in the Hill Country, it grew far bigger than further west on her own drier range. The oak and cedar mixed in with the mesquite told one why. Neither rival species could delve as deep for groundwater. That meant that while such water lay heartbreakingly deep for a nester with a pick and shovel but no dynamite, the permanent water table couldn't be more than about twenty to thirty feet down. The trees, of course, took advantage of cracks in the hard but brittle limestone. Try as one might, it was tough to spot the windmill of even a tube well in such a literally hard country.

As the natural game trail they'd been following climbed over a rise between two gigantic molars, Ki swung off it to forge along the contour line across a slope of dry grass strewn with rock slabs the size and color of fallen tombstones. Lone Star didn't ask why as she and her two ponies followed Ki's lead. They'd left Austin under cover of darkness, and checked more than once to make sure they'd not been followed. Nonetheless, folks not wanting to be followed would have been mighty dumb if they'd ridden like sore thumbs against a cloudless cobalt sky with the morning sun's beams shining their way as if they were fool actors up on a stage.

Ki led them around the rise, their heads below the horizon, as everyone out this way had long since learned from Mister Lo, the Poor Indian.

Lone Star was reminded once more of that infernal Custis Long, and it hurt as she recalled that time in that hotel room when, sharing a smoke afterwards, he'd pointed at a Currier & Ives print across the room and observed that the artist who'd depicted all those painted and befeathered Indians lined up on a rise had likely met few painted and befeathered Indians in the flesh.

She knew her old friend and all-too-occasional lover had scouted for the army during the Custer Scare and the more recent Shoshone Trouble up around the South Pass. But there'd been no need to explain to a girl who'd brushed with Comanche wearing pigtails. Indians never said "How!" or posed dramatically against the sky like fool statuary meant to be admired at a distance. George Armstrong Custer had found that out the day he tripped over close to ten thousand Lakota, Cheyenne, and Arapaho while suffering the distinct impression he was chasing a war party of about thirty. The open range west of Longitude 100° only appeared that open to the green or careless. She knew nobody

43

more than a few furlongs off in any direction could see her or her much taller companion, for the same reasons neither she nor Ki could be certain about who or what might be waiting for them in the very next draw to their west.

As if reading her mind, Ki slowed his own mount to a Comanche raider's creep, and casually hauled his saddle gun from its boot as he rose higher in his stirrups, rounding the gentle bend.

Lone Star dropped a casual hand to the grips of her Colt Special. Then, even before she could peer into the next draw west, she could tell from Ki's more relaxed posture that he approved of the view.

As she followed, they found themselves in a pleasant dell just aching to be settled by some deserving outfit. The slope to the north was well timbered, mostly with ancient oak that could feed many a foraging hog while screening the wide flats below from the sometimes wicked winter winds. Two thirds of the flat floor was dry enough for gramma, indicating it didn't flood often. Closer to the eastward gap draining the dell grew sedge and big bluestem, tall enough to hide a grown man if he didn't mind squishy boots. Reining in beside Ki she observed, "It's an all-summer *cienaga*. There must be some clay under that swampy end, and I'd bet on well water most anywhere else a body wanted to go down a few yards with a posthole digger."

Ki nodded, although with less intent interest. Since his arrival in the American Southwest the man called Ki had picked up nearly as much Spanish as English, Spanish in some ways being easier for anyone raised in his mother's tongue to pronounce. So he knew that *cienaga* was intended by Lone Star to mean more than simply "marsh." Anglo Texans, picking up tricks of the trade from the original vaqueros, had tended to adopt Spanish words to split hairs as they learned the ropes of their new way of life. To a Texan "gulch" was good enough to decribe the familiar results of erosion, east or west, while arroyo was reserved for a really serious gulch, and a canyon was even worse.

Ki knew she'd have called a regular marshy meadow by its Anglo name. To a Texican of the cow persuasion a *cienaga* was a valuable patch of evergreen wetness in a land that could get mighty parched between summer rains. As if to prove his unspoken point, she rose in her own stirrups for a good gaze all about as she decided, "Something, or some*body*, has to be spooking would-be settlement in these parts. This sweet little glen would be perfect

44

for a young couple starting a family and their own herd. Look at all that water, timber, and ungrazed grass just waiting to be claimed by anyone with a lick of imagination or ambition!"

Ki agreed it sure beat all,—in Japanese, because he was starting to feel better. They rode on, being careful about exposing themselves against the sky, and that was doubtless the reason they rounded a rock-strewn swell to surprise a pair of young Mexicans branding a yearling they'd roped and dragged to their modest mesquite fire in a chalky wash. As the one who'd been holding the running iron spied Lone Star and her *segundo* riding thoughtfully in, he dropped his guilty little secret and started to go for the old Patterson Convertible strapped cross-draw around his bell-bottom chaps. He decided to just grin up at them, sickly, when he found himself staring into the unwinking barrel of Ki's saddle gun. The youth standing closer with his back to them tensed as if to make some sudden move of his own. He decided to turn around slowly, hands polite, when his comrade hissed, *"Pero no! Es desperado, yo espanto."*

Everyone there knew why he had every right to feel hopeless fear. Many a blonder boy had been executed out of hand in cattle country just for having a running iron in his saddle bag. These young scamps had been caught in the act with their iron heated red and a hitherto unmarked maverick about to be wearing a brand its own mama had never seen before.

The unwritten agreement about running irons was that no honest human being had any call to tote such a wicked instrument of the devil around. Therefore, any son of a bitch caught branding any critter so free-handed deserved to die, *poco tiempo* if not sooner.

On the other hand, the unwritten maverick laws varied a mite from range to range, and could be interpreted more ways than one, depending on how tough one felt.

The original Texas maverick had been a human being, or at least a lawyer answering to the name of Samuel A. Maverick of Galveston. Along about 1845 Lawyer Sam had taken possession of a beef herd on Matagorda Island in lieu of unpaid legal fees. Hardly knowing which end of a longhorn the chips fell out of, Lawyer Sam had paid little mind to his untended herd, guarded mostly by the salt water all about his duney range. But he knew enough about the basic facts of nature to assume that, cows being cows, his herd should have shown *some* natural increase by the time he decided to sell it off in '53.

It hadn't. When Maverick had his herd brought ashore and tallied he found it had, if anything, shrunk a mite. So being a lawyer, he took some neighbors he suspected to law, accusing them of helping themselves to his poor unguarded beef.

They pleaded not guilty. For while they'd indeed helped themselves to many a lonesome-looking longhorn out on the Matagorda dunes, they wanted it distinctly understood they'd never, ever, even cast a covetous eye on a single cow bearing the brand of good old Sam or any other owner.

That would have been a sin. It said so in the Good Book. Just as the common law of Spain, from whence had come the Hispano-Moorish longhorn by way of Mexico, decreed it was the *duty,* not just the right, of every stock breeder to brand his damned stock, lest just such misunderstandings between honest neighbors arise.

So Sam Maverick's case had been thrown out of court, to the delight of most everyone else, who'd of course, and right soon, dubbed the old boys who'd grabbed all that unbranded stock "mavericks," making the object of such windfall roping a maverick.

The murkier part was that despite the legal precedents set in the original Maverick Case, there was some dispute, some of it noisy, as to just what might constitute a lawful maverick.

Some owners contended, at gunpoint, a calf dropped by any damned cow bearing their damned brand was theirs to brand, keep, and cherish any god damned time they got around to it. The two Mex kids Lone Star and Ki had just caught up with no doubt subscribed to a much looser interpretation of the code, claiming any unbranded stock, whether it was still dragging its umbilical cord or not.

The critter getting back to its hooves, now that Lone Star could study it, seemed a tad big to be running about unbranded, although not more than six or eight months old. So the maverick part was sort of marginal. It was that running iron cooling in the shortgrass at the moment that could still get someone killed in these parts.

As Ki went on covering the two scared kids, Lone Star smiled down at them, not unkindly, to say, "One can see the two of you know these hills better than my *segundo* here and me. We have been searching for cows, other cows than that one, one hopes, branded Circle Star."

The artistic young Mex who'd just dropped that running iron made the sign of the cross and protested, "As Jesus be our judge, we have enough troubles, *señorita bonita*! Everyone who deals in *carne de vaca* knows the *Starbuck* brand! *Pero* their herds graze far to the west of this disputed range."

His fellow *maveriquero* pointed at the now-distant *ternero*, grinning back at them from atop a rise to the north, to assure Ki and Lone Star, "As Jesus be our judge, that stray we were only having a little fun with wore no brand at all. My brother and I are only men of some ambition, not *ladrones.*"

Lone Star was too polite to point out that Jesus wasn't the one in a position to judge anyone around there at gunpoint. She smiled in a way that usually made grown men feel wistful and said, "The Tejano maverick laws are similar to the Mejicano views—neither notion strays all that far from English common law on property unclaimed by any taxpaying owner—or as our own kids put it, finders keepers."

By now the discarded running iron had cooled back down to scrap-iron gray but set the grass roots around one end to smoldering. The kid who'd dropped it took a step forward to stomp the rising tendrils of smoke lest the grass fire get serious. He shyly asked Lone Star why Ki was still pointing that Henry at them if there was to be no argument about recent events.

Lone Star sighed and explained, "My *segundo* feels protective in strange surroundings. You said this range was disputed? Disputed by whom, *por favor?*"

The one who'd been holding the maverick rather than the running iron, who seemed to know a mite more about gringo stock folk, waved an expansive hand at the rocky slopes all about. "A good half day's ride to the northeast one might find the hacienda of the *muy peligrosos* Sanfords. They brand Lazy S. A little farther to the west range the Grayson brothers, and they are more than dangerous. They are *loco en la cabeza!*"

The young Mex who'd just put out a budding range fire nodded and chimed in. "The Graysons were here in these hills before the Caddo or Comanche, if one is to believe everything they say."

His friend pointed out, "Is not healthy not to believe any of the Graysons, and the one called Rafe has been known to gun an hombre of our *raza* who was nodding in agreement!"

Lone Star nodded grimly and replied, "We've heard of these Grayson boys. What's the story on that Sanford outfit?"

The same Mex explained, "They settled near wood and water just a few years ago. It is said, one does not pry, El Capitan Sanford rode for El Norte in that war you people had a few years ago. Whether this is true or not, the main dispute seems to be some disagreement between Austin and Washington regarding that homestead law of El Presidente Lincoln. Since our *raza* does not seem to be included, you must forgive us for not understanding it at all."

Lone Star frowned thoughtfully and explained, more for Ki's information than anyone else's, "Texas passed its own laws as to land, water, and mining claims, back when it was still a republic. When she entered the Union back in '45, Texas reserved the right to manage such matters her own durned way."

"But then Texas threw in with the Confederacy, and guess who won," Ki pointed out with a dubious smile.

To which a proud daughter of Texas could only reply, "Maybe so. All bets were off with carpetbaggers in the catbird seat, until just recent. My late father knew what he was doing when he voted for Rutherford Hayes in the election of '76. Hayes may have been Republican, and we heard he'd ridden against us as a one-star general in the war. But my father said he'd ridden brave in the Shenandoah Campaign after he'd been badly wounded at South Mountain, and better yet, he stood for civil service reform and solid currency."

Ki smiled thinly and said, "That's why he'll no doubt lose in the next election. But could we stick to what this range dispute was all about, Jessie?"

Lone Star shrugged. "We're going to have to ask one side or the other if we want the details. If you'd like an educated guess, I'd say that Sanford bunch thinks it's operating under U.S. federal land use regulations, whilst the Grayson boys feel Texas law and their old-time religion is still good enough for them."

Turning back to the Mexican kids she nodded graciously and said, "You've been very helpful and it's been nice talking to you. Why don't you just go with God, clear off this range, and we'll not have to tell any fibs for you when we show up at the Grayson spread."

The one who'd been caught in the act with that running iron left it right where it was, and turned on one heel to head for their half-hidden ponies in a mesquite clump across the draw, neither looking back nor commenting further on what they all recognized as an act of signal mercy.

His comrade, whether more grateful or simply more talkative, smiled boyishly up at *la señorita bonita.* "You go with God too, *dama mia. Pero* do not expect to find God anywhere near those *muy malos* Graysons!"

Suspecting he might not be getting through to her, the Mex turned to Ki to add, "*You* talk to her, Señor Chino. Make her see those wild ones are not the sort of men even an ugly woman of virtue would wish for to associate with, eh?"

Ki shot an amused glance at the lady they were talking about as he replied, "I've been trying to get through to her since we rode out of Austin, and so far, I've had no luck convincing her this game's not worth the candle. You might say she has a mind of her own."

The Mex sighed, made the sign of the cross, and murmured, "The Graysons have no minds at all. They will probably kill you. Do we have to go into what they will want to do to a beautiful woman?"

★

Chapter 5

By this time Longarm had filled out all the pesky papers required by the City of El Paso and the State of Texas. In return some more reasonable Rangers had pawed through wanted fliers, old and new. They'd decided the two unfortunates who'd been laying for Longarm had to be a recent graduate of Yuma Prison over in Arizona Territory and his protégé and punk, a cowhand wanted for backshooting a colored shoe-shine boy in Globe for the day's profits. His handle had been Wiltz. The older one, who'd died wearing pissed-up purple prison-release pants, had been aptly named as well. His last name had been Potter. They'd called him Pot Shot Potter, unimaginative as that sounded, because he'd been known to rent his gun hand by the hour but preferred to take care of his client's enemies from cover if not from the back. His last known victim, if anyone could prove it, had been an Arizona rancher making a heap of noise about some missing stock. When Longarm asked if anyone knew who Potter had potted the rancher for, the Rangers allowed that was still up in the air. The murdered rancher had been grazing his cows along the lower Gila when he'd suddenly noticed how few he had. Nobody knew how or why he'd decided some mammy-jamming sons of a one-legged whore, as he'd put it, had driven his purloined beef toward the Southern Pacific loading ramps at Globe. Nobody around Globe had seen hide nor hair of the poor gent's beef before he'd been found facedown in an alley behind a saloon, shortly after a loud and red-faced conversation with the late Pot Shot Potter.

Longarm put all of that down in his notebook with a stub pencil and a grain of salt. Gents were always being found facedown in cow towns after indulging in noisy war talk, and folks always tended to assume the dirty deed had been done by the nearest mortal with a gunslick's rep.

On the other hand, old Potter and his lover boy had been laying for *him* more recently, and while he'd yet to accuse anyone in these parts of stealing cows, it was worth noting he was looking for a lady who'd just lost some stock.

Passing out smokes and shaking hands all around, Longarm left the Ranger station to retrace his steps to the intersection the D&RG depot shared with Western Union. He was commencing to feel the Texas sun, early as it was, through the tobacco-brown tweed of his frock coat and vest by the time he made it inside again. So he hauled off his coat and laid it, folded, at one end of the counter before he got to work with that same pencil stub and some handy telegram forms.

He brought his home office up to date on his surprising reception in El Paso with his first message, sent collect at nickel-a-word day rates. He left out the dirty parts involving Miss Messy, but as the clerk took the block-lettered blank from him Longarm said, "I know all about your company policy, and I hope you understand how much of your wires get to go across federal land betwixt towns. As you'll see while you're sending that official federal report, I've just reason to suspect I was set up for an ambush by wire. So now you're fixing to show me any and all telegrams wired here to El Paso from your branches up the D&RG right of way—from, say, Colmor to Las Vegas betwixt last sunset to last sunrise, right?"

The Western Union clerk had doubtless had this same discussion with state and federal lawmen in the past. He was loyal enough to company policy to protest. "That could be a heap of messages, ah, Marshal."

Longarm smiled thinly and replied, "I'm only a deputy marshal and that's all right. I enjoy reading when it's too early to drink and too hot to screw. We're talking about premeditated murder here, pard."

So the Western Union clerk dug out all the incoming traffic sent from north of Las Vegas in the darkness before dawn, and in point of fact there wasn't too much and none of it seemed either dirty or all that interesting. He had to read through it all twice before he figured out Miss Messy's code. She'd naturally signed it with another name, and addressed it to a business associate named Jones. That and the fact it had been sent from Colmor care of this branch office, instead of delivered to any El Paso address, inspired Longarm to read more carefully. Once he did, it was easy enough to make out what she'd really meant to convey with:

"JUNIOR FAILED HIS EXAM AND HAS DROPPED OUT OF SCHOOL TO SPEND SUMMER AT HOME STOP ARRIVING ON MORNING TRAIN AND TRUSTING YOU TO SEE HE GETS RIDE TO DESTINATION STOP SIGNED MASON."

Handing the copy back, along with a cheroot, Longarm said, "That has to be the way they knew I'd be getting off this morning. Now I got me another serious message to get off."

So the clerk lit up and went back to send Longarm's first wire to Billy Vail, while Longarm composed his query to anyone at the Circle Star who might have an answer.

He left off addressing the blank until the clerk rejoined him, assuring him his message to Denver would be delivered at the Federal Building within the hour. Waving the second yellow blank in an undecided way, Longarm explained, "This goes to the privately owned telegraph set of Miss Jessica Starbuck, out to her Circle Star. I disrecall the numbers you boys use to hitch her up with your own wires. I know you can, because you've done so before. Running her Starbuck Enterprises from her rambling ranch house calls for heaps of telegraph messages in every direction. I swear you'd think she was a pretty little spider-gal dwelling in the center of a big old copper web."

The clerk sort of sniffed and said, "We handle plenty of traffic for Starbuck Enterprises. There's no way for Miss Jessica to get in touch with her West Coast branches without our relaying wires both ways here."

He took Longarm's message, saying, "I can send this for you easy enough, if you want to waste your time and mine. Since I've already bent company policy all out of shape this morning, it might save us both some bother if I told you neither Jessica Starbuck nor anyone else in a position of authority will be there to respond to this. I just told you we relay lots of messages to and from Starbuck Enterprises. I can't let you read any of the backed-up traffic. I'm more afraid of Miss Starbuck than a mere telegraph company. But I can tell you she's not there, and it gets worse. She and her foreman left word they could be contacted at the hotel she owns in Austin, if it was important."

"Why is that worse?" asked Longarm. But knowing Jessie, he wasn't too surprised when the clerk replied, "They're not there either. A heap of folks, including Uncle Sam and the State of Texas, have been trying to track them down by wire since yester-afternoon, to no avail. Nobody at the hotel knows where she and her foreman were headed, or even when they left. They never checked out. At least one Ranger captain who seems to think he's her uncle has ordered a search party out in case she's been kid-napped."

Longarm thought a moment. "I doubt anyone could abduct Jessie Starbuck and her Oriental *segundo* from her own hotel in the middle of a fair-sized city without someone noticing all that noise. Last I heard, she was missing some beef way closer than Austin. She must have headed there because it was the state capital and she wanted to go through some records."

"She's not there now," the telegraph clerk pointed out.

Longarm shrugged. "She must have found some records worth following up on then. Lord knows where in thunder, or even Texas, she might be right now. I'd have to read the same records, the same way, and I doubt my own boss wants me to."

He scowled a bit, then reached out for the form he'd just handed over, saying, "Let me reword that some. If the lady of the house ain't home, anyone who is would still know whether or not they'd accepted delivery of a swamping crate with a heavy oak desk inside it."

He crossed out some of what he'd written and blocked in more simple directions before he handed it back. "I hope you can still read this. You see, my main mission is to recover that fool crate of furniture. Jessie Starbuck's a big enough gal to look after her own herd, and she'd have come home by now if she hadn't come up with some notion as to where her beef went and who might have stolen it, the poor bastards."

The clerk said they'd have his revised message at the Circle Star in no time, assuming anyone there could take down incoming Morse.

Longarm winced. "I wish you hadn't thought of that. I ain't certain how many of the household staff can even read or write plain English. I asked for a direct yes or no as to whether they have that fool crate at the Circle Star. How long do you reckon I ought to give 'em before I despair of a sensible answer?"

The clerk shot a glance at the Regulator Brand clock on one wall. "I can get this right off. Since there'll be no door-to-door delivery involved, you ought to know in no more than an hour if we get any answer at all."

Longarm picked up his coat, leaving it draped across his left forearm but making sure his cross-draw gun grips stayed clear. "May as well give 'em a mite longer. Whether I push on from here by rail or bronc, it's too blamed hot outside right now to contemplate. So I'll be back after mayhaps a shower, shave, something to eat, and iced beer."

The clerk wisfully agreed that was better than a ride out to Fort Bliss, or even a train ride, during the usual siesta hours of summer. So they shook on it and parted friendly.

Back outside, the Texas sun was blazing so white that everything in sight seemed drawn with chalk or shaded with India ink. Longarm wisely clung to such shade as there was on his side of the deserted dusty street as he made his way first to the nearby depot. So he never noticed the narrowed eyes glaring at him from the deep shadows of an arcade across the way. He wasn't expecting anyone to peg more shots at him in the middle of town in broad-ass daylight, and since the killers staring soberly at his back at the moment would have been the first to agree such a move could get a boy's neck stretched in the State of Texas, they just muttered about the next sneaky moves they might try now that the tricky son of a bitch had blown away Potter and Wiltz.

Before he'd done that at dawn by getting off his train in a less usual way, Longarm had commended his personal possessions to the train crew. So unless he'd been betrayed after tipping two porters, his McClellan, Winchester, and other possibles figured to be waiting for him in the baggage room.

They were. The elderly fuss in charge groused about Longarm not having a proper claim check, and said them fool niggers should have given him one. But in the end he settled for a sincere apology and a smoke. Most everyone but Billy Vail seemed to admire those three-for-a-nickel cheroots. Vail was the only human being Longarm knew who smoked horsehair rope.

Packing his old army saddle with everything else, including his frock coat, lashed to its brass fittings, Longarm headed next for the Vista Linda Hotel just across the way. He'd stayed there in the past. So he knew the *vista linda* they were talking about was the pretty view of the not-too-distant Cerro Alto to the east by northeast. The vista of those smelter stacks to the west was sort of dreary.

The lobby of the Vista Linda was just brown gravy dark and drab. The usual old cockroaches you found loafing in the lobbies of third-rate transient hotels were using the chairs and spittoons provided by the management. Longarm felt no call to pay them any more mind than they seemed to be paying *him* as he dropped his McClellan by the desk and bet the old gent behind it that they couldn't hire him a room and running water for four bits a day.

The clerk snorted in disgust, "Why don't you ask for dancing gals nekked whilst you're at it? We can hire you a plain old flop for six bits, this establishment being so refined and handy to the center of town. If you want a corner sink with genuine running water it'll run you a dollar a day, with the shithouse and bath just down the hall."

Longarm started to settle for the bare neccessities. Then he reflected that they'd probably let him charge the room to his expense account and that pissing in a sink had running down any hall beat by miles. So he plunked down a silver cartwheel and the clerk rang a handy cowbell for a skinny kid in a monkey suit, saying, "William, take this gent and his gear up to Room 3-F."

So William did, earning himself a dime for packing the McClellan up to the third floor and handing Longarm the key. As soon as he was alone Longarm peeled off his vest, shirt, and undershirt to see if that corner sink really worked.

It did, though anyone who'd wanted hot water or even truly cold water would have been out of luck. Tepid tap water on a ragged but clean enough washcloth did so much for Longarm's hide that he dropped his pants to rinse off his sweaty balls while he was at it.

Letting the oven-hot but bone-dry air of El Paso dry his hide, he got out a fresh shirt and underpants. The shirt would be enough alone, though he put his vest back on open, rather than leave his watch and derringer behind with no vest pockets to pack them in.

Then feeling a mite better, even as it kept getting hotter, he let himself back out in the hall to lock up with a sliver of match stem wedged in the doorjamb near a bottom hinge. He doubted anyone would want to lay for him inside during daylight hours, and he wasn't planning on spending the night. But it paid to be careful, as the late Wiltz and Potter had learned only that morning.

Downstairs, he kept the key but told the old room clerk he'd be back for a lie-down as soon as he'd stuffed his gut, should anyone ask for him. The clerk asked where he meant to do all that eating and drinking. Longarm said he was still working on that, not having been in El Paso for a spell.

Then he strolled out, softly singing "Farther Along" as he passed the first chili joint to the west, with the sun at his back, and decided to leave the inviting interior to all those buzzing bluebottles. For while bluebottles were pretty enough as flies went, Longarm had never gotten over a certain distaste for the shiny little buzzers since he'd pulled burial detail in the warm months after Shiloh. He felt sure those bluebottles buzzing over the counter in yonder had only smelled spilt chili con carne. But once you'd seen bluebottles laying their eggs in the open mouth or staring eyes of battlefield casualties, you just never felt like eating in their buzzing company any more.

He didn't think much of the sissy tearoom he passed next. He swung the corner to follow darker shade south toward Mexico, hoping he'd find a more inviting place before he walked that far in this heat.

There was nobody dumb enough to be out on the walk with him at this hour. It had to be pushing high noon. So he felt free to sing, out loud:

Farther along, we'll know more about it.
Farther along, we'll understand why.
Cheer up, my brother, walk in the sunshine.
We'll understand it all by and by.

So how come he was hearing "Aura Lee" at the same time he was singing "Farther Along"?

He paused in the shade of a feed store canopy to light a smoke and listen. He could barely make out the strains of that old war song, popular with both sides, being played on some distant piano and not too well.

Longarm shook out his match, muttering, "If that's who I think it is playing that dumb piano so awful, there figures to be a saloon wrapped around her, and where one finds a saloon with a piano, one generally finds a fair free lunch as well!"

So he tracked down the source of the tinny tinkles about poor Aura Lee, who'd died of the consumption, clap, or whatever before her soldier boy in blue or gray could ever get back to her.

He had to cut through the next block by way of a fetid alley. Then at last, he entered the side door of a corner saloon, to find himself gazing fondy at the rear view of a voluptuous hourglass figure in screaming-red fake silk. Miss Red Robin's bright red hair was fake as well. Longarm knew for a fact she'd been born a brunette. He knew this more certainly than many another man who might have admired Red Robin's looks much more than her piano playing. For while Red Robin was a free thinker for a natural brunette, she prided herself on being a professional musician, awful as that might sound in every way, and hence was not inclined to entertain the customers where she might be working once she got off work.

Longarm had gotten to know her in the more Biblical sense because she'd been on the run from the law when first they'd met in other parts of Texas. They'd both agreed, in the end, the joke had been on her for seducing a lawman who'd had nothing on her. Her crime of passion hadn't been federal to begin with, and the silly bastard had lived after all.

Since then they'd met in other parts of the West, and had had to find other excuses to leap in bed together. Like old Kim Stover up on the Bitter Creek Range, that high-toned widow woman on Sherman Avenue back in Denver, and of course Jessie Starbuck, Red Robin was more than just a great lay. Thus, a man with a wandering job and a tumbleweed heart had to be careful around such temptations, lest he hurt an old pal or his own fool self.

The saloon was nearly deserted at this hour, and the lady in red was apparently playing mostly for practice, still unaware of him. So Longarm was tempted to just back out, quietly, and find a place that was safer for both of them.

Then, without turning her head but tooling more softly on the keys, Red Robin called out, "Damn it, come in or go 'way and shut that damned door, Custis. Downtown El Paso stinks of over-seasoned tamales and baked horseshit at this hour."

He stepped inside, shutting the side door behind him sheepishly, as Red Robin swiveled on her shapely behind to soberly ask, "Do you think I'm getting any better, Custis?"

He was sure she was talking about her piano playing. There was no room for improvement as far as her face or figure went, unless one could have talked her into less henna rinse and war paint. He knew nobody could. He'd tried to tell Red Robin she'd look high-toned and even prettier than the Princess of Wales if only she'd calm down a bit. She'd allowed she wanted to be noticed more than she wanted to pass for any fool princess. So on this occasion Longarm just told her she looked swell as ever and that he could tell she'd been playing "Aura Lee," right?

She sighed. "I get lots of requests for that and the one about the mockingbird that sings on Sweet Hattie's grave, if only I could remember the damned dirge. How did you know I was here, Custis? I'd be lying if I said I was sorry to see you right now. But I suspect I'll be sorry afterwards, you brute."

He said he'd only been searching for food and drink, and added, "I ain't sure I'll have the time to be brutal, Red Robin. I'm on a serious case and just looking to kill some time, comfortable, whilst awaiting the answers to some telegraph wires. How did you know it was me just now?"

She lowered her big bedroom eyes from his gaze, murmuring, "I knew someone was stuck there in that doorway undecided. After that it was simply a matter of familiar tobacco and, ah, other smells, along with who might be so hesitant to stay or leave. I ain't sure I want to shack up with you again either, damn both our weak natures."

Longarm gulped and shot a guilty glance at the old barkeep closer to the front entrance. The cuss didn't seem interested in their conversation. Longarm still felt his ears burning, even after Red Robin softly added, "Old Jim is half deaf, and them two old-timers playing checkers by the window barely savvy English."

Longarm said he was glad, and asked where they might have the free lunch, since he failed to see any at either end of the bar.

Red Robin rose from her upright, inspiring upright feelings in him as well. "They'll put out some deviled eggs and pickled pig knuckles later. It's too slow as well as too hot right now. Let's go upstairs and I'll treat you right, Custis."

He said, uncertainly, "You're right about how hot it's got, and I'm really hungry, Red Robin."

She smiled. "So am I, more ways than one. I was only down

here practicing so's the food and beer I ordered would have time to cool off. Come on, Custis. I'll show you some modern wonders they just got in these parts."

So he went with her. Most men would have. She yelled at the old barkeep, who just nodded their way, blankly, whether he understood what she'd said about the quitting-time crowd or not. She led Longarm through a beaded curtain into darker parts of the old adobe pile, and from there up a wooden stairway to the quarters the management had assigned to her down the second-story hallway. He noticed she let them in with a key. He was glad to see they didn't have to worry about surprises once they were snug inside her corner suite.

She'd naturally closed the shutters of the windows on either wall of her corner room, but they still would give cross-ventilation should the breeze ever pick up at all.

He tossed his hat on a sofa, and might have followed it on down. But Red Robin shook her red head and said, "Not here. In yonder." So he followed her into a smaller room where a big oaken icebox loomed near the head of a modest bedstead. But the temperature of her combined pantry and bedroom was what struck him the most. For while it would have been dumb to call the place really comfortable, it was still a good twenty degrees cooler in there.

Red Robin opened the icebox to let what looked like a whole Frisco fog roll out and spill around their feet. She dared him to guess what she had in there instead of the usual ice.

He laughed and said, "I've seen dry ice before. They got one of them dry ice plants up in Denver too. It sure takes some getting used to, though. Do you know they didn't even know how to manufacture plain old *water* ice when I was starting school? They used to cut ice from frozen ponds in wintertime, and sell it through mayhaps half the summer preserved in sawdust. I think it was along about '34 a cuss called Perkins discovered you could get below freezing by compressing and evaporating stuff like ethyl ether. But he never tried to market his notion. A Doctor Gorrie, over to Florida, got to making artificial ice to cool his fever wards, and it was only natural Thadeus Lowe was cranking out summer ice in commercial quantities right after the war."

As Red Robin took out the bucket of beer and pasteboard box of food, Longarm peered in around at her at the big block of fuming carbon dioxide she'd had delivered that morning. She warned him not to touch it, saying, "It's so cold it can blister your skin like hot coals. Ain't that something?"

He nodded. "I told you they got a new Linde plant up to Denver. Linde is this pumping wonder who compresses stuff like ammonia to get things colder than cold. I just read where he's invented ways to make whole warehouses colder than Greenland. I swear I don't know what the world's coming to at the rate they keep inventing things. Is that blue cheese I smell, now that it's commencing to thaw, or could someone around here be getting passionate?"

Red Robin laughed. "Both. Shut the icebox lest all that dry ice steam away. I really like not having to worry about it melting like regular ice. That damp dew on the outside of the icebox is just from the cold coming through. It won't amount to much on the rug, and meanwhile, ain't you glad I brought you up here?"

He allowed he surely was as he sat on one end of her bed to get at the tray of good things she'd spread out for them. As he stuffed a slice of salami rolled around blue cheese in his mouth with one hand, and reached for an earthenware mug of cold beer with the other, he noticed Red Robin was still on her feet, peeling out of her tight red dress.

That didn't surprise him as much as the fact that she'd been wearing nothing at all under it. As if reading his mind, she calmly declared, "It's too hot for underthings and I don't want to sweat this dress up, ah, entertaining you."

He said that in that case he might as well shuck his vest and gun rig at least. But somehow, by the time he'd hung them over a bedpost, while Red Robin reclined on the far side of the tray naked as a jay, he figured he might as well just keep going. So he did, and after they'd both enjoyed a few more bites and sips that way, across from one another, it seemed only natural to get the damned tray out of the way so they could nibble one another right.

As ever getting back together with an old pal, Longarm was struck by how swell it felt sliding one's old organ-grinder back where it seemed it had always belonged. He knew wryly that mounting the same gal the same way, night after night, could get to feeling more like work than pleasure after a three- or four-week honeymoon. That was another good reason for a young and healthy lawman to stay single. And yet, after not having had Red Robin for a spell, the very fact that he'd had her before made entering her less uncertain than it might have been had this been the first time.

As if to prove she felt the same magic, Red Robin spread her soft thighs wider, hugged him down against her big marshmallow breasts, and hissed, "Oh, Jesus, yes, Custis, yessss!"

So he let himself go, knowing just how many thrusts it would take to make her come, and as ever, they came almost as one in a mingled moaning of mutual satisfaction.

Then, since they were old pals who didn't have to prove anything, they did it again, with a pillow under her hips this time, and agreed they both felt like eating some more.

It was a swell way to kill an otherwise tedious afternoon in El Paso. They had more than enough food and drink to satisfy the two of them. He had to satisfy them another way after Red Robin, feeling playful, spread stinky cheese on his flaccid virility and got it all worked up again, cleaning it off with her sassy lips and darting tongue.

They finished dog-style by unspoken agreement, since that was what old friends were for. He didn't ask why she was crying all over his bare chest afterwards, as they lay sharing a smoke with dry ice vapor swirling all around the bed. He let out some smoke, patted her bare shoulder gently, and said, "I know, honey. I'd like to spend at least the weekend here in El Paso too. But I told you earlier I was down here on important beeswax."

She sniffed and murmured, "I know how important I am to you, damn my weak nature."

He assured her, soothingly, "I'm just as weak-natured about you, as you knew damned well when you dragged me up here for some of your swell cheese delights. I'll tell you true that if I was only after Frank, Jesse, or The Kid, I'd be tempted to shirk my duty till at least that inevitable morning when all you gals chide a man for having less ambition than the cuss across the way."

She protested, "Custis, that ain't fair. You know I've got at least as much gypsy in my soul as you. Do you recall that time we met like this halfway up that peak in Colorado?"

He chuckled. "Fondly. The point is that this time Billy Vail sent me out on a chore so important I ain't allowed to tell nobody about it. Suffice it to say, I've got to get on over to Austin or out to a sort of remote cattle spread, depending on the answers to them wires I sent earlier."

She snuggled closer and began to toy with his love tool as she murmured, "They're not paying me all that much downstairs. Could I come with you, hon?"

He laughed louder than she thought polite and told her, "You

61

just did. I'm sure taking you along where I'm headed could lead to more excitement than I'm prepared to cope with, amusing as it sounds."

She persisted. "Pretty please with blue cheese on it?" Then they both heard a loud rumble somewhere in the distance. There was no way to see outside from where they lay listening to the fading echos. She said, "Praise the Lord. A late-afternoon gullywasher is just what we've been praying for, as long as it's over no later than, say, seven or eight."

He nodded. "There you go, Red Robin. The boys downstairs will be flocking in to hear you by the cool shades of evening after a good summer cloudburst."

He listened a few more seconds before he added, "Don't hear no hail or even rain on the roof yet. That means a longer than usual summer rain once she starts."

He sat up, the almost-shot cheroot gripped in his teeth, as he swung his naked feet to the foggy rug, "I'd best get on over to Western Union while I can do so halfways dry. I have a slicker tied to my saddle, over to the Vista Linda, but . . ."

"Go ahead if you just can't stand my company now that you've come in me," Red Robin pouted, as if to prove even old pals could be pains in the ass once they'd used and abused a poor boy.

He hauled her in for a soothing kiss and then, since she grabbed him indelicately again, they wound up saying adios the best way men and women could communicate with one another.

The next time he tried to get up she let him. So he cleaned up, got dressed, and got going before she could fuss at him some more.

The first thing he noticed, back out on the streets of El Paso, was how brightly the sun was still shining from a cloudless sky.

As he strode up the shady side of the street he felt just glad he was still in town with mostly 'dobe walls looming well above the pancaked crown of his dark Stetson. For lightning, wet or dry, was a mortal danger to man on horseback on open range, and dry lightning was the kind both cowboys and Indians were allowed to say they were scared of. He'd read where a bolt from the blue had once turned back a Mongol horde by sizzling down from a cloudless sky to set other high plains afire and scare those Mongols shitless.

A rider caught alone on the plains by broody clouds and a tingle in the air could always dismount and hunker lower than his saddle horn with his fingers crossed and his balls puckered. But there was no way to anticipate *dry* lightning. It struck willy-nilly and you just had to study on something more cheerful, like how long was forever or how high was up. A body cursed with any imagination had a hard row to hoe in this vail of tears.

Fortunately, dry lightning was so rare that Longarm had only seen it a couple of times, and had never been hit by it in the thirty-odd years he'd been exposed to the Good Lord's wry sense of humor. So he'd about forgotten about the threat of an afternoon storm by the time he'd made it back to the Western Union.

He found answers to some of his earlier questions waiting for him. Leaning against the counter Longarm read Billy Vail's advice to let El Paso claim the modest bounty on Pot Shot Potter as long as they were willing to bury his trail punk as well. Vail's wire ended with a plaintive request for any news about that confounded crated desk from Queen Victoria. Some blabbermouthing maniac from the State Department had allowed to Lemonade Lucy Hayes, the First Lady, that yes, the blamed desk intended for the damned oval office had arrived in these United States from England, but that no, it wasn't in the oval office just yet. They called the President's pleasant-looking but mule-stubborn wife Lemonade Lucy because she sided with the Women's Christian Temperance Union—and to hell with the political advantages of wine or worse at any dinner *she* might be giving at the White House. Billy Vail said she was anxious to try some of her swell lemon-oil furniture cleaner and a coat of carnauba-palm wax on the brine-seasoned oak Queen Victoria had written her about. No doubt Queen Victoria would be asking about that infernal desk any minute now as well.

Longarm lit a smoke, noting he was running low, before opening the telegram from Jessica Starbuck's private telegraph station. After he'd snorted and cussed a time or two, the curious clerk, who'd after all taken down the message from the Circle Star an hour or so back, asked how come. "It looked like good news to me—just typing what they sent, of course."

Longarm explained, "It is and it ain't. I get to forget that cuss who signed for a crate in Washington on the Brazos. He was a neighbor who'd delivered a dray load of hides, and figured to get in good with Miss Jessie by saving her a needless trip."

The clerk nodded. "Right. As I recall, they say he dropped that mysterious crate off at the Circle Star this very morn. So now Miss Jessica Starbuck has it and all you have to do is—"

"The asshole of a *tercero* Miss Jessie and her *segundo* left in charge put the damned crate aboard a damned buckboard and ordered his *muchachos* to deliver it to *la patrona* in Austin, *poco tiempo*! So Christ only knows where it might be right now, and I don't have Christ's mailing address!"

Sticking the telegrams in a hip pocket till he could get around to writing down all the names involved, Longarm spun about to scribble a hasty message back to that overly helpful assistant foreman at the Circle Star. He knew he wasn't supposed to say too much about the contents of that crate. He figured it was safe to say he'd personally tear the *tercero*'s head off if they didn't overtake that buckboard and get the crate back to the ranch or on to Austin, depending on where they caught up with it. Either way, he should sit on the damned thing till Longarm could claim it personally in the name of the federal government.

The Western Union man, who was starting to keep up with the case as well by now, opined that that ought to do it. Longarm grimaced. "Lord willing, the creeks don't rise, and Comanche don't take an unhealthy interest in a lighty laden buckboard moving sudden as well as solo. Meanwhile I'd best catch me a train headed east. If that crate ain't headed back to the Circle Star by the time I reach San Antone, my best bet would be to keep going in hopes of meeting up with it in Austin before Miss Jessie Starbuck carves her initials in it. I'm supposed to deliver it to its rightful owners unused."

The clerk said he'd get the latest message on the wire *poco tiempo*. Longarm went next to the depot to book an eastbound seat and pick up a timetable. As long as he was there he strode over to the tobacco stand at one end of the waiting room to replenish his supply of cheroots.

The slicker taking advantage of the traveling public said the same brand sold two-for-a-nickel. Longarm asked how much his mother and sister might charge, but sprang for two bits worth anyhow. He still had to recover his possibles at the hotel, speaking of wasting money on the road.

He turned from the tobacco stand, tucking the ten fresh cheroots in a shirt pocket under his vest lest they get in the way of his telling time or drilling someone with his derringer. Suddenly one of those same El Paso copper badges he'd met there that morning came in off the front walk to spy Longarm, go frog-belly pale, and stammer, "Be you a haunt or could I be dreaming all this shit?"

Longarm smiled uncertainly. "I don't see how this could be your dream, considering all the fun I've been having this afternoon. Why would I be a haunt? It was me as *won* this morning, remember?"

The roundsman protested, "You just got blowed to smithereens at the Vista Linda, along with one whole corner of the hotel! They think the gaslights must have been going quite some time in your room unlit, and whatever happened, your army saddle, Winchester, and what we took to be bits and pieces of *you* wound up scattered across the Vista Linda's flat roof!"

Longarm whistled softly. "That old spoilsport who said virtue was its own reward never had some son of a bitch out to do him dirty with dynamite, I'll vow. Fool that I am, I told a whole lobby filled with strangers I'd be back at the Vista Linda for an afternoon siesta once I'd grabbed a bite to eat. You say my saddle and Winchester survived the results?"

The copper badge nodded. "You know how old saddle leather and steel get, once they're burnished with all the nicks and scratches there's room for. It must have been your spare shirts, socks, and such that made the boys figure you'd been more blowed apart. There was all sorts of plaster, lathewood, roofing, and such all over creation as the fire department was hosing the hotel down. You say it was dynamite, not gas?"

Longarm headed for the scene of the crime, the roundsman in tow, as he replied, "I wasn't there. It could have been blasting powder. If anyone had been inside my hired room long enough to turn on the gas lamp without lighting it, they'd have noticed I wasn't there. So how do you feel about a bomb, dynamite or black powder, tossed over the transom?"

The roundsman said, "Awful. You're sure lucky you was somewhere else at the time. Ah, would you like to tell me where you was instead?"

Longarm shook his head and primly replied, "A man who'd kiss and tell deserves to get blown up in bed with bombs. Let's go find out whether I need a new saddle and saddle gun or not."

★

Chapter 6

He didn't. The already battered McClellan he found waiting for him in the police tack room needed no more than a wipe off with a damp rag. The Winchester in its saddle boot hadn't been begrimed with plaster or 'dobe dust at all, and the possibles stored in his saddlebags had been protected as well. It had only been stale socks, underwear, and that one old hickory shirt they'd taken for his mortal remains.

As Longarm boarded an eastbound Southern Pacific combination that afternoon, the folks he was hoping to catch up with in Austin were as aware as he that the day was shaping up to be a scorcher, although dry lightning was the least of Ki's worries, over in the Hill Country, as he kept urging the lady known as Lone Star to quit while she was ahead.

She was willing to agree this protracted search for purloined beef that might not be anywhere in these hills could be costing her more, in the form of neglected business chores, than that many cows could be worth. But like Lemonade Lucy Hayes, Jessica Starbuck had a stubborn streak to go with her outwardly serene approach to life.

As Miss Jessica Starbuck of Texas, Lone Star had naturally been presented to the first lady ever dubbed The First Lady by the press. The young Texican heiress, on a business trip East, had gotten along right well with the more matronly and smilingly stubborn mother of eight. It just wasn't true that lemonade flowed like wine at the White House. During the dinner Lone Star had enjoyed there they'd served her a hollowed-out orange filled with a refreshing rum sherbet. Lone Star neither knew nor cared whether the rum flavoring was artificial, as some said, or real Jamaica rum, as others insisted. The point had been that nobody had gotten falling-down drunk, and all the Hayes children had been as well behaved as their mother's guests. A lady who knew her own mind didn't have to put up with any nonsense off anybody.

Lone Star was saying as much to Ki as they wound around yet another bend in the maze of rolling rocky slopes. Ki murmured something rude about all womankind in Japanese, then insisted, "Jessie, if those cows are anywhere in these hills, and we don't know they are, they could die of old age, and so could we, before we ever found them! You can't see a country mile in any direction amid all these half-timbered outcrops, and even if you could, we're talking about over thirty thousand square miles!"

To which she demurely but stubbornly replied, "Pooh, we don't have to search every draw. We've a rough idea where those Graysons graze stock, and I told you about them using a chevron trail brand."

Ki shook his head and replied, "No, you didn't. That brand inspector in Austin told you they brand Lazy Triangle. That's not what that vaquero read when he spied your cows moving up that draw, many a mile from here—if he spied any of your cows at all. Has it occurred to you the boy could have simply been trying to curry favor with you, Jessie?"

Lone Star scowled and almost asked a dumb question. But as a self-appointed tracker of crooks great and small, she'd long since learned what every lawman, or lawwoman, knows about eyewitnesses.

Eyewitnesses got things wrong a lot. Innocent folks with no good reason to lie were forever throwing dust in the law's eyes in a sincere attempt to help. When asked a question, most folks would rather answer any fool way than allow they simply don't know. So it was perfectly possible a young range rider, who'd seen most anything while out on the range alone, had convinced himself he'd seen something that might help. Custis Long had told her more than one tale of side trips to dreamland, inspired by eyewitnesses with no sensible reason to dream such whoppers up.

On the other hand, nine out of ten times one could bet on fire where a halfway honest informant had reported smoke. No cow thieves would ever be caught if anyone trying to cut their trail refused to trust folks who said they'd spied the rascals. So as she brushed a buzzing horn fly away from her face with her free hand, Lone Star told Ki, "We're over halfway to the Grayson spread. We'll scout them regardless of how they might brand, and if they don't have any Circle Star stock out yonder in the middle of nowhere, we'll head back to Austin and take her from there."

"Then you're not giving up on those missing cows, no matter how much it costs you?" Ki asked, knowing full well what her answer would be.

Ki was mildly surprised when she said, instead, "Get out of my face, you fool fly! Do I look like I'm sprouting horns? Go find a calf with budding horns to lay your pestiferous eggs in. Hasn't anyone ever told you why you're called a horn fly?"

Ki slapped at another specimen of the same species, also surprised. The Texican horn fly, while a bane to the Texas cattle industry, seldom pestered humans, horses, or anything else but horned cattle, sheep, or goats. The adult horn fly subsisted on the same food or filth as the common housefly. It wasn't nearly as pesky as the biting horsefly, unless it was in a family way and laid eggs where a cow had a wire cut or an irritated hide around the roots of a horn. The tiny eggs hatched out to be horrible maggots that could sicken a cow to death or drive it to killing somebody else because of their awesome itching. Since both Ki and Lone Star knew all this, Ki could only nod and stand taller in his stirrups for a look about when Lone Star called back, "There has to be a herd of tormented cows within the hunting range of all these infernal horn flies!"

Ki called back, *"Dotira o erabimasita ka?"* as he indicated the nearest limestone ridge. Lone Star nodded. *"Hai.* I'll try the other way." As she tethered her pack pony to a handy mesquite, Ki did the same with his so they could fan out to back-track those flies.

Lone Star heard the lowing and rope slaps of a herd on the move as she topped the rise to their north. Nothing was moving in the next draw over. But she nodded thoughtfully at the faint haze of dust against the northern skyline and called out to Ki, way to her south.

Ki spun his pony to use Plains sign, wigwagging his spread fingers at shoulder level to indicate "what, where, or why?" Lone Star made the Indian sign for cow, it looked as if she was milking her left thumb. Then she signed for him to hang back and cover there as she rode in. She'd turned in her own saddle to ride over the rise before Ki could sign a firm negative back at her. To anyone who'd never chatted with Kiowa or Comanche at a safe distance, it might have looked as if Ki was writing something on his left palm with his right trigger finger.

Lone Star loped down the far side and across the intervening draw. She headed for a clump of wind-gnarled live oak in a saddle of the next rocky ridge. But even as she was riding for the cover two men in Texas hats and faded denims, who'd obviously dismounted on the far slope to bull through the live oak on foot with their saddle guns, broke cover to hail her, guns held politely enough at port arms.

Seeing they had the edge on her no matter what she did next, Lone Star waved as if she'd been seeking high and low for the both of them and rode on up the slope.

As she reined in at conversational range she saw the younger of the pair had Indian or part-Indian features as well as a Winchester '66 Yellow Boy. The somewhat older and more Anglo hand to her right packed the more recent and popular Winchester '73.

Leaving her own Colt and Winchester right where they were, Lone Star smiled down at the unseemly pair and innocently trilled, "Howdy. My friends call me Jessie and I'm looking for the Grayson outfit."

"You found it," said the older and meaner-looking one. "We beat you up to this live oak on account we heard you calling out to someone just now. Would you like to tell us who that might be, ma'am?"

She tried to smile more warmly, noting it didn't seem to have much effect on either, as she replied, "I was calling out to you all, of course. I had you figured in that draw I just crossed, and I was told long ago never to ride in on a herd on the move without letting anyone know I was coming."

The older one with the younger carbine smiled up at her grudgingly and said, "You was told right. I'm Rafe Grayson. This here's Chief. We calls him that on account nobody can pronounce his true Comanche name."

"I was sprinkled Ian Gordon and my daddy was a Comanchero trader, not no chief," the young breed protested. But his obvious boss just snorted and said, "Backtrack this lady's pony and tell us how truthful she might be, Chief." Then he nodded curtly at Lone Star. "You'd best come along with me, ma'am. Watch your pretty face punching through them live-oak branches."

Then he ducked under some branches to vanish from sight for the moment. Lone Star saw her chance, but decided not to take it. So far they'd been acting reasonably, despite the mean things she'd heard about them. She was never going to get a good look at their herd by running away from it. The one called Chief was already heading down the southern slope afoot. She knew he was no danger to Ki whether he caught her in any fibs or not. So she reached her free hand up to hold on to her hat brim and protect her face as she spurred her pony through the wall of fat green leaves and skinny brittle twigs.

As they came out the far side she spied Rafe Grayson well down the slope ahead of her, still afoot, not looking back, as he headed for the trio of ponies waiting halfway up the north slope with their reins grounded in the grass. Down below, a strung-out herd of longhorns moved along the bottom of the draw like a big brown snake enjoying a dust bath. There were other Grayson riders up and down the draw, of course, but none close enough to worry an armed and dangerous woman. So Lone Star relaxed a bit as she walked her own pony after Rafe and the three cow ponies further down.

The *three* cow ponies?

And then the braided reata thrown from behind her, by an expert roper, dropped lightly around her head and shoulders to pin her elbows to her waist, yank her rudely from her saddle, and deposit her on the grass with a bone-jarring thud.

She'd fallen off her first pony as a child, and might have survived this fall as bravely had not Rafe Grayson whirled with a rebel yell to dash back up the slope and kick her in the head as she struggled to sit up.

Then she was six or seven again and that infernal paint pony had balked at a fence and dumped her in the dust in her Sunday-go-to-meeting riding habit, and now she was going to get it for being such a tomboy, riding bareback and astride in pantaloons and skirts.

Then she noticed she was riding even sillier, facedown with her derriere in the air across the saddle, wrists bound behind her and her legs dangling down the far side. She'd lost her hat as well as her gunbelt amid all this confusion of kicked-up dust and swirling stars. She shook her blond head to clear it. She still couldn't see much more than dusty grass and the hooves of the pony they'd bound her over. It wasn't the bay she'd been riding. It was a big-ger roan. The center-fire Mex saddle was unfamiliar as well. The slender figure leading it, mounted on Lone Star's roping saddle and bay, noticed she was back among the conscious again. He told her, quietly, "I'm sorry Rafe booted you after Lopez roped you, ma'am. I'd have settled for just disarming you and tying you up, had it been up to me. I know that can't be a comfortable way to ride. But we're almost there."

She sucked in some air on an upward jolt, and conserved it by speaking even more softly as she replied, "I could tell you had better breeding, ah, Ian? Would you mind telling me why you all have taken me captive and how far we might be from the Grayson home spread?"

Chief, or Ian Gordon as he preferred to be called, told her, "Rafe took you prisoner because you was trespassing on Grayson range, or mayhaps because he's just like that, ma'am. We ain't taking you all the way home with us just yet. We'll be stopping at a line camp Rafe and his brothers built for their daddy, Old Grizzly Grayson. Lucky for you, most likely, old Grizz was run over by my own momma's kin back '74. The line camp he ordered built over the only tank for miles is where we're herding this new stock. Given plenty of water and tolerable grass they ought to stay put without our having to watch 'em too severe."

Lone Star said she knew a thing or more about grazing stock on marginal range. By craning her neck uncomfortably she could make out some of the closer cows they were talking about. She didn't see any branded Circle Star, and it was true this outfit's trail brand seemed to be a complete triangle. That didn't mean they couldn't run an open V to a triangle at any stage of the game, whatever their game might be.

Letting her head and dangling blond hair loll down at stirrup level some more, she asked the part-Comanche in a conversational tone, "Who killed the old daddy of all these sweet lads? Tosawi, Parra-Wa-Samen, or Uncle Quanah Parker?"

Chief blinked, frowned, and demanded, "You call Ten Bears of the Yamparika Comanche by his Comanche name? You call Quanah, son of the great Peta Nocona, your *uncle*?"

To which she modestly replied, "Well, he was only in his thirties when he decided to come in, and my own father was one of the few trusted Texicans he asked to speak for him. Quanah and his band hid out on our range a spell before the B.I.A. decided it made more sense to feed 'em than to fight 'em. As you likely know, Uncle Quanah was the love child of a Comanche chief and Miss Cynthia Ann Parker, carried off as a child by raiders who'd objected to the location of her real daddy's ranch, and raised to womanhood by otherwise kindly Indians."

Chief grumbled, "I know all about Quanah and his poor momma. The Texas Rangers rescued her, or thought they had, just afore the War Betwixt the States. She was returned to her white kith and kin along with a baby breed daughter, Miss Topasannah. But all she could do was grieve for the two breed sons she would never see again, and they say she starved to death, deliberate, after Topasannah died in '64. I still don't see how that makes her oldest boy, Quanah, any kin to *you*."

Lone Star patiently explained, "The term was meant honorific. He was a friend of my father and a guest under our roof. What else was I to call a poker-faced older man who gave me wampum work for my sixteenth birthday? Santa Claus?"

Chief chuckled dryly. "Yes. It's Comanche custom to adopt anyone they don't intend to kill or sleep with as younger kinsfolk. Quanah gave up five or six years ago, right?"

She dimpled up at him to primly reply, "It's none of your business just when I might have been sweet sixteen. Uncle Quanah had been considering such options long before he came in formal. The bloody siege at Adobe Walls must have matured Uncle Quanah a mite. Buffalo rifles with telescopic sights can mature anyone aboard an Indian pony on open prairie. Uncle Quanah once told us that after they were beaten off at Adobe Walls, some of his followers set out to slaughter their medicine man, Isatai. He made 'em stop. They were already having enough trouble with bad medicine. But from that day on he thought less about medicine and more about the spirits his white momma had talked to. After Three Fingers Mackenzie served up more bad medicine and artillery fire at Palo Duro in the summer of '74, Uncle Quanah had had enough. He and his Kwahadi band were the last survivors of Palo Duro to come in, but come in they did, and now Uncle Quanah's living white as you."

She hesitated, then added, innocently, "Maybe whiter. Last I heard he was helping white settlers set up land deals and encouraging Indians to get educated. Uncle Quanah's a *soldado muy hombre* who, having fought and lost fair and square, abides by the laws of Texas and doesn't go stealing cows and kidnapping women!"

Chief scowled. "Bite your tongue, girl. We got this herd cheap but lawsome, and it ain't for me to say whether you've been abducticated or placed under arrest. What gave you the right to pussyfoot around on other folks' range and then lie about it when they asked you some simple questions polite?"

Lone Star sighed, staring down at a horned toad staring back up at her from a fresh hoofprint because it was too squashed to run off. "I might have known you'd cut the sign of that pack pony as busted loose when first I heard you boys over in this draw. I'll bet you thought that meant I'd been riding with yet another gal. You never caught up with old Blacky, right?"

"Not on foot," Chief said thoughtfully. Lone Star had always found men who thought the most easy to confuse.

Chief muttered, "The runaway's a black one, packing supplies or Lord only knows who else. How's that for reading sign on summer-kilt grass and slickrock?"

She sighed and said, "Suit yourself. Blacky will come in for water once he sees how the rest of us are being treated, and you'll be able to see for yourself. Meanwhile, do I really have to ride with my head all adangle like this, Ian? You could guard me just as hard if I was seated astride with my hands still tied behind me, you know."

Chief said, "I would if Rafe was calling a trail break. Only he ain't and he ain't likely to, this side of that line camp. He wants this herd settled in near water, used to the surrounding range, well ahead of sundown."

Lone Star told him she knew about bedding a herd for the night on new range, and added, sweetly, "I forgot a Scotch Comanche couldn't ride fast enough to catch up with strolling cows."

It worked. Chief led Lone Star's mount to one side upslope and demanded to know, as he reined in, how in thunder he'd become a Scot as well as Comanche. She said she'd tell him as soon as he got her head up so all this blood could drain from her poor brain.

Chief dismounted, grounding her lead line as well as his own reins, and reached up to grab her hipbone on either side and haul her off. As she landed on her numbed feet with her hands bound behind her, she found her bare fingers brushing the fly of his sweaty denim jeans. But he resisted any temptation he might have felt to thrust forward. He let go of her left hip and shifted the grip of his right hand in a helpfully indelicate way as he reached around the front of her for a left stirrup. "Lean back agin me and get your foot planted firm enough to lever the rest of you aboard, ma'am."

She did, her own breath catching as she leaned her silk-clad back against the muscular youth. She knew this was a mighty odd time to be admiring masculine charms, even though the young breed was nice-looking in his own exotic way and she hadn't had any for a spell. It still felt pleasantly exciting when the surprisingly strong young cowhand put his right hand in a friendly position to boost her, or goose her, aboard that Mex saddle she'd been riding in a far less dignified manner up until then. She almost went over the far side. A less skilled rider would have, with both hands tied so awkwardly. Chief grabbed her left thigh as he saw he'd put her aboard harder and farther than intended. When he saw she was staying in that saddle come hell or high water, he kneaded her firm thigh with more admiration than lust, saying, "You sure got powerful, ah, limbs, ma'am."

She nodded down at him. "I was riding before I was walking, or so they say. I can't recall learning to do either. I was walking and riding pretty good as far back as I can remember."

Chief said that likely accounted for the way she was built under her riding skirts. Like most halfway decent men of his era, he'd learned to say plenty about female anatomy without using any down-right improper words such as "leg" in mixed company. As the properly brought up young breed was remounting his own pony they were joined by the rougher Rafe Grayson, who demanded to know what in thunder they were doing back there, and crudely added, "Don't go trying to change your luck with white meat unless you clear it with me and my brothers first."

Chief flushed a shade of darker brown, which was close as most Indians could get to showing embarrassment, or rage, as he protested, "I was just setting her upright in the saddle so's we could both move faster if we had to."

Rafe stared thoughtfully at the captive blonde, shrugged, and declared, "Just make sure you hang on to her in any position and gun her if she makes a break for it. That goes for any attempt her pals might make to git her back too!"

Chief nodded. "I've been studying on that, Rafe. The lady says she was leading three pack ponies and that one busted loose when it sensed this herd."

Lone Star volunteered, "Blacky's an old nag who remembers the buffalo over on the Staked Plains. She must have shied at

74

the notion of mysterious hooves coming her way in considerable numbers."

Rafe ignored her to scowl at the young breed. "You had another rider lighting out to the south when he spied you coming."

Chief said, "Might have been a *she*. Might have been nobody at all, like she keeps saying. I never saw the black brute in question, Rafe, and that's something to study on as well. I *would* have seen it, soon as anyone riding it should have seen me afoot in brush, unless, like she says, that fourth pony had lit out over the rocks to the south well before we caught her."

Rafe grimaced and said, "Gun her either way at the first sign of trouble. I got a herd to punch on home."

He reined his own mount to ride back up the lowing column of cows. Lone Star called out, "Before you go, sir. Would you mind telling a gal just why on earth she's being treated so mean? We met on open range and we're still on open range, federal property, no matter what you or your rival stock folk might say."

Rafe smiled crookedly and told Chief, "I told you how slick she might be as you and Lopez was loading her aboard, remember?"

Chief shrugged. "I remember you saying she was some sort of honorary female Ranger. I still say I've never heard tell of the Texas Rangers having a female auxiliary."

Rafe told him, "There's a heap of things you've never heard of, you poor benighted heathen. I knew who she was the moment I spied that shiny star pinned to her hat. We got us the one and original Lone Star, Jessica Starbuck from the mesquite country further west. So don't you go dropping your guard around her, boy. For if she don't tear your fool face off, me and my brothers will, hear?"

Then he spun his pony to lope west through the haze of dust and out of sight. Chief spurred after Rafe and the others, or most of the others. The tail of the herd was just passing now, with a pair of unhappy-looking drag riders in tow, faces covered with kerchiefs and otherwise so dusty it was hard to tell whether they might be Mex or Anglo.

Chief led the captive Lone Star along a contour line of the draw, above most of the stirred-up dust. As he slowed to the pace of the plodding herd, closer to the head of the column, Lone Star suggested, "You boys must have something you're anxious to hide, if you took me for some kind of law."

Chief said, "Never you mind what we might or might not want to hide from any law, ma'am. You was going to explain that remark about Scotch Comanche as soon as I made you more comfortable, remember?"

She nodded. "Gordon is an illustrious Scotch name, making your Comanchero daddy a gent of some quality, whatever he was doing in Comanche country with trade rifles and firewater. My own father kept a fair library over at the Circle Star and we had Logan's *Illustrated History of the Scottish Clans.* As a girl I studied it on many a rainy winter's day, and liked to picture myself gussied up like a highland lassie. There was this one Miss Sinclair who got to go barefoot in a ferocious red plaid, and Miss Mac Nicol got to wear a ruby brooch I really admired. I forget how the old boy named Gordon was dressed. But I remember the book said Ian was the highland way of spelling John, and that the highlanders were the warrior bands of their nation."

Chief looked pleased. "I never knew my name was John before. I mind I heard somewheres about Queen Victoria setting great store by her Scotch soldiers in India. Nobody never told me Gordon was a Scotch name, though. You say they're *quality* Scotch?"

"Some of 'em are earls—that's Scotch for a gent a mite higher than a chief," she replied, racking her brains for more about Clan Gordon in that fool book. "They've even written a song about Miss Peggy Gordon, if I could recall it. She must have been a real looker, breaking hearts the way she did in the old country."

Chief asked her to sing it for him. Before Lone Star could reply they were joined by another youth in *charro* duds and a bigger hat. He called out, "*El patron* said I was to watch this *muchacha* and rope her again if she made a break for it, Chief."

To which the breed primly replied, "I'll thank you to call me an *earl* if you can't get my Christian name right, you ignorant greaser."

★

Chapter 7

If you believed illustrations by Currier and Ives, some steam loco-
motives of the day could get up around a hundred miles an hour
on selected sections of Eastern track. Given the trackage of West
Texas it took guts to average thirty or forty miles an hour. So
the day was well shot by the time Longarm reached the transfer
point at Alpine, north of the Big Bend and still west of the Pecos,
courtesy of the pokey Southern Pacific.

It got worse. They told Longarm and the other Austin-bound
passengers they could expect a longer delay than usual, thanks
to some repair work down the grade between Marathon and
Sanderson. So Longarm toted his saddle and possibles clean off
railroad property, and stowed it all behind the clerk's desk at the
Cathedral Hotel. The hotel was named for a nearby mountain one
could see from the windows facing south upstairs.

Longarm was thinking ahead. At the rate they had him going
he'd arrive in San Antone at too ungodly an hour to wire anything
but night letters nobody would answer for a spell. So he hired a
flop for the night there in Alpine, with a view to either going on
to Austin through San Antone, or hiring a livery mount to head
elsewhere, depending on some answers.

Pocketing his hotel key and change, Longarm retraced his steps
to the Western Union across from the railroad depot. Had Alpine
not been the county seat as well as the junction where the Southern
Pacific met up with the Panhandle & Santa Fe, neither the depot

77

nor telegraph office might have been so imposing. A traveling man had to know where he might be getting his fool self stuck for the night.

Knowing before he'd arrived that he'd have at least a forty-five-minute layover in Alpine, Longarm had directed some folks he'd wired earlier to reply, if they meant to, care of Western Union's Alpine branch. The telegrapher on duty there was a pleasantly plump little gal with her mouse-brown hair pinned up severely and an unpleasant manner of dealing with strange men. When Longarm told her who he was and what he wanted, she told him that was easy for him to say but that she'd like some proof.

Then she got out a magnifying glass to go over the federal badge and identification papers he'd spread on the counter between them. She must not have detected any trickery. She slid it all his way and put her big lens back under the counter, saying, "I didn't mean to be unkind but one can't be too careful this close to the border—on a mountain pass as well."

He nodded soberly. "Lot's of folks take me for a Mexican bandit since I've got so suntanned out this way. You were fixing to tell me if there were any messages here for me, right?"

She dimpled slightly and confided she'd have never asked for proof of his identity if she hadn't been holding more than one for him.

She handed over a sheaf of yellow envelopes. He resisted the impulse to reach for a smoke, lest she cloud up on him some more, and just tore each envelope open to read. He resisted the impulse to cuss as he found out that nobody up at the Circle Star could tell him where that damned desk on that damned buckboard might be, or where in thunder Jessie Starbuck might be since she'd lit out with Ki from Austin on a mission to points unknown, and that Billy Vail still wanted to know how he was coming along with those delicate state secrets.

Longarm picked up a Western Union pencil better than his own and started tearing blanks off their telegram pad to fuss back at everybody. He told his home office where he was and why, figuring that would hold them for now. He wired that fool *tercero* up at the Circle Star to sit on that crate if his vaqueros brought it back, to run it to the nearest railroad town if they caught up with it closer to such a town than the ranch, and in either case, not to open the crate if they knew what was good for them.

Then knowing what a long shot it was, he wired Jessie's hotel and office manager in Austin to hang on to that crate and wire him direct and collect the moment it arrived.

The chubby little telegraph clerk, who had to read everything he'd blocked in as she counted the words at a nickel a shot, must have been the one who'd taken down the messages he'd just read. She said, "I know this is your business and none of my own, Deputy Long, but am I to understand some fool Mexicans have started out for Austin with government property aboard a buckboard? I've a general idea of the distance. We relay lots of messages from Mexico to that Starbuck outfit. Hauling freight that far by buckboard would take them over a week, Lord willing and the creeks don't rise."

He nodded soberly. "The boys involved were all Tex-Mex with notions of cross-country travel left over from less complicated times. I noticed, trying to route my ownself from El Paso to Austin, that you just can't beeline worth mention by rail."

"There's a railroad running fairly close to that big ranch and right through Fort Stockton, isn't there?" she said.

He nodded. "Miss Jessie Starbuck's got more than one private railroad car as well as more than one ranch. I almost headed for Fort Stockton my ownself, before a quick look at the map showed me there's no rail connection from there to Austin unless you'd like to ride to hell and back."

He squinted his eyes half shut for a better picture of his mental map. "That young *tercero* likely thought, at first, to run that crate over to Fort Stockton and ship her by rail from yonder to Austin. Then he figured, or somebody told him, how the Panhandle & Santa Fe swings way north to head up into the Texas Panhandle instead of Austin, Houston, and such. So he said to just keep going, the idjet."

She blinked her eyes. "Wait a minute. That Panhandle & Santa Fe runs through here as well, right?"

He nodded. "That's what I'm doing here this evening. Depending on some answers to them wires, I can light out from here to Fort Stockton, Santa Fe, the Circle Star, or even on over to Austin. Makes a body feel like a big smart spider in the center of a web."

Then Longarm chuckled. "I ain't been a spider long enough to enjoy flies for supper, though. I reckon I'll go exploring for some chili con carne or *migas*. You'll still be on duty should I return in about an hour, right?"

She stared wistfully out through the front glass at the lengthening shadows. "I don't get off until midnight. If you like *migas* try the Cazares Comedor around the corner and down past the barber pole. They make the best *migas* this side of the Rio Bravo."

He said he would and meant it, figuring any gal who called the Rio Grande by its Mex name ought to know Mex cooking, blue eyes and brown hair or not.

He found the small diner where she'd said it might be, open to the street and cool shades of evening as it sent its tempting odors out to say, "*Buenoches, amigo. A 'onde va?*"

So seeing he'd been invited to seek no further, he turned in to take a seat at one of the four candlelit blue-painted tables. He told the shy and pretty *muchacha* who came out from the back kitchen that he couldn't make up his mind between their *migas,* their chili, their tamales, or their chicken enchiladas, now that he could smell them all at once.

She said his nose had missed the briskets of barbecued ribs they had on special that night. He sighed and decided he'd best order *migas* and ribs with a pitcher of *cerveza.* You didn't have to order lots of tortillas to smother the fire in a good Tex Mex joint. They knew what their own cooking tasted like.

The young waitress was back in no time with more grub than he thought he'd just ordered. It was easy to see how that West-ern Union gal had developed that cute little extra chin if she ate there often.

Migas were a Tex-Mex invention whipped up with scrambled eggs, tomatoes, red and green peppers, torn-up tortillas, and Lord knows what all. It took extra mouthfuls of corn-meal tortillas and Mex *cerveza,* brewed German-lager style, to put the fire out between swallows.

Barbecued beef ribs, big and greasy as obtainable, were one of the Anglo Texan's nicer contributions to Tex-Mex cuisine, oth-ers being grits and gravy—unless, as some contended, it was the American Indian who introduced hominy grits to the Old South. The sauce they'd used to barbecue this particular brisket had less brown sugar and more tabasco than an Anglo Tex cook might have used. When his waitress asked him anxiously, noting he was armed, whether he found their cooking too spicy, he assured her, in Spanish, " Not at all. As one travels north they use less and less pepper, until by the time one orders chili in Montana, one may as well be ordering Boston beans."

She had a pretty laugh to go with her Spanish features and Apache eyes. It was hard to say whether she was worried about his digestion or trying to flirt. Apache eyes could be mysterious.

When he failed to flirt back he was left to finish his supper in peace. He'd have ordered dessert if it had been an Anglo beanery. Since it wasn't, he just paid for what he'd had and quit while he was ahead. Mex coffee wasn't bad, but their notions of apple or mince pie took getting used to, and he'd had enough of such notions for now.

Out on the streets of Alpine the shadows were long and purple indeed, and the sky above was tomato to the west and eggplant to the east. There was still enough light to consult his pocket watch. He figured he'd given that little Western Union gal long enough. So that was where he was headed when, rounding the corner, he spied fresh lamplight in a coffee shop across the way and decided, "It's early and I'd really like some home made coffee and cake to top those spicy ribs off."

So he sidestepped off the walk, and that still might not have saved him had not someone somewhere to his rear called out, "Brazo Largo! *Cuidado!*" to send him over a watering trough just ahead, headfirst, as all hell busted loose behind him!

Brazo Largo was simply Longarm in Spanish, while *cuidado,* of course, meant "look out." So he was more annoyed than astounded to hear bullets thunking wetly into the wooden watering trough as he sprawled in the dust and powdered horseshit behind it, his own gun gripped in one big fist while he pondered his next move.

Sticking his head up from behind his soggy cover didn't sound like such a smart one. In the tricky light he saw, at second glance, there was a gap between the dirt he now lay in and the plank walk he'd just jumped from. So he rolled under it, and proceeded to snake toward the source of those mysterious gunshots on his belly and elbows, past the cover he hoped they still thought they had him pinned behind.

But there were no more shots, and by the time he'd crawled far as the corner he'd just rounded, there were boots clomping on the planks above as well as back and forth out there in the street. He still lay doggo till he heard that same familiar voice calling, cautiously, "Hey, Brazo Largo? Where the hell are you?"

Longarm rolled out from under the walk, making a pilgrim in high buttons and a derby hat shy like a spooked pony, and got to his own booted feet, dusting off his tweeds with the battered Stetson in his left hand as he kept his .44-40 ready for action.

A slender figure, almost as tall as Longarm and clad all in black *charro*-style, was putting his own .45-55 away. As they got within conversational range in the broody sunset, Longarm recognized the high-toned Hispanic features of El Gato, as the handsome young cuss sporting the big black sombrero was called. El Gato was hard to mistake for a normal border Mex in that spooky outfit, with all the silvery braid and conchos others admired replaced with black jet or painted over with stove polish. As they shook hands in the street El Gato said, "He was Anglo. Dark suit and hat, crushed north-range-style. I missed him too. I didn't go for this widow-maker until he'd already drawn on your back. I gave my own show away by shouting that warning. He was running and bobbing over *that* way, pegging rounds your way as I was trying to nail him. He ducked through that gap across the street. I don't know if I winged him or not. Now you know as much as I do."

Longarm holstered his own six-gun as he soberly replied, "Not half, El Gato. For openers, how come you was pussyfooting along behind me instead of calling out to your old pals?"

The Mexican bandit or liberator, depending on whom one might ask, smiled shyly and explained, "I am not north of the border this evening, should anyone wish for to question my whereabouts. Knowing your devotion to your Tio Sam and your admiration for El Presidente Diaz, I did not wish for to burden you needlessly with my own little secrets. *Pero* when I saw that other hombre throwing down on your back, I thought it best to risk possible trouble with the law. Am I in trouble with the law, *amigo mio*?"

Longarm said, "Not if you let me do the talking, you fool Mex." Sure enough, an older man in a worn blue shirt with a shiny brass badge was heading their way with a ten-gauge scattergun and a wary expression.

Longarm called out, "I'm the law too, and yep, that was us you just heard discharging firearms within your city limits, ah, Sheriff. We had to. Some son of a bitch who run over betwixt yonder store fronts was discharging at us first."

The older man kept his muzzle aimed politely down as he quietly suggested he was only a Brewster County deputy and that he'd sure like to see some proof if he was talking to another lawman.

Longarm always packed his billfold well away from his side arm lest others mistake his intent when he went for his badge and credentials. The older deputy sheriff recognized the federal badge and printed identification at first glance, and seemed more relaxed as he asked, "Betwixt them two buildings, after trying to backshoot you, you say?"

Longarm nodded. "Dark suit. Low-crowned hat. That's the best we can do. It was all over fast, as you must have just noticed. Neither of us got a good look at the cuss, and I just can't say what made him so moody. Why don't we all get out of this hot sunset and mull it over sitting down?"

The local law allowed talking was a thirsty chore. So the three of them retired to a nearby saloon the deputy sheriff recommended. Longarm had really wanted that coffee and cake, but what the hell.

They found a booth near the back of the hole-in-the-wall workingman's saloon. The light was a bit better, thanks to a sputtering coal-oil lamp someone had just pumped to full pressure in the center of the pressed-tin ceiling. It was easier to see the older lawman needed a shave now. He shot a keener look at El Gato as they all sat down, musing half to himself, "No offense, señor. But you sure resemble a young cuss *los rurales* have a handsome bounty posted on."

Longarm said, "Old Roberto Capucha here ain't wanted by the law in these parts, and he just now saved my bacon from a backshooter. So Viva Mejico and fuck her current government, and we'll all get on better if we stick to *Anglo* owlhoot riders. Have you had any banks held up or stock run off of late, pard? In all modesty, I've a rep for rounding up such rascals, and some rascals have been acting awfully anxious about me ever since I left Denver."

The Brewster County lawman said they hadn't been having a crime wave of late. Then a weary-looking breed in a dirty shirt and clean apron came over, and the lawman added they'd all like some tumblers and a pitcher of draft.

Meanwhile, Longarm passed out cheroots, and as they lit up he asked El Gato if he recalled the time they'd first met, riding the Laredo Loop down Mexico way. The vaguely sinister young Mex with no visible means of support nodded soberly. "I have been considering those Anglo cow thieves using my country as a detour for to move stolen stock between your Texas and Arizona Territory. It was the first thought I had when that *cabrone* threw down on your back just now. *Pero* between yourself and *los rurales,* little gringo stock has been moving about south of the border."

Longarm asked, "What about Mex stock—let's say, seized in the name of the Causa de Libertad?"

El Gato looked away, murmuring, *"Quien sabe?* Anything is possible in a country governed by ogres. *Pero* that was an Anglo wearing his hat in the northern fashion, not a Mexican liberator of beef, just now, no?"

Their beer and glasses were brought to the table. As the old deputy sheriff poured, Longarm softly confided, "A lady we both know and admire, name of Jessie, just lost about a thousand head. Even as we speak, she and her *segundo* are out hunting for them. What if some poor dumb cow thieves think I'm out to join in the hunt?"

El Gato reached for the beer the deputy had poured him, nodding his thanks as he told Longarm, "Hombres have been shot in the back, or even the front, for less. *Are* you on your way for to help Jessie recover her stolen beef, amigo?"

Longarm reached for his beer as well, growling, "Mean as it sounds, stealing cows in Texas ain't a chore for the Denver Federal District Court. I ain't supposed to tell nobody what I want with the lady robbed by others. So don't ask no questions and I'll tell you no lies."

The deputy sheriff brightened. "Say, we must be jawing about Miss Jessica Starbuck and her stolen cows, now that I study harder on your words, Deputy Long. We got us a bulletin on them cows a few days back. The Rangers have been keeping an eye peeled for 'em all along the border too. But that can't be the way the thieves druv 'em. You say that old boy who just tried to backshoot you is in cahoots with the same gang?"

Longarm sipped some beer. It was warmer and flatter than the brew he'd had with his ribs. He grimaced. "Had you really been paying attention you'd have heard me surmise it works more ways than one. Someone could be worried I was after cow thieves. Someone could be worried about me catching 'em at something else."

They both seemed to want to know what else was left. Longarm shook his head. "I just told you I ain't supposed to talk indelicate about delicate matters. I can say, since I've sent wires about it all

84

over creation, a certain item of government property was delivered to Jessie Starbuck by mistake, after which it gets even sillier. They want me to catch up with it, her, or both, just so's it can be sent to its proper destination."

"What's a post office mistake got to do with stolen cows?" asked the deputy sheriff in a sincerely puzzled tone.

Longarm didn't want to repeat himself or, worse yet, say too much. So he simply inhaled some smoke and suds to let El Gato muse, half aloud, "A hired gun following you down from Denver might have his hat crushed in the northern fashion. North plains riders stealing Texas beef could account for the reasons nobody *I* know has heard a thing about that many *vacas* on the move, eh?"

The older lawman stared at the younger Mex thoughtfully through the drifting tobacco smoke as he slowly nodded, as if to himself, and said, "Right. Roberto Capucha *does* translate, half-ass, as Robin Hood. And you do fit the description on them Mex fliers, El Gato."

The Mexican purred back softly, "And what if I do, *viejo*?"

To which the wise old county lawman thought it best to reply, "Like our pard here says, you ain't wanted for shit on *this* side of the Rio Grande." Then he made an elaborate show of consulting his own watch before he added, "It's been nice talking to you kiddies, but I'm still on duty and it could mean my job if the high sheriff caught me swilling beer in here with my pals. So I'd best just get it on down the road, hear?"

He rose, dropped some coins on the table, and headed for the door. Then Longarm observed softly, "He's more likely to wire *los rurales* in Ojinaga than he is to try for you here in Texas, amigo."

El Gato said, "I know. People are always wiring *los rurales* about me, as if those *cabrones* meant to share the reward with other rats. *Pero* do not worry about them grabbing me by my *cojones* anywhere near Ojinaga. A man of prudence never jumps the border near a railroad town, or for that matter, any town at all. El Rio Bravo rolls through many a desert mile where one can cross by broad day with no fear of discovery, eh?"

Longarm nodded. "That brings us back to Jessie Starbuck's missing cows."

But El Gato shook his head and firmly insisted, *"Pero no.* One might say I am well informed about such matters. As we established when first we met, along the Laredo Loop, my *muchachos* and me have enough trouble with *Mexican* lawmen. Is true we might steal a cow in Mexico for to convert it to cash for La Causa up this way. We do not run *Texas* stock *south*. If we did, the price we got for it would be too low for to justify the risk, eh?"

Longarm nodded. "Have any Mex cows in serious numbers crossed the border into Texas lately?"

El Gato sipped delicately at his beer and looked shyly away as he replied, "Like yourself, I may know things I am not at liberty for to talk about. I fail to see how stock stolen from backers of the ghouls who stole our government off the grave of Juarez could interest any honest Anglo."

Longarm agreed El Gato sounded innocent as ever, but added, "I'd likely feel up to writing you off entire if I had a better notion what you *have* been up to up this way, *amigo mio.*"

El Gato looked pained. "Like yourself, I find one must pass through this mountain railroad juncture for to get anywhere else. Would it help you if you knew I have just been in San Antonio for to collect some *dinero* owed La Causa by a slow payer? You have my word nobody involved cares a *higo* about Jessie Starbuck's herd or your mysterious government shipment."

Longarm sipped beer thoughtfully. "What *did* you sell some slow payer of the gringo persuasion in San Antone then?"

El Gato shook his head. "I do not ask how often you play with yourself, and what my sheep and I may do in private is none of your concern either. I just told you nobody I know could be involved in anything you could be working on. What more do you ask, a dance with my sister?"

Longarm shrugged. "That reminds me of a pretty little thing over to the Western Union, and I got a night train to catch as well. It's been nice talking to you and thanks, *amigo mio.*"

They shook on it and parted friendly. By now it was much darker outside. The brighter stars were winking down from a deep purple sky. Freetail bats were fluttering around the street lamps like big-ass miller moths. They were doubtless after the real bugs attracted by the lamplight. Like the longhorn and lots of other Texas flora and fauna, freetail bats were strays from Old Mexico. Down yonder they'd started out as cave dwellers, and followed the Spanish padres and other settlers north to more open range when they discovered the barns and bell towers of mankind worked just as good as the far less common caves provided by Mother Nature. Mexicans thought freetails brought good luck. They surely kept down the bugs. Most Anglo gals were convinced bats of all persuasions existed only to tangle their fool selves up in some screaming female's hair.

The pleasantly plump little gal at the Western Union office had two pencils instead of bats in her mousy brown hair as Longarm rejoined her. She seemed glad to see anyone, and when he asked, she confirmed business had been slow. She'd only had one other customer since last they'd spoken, and that had been over half an hour back. When he asked how his own trade with her and her outfit had been going, she cheered up and handed over some more telegrams, observing, "I had to pay attention as I took them off the wire, naturally, and I have to say nothing new reads like nothing new to me."

He read every damned one anyway, leaning against the counter as he managed not to curse out loud. It wasn't easy. He saw he could have saved some traveling time and the hire of that hotel room had he not been so smart. All he'd gotten out of all the wires he'd sent from here so far had been a fair Mex meal and an attempted assassination.

He reached absently for a smoke, remembered his manners, and mused aloud, "Nobody I can think to wire would be anywheres we could reach 'em at this hour, and there's a night train bound for San Antone and Austin coming through the junction well after midnight. Are you afraid of bats, ma'am?"

She blinked, laughed incredulously, and asked what on earth bats could do with either telegraph messages or train schedules.

He smiled softly and explained, "You said you got off at midnight. That'd give us time to see you safely home through the clouds of bats outside this evening. You could put my hat on if you don't want me shooting bats close to your pretty head."

She laughed and started to say she thought freetails were sort of cute. Then she wondered why any new girl in town with her own lonesome quarters and a bit of a weight problem would want to say a thing like that.

But even as the two of them were flirting inside the lamp-lit telegraph office, the same hired gun who'd tried for Longarm earlier was lurking in the darkened doorway across the way, his right thigh throbbing under the silk bandanna wrapped around the flesh wound from El Gato's sixgun, and his own weapon, a monstrous Walker Colt Conversion, waiting six-in-the-wheel for another crack at that fucking federal lawman's broad back!

87

Chapter 8

By now there were far more stars, and bats, in the night skies of the Hill Country. The Grayson herd, gathered about their remote line camp in a deep and partly timbered draw, had accumulated clouds of blood- and crud-sucking bugs in their travels, and now the freetails were skimming back and forth above the restless horns of itchy cows, enjoying a good feed.

Seated by an outdoor supper fire with her back to the limestone rubble wall of the rambling shelter used in colder or wetter weather, Lone Star was paying more attention to the roughly dressed and rough-talking men around her than she was the stars, the bats, or even the beef stock bedded on the dusty grass across from the spring-fed tank that justified this line camp, hideout, or whatever.

She'd had plenty of time to study brands before they'd run the herd into this particular draw near sunset. Not a cow she'd seen so far wore the Starbuck brand or any other marks she recognized as West Texas. She suspected a good many of them had been marked down Mexico way. Anglo outfits tended to use stamp brands that were simple to describe as well as read from a rifle shot away. You didn't have to draw a picture of, say, a lazy K or a rocking H to have the law looking for stolen stock branded with the letter K lying down or the letter H perched atop a simple inverted arc. Any Texican who read brands would know, without looking, a Circle Star had to be either a big letter O followed by a simple star, or maybe the star inside the circle. But Mex rancheros branded more artistically, many vaqueros having an uncertain grasp of the alphabet and Arabic numerals to begin with. A heap of cows chewing their cuds over yonder wore an ornate brand she'd decided to call an upside-down Mex sombrero or maybe the simplified outline of the head of a chongo steer, a kind of longhorn with its horns grown freaky, pointed down instead of the usual way. Another brand on a heap of those mysterious critters seemed a simplified rendering of a pair of dice, rolled snake eyes with a single dot in the center of each square. She hadn't seen one brand either the Graysons or their rivals, the Sanfords, might have registered as their own.

As if to remind her even more of Old Mexico, that young Mex who'd roped her so roughly was strumming an after-supper guitar a good deal more gently. He seemed to be trying for "La Paloma." She hoped she was wrong. "La Paloma" was a sad old song, even when it was played right. It sounded sadder when it wasn't.

The youth called Chief came around the fire from the chuck wagon, packing a couple of tin cups. He hunkered down beside Lone Star to shyly hold one out to her, saying, "This ain't coffee, ma'am. Seeing you won't be called upon to guard the herd tonight, I asked the cook to brew you some hot chocolate."

She took the hot cup gingerly, with a smiling nod of thanks. It could have been asking for more trouble than she was already in to ask when, where, or with whom they expected her to turn in. It was still early and, so far, even Rafe Grayson had been calling her "ma'am." She sipped some chocolate. It was a bit bitter as well as thinner than *she'd* have made it. She still said, "This is just what I needed after grits with no gravy and *refritos* without enough salt, Ian. But about that hat I was wearing, earlier . . ."

Chief shook his head. "I asked Rafe if I could ride back to where we captured you. He said no. He said you need that hat you was wearing back yonder less'n I need a bullet in my Comanche head. You see, we got us a couple of riflemen hanging back and watching out for uninvited company dogging our trail. I told Rafe I was sure I could ride for your lost hat and get back while the light was still good, but he said not to chance it. Rafe can be real cautious at times."

Lone Star sipped more watery chocolate, choosing just how she might question the friendly but not too bright young breed further without inspiring him to clam up. She'd already discovered none of these boys felt inclined to discuss the stock they'd been herding over uncharted rolling range when she'd stumbled on their little game, whatever it might be.

Across the fire, the Mex strumming that guitar hit a truly dreadful chord, and obviously tone-deaf, decided he was as as likely strumming "La Golondrina" and started singing that instead.

Lone Star wasn't the only one there who winced. Someone called out, "Stop torturing that git-fiddle and let somebody strum it as knows how!"

Another hand volunteered, "Chief plays better than most. Surrender that instrument of torture to Chief and give the rest of us a break, you infernal coyote caught in quicksand!"

The vaquero who'd been trying in vain for *some* damned tune joined in the laughter. The guitar, whoever owned it, was passed around the fire to Chief, who modestly stubbed a few melodious bars, twisted a tuning key, and launched a fair rendition of "Old Kentucky Home."

When Lone Star and everyone else applauded that effort, Chief tried for "Old Folks at Home" and then "Jeanie with the Light Brown Hair." Lone Star got the impression he and the boys admired soft sad songs around a campfire of an evening. Most cowhands, like most soldiers, did. Such tastes seemed to go with otherwise violent natures.

Hoping to keep everyone soft and gentle as Jeanie's hair, the captive girl tried to encourage the Comanche breed to sing another sentimental ditty. Chief said, "I'm running out of mushy ones. I wish I knew the one about that pretty Scotch gal, now that you tell me I'm Scotch on my daddy's side."

Lone Star smiled and softly sang the first few bars of "Peggy Gordon." Chief nodded. "Go on. That's pretty. Do you know how to twang this git-fiddle?"

She nodded, and took the guitar from him as another hand across the fire muttered, "Hot damn, she's talented as well as pretty."

Lone Star ignored the remark, and the lewd chuckles it seemed to inspire, as striking her own key and feeling not a little awkward, she began.

Och, Peggy Gordon, thou art my darling.
Coom sit thee doon upon my knee.
Coom tell to me the very reason
Why I've been slighted so by thee!

They liked it. So she kept going as, up on the dark limestone ridge to their north, her *segundo* and would-be rescuer, Ki, listened in mingled amusement and wonder.

Ki had her lost hat in a saddlebag, *shuriken* and all. He'd almost been spotted recovering it. He would have been had not he been trained to scout more ways than one.

Thanks to the late Alex Starbuck and Comanche as well as vaquero tutors, the man called Ki knew all the Texas tricks of scouting on or about cattle country. So he'd half expected those cowhands holding Jessie down below to have outriders guarding their trail well back indeed. After he'd spotted them first, it had been simple enough to wait them out before ghosting over afoot to recover Jessie's hat, and then read the other signs occasioned by her being roped from behind while following some two-faced sneak on foot.

Before he'd seen his first blade of Texas shortgrass, Ki had been trained in more than one martial discipline of his mother's culture.

Bushido, or the way of the warrior, could be roughly divided into the fighting skills of those allowed to carry at least two swords in public and those forbidden on pain of death to pack any knightly weapons at all.

The *samurai* or armored knight of Dai Nippon was supposed to fight with semi-suicidal or downright suicidal bravery, scorning any cute tricks as he simply waded into the enemy, in any numbers, to slash and stab while screaming "*Banzai!*" until he'd won or been killed or killed himself. A *samurai* was not allowed to *lose* like lesser men.

Although the child of a *samurai*'s daughter, Ki had been forbidden full *samurai* honors by more rigid members of the warrior caste, and been forced to live the semi-outlaw life of the *ninja,* or Japanese fighting man without a fancy pedigree.

Ninja training was, in a word, sneaky. Often employed by high-toned Japanese to go where *samurai* didn't and do deeds forbidden by the fancy code of Bushido, *ninja* seldom yelled "*Banzai,*" and almost never tried anything suicidal. Most of the razzle-dazzle martial arts the gentlemen of Dai Nippon were notorious for in the rest of the world consisted of time-tested *ninja* tricks.

One he'd been taught, as a street kid learning to survive among slum dwellers who literally ate little boys on occasion, involved trailing dangerous people who seemed to be worried someone might be trailing them.

Like a deer stalker anticipating where his target might be headed, rather than sniffing where everyone knew it had been, Ki had swung far wide of the slowly moving herd that afternoon to scout far out ahead, in hopes of figuring where it might be going. He'd found the obvious line camp down there long before any Grayson point riders would have noticed him exploring the whole layout afoot, his own mount hidden a couple of country miles away in other thick timber. Like many an Apache before him, Ki had long since noticed how tough it was for an enemy on horseback to spot a man afoot in any halfway decent cover. The weakness of most mounted fighting men, be they *samurai,* Sioux, or the good old boys, was that they just hated to move about afoot and seldom expected anyone half as tough as themselves to want to.

Crouched amid wind-tortured trees atop the rise right now, Ki counted the ways he knew down into that draw, thanks to his earlier explorations that afternoon.

He'd left his useful but possibly awkward Winchester with the pony hidden three draws away. But he naturally had his sixgun with him to back his more silent weapons. Ki preferred *ninja* weapons as well as *ninja* methods when taking on superior numbers with only the element of surprise in his favor. But Ki wasn't a sap about the pros and cons of both cultures he knew. Admiral Perry had steamed into Japanese waters with big guns, a lot of big guns, and nothing more tricky the boy Shogun had been able to come up with had made Admiral Perry go away.

There were nine cowhands listening to Jessie sing around that fire. There were a couple more slowly circling the bedded-down herd on their ponies. There was no saying how many night pickets the obviously cautious leader had posted further out. So blasting in with his six-gun or even going back for his Winchester didn't sound too safe. They had Jessie down there with a stone wall at her back, and if even one decided to prevent her rescue by simply gunning her . . .

"*Hai,* we have to wait and see where they bed her down, away from that firelight, and then maybe if we work in whichever way is less guarded, picking off anyone in the way as quietly as possible . . ."

Then Ki froze solid, every hair atingle but not even his lungs working as he felt cold steel against the nape of his neck and the

92

even sneakier night crawler holding the gun drawled, quietly, "One fart loud enough to notice and you're one dead Chinaman."

Ki softly murmured, "I'm not Chinese and who's farting?"

So the one who had the drop on him chuckled. "*Bueno,* whatever you might be. Now my sidekick, Joe, aims to pat you down for weapons overt or hidden, and you're going to hold still as a bump on a log whilst he does so, ain't you?"

Ki didn't answer. Joe searched him anyway, getting everything but the *kogatana* sheathed under Ki's collar, just below the gun barrel pressed against his nape and almost touching the hilt.

Joe said he was harmless, showing how much Joe knew, and the one who'd gotten the drop on Ki said, "We'll see. You're fixing to rise to your feet slow and easy, mister. Then we're fixing to take you to our boss lady. It'll be up to Miss Billie to say what we get to do to you then. Don't try shit if you don't want me to do you afore she says I can, hear?"

Ki said he followed their drift. As they led him away from the soft strains of "Peggy Gordon," Ki was able to determine there were three of them, and wryly noted he and the Apache hadn't invented night patrols afoot in cow country after all. They walked him a good two miles, away from his own mount and extra weaponry, before they marched him down into a darkly timbered draw, calling out they were coming.

Down amid the oak and scrub cedar they had a tiny Indian fire going under a monstrous coffee pot. As well as he could tell by the faint ruby glow of mesquite coals, the figure rising on the far side seemed too shapely to be a short man. He was sure it was a woman, a fairly young one, in white cotton and bleached buckskin, when she demanded to know why the son of a bitch— probably meaning him—was still alive. She added, "Didn't you pass even one handy hanging tree along your way?"

The one who now had his saddle gun in the small of Ki's back replied, defensively, "We can't prove this one's a Grayson rider, Miss Billie. To begin with, he's some sort of Chinaman or worse, and the Graysons don't have nobody like that riding for 'em. After that, he's even more mysterious. We got the drop on him from ahint as he was scouting the Graysons from a wooded rise, sneaky as us."

The mysterious Miss Billie kicked some fresh kindling and air into the coals at her feet to shed more light on all concerned. As

93

she regarded her uninvited guest with interest, Ki could see she was a statuesque brunette, a little older as well as a little bigger than Jessica Starbuck in every way. She seemed to like what she saw well enough to smile back at Ki, although uncertainly, as she said, "As likely part Sioux as part Chinee. Too tall, lean, and mean to qualify as a runty Comanche or Chink. We're waiting to hear your tale, stranger."

Ki said, simply, "Your boys are right. I was scouting that line camp with a view to slipping in and getting back out with my own boss lady. They call me Ki. I'm *segundo* to Miss Jessica Starbuck of the Circle Star. They kidnapped her earlier today. I don't know why. You say they're called the Graysons? We were headed for the Grayson home spread when we ran afoul of them so far from home."

The other woman dressed so cow in a man's work shirt and buckskin skirts said, "I'm Billie Sanford. My daddy owns the Lazy S, and just where our range leaves off and the Graysons' range commences is a matter of some dispute. I've heard tell of Jessie Starbuck. They say she's all right. But how come you all were out to call on them mean Grayson boys if she's all right?"

Ki explained, "We're missing Circle Star stock. At least a thousand head. The only possible witness to our misfortune allowed the thieves might have been moving them trail-branded with a big triangle. We were told in Austin the Graysons trail-brand something like that. So add it up, ma'am."

Billie Sanford did. "There's nothing I wouldn't put past 'em. Guess whose beef they got bedded over in that other draw! The sons of bitches would lift the pennies off a dead sheepherder's eyelids."

The fire was dying back down. Ki could still make out the busty Billie's pouty face as he frowned thoughtfully and replied, "I know for a fact they've abducted at least one innocent maiden. I can't recall spotting any Lazy S brands on those cows they've been driving all day, though."

Billie Sanford said, "We never got the chance to mark 'em and brand 'em. They were stole *afore delivery* by them ornery Grayson brothers."

She hesitated and let the light die down between them some more before she continued, defensively, "We made a deal for some Mexican stock from a . . . supplier we've dealt with in the past. Since you raise cows in Texas you likely know how tough it can be to increase one's herd natural, with the price of beef going through the roof back East."

Ki nodded soberly. "We buy Mexican stock from time to time. We try to get a proper bill of sale to go with it, conditions down Chihuahua way being so unsettled. I take it the beef you bought crossed the border open and above board with everything on paper tidy?"

She sniffed grandly. "Don't mock me, Mister Ki. Ask me no questions about papers and I'll tell you no lies. Suffice it to say, none of us ever stole one head of that herd, however the Mexicans selling it to us might have rounded it up. We paid in advance, cash. After that the deal was for the Mex drovers to leave the herd in a certain draw southwest of our home spread, untended and unwitnessed as my boys and me took possession under the Texas maverick code. But then, before we could manage—"

"Let me guess." Ki said, interrupting with a wry grin. "Before you could round up all those, ah, strays from Old Mexico, your rivals, the Brothers Grayson, beat you to them, and now they're almost home free with them, trail-branded and . . . Why have they grabbed Jessica Starbuck in that case, the cross-grained idiots?"

Billie Sanford nodded grimly. "You just described 'em accurate as hell. I told you they'd steal the pennies off a dead man's eyes. They'd doubtless enjoy gunning the mourners to get at the corpse. I know what you're thinking about the ownership of that herd being their word against ours. They still know they're guilty, and you know how a dirty dog with a guilty conscience tends to act. They may think Jessica Starbuck can prove something. Or maybe they just grabbed her because she's good-looking as some say."

Ki felt a big gray cat get up and turn around a time or two in his gut as he muttered, "Let's hope not. So far, they seem to have been treating her like a lady."

Billie Sanford shrugged. "It's early yet, and like us, they might be waiting for Jake and Alvin to ride in. Alvin is the one your boss lady has to worry about. Both Rafe and Jake Grayson have been known to rape a gal now and again. But Alvin's the one who's mad-dog mean enough to mess gals up, even do they say yes."

Ki didn't ask how she knew this. He said, "They're holding Miss Starbuck against her will no matter how they plan to treat her. So with your permission and my weaponry back, I'm going back to convince them of the error of their ways."

Billie Sanford shook her head imperiously. "You don't have my

95

permit to go nowheres, with or without your six-gun, handsome. I've sent a rider for some extra gunhands. Ain't nobody in these parts likes them dreadful Grayson boys. Once we gather a big enough bunch we'll ride in together to finish off the Grayson outfit once and for all. You'll be welcome to tag along, and we may even give you back your gun rig, subject to your sensible behavior in the meantime."

Ki frowned. "Your bloodthirsty plan's likely to get Jessie Starbuck killed in the cross fire. It's certainly against all common sense as well as the Texas criminal code!"

She sniffed grandly again. "We'uns follow an older code. The feudal code of the hills back home. Us Sanfords hail from the County of Harlan in Old Kentuck, where men are men and it ain't too safe to cross the women. Those trashy Graysons stole our cows. It ain't the first time they've hit us, and they've been as mean to others. So you just wait and see how much fire I mean to lay on the sons of bitches, crossways, sideways, and anyways! I'll tell the boys not to gun no gals in the Grayson camp, though."

Ki shook his head. "They'll be shooting back as wild, and wild shooting has to lead to wild shots, Miss Billie."

The well-endowed young cattle baroness shrugged. "They shouldn't have got so wild with other folks' property then. It ain't as if I *want* to endanger your boss lady or even the hired help of the Grayson boys, handsome. We've tried other ways to make 'em leave us alone. Even as we speak my poor old daddy is over to Austin trying to get a warrant on the rascals so's the Rangers can arrest 'em."

Without taking time to think Ki said, "Neither the state courts nor the Rangers are apt to act on a mavericking case, Miss Billie. You should have had your Mexican . . . importers slap your own Lazy S on those cows before they left them to be sort of found by you. As things stand, it looks like a case of finders keepers."

"I just said that," Billie Sanford declared, "I told my poor old daddy he was wasting his time. But I swear he's one stubborn man. At least his riding off to the state capital, leaving me in charge, offers the rare opportunity to settle this feud Harlan County-style!"

Ki whistled softly and murmured, half to himself, "In other words we're talking about an unauthorized as well as lawfully dubious raid on a rival cattle outfit."

It had been a statement rather than a question. Billie Sanford still smiled as if she'd been complimented. "You're learning, handsome. Meanwhile, you'd best stick tight as a tick with me till we're ready to move on the Graysons. My boys will swat you like a fly if they see you hop ten feet from me without my permit. Come on. There's some white lightning in my bedroll and we might as well get comfortable as we await the coming battle."

Ki hesitated as she turned away. She hadn't strode far before a hand called Jeff growled, "You heard Miss Billie, stranger." He cocked his gun by way of emphasis. So Ki strode after her.

The buxom Billie led him through a wall of interwoven mesquite to a barely visible square about the size of your average picnic blanket, surrounded by but not directly under any mesquite or live oak. She dropped her shapely self upon it, patting the stiff canvas invitingly. So Ki sank down beside her, to discover he'd been right about her having spread her bedding with range savvy. Come sunrise, if she wasn't out shooting the world up, the trees would offer shade well on to high noon and privacy throughout the day. But should the weather turn nasty, as it could at any time in these hills, Billie's bedding lay clear of leaf drip and lightning strikes. Country folks in Japan as well as Texas held that oak trees were more apt than any other to draw lightning from the sky to the ground. So the notion was no doubt based on some true quirk of nature, perhaps the density or moisture content of the species. In the high country pines were struck more often than aspen, although it was dumb to be under *any* sort of tree when the horrendous electrical storms of the American Southwest were brewing.

Billie Sanford had dug a mason jar from somewhere in her bedding as Ki adjusted to his new surroundings, ready to move the second he could be more certain he was moving right. In the faint moonlight filtering through the shimmering leaves he could see she'd tossed her sombrero aside. Whether she was still wearing her gun or not was less clear, the way everything shimmered uncertainly in the shifting salt and pepper of moonlight and inky black shadows—mostly the latter.

She took a healthy swig from her jar, gasped for air, and held it out to Ki. He took it. That gave him the chance to roll closer, but he still wasn't sure whether that was a gun rig around her hips or the way her riding skirts had bunched. He was certain the shapely left knee she had drawn up and aimed his way on the canvas dew cloth between them was bare. He wondered idly what she was wearing

97

under that fringed split skirt. As he tasted the corn liquor in the jar, assuming it was that and not paint remover, Ki suspected he just might be able to find out if he could get *her* to inhale some more of this concoction.

The question was whether he wanted to get under her skirts or not. Ki had the same carnal appetites as most other healthy young men. But he'd been trained to control them by the same culture that had introduced him to sex at an age when most American boys were still working on what those words the bigger boys wrote on the outhouse walls really meant. He'd learned to take pleasure in the unfair sex, and vice versa, even as he'd been learning the martial arts of the Orient. Hence, just as he knew it felt far better to stab a woman's flesh with one's own than it might to sink colder steel into the flesh of an enemy, he knew only a *bakujin* cared more about pleasure than more serious matters. *Bakujin* translated loosely as a dumb asshole, and his job was to rescue Jessie Starbuck, not to trifle with Billie Sanford. But Ki still made his naturally deep voice go tomcat-purry as he told her it was great stuff, handing the jar back after pretending to drink more than he had.

She sounded sort of feline herself as she lapped up some more white lightning and replied, "My poor old daddy makes it himself out back in the blackjacks where the pesky Rangers never go. Daddy holds it's no beeswax of the state or country law what a body might choose to do with his own corn mash and spring water on his very own claim. I don't see why the Rangers have to tell the durned old federal revenue snoops about private manufacture in any case. Do you?"

Ki chuckled, as deep and sultry as he knew how, and confided, "What the revenuers don't know won't hurt anybody. A lot of Mexicans feel the same way about home-brewed *pulque*. I'm not sure whether it's the federal liquor duties Washington is worried about, or whether ladies like Lemonade Lucy Hayes just don't want anyone to get drunk. Some say cracking down on the sale of trade liquor to reservation Indians was her doing. Old U. S. Grant seemed too drunk himself to care. *I* don't care, drunk or sober. Where I grew up every farmer worth his salt converted part of his rice crop to *sake,* and nobody cared if anyone wanted to get *sake ni yu,* or falling-down-happy, on his own *sake.*"

Billie lapped more corn liquor, and handed the jar back to Ki as she said, "Damned right. It ain't natural, expecting folks to pay extra tax on stuff they make on land they've already paid taxes on. That's double taxicating, and that's what Great Grandaddy Sanford fit the Redcoats over, long ago and way back East."

Ki didn't answer as he made a pretense of drinking from the jar. They'd already established she was a free thinker when it came to any legal restrictions on mayhem or moonshine. Ki found it more interesting, as he explored the level in the jar with his tongue, that *she* was pretending to drink more than she really was as well.

Lest she catch him the same way he'd just caught her, Ki took a good swig this time, and passed the jar back with a strangled noise. He let the white lightning dribble silently away as he made a pretense of getting more comfortable on the bedroll. The fact that it made him smell like he imagined Daddy Sanford's blackjack grove did would only authenticate his drunken state, if getting him drunk enough to hang on to was what she had in mind.

Her voice sounded drunker than she had any right to be as she yawned and declared, "I sure feel sleepy of a sudden. I swear I'd suggest turning in if it didn't sound so forward. Where's them parts where folks make white lightning out of rice and talk so funny about it?"

Ki took back the jar she was holding out to him again as he told her, "Your people call it Japan. My own daddy was American, like you all. That's about all I can say about him for certain. My mother was a lady of the Nippon-no persuasion. *Sake* simply means wine in her tongue, see?"

He determined that, again, the girl had been faking the amount she'd really inhaled, but Billie managed to sound drunk as a skunk when she replied, "Oh. I heard tell Japan Land was close to China. That's likely how come you look sort of Chinee, only better. So tell me true, Japan boy, is it true what they say about Chinese women?"

Ki laughed, sincerely enough, and replied, "To begin with, I just told you I was part Japanese, not Chinese, but speaking as an . . . ah, man of the world, I can assure you anything you heard about the private anatomy of Chinese ladies is simply not true."

She sounded disappointed as she took the jar back, muttering, "Oh. Does that mean Chinee boys, or Japanee boys, are hung to pleasure natural women in the natural way?"

He moved closer to lay a casual right hand atop her left hip as he replied, "I can't speak for other Oriental gents, Miss Billie. But in all modesty, I've never had any complaints about my natural ways."

She wasn't wearing that gun she'd had on back at the fire. That meant she'd tossed it aside with her hat. That meant good or bad, all depending on where it lay in the dry grass all about.

Had she still been packing it he'd have disarmed her already. If she suspected he might be groping for it in the dark, she'd doubtless get to it first, and she'd already proven just how impulsive she was.

As if to prove Ki right she leaned toward him, even as she purred, "Oh, heavens, what are you doing with your hand on my poor maidenly flesh, good sir! Did you think I meant my innocent questions as an invite to get forward?"

Ki answered, "I did," and reeled her in for some skilled kissing as they flattened side by side on the canvas, his free hand sliding around and down to her tailbone so he could press her pelvis firmly against his own.

She tongued him back, and began to grind her pubic bone against the erection they could both feel dawning in Ki's jeans. She tried to say she wasn't that kind of a girl as Ki got to work on her waistband, their tongues entwined in a serpentine mating ritual, and by the time they managed to say it out loud, she *was*.

"Oh, Lord have mercy!" Billie sobbed as she wrapped her shapely naked limbs around his waist, making him glad he'd only moved his pants down enough to get into her as he felt the spurs on her boots inspiring his bounding buttocks to full gallop. He in turn inspired her to climax half dressed as well, knowing she'd feel far less shy once she'd enjoyed his ejaculation in her lusty young innards.

He was right. She protested and asked, "What if someone comes?" But she laughed like hell, and allowed Ki to strip her once he'd pointed out, "Someone already has, and if your hands don't know better than to bother you in your own bedroll, you haven't got them trained worth spit!"

He was pleased to note she agreed. She was pleased to get on top and ride his asparagus stalk, squatting on her spurred boot heels but otherwise naked as a jay and enjoying the way he was rolling her naked nipples between thumbs and forefingers as she bounced teasingly for both of them.

But all this wasn't doing much for Jessie, still a prisoner in that other camp. So Ki suggested they finish right and they did, although not exactly the way Billie Sanford might have expected when he re-entered her from on top, with one of her bare knees hooked over either of his elbows. She gasped, "Lordy, not *that* deep, darling!" giving him the excuse to shift position just a bit and knock her out entirely with a little romantic pressure on a nerve center few sex maniacs had ever been told they had.

As Ki finished in her vulnerable unconscious flesh, making it tighter than ever with the inspiration from another pressure point, he felt a rush of mortification at his own weakness. For he'd only seduced the seductive little minx, if that was what he'd just done, to get away from her and her riders. Why was he still screwing her now that he was free to go?

He told himself to withdraw and get going now that he could. The hour was late and Ki didn't know whether Jessie was being subjected to this same treatment, or worse, while he humped away at this crazy cowgirl instead of riding to his employer's rescue.

But Ki was inside her, with a raging erection, and so kept humping and hoping another few thrusts would do it. Ki had much better control over his own body functions than the average humper of unconscious beauties. But thanks to having come in her already more than once, he found it a hard row to hoe, and decided, as many a man before him had, without meaning it any more, that he'd bounce about a hundred more times and then pull out no matter what.

It was a good thing he did. From the mesquite south of Ki's moonlit bounding buttocks, the faithful Jeff stood watching, rifle in hand and jaw muscles rippling as his job and jealousy warred within him. Jeff had long admired his boss lady, but had never had her, even though this was far from the only time she'd bedded a passing stranger who'd tickled her fancy. Jeff watched as long as a natural man could have been expected to abide. Then he turned away to head back to join the other boys at the coffee fire, and to hell with orders.

Miss Billie had told her boys to back up her play and gun the stranger if he made a break for it. But that infernal Chinee wasn't going no place but up Miss Billie's ring-dang-doo, and what the hell, she could give a holler if she wanted any other men around, right?

★

Chapter 9

And so even as Ki was abusing himself with the body of a woman Lone Star had never heard of, the captive he was determined to rescue was beginning to think she was going to have to get herself out of her own fix. By now she had a better grasp on the fix she was in, thanks to the hardly modest talk around that infernal fire. These boys had mavericked most of their good-sized herd from others who'd doubtless had little if any more right to them, under Mexican if not Texican statutes. The reason they kept the fire so bright and seemed intent on staying up all night had something to do with the rival Lazy S and other outfits new to the Hill Country, and thus without property rights recognized by the Brothers Grayson or other such good old boys.

As she sat with her back to the freestone wall, facing the fire on her rump with both knees drawn up, Lone Star, being a woman used to wearing skirts, was all too aware of one hatchet-faced cowhand across the way, desperately trying not to let it show as he reclined in the grass on one elbow, trying to see what might show as he cast sneaky glances at the shapely young blonde across the way. Lone Star knew how much anyone could see up under her loose divided skirts. For she'd have never been sitting this way had anything important been exposed. Divided riding skirts were of course and in fact more like the loose pants once worn by pirates than true skirts. They made a gal seem modestly attired in proper if rainy-suzie-length skirts, ending about at the level of her boot tops when she was standing or walking upright. When she was seated like this, one could more easily see a bare leg loosely covered by each half of the buckskin garment. Nice girls of the day didn't *have* legs, according to Queen Victoria and the fashionable young things in *Frank Leslie's Magazine*. But in point of fact, from directly across the fire, that hatchet-faced Romeo could see her shins from boot tops to kneecaps and, by craning some, the backs of her firelit thighs, almost to where it really counted. She knew the low-slung crotch of her riding skirts hid the fuzzy sight the poor simp was so anxious to peek at. She knew he had as much chance of satisfying his curious nature as poor Peeping Tom had had in Coventry Town when Lady Godiva rode through astride, with a whole white horse between her spread-open groin and the eyes of mankind. She wondered, idly, what the ugly mutt would do if she let him see a little more of her. The one good thing about singing around a camp fire with the boys was that there was some safety in numbers, she hoped. They said even The Kid and the James-Younger boys took some pride in acting well-mannered toward women. If they'd meant to gang-rape her they'd have tried, or even done so, by now. Things had gotten pleasanter since she'd sung them a few songs and passed the git-fiddle on. If only they'd let the fire die, or let her turn in, as she'd asked more than once. But Rafe kept saying it wasn't safe. That everyone not out on picket guard had to stay by the fire where he could account for 'em until his brothers and some other boys showed up. Rafe clearly expected some sort of showdown with those other outfits. But every time she asked, they told her not to ask.

A freetail bat swooped lower than usual to nail a moth attracted by the fire. Lone Star flinched despite herself, more for fear the poor bat would catch fire than for fear of night critters. But the hatchet-faced hand across the way laughed and told her, "Don't you worry, missie. Them bats ain't out to get in your hair. Not no hair I can see from here leastways."

Lone Star stared skyward with more interest than she really felt as she perhaps unconsciously spread her knees a bit wider, innocently saying, "I'm used to freetails. They do more good than harm around skeeter-pestered stock. It's odd to see so many, though. I know there's plenty of stock and lots of bugs in this draw this evening, but that breed of bat holes up by day in natural caves, right?"

The hatchet-faced one hunkered lower to peer higher up inside her skirts. It was the kid called Chief, or Ian Gordon, who told her, "We got heaps of caves in these here hills, ma'am. That there tank you can just make out from here in the moonlight is fed by water running up from limestone caverns measureless to man."

Another hand who knew his way about those parts volunteered, "That can't be where all them bats go at daybreak, though. You can see the big old hole all that water comes up from. It's cavesome as you say, but the water never drops low enough to let sunshine or bats get through. Them bats likely fly in and out some sinkhole higher up, on any ridge you'd like to guess at. I've never seen it my ownself."

There was a general mutter of agreement. The Mex who'd roped her opined there were likely lots of modest sinkholes, hidden by trees and scrub by the grace of the Mother of God. For had there been any a *vaca* or *caballo* could break a leg in, he felt sure he'd have heard about them by now.

A pudgy hand called Slim idly strummed the git-fiddle and asked if the lady knew the words of "Old Paint." Lone Star did. It was a herding song made up along the Goodnight-Loving Trail by some now-forgotten hand who'd left no explanation for some of his lyrics. Unlike many a so-called folk song, made up and then copyrighted by the likes of Stephen Foster, "Old Paint" was the genuine article. Bets had been made about it and never collected. Nobody could say who'd made it up or what could have happened to him, save for the fact he'd surely gone under to Indians or some other occupational hazard before he'd found out his song was famous enough to be printed and published these days.

Lone Star didn't want to attract any more attention to herself as she leaned back farther, pretending not to notice how that one hand across the way was sweating, no doubt from having his fool face almost in the fire by this time.

Lone Star started to move her limbs to a more maidenly position. She knew Ki was somewhere out there, and she didn't want him to find these morons fighting over her when and if . . . Or did she?

Turning slightly on her rump, as if to listen more intently to Slim, Lone Star, wearing nothing under her riding skirts, gave her hatchet-faced admirer a free lesson in gynecology, trying not to blush as Slim twanged on about riding Old Paint and leading

104

Cheyenne in the company of some long-forgotten hands called The Pirate and Snuffy. She knew she had unusually pretty privates. More than one lucky lover had told her so, and that comical Custis Long had once confided, while inside her, he felt guilty about violating the pure-food laws, bless his sweet hide and what he liked to call his old organ-grinder.

She risked a sidelong glance to note the one she was teasing was staring bug-eyed and sort of drooling now. She was hoping he'd suggest a stroll in the moonlight. If Rafe Grayson indulged them, she was good as gone. The poor simp was only a little over six feet and couldn't weigh more than a hundred and seventy-five. She'd let him kiss her and respond with passionate thumbs to both pressure points at the base of his skull. If that didn't do it, there was always the old reliable knee in the groin followed by a kick to the breastbone.

She shot him another sidelong glance. Their eyes met. She looked away. It wasn't enough. Her hatchet-faced admirer sprang to his feet with a strangled sob and roared, "That tears it! She knows what she's been doing, the prick-teasing little sass, and now I mean to *get* me some of that old ring-dang-do she's been winking at me like the whore she was born!"

Then, as Lone Star slid her back up the rough wall, he proceeded to come her way, smack through the fire, scattering hot coals and attracting surprised curses from all sides as he tore at the buttons of his bulging jeans.

Lone Star faced him with an expression of calm resignation. She wanted him to drag her off into the dark, away from the others. But the breed kid called Chief sprang to his own feet, interposing his own slender form between the captive blonde and her would-be rapist as he demanded, "Have you gone loco, Gash? This lady ain't with you, you horny bastard!"

That reminded the one called Gash of the gun slung low on his own right hip in a waxed tie-down holster. He let go of his own crotch to hover the same hand like a hungry buzzard near the mock-ivory grips of his double-action Remington as he declared, "Somebody give that fucking Indian a gun as good as mine and stand well clear. For you all just heard him call me a bastard, and nobody does that and lives, even if he *knows* who his *own* daddy might have been!"

The one called Slim, who'd naturally frozen with his git-fiddle, murmured, "Boss? Ain't you gonna stop it?"

Rafe Grayson stayed put on his haunches, well clear of both the fire and what was going on so close to it, as he observed, "I'd say both you boys may have acted with more haste than common sense. That female don't get screwed at all unless she gets screwed by all who want some, Gash. As for you, Chief, it's just plain foolish to remark on a white man's probable parentage when he's packing double-action and you've only got an old dragoon thumb-buster to back your bluster!"

"I ain't afraid of the silly cuss," Chief blustered.

To which Rafe replied, "Nobody asked if you was afraid, you cross-grained Comanche. We're discussing your protracted existence, not your pride. Tell Gash you're sorry you called him what you called him and we'll say no more about it, hear?"

Chief hesitated, then shrugged and said, "I'll apologize for calling you a bastard if you'll stop acting like one, Gash."

It wasn't enough. Gash purred, "I want you to get down on at least one knee and say it humble, Indian. I want you to make it public that you spoke out of turn to your betters because you was taught no manners by your own white-trash daddy and his stinking squaw."

Chief must have thought he had a better idea. Lone Star gasped out, "No, Ian!" as Chief slapped leather.

The breed was good. Gash was simply better. They both had their guns out about the same time. Then Gash fired, twice, in the time it took Chief to cock his single-action horse pistol. The better-natured youth crashed back against the same stone wall and Gash fired again, even as Chief's knees were buckling and he was already dead on his feet. The lifeless kid let go his unfired gun and pitched forward to land facedown in the fire. As a couple of the others sprang up to pull his already sizzling form from the flames, Gash holstered his smoking six-gun with one hand and grabbed Lone Star's wrist with the other, growling, "That was that and this is this. You and me are about to fuck like rabbits in the greenup time, little darling!"

She didn't resist. As he started to drag her away, Slim soberly asked, "Boss?"

Rafe muttered, "Let 'em go. You just seen Gash kill one man for that pussy, didn't you?"

Slim replied, "I did, and Chief was a good old boy. Ain't we fixing to do nothing at all about Gash gunning him like that?"

Rafe shrugged. "I'll tell my brothers when they get here. We'll figure something out. In the meanwhile I don't want to lose more gunhands with them pesky Sanfords out looking for us and them cows. So let old Gash fuck the pesky gal if he wants. It won't hurt neither one of 'em all that much."

An unshaven tobacco-chewer across the way spat into the fire and got to his own feet, announcing, "In that case I mean to ask for sloppy seconds."

As he turned from the fire most of the others laughed nervously. Then a shorter, greasier one with a drinker's nose said, "Hell, I'm on fair terms with old Gash as well. Once he's had his own way, I'm sure he'll be willing to share the good things of life with his friends!"

Nobody else, to their dubious credit, seemed to want any part of the action. That still left Lone Star out in the moonlight, being marched toward a grassy mound so her pretty little ass would be aimed right, Gash said, while those two others tagged along, calling lewdly helpful suggestions and informing their victim-to-be that the fun for her was just starting.

Gash led Lone Star up to the mound and spun her around to face him. He growled, "You can take off them duds or we can rip 'em off for you. It's all the same to us, girl."

Lone Star faked a little sob and pleaded, "Please don't tear my nice silk shirt, sir," as she began to unbutton herself down the front. She knew the effect her bare breasts in moonlight had on most men. All three moved closer for a better look, and the tobacco-chewer moaned, "Jesus, Gash, fuck her so's me and Amarillo can get at them sweet titties too!"

Lone Star didn't like the odds. All but one were far bigger than she was, even if they hadn't been wearing more weaponry. On the other hand she doubted she'd get a better chance at the knife in her boot, and she knew she was right when Gash growled, "She's starting to stall us, the shy little cunt. Amarillo, get ahint her and hold her whilst me and Snotty strip her down."

As he reached for Lone Star's waist-fasteners he asked her, conversationally, "Have you ever sucked one cuss whilst another fucked you frontways and yet another shoved it up your ass, girl?"

Lone Star smiled up at him sweetly to reply, "Ooh, that sounds like fun!" just before she chopped him across the throat with the edge of one dainty-looking but work-hardened hand.

That was it for Gash for at least an hour, if he ever recovered at all. But the stocky Amarillo, already moving around behind her

107

when she made her move, naturally threw a roundhouse right at the side of her blond head.

She'd expected he might, and so she'd ducked all the way down on her haunches as he began his swing, then reeled off a good six paces as he tried to recover from his mighty punch through thin air. That left the taller one called Snuffy, yelling loud remarks about treacherous bitch wolverines as he loomed above her, going for his gun with an ungallant lack of other inspiration.

But as Lone Star sprang back up, with catlike grace that inspired Snuffy to flinch back a pace, she had her own weapon out, the razor-honed *kogatana* fashioned in far-off Nagasaki by a famed swordsmith who admired the mistress of Starbuck Enterprises. She proved he knew his business when she sank the *kogatana* deep into Snuffy's bladder, keen edge up, and ripped him open to the breastbone, spilling his severed gun rig as well as ripped-open guts on the grass. Then she was running, open shirt flapping, knife in hand, while Amarillo pegged pistol shots her way, wailing, "Help! For Gawd's sake call out the cavalry! She ain't no play-pretty, she's a fucking one-woman bayonet charge!"

And then, as all hell busted loose behind her, Lone Star made it to the moonlit limestone tank and hit the spring water in a head-long dive.

As she knew from having watched them water their herd before sundown, the tank was saucer-shaped all around its edges. The stock had been able to wade in well above their forehocks, which was deep as most cows ever wanted to wade undriven. So the bullseye center of the roughly round tank had to be where spring water ran in from that submerged cave. She swam underwater to roughly the middle, knife gripped between her teeth, then surfaced just long enough to check her bearings and take a few deep breaths. She'd have taken more had not someone shouted, "There she is! Git her, boys!" So she ducked back under just as the first bullets inspired ear-splitting spouts all around where she wasn't anymore.

She dove down and down with her eyes open, although not seeing much in the dim moonlight filtered by less than crystalline water. She found one jagged edge of the sinkhole in the center of the tank. She was able to move deeper, faster, by gripping hand-holds and pulling. It still took a million years, and she was running out of breath before, a quarter of the way around, she found what seemed an opening about the size of a storm drain in the otherwise vertical wall. She pulled herself in, headfirst and faceup, to claw desperately at the handholds above her. For by now her lungs were bursting and it was already too late to turn back, even if she hadn't just inspired one killing and personally killed one or two others back there. But if this infernal underground creek didn't let her up for some air fast, she knew she was done for no matter what!

★
Chapter 10

Farther west in the railroad town of Alpine, the Western Union clerk who'd caught the graveyard shift had just strolled in to relieve Miss Kathy Turnbolt, as the pudgy little gal was called. That was one of the less interesting things Longarm had learned in the past few hours as he'd kept her company during a mighty slow night. Western Union frowned on its help disclosing the contents of one customer's telegrams to another. Longarm had often had to threaten and cajole to get any information at all out of telegraphers more concerned about their jobs than even federal law. But fortunately Kathy was sort of stupid as well as sort of pretty, if one admired them pear-shaped. So she'd seen no harm in jawing about earlier visitors. One morose-looking individual who might have hurt one leg one time, from the way he strode in, had wired his Aunt Felicia in Austin about a shipment from Denver arriving as expected but with a number of parts badly damaged and the big wheel missing entirely. Kathy had thought the limping cuss had likely meant a machine of some kind. She'd searched high and low for a carbon, saying she was sure she'd filed it somewhere around there. But Longarm had told her not to fuss about it because, if he was guessing at all right, he knew how many parts he might have damaged and where the big wheel they were after might be. She'd asked if he knew the limping man who'd wired Austin, and Longarm had said, "We may have met

110

earlier. I can't wait to ask him how, or who, his Aunt Felicia might be."

They'd also established she could indeed use some company on her way home, along a dark side street and past the tumbledown picket fence of a mighty spooky graveyard the Mexicans held to be severely haunted. Kathy said they kept the graves over at First Methodist nicely tended, so the dead *there* were likely at rest. But the Mex one she had to get past went with an old abandoned mission, either Jesuit or Dominican, and some said the forlorn haunts left behind in a strange land tended to moan and gibber among the weed trees and half-toppled tombstones over yonder.

Longarm assured her he wasn't afraid of haunts, and that he'd in fact scared more than one of them in his time. So as they left the telegraph office, being a woman, she naturally wanted to know all about his previous adventures with haunts.

She was clinging sweetly to one arm and smelling of violet toilet water as they strode in step. So he told her modestly about the time land-grabbers had sicced a *wendigo* or evil spirit on the Blackfoot up Montana way. He skimmed tersely over the tale. It always reminded him of poor old Roping Sally, a sweet screwing tomboy who'd been murdered by that all-too-solid evil spirit. He said, "I had an outlaw I'd already gunned come after me for a rematch one time. Leastways, that's what the killer pretending to be the late Cotton Younger wanted us all to think. My point is that every haunt I've ever heard of comes in only one of two varieties. Total imagination or fake. I've always hankered to meet up with a real haunt. So far they've disappointed me."

She shivered and clung closer, demanding, "You say you'd *like* to see a haunt, a *real* one?"

He said, "Of course I would. It would offer some assurance to a man who figures on dying, sooner or later, whether by gunfire or something more natural. I don't know about you, Miss Kathy, but I've never really enjoyed the notion of dying. I like it here too much."

She half sobbed, "I don't want to die either, *never,* hear?"

He told her, soothingly, "The Good Book says it won't be so bad when the inevitable catches up with us. My point about haunts is that dying might not be so scary if there was any chance you'd get to come back sort of scary."

"Even if all you got to do was gibber and moan?" she demanded. To which he thoughtfully replied, "That sounds like more fun than just lying there amid the daisy roots. The Horse Indians say everyone has four haunts. When you kill, say, a Cheyenne, one of his haunts gets to hang about this world and get back at you and his other enemies. That's how come Cheyenne mutilate the trigger or bow fingers of the enemies they kill. Makes their haunts less dangerous."

He stopped walking and talking as they came to what she said was her corner. They were either stirring up echoes with their own heels, or the streets of Alpine weren't as deserted as they might appear at that hour. She asked why they'd stopped. He shrugged and said he might have been spooked by some long-dead Indian. As they turned the corner the brooding figure who'd been limping after them thought it safe to limp on, hugging the shadows on the far side of the street sort of pleased with himself. It hadn't been easy to forgo the easy shot at Longarm through the plate glass of the telegraph office. But a hired gun who'd killed before liked to kill with the odds in his favor. Backshooting for hire was only the first row a poor killer had to hoe. He had to get away, clean, after putting his target on the ground. He knew other lawmen were apt to stake out the rail depot once they'd heard gunplay anywhere in town. So he had his pony tethered in a handy municipal park with filled canteens and enough grub to last a man on the owlhoot trail quite a spell. As he limped on after Longarm and that gal, he planned to wait till they were near that old Spanish mission, without witnesses to worry about, then backshoot 'em both. Dead men, or dead women, telling no tales.

But as Robert Burns had long ago observed, the best-laid plans of mice and men could surely get fucked up. In this case the hitch was El Gato, who'd been looking for Longarm when he'd noticed somebody more sinister on the dark streets of Alpine.

El Gato, The Cat, had earned his nickname from both friend and foe because he was simply a sort of a freak. His feline smile and pantherish movements alone might not have done it. The handsome young outlaw—or liberator, as he preferred to be described—had been born to perfectly normal parents with the uncanny night vision of your average alley cat.

It was not true, as some feared, that El Gato could see in total darkness. But like his namesake, he could see an astounding amount if there was any light at all. Since, unlike a real cat, El Gato was literate and in fact well-educated, he could and often did read newspapers and reward posters by starlight. The dictatorship of El Presidente Diaz printed an awesome lot about the desperado known as El Gato, and if *los rurales* ever got their hands on him . . .

But this evening he was safer up in Los Estados Unidos, where even U.S. Deputy Marshal Custis Long agreed no man who shot *rurales* on sight could be all bad. So he concentrated on the limping figure he'd spotted first. Had the man tailing Longarm and the girl looked back, he'd have seen nothing. El Gato was even better at clinging to shadows, and was also clad in ebony from head to toe. The *cabrone* was rounding the corner after Longarm and the *muchacha* now. El Gato broke cover and darted across the dimly illuminated street like a shadow cast by the clouds scudding across the moon above.

Meanwhile Longarm had just been given the dismal news about where they were headed. Kathy had her own room, it was true, in a boardinghouse presided over by an old bat even Kathy described as fat. And Longarm had just gotten to like the way Kathy's broad hip brushed against his thigh as they strode arm in arm. It was tough to picture just how she might look with her bodice and pleated skirts off. He had to take it on faith she had legs. Her pelvis bulged big enough for twins below her surprisingly slender waist. Even allowing for strong corset stays, the broad-hipped little gal was almost petite from the hips up. He'd been looking forward to giving her a sort of medical examination, but he failed to see how they'd play doctor with a fat old landlady watching. So he'd likely have to settle for a peck on the cheek and a frustrated pecker as he boarded that pre-dawn combination for Austin, cuss all old ladies who'd forgotten how it felt and didn't want anyone else to have fun.

At this hour most of the houses they were passing were dark as moonlit buffalo skulls. Nobody with a lick of sense left coal-oil lamps or even candles lit after bedtime, and few had call to be up after midnight in a world that rose with the chickens. So he had to agree some of the dark windows they passed seemed spooky. Although he'd seldom worried about that simple fact of Victorian life before.

She confided that on more than one occasion, passing a house up ahead at this hour, she'd been scared skinny by what she hoped was a little old lady who sat staring out a bay window at all hours, dressed dark as the unlit room behind her so her pale face and white hair seemed to be just floating there, staring out with no

113

more expression than a window dummy, or a propped-up corpse.

Longarm followed her drift when she suggested they walk on the far side. But they hadn't gone far before she whispered, "Oh, Lord, we're coming to that graveyard I told you about!"

He could see they surely were, and that the long-neglected pickets did sort of resemble the bared ribs of some long-dead monstrous dragon, or at least a swamping snake. The moon was bright enough, but there were no street lamps up this way. So everything on the far side of the eerie pickets looked like tarnished silver against black velvet. Spanish-speaking folks had always gone in for more elaborate grave markers than most, and he had to allow some of those silvery stone forms staring back at them looked mighty broody, or even drunk. Alpine got enough winter frost and summer thunder each year to have tipped the stone figures every which way. Since the graveyard was Mex instead of, say, Congregational, more than one carved figure was a skeleton, held together by stone grave-shrouding. Longarm had just told her they sold candy shaped like skulls on the Day of the Dead down Mexico way, when an owl hooted from an overhead pine limb and poor Kathy tried to climb over or under him—it was hard to say.

He held her against the front of him, comforting her and trying to ignore the way she was discomforting *him,* as he told her it was only a lively owl and not a dead Mex. She was still shivering like a half-drowned kitten, and the way she shivered her broad pelvis against his pants accounted for his discomfort. She seemed to be crying as well. He said, "Aw, don't do that, honey," and kissed her to secure her from the things that went bump in the night. He hadn't expected her to kiss back with such enthusiasm. But he didn't want any gal to think he was a sissy. So as she ground her odd body against his normal feelings, he checked all her teeth for cavities with his tongue too.

She had neat little tits for the big rump she'd been cursed, or blessed, with. They were only a tad larger than the average woman's and firm as fresh-baked corn bread. He knew he'd never know unless he felt her up further, and sure enough, her heroic buttocks were as solid, and almost as big, as the rump of a burro. As they came up for air Kathy sobbed, "Oh, Custis, what are we ever to do?"

He sighed and said, "Get you on home, I reckon. As I said, that was only an owl bird, and what we've been doing to one another ever since is just cruelty to animals."

x

114

She buried her face against his tweed vest and murmured, "I know. I want you so bad I can taste it. But there's simply no way I'd ever get you up to my room."

He blinked in surprise at the bold invitation, but managed not to let it show as he soberly suggested, "I got me a hired hotel room back yonder. I get to take anyone I want upstairs."

She gasped, "You can't be serious! I *live* in this town, and folks I don't know tell me dirty things about poor gals I've yet to meet! I'd have to leave town, if not Texas, once it got about that I'd been seen going up to a strange man's hotel room!"

He protested, "Aw, I ain't so strange, honey."

She giggled, grinding her big but surprisingly firm belly against the bulging front of his pants as she replied, "My feelings for you are only natural too. I was, ah, engaged one time, and once the loaf's been cut it does seem harder to refuse mankind one more little slice. In a small town like this a girl can't be too careful, though, and to tell the truth, I'd have never invited you to carry me home after midnight if I hadn't known you were just tumbleweeding through."

He kissed her some more, a palm planted firmly on either firm buttock. Then he said, "Bless your pragmatic hide, I'd like to tumble like hell with you too. But seeing your place is out, and my place is out . . ."

"What's wrong with yonder graveyard?" she coyly inquired, adding, "Nobody in *there* is likely to gossip about a little harmless fun."

He laughed, and started to ask what had happened to her fear of the dead. But that would have been a stupid thing for a man with such an erection to ask, so he simply scooped her up in his arms and gallantly stepped over a broken-down section of fence.

As the two of them vanished from view, the killer who'd been trailing them moved out into the moonlight across the dusty street. But before he got far, a ton of bricks landed on him from behind, and by the time he figured out where he was, facedown in the dust, El Gato had disarmed him and grabbed a fistful of hair in one hand while shoving a gun muzzle against the base of the victim's skull with the other. The man he'd jumped had been wounded before, and he groaned, "You're hurting me, damn you!"

El Gato replied with a boyish smile, "*Abono,* I have not even *tried* for to hurt you yet. I say without boasting both my parents were almost pure Spanish. *Pero* I do know a few old Yaqui tricks.

115

You have heard, perhaps, of the Aztec-speaking tribe even your own Apache consider cruel?"

His captive must have. He half sobbed, "What do you want of me, damn it? You've got my gun. My wallet's in my hip pocket. You're sitting on it."

El Gato purred, "Later, as I leave perhaps. Right now I wish for to know who sent you after Brazo Largo, you call him Longarm, and for why."

The hireling he had pinned between him and the dirt tried, "Who's Longarm?" and then wailed, "No! Don't! I'll tell!" as El Gato shifted his weight to grind the man's face in the dirt with one hand and poke the gun muzzle at one kidney hard.

El Gato let him get his breath back as he said, conversationally, "*Bueno.* For to save some more *mentiras,* it was I who shot you while you were attempting to shoot Brazo Largo in the *dorso,* you cowardly *cabrone.* I am less interested in how you are called than I am the name of the *ladrones* you must be working for. Who are they and for why did they send you after Brazo Largo? Has it anything to do with that *misterioso* crate he has been seeking?"

His captive groaned, "I don't know anything about any fucking crates. They don't want him getting together with that fucking Lone Star!"

El Gato hurt him again, hissing, "The open mouth gathers flies when it is not careful. La Señorita Starbuck is also on good terms with me and mine, you *rata puerco!*"

His victim assured him no disrespect had ever been intended for such a Texas rose, and the more mollified Mexican eased up a bit with that gun muzzle, saying, "*Tanto mejor.* Now you are going to tell me who does not wish for my friends to join forces, and for why, eh?"

The man with his face to the dirt was learning. He groaned, "The big cheese answers to Kellog, King Kellog. I know it sounds dumb but that's what he wants to be called. I don't know the real names of his backup. He hired me and my pals direct, by way of the underground telegraph."

El Gato nodded thoughtfully. "Brazo Largo said he thought some of you had just gotten out of prison. I know how this underground telegraph works. Your King Kellog heard you were looking for work and the rest we know. Now you are going to tell me what this King Kellog fears once Brazo Largo and La Estrella Soledad get together, eh?"

116

The man on the dirt groaned, "I'm not all that certain. I suspect King Kellog stole something from that sassy . . . Ouch! Pretty little thing! Last I heard tell, Lone Star and that big Chinee who rides with her were out looking for it. Mayhaps Kellog fears a real paid-up lawman like Longarm can put 'em on his trail, and once that happens, we all know Lone Star ain't as bound by legal niceties."

El Gato thought. "You might well be telling me all you know. I for one would hesitate to tell much more to such a pathetic, how you say, punk?"

His victim protested, "I'm no such thing. I never bent over for nobody, all the time I was in prison. But I've told you all they ever told me. So you can kill me if you want to but that's all I can tell you!"

So El Gato killed him, because he wanted to, with a few silent but solid blows of his heavy gun barrel. Then he helped himself to the freshly killed killer's wallet and gun rig, for both Longarm and La Causa, before rolling the body under the plank walkway, out of sight for now if not out of scent in a warm day or less.

El Gato had seen his old pal, Brazo Largo, tote that big-assed *muchacha* into the graveyard across the way. El Gato doubted he'd done so to bury her. So he strolled back the way he'd come to the nearest corner, sat down on the edge of the walk, and lit a *claro* to wait out his *amigo lascivo* as, over on the far side of that graveyard, Longarm was discovering further advantages of pear-shaped women.

For openers, one got the delights of two pillows under a rollicking rump without having to shove any under her. She said she didn't mind doing it on firm sod. He believed her. It wouldn't have been polite to ask her if she'd ever done it right here in such a handy but sort of spooky love nest. He suspected she might have. She'd led him directly to this corner of the graveyard, shyly suggesting she'd been here alone by broad day, maybe to place flowers on the graves of some long-dead greasers. However Kathy might have learned about this secluded spot between the rear wall of a family vault and the back fence of the whole place, they were hidden by the ebony shade of twisty old evergreens, and though she'd resisted the scandalous notion at first, he'd convinced her it would go easier on their duds and far nicer on their passionate flesh if they stripped down for some nude alfresco fun. Once she'd agreed anyone who caught them back there was certain to guess what they'd been up to anyway, even if they were in full suits of armor, she told him with coos of delight that his naked body felt just grand atop hers. And he couldn't have agreed more. For aside from the simple fact it always felt better that way, he'd been dying of curiosity about her unusual body.

There was just enough filtered moonlight to see what he was up to as he got down and dirty with her, naked save for her high-button shoes and striped knee socks. As he got her fat thighs well spread to prong her from a stiff-armed push-up position, he could see she was indeed built like a totally fat washerwoman from her slim waist down, while all the parts a man usually kissed were those of an almost slender young girl.

Her lusty young love-maw, taking all he had to give and moving up to meet his every thrust, was another interesting blend of female odds and ends, as if she'd been put together by a sex-mad Doctor Frankenstein, only prettier than that critter Miss Mary Shelley wrote about. Kathy's hungry vagina was tight as hell, but apparently deep as the ocean. No matter how deep he managed to thrust, she kept begging for it deeper, a tight velvety sheath that clung to every inch of him going either way. But she still kept coming far more than he, and he found it easy to keep coming amid such pleasant surroundings.

She seemed just as pleased, and it was easy to see what a problem she might have in a tiny Texas town with such unslakable appetites. He said as much when they took a breather, sharing a cheroot a nice girl shouldn't have been sucking on either.

She snuggled her unbound head against his bare shoulder as they both let the dry grass soak up some of their sweat, saying, "I know. It hardly seems fair. Girls like to do it as much as many a man, but only men are allowed to admit it. I wish we got to approach the subject like you all. If I was in charge, a girl like me with a taste for travel and an itchy crotch could live free and easy as any other telegraph tramp. I've ever wondered what it would be like to be free to fuck without being called bad names."

He patted her bare shoulder, blowing smoke out his nostrils, and assured her, "You'd likely make most men proddy. I've known a few such gals in my time. They even spooked *me* a mite."

Kathy laughed. "What did they do, whistle at you as you passed their beauty parlor?"

He laughed too. "It wasn't that part as spooked me. You might have noticed just now I like lusty ladies just fine. It was that part

118

about 'em living so mannish in other ways as gave me pause. I mean, what's a poor boy to do when he asks a gal out for supper and she suggests a fancy place he can't afford, and then grabs the tab and tips way more than he might have?"

She started to reach for the cheroot, decided she'd rather grab for something bigger, and observed, while giving him a gentle hand job, "I'd never do that. You must meet some mighty rich as well as independent women in your line of work. Were they crooks you got to arrest as well, you horny rascal?"

He sighed. "My boss frowns on his deputies screwing ladies in handcuffs. Their lawyers can make such a fuss about it in court. I was only referring to some ladies I'd met socially in my travels. A couple were rich widows and another an heiress."

"You mean like Miss Jessica Starbuck?" she demanded, gripping his dong more possessively as it began to rise to the occasion.

He made a mental note she might not be as dumb as she seemed, that being easy to manage, and backtracked by saying, "I don't recall my sending any mushy wires to the Circle Star by way of Western Union in recent memory. I do recall a cattle queen I met up in the Bitter Creek Range who mortified me in Chicago by paying my way at a pricey hotel as if I was one of them French giggle-glows. But you have my word she wasn't even kin to Jessie Starbuck."

Kathy was truly jerking him off now, sitting up on her broad bare ass as she pouted, "You'd have never been in no grand hotel with her if you hadn't wanted to stick this mean thing in her, I'll betcha!"

He laughed lightly. "No bet. When it's stiff as that it hardly cares *where* I stick it, albeit in the cold gray dawn I'm usually happier to recall it coming in a modest little sweetheart such as that mousy telegraph gal who dwells in a strict boardinghouse and looks as if butter wouldn't melt in her mouth."

She laughed and lowered her lush lips to the chore she'd been working at, her unbound hair brushing his belly as her head bobbed up and down. He knew right off she'd done that before too. Women could be divided into those who knew how to give French lessons and those who scraped with their damned teeth. Someone, bless him, or her, had at one time told Kathy the whole trick was to pull both lips in over one's teeth, as if mocking an old crone with her false choppers out. It helped if the resultant opening was kept nice and wet with occasional tongue licks—and, right, she knew that too. So it felt as if she'd somehow grown a tight pussy in her pretty face.

But there were better places than even a pretty face for a man to finish, and she must have expected him to shove her over on her bare back and big rump in the grass, judging from the way she spread her huge thighs and sobbed, "Yes, oh, yesss!" as he shoved it, hard, where they both liked it best.

Once they'd climaxed that way, so hot, they still wanted more, and so he gave her some dog-style as he grinned down at her horselike behind in the dim light. He'd once heard about this German cavalryman they'd caught doing this to his mount. They'd wanted to shoot him. But Frederick the Great had said it made more sense to transfer him to the infantry. Longarm had always wondered what sense *that* made, if it made any at all. He'd never tried humping a real horse himself, even though it always got everyone red-faced and giggly when they watched a stud servicing a brood mare. A mare in heat surely winked her big old ring-dang-do at the world as she was waiting to have it filled. He'd often heard it remarked, and he'd often agreed, it would be grand to meet a gal with privates like that, on a more human scale. So now, as he felt Kathy contracting in passion on his questing shaft, he shut both eyes and pictured a hot little pony, instead of her, as he clung to her hipbones and slammed against her equine ass. It sure felt nice and dirty. He idly wondered if he might be getting touched in the head. Like many a man, and likely many a woman, he'd often inspired himself to keep going by picturing, say, a Cheyenne squaw as he humped an Irish redhead, or vice versa, but this was about the first time he'd indulged in bestiality with an all-too-human being.

Somewhere out in the night some other asshole was singing "Green Grow the Lilacs," which was bad enough, only he was singing it in Spanish, which was weird.

Mexicans called a North American a "gringo" as he might call them "greasers" because "Green Grow the Lilacs" had been a marching hymn sung first by Houston's Texicans and then by Zach Taylor's troops in the Mexican War. Having no notion what a "green grow" might be, they'd settled on gringo in describing the ornery strangers from north of their Rio Bravo.

Longarm had never heard the old song sung in Spanish for obvious reasons. As he listened, enjoying his pony ride, their unseen singer *de la luz de la luna* got to the part about green lilacs sprouting from the ass of someone called Brazo Largo, and Longarm caught on.

The singing made Kathy proddy as he prodded her. She arched her spine to take it deeper but protested, "That fool Mex is likely to attract attention to these parts with his drunken wailing, and I'm usually home by this time, cuss all Mexicans and landladies!"

He pounded harder and brought them both to full climax, as any true gent in his position might have, then agreed it might be best if they quit while they were ahead.

They got dressed and Kathy pinned her hair back up, quietly crying as she considered they might never meet so swell again. He kissed her, and assured her he always changed trains at Alpine when Billy Vail sent him down this way. So she kissed him back and stopped crying.

El Gato stopped singing, from the inky shadows down the way, as he saw them leave the graveyard together. The cat-eyed Mex trailed them as discreetly till he saw them turn in at Kathy's garden gate. Then he relit his cigar, knowing Longarm would no doubt spot the flare of his match. It still seemed to take a gringo an unseemly amount of time to get rid of a *puta* one had been screwing *that* long, Madre de Dios. Then, at last, he saw the tall deputy ambling back his way and broke cover. Longarm joined him, muttering, "I'll grow you some green lilacs, you sassy Mex tomcat! It's way after midnight and I thought we already parted friendly."

El Gato replied, "*Sí, me también, pero* I was on my way for to tell you about something I had just learned when I spotted that gunslicker we'd met earlier. So I followed him as he followed you, with interesting results."

El Gato kept the dead man's gun rig but handed over the wallet as he brought Longarm up to date in a few laconic words. Longarm put the wallet away to examine later by better light. He didn't ask if there might still be any money in it. He asked what else El Gato had been hankering to tell him.

The deadly young Mex said, "Some, how you say, business associates of mine made a delivery over in the Hill Country between San Antonio *y* Austin. That is to say, they tried to. Some Anglo *ladrones* stole the herd. My own friends lost no *dinero* in the transaction. It was their Anglo customers who got burned. Their name was Sanford. Not evil people but perhaps a little excitable."

Longarm thought. "Well, Jessie Starbuck does seem to be hunting for stolen stock over yonder. But after that I just don't know. Billy Vail never sent me out after cow thieves this time."

El Gato insisted, "*Ladrones de vacas* come in two sizes. Most are poor but dishonest small holders who get perhaps a little sloppy with their roping and peddle an occasional side of beef to local butchers who ask few questions when the price is right."

Longarm nodded. "Right. The other kind is the kind as steals stock wholesale, by the trainload. They ain't as common these days, for the simple reason it ain't easy to drive big herds far over half-settled range without nobody noticing. Such rascals usually have some sneaky plans on getting all that beef from point A to point B without the whole world having to know about it. Let's go on back to that taproom across from the depot, so we can jaw about it more comfortsome while I wait for my fool train."

El Gato dryly observed he'd be anxious to rest too if he'd just been playing slap-and-tickle in a graveyard. As they strode side by side along the dark street El Gato observed, "That *cabrone* I left under the walk back there was unable to tell me exactly what the mastermind he'd been hired by had stolen. *Pero* Jessie Starbuck, as herself, has that mysterious crate you are after while, as Estrella Soledad, she is in hot pursuit of *ladrones de vacas*. Is interesting what you just said about *cabrones* who steal *vacas* in great numbers, no?"

Longarm nodded grimly. "I wouldn't be chasing all over creation after the lady called Lone Star if I didn't suspect there could be *some* connection. It's just that I'll be switched with snakes if I can figure any out!"

★

Chapter 11

Longarm caught the eastbound combination along about quarter to four, cleaned himself up in the gent's room, found the bar in the club car closed for the night, and propped himself solo in a coach seat to catch up on his beauty rest as the trucks clicked soothingly ever eastward under him.

Over in the Hill Country to the east, the man called Ki waited till sunrise before he strode downslope into the Grayson line camp afoot, waving a white kerchief aloft on a crooked mesquite branch.

They'd spied him coming long before he made it to the sprawling stone walls across the big tank from grazing herd. Ki had expected them to. In the pre-dawn darkness he'd crept all around them without being able to learn spit about Jessie or even her three ponies. It was as if she'd never met up with this outfit, only he knew for a fact she had.

About half the Grayson hands were already up, sipping joe around the kicked-up fire as they waited for Cookie to rustle up some grits and gravy. Rafe Grayson called out, "We can coffee you if you come in peace for any sensible reason, or gun you if you'd rather. So be careful how you choose your words, pilgrim."

Ki removed the kerchief from the stick to throw one away and put the other in a hip pocket as he carefully replied, "I came in to make a deal. I'd be *segundo* to Miss Jessica Starbuck, whom I suspect you've already met. I don't know why you grabbed her.

123

But I want her back. In return I'm offering information that could save your young and impetuous asses."

The short dumpy Amarillo growled, "Let me do it, Rafe. He's with that she-devil as got Chief kilt, half-kilt Gash, and kilt poor old Snotty entire!"

"Opened him up like a watermelon she did!" opined another, adding, "Let's open this pal of her'n up the same way!"

But Rafe shushed them and told Ki, "We'd like to hear what you got to sell, Chinaman. It better be good."

Ki ignored the remark about him being a Son of Han and said, "First you tell me where the lady might be. Then I tell you about another lady who means to do you dirt."

Rafe wrinkled his nose. "Oh, Billie Sanford? We ain't afeard of that Kentucky spitfire. Her daddy was a sissy as well. Rid for the North like the nigger-loving scalawag he was born. Where might they be, with how many gunhands, to hit us when?"

Ki insisted, "You were about to tell me about that other lady, weren't you?"

To which Rafe replied, "Mayhaps I was and mayhaps I wasn't. We don't have her now, dead or alive. Look around if you like, after you tell us more about them pesky Sanfords."

Ki had already looked around all he'd cared to. But if Jessie had been set free, or freed herself, where could she be? He'd scouted the ridges all around before he'd felt forced to take this risk. He'd spotted one distant rider, male, leading some pack ponies to the northeast. Jessie Starbuck could leave less sign than your average Comanche once she'd put her mind to it. But if she'd escaped, where was she? She'd surely known he was ghosting along after her. She'd have surely scouted for him, or at least left clues to tell him which way she was fleeing.

Ki told Rafe, "I'll take your word she's not here. What was that about her hurting somebody?"

Rafe snorted, "Shit, she never hurt nobody, Chinaman. She got one admirer shot dead, knocked another out entire, and disemboweled the third."

Ki repressed a knowing grin. He didn't think this would be a wise time to say, "That's our Jessie!" out loud. He asked what had transpired next. Rafe pointed at the nearby tank. "She committed suicide, we hope. Dove headfirst in yonder tank and never come back up. It's too deep to see bottom, out in the middle. But bodies usually pop to the surface after they've been down there long enough to get stinksome. Meanwhile that water won't hurt the stock, and we uns got better stuff to drink."

Amarillo exulted, "I can't wait to see her bobbing about out yonder, all bloated up like she's fixing to have triplets. Drownded men float facedown whilst drownded women float faceup, ain't that a bitch?"

Ki stared heartsick at the innocent surface of the welling spring water, numbly wondering why Jessie had done such a desperate thing, even as he hoped she hadn't. If they'd seen her hit the water in poor light, and she'd slipped out on the far side, among all those cow legs . . . Then Rafe Grayson dashed his hopes by spitting and adding, "We searched all about, high and low, with lamps and torches for the loco little gal. Some say yonder water comes outten an underground spring big enough for a body to swim into, if said body belonged to a mermaid. I doubt she could have found any such opening in the dark. If she did, she may *never* come up, and Lord knows what it'll do to the taste afore she's rotted away entire."

Another hand said, "Stock spooks at the smell of Mister Death, but that's an awfully big tank and she was a mighty small gal, Rafe."

Their leader shrugged and told Ki, "Now you know what happened to the late Lone Star. Yep, we knew who she was and all about her half-ass vigilante riding. The two of you was riding after us in league with Billie Sanford, right?"

Ki shook his head sincerely. "You've really got things all tangled up. I just escaped from Miss Billie and her bunch. Miss Starbuck never even met 'em. I can tell you flat out we were headed for your main spread to question you about some missing Circle Star stock."

Rafe protested, "We ain't got none. You can see for yourself. Lone Star agreed she'd been barking up the wrong tree before she turned into a homicidal lunatic on us."

Ki nodded. "I'm sure you boys were treating her like a lady, but you know how some women get. Miss Billie Sanford's the one who's mad at you now. She seems to feel at least some of those cows across the way were meant for her. She knows where they are. She knows how many of you there are. She's waiting for your brothers to ride in so she can make a clean sweep. I'm not sure how many guns she means to lead against you or which way they'll be hitting you from. They captured me the same way and no doubt for the same reasons you captured Miss Jessica. I got away before I was able to learn their full plan of attack, but if I were you I'd let her have the fool cows without a fight."

Rafe sneered, "It's a good thing I ain't a yaller Chinaman then. Nobody gets a cow off this child without a fight, you crybaby!"

Ki cocked a brow. "Do I look like I'm crying? It's no skin off *my* Oriental ass if you all go under defending your right to be pains in the asses. I do know enough to say you may be just within Texas law as it pertains to mavericking. Billie Sanford doesn't give a shit, and she won't attack at all until she's sure she has the firepower to finish you off once and for all. I got the impression, just talking to her, she doesn't hanker for long engagements or long feuds. Jessica Starbuck was traveling in the company of a saddle bronc and two pack ponies when last we parted. Are you trying to tell me they might have drowned as well?"

Rafe looked away, muttering, "Never mind what happened to her ponies. There's some things it's best not to know for certain, and her other sins lie buried where they'll never be noticed. You'd best give old Amarillo that gun afore you set down for some coffee, Chinaman."

Ki started to object. He heard the soft snicks of more than one gun hammer behind him. "I'd just as soon move on, before that other bunch fires from the trees all about, if it's all the same with you."

"It ain't all the same with me," snapped Rafe. "You just allowed you've been riding with Lone Star and doing Lord knows what with Billie Sanford. How do we know you didn't come in to spy on us, counting heads and sizing up our defenses whilst feeding us bull about the other side?"

Ki sank down on his haunches, deciding he may as well have that coffee for his otherwise vain efforts. "*Baku-jin sorei na!* I had you all sized up before I came in. Anyone could, from either wooded rise north or south! You don't have a full rifle platoon down here, and yonder tumbledown shack won't do you much good in the long run."

Rafe shrugged. "Them walls are solid rock. Up on the Canadian River a handful of good old boys stood off the whole Comanche Nation ahint *adobe* walls!"

Amarillo chimed in. "Damned right, and all the South Cheyenne, Kiowa, and Arapaho as well. Everyone's heard of the Adobe Walls Fight."

Ki had, as a matter of fact. Jessie's "Uncle Quanah" had been there in his misspent youth and liked to brag about it. Ki didn't think this was the time to pick nits. If it had been he'd have pointed out that Adobe Walls had been a big well-appointed trading post, manned by sure-shot buffalo hunters armed with scoped rifles, and attacked by a large war party of allied Indians, not anything like a single nation. He did feel safe to point out, "The buffalo hunters at Adobe Walls were picking off Indians at a mile with scoped high-powered plains rifles, and it was still a near thing. Neither you nor your brothers paid a dime for any of that stock across the way, Rafe. Billie Sanford would doubtless do you dirt in any case, but I can't see anyone else backing her play if they could recover all that stock without bloodshed!"

"Bloodshed goes with raising stock and holding on to your range," growled Rafe. "We could likely replace the cows. Range is another matter. Range is getting ever tougher to hang on to as the country fills up with pesky strangers. We Graysons hold all the range you see around you because we've never backed away from a fight with nobody. Do you 'spect us to back down to an infernal *girl*, you Ching-Chong asshole?"

Ki was still waiting for that coffee, perhaps in vain, as he kept a straight face and soberly replied, "No offense, but we took the liberty of scanning some maps in Austin before riding out to have all these dumb misunderstandings with you. If one wanted to be picky, one could point out that we're a good hard ride from the home spread platted in your name. Despite your squatter's claim to this particular draw, we're on open federal range at the moment."

He didn't get any argument. Rafe nodded. "There you go. It don't belong to nobody, on paper. As for who gets to graze it, it's a simple matter of being tough enough to hold however much of it. Billie Sanford and her mealy-mouthed daddy ain't the first who've tried to crowd us Graysons. Indians, greasers, and even some Texans I'd as soon not talk about lie buried hither and yon on this here land. We got some of our *own* bones buried in this here land. Ain't nobody gonna take this land from us, and I'm still waiting for that fucking gun, Chinaman!"

Ki was tempted to give his sixgun to the bastards a bullet at a time. But there were other ways to kill, and they tended to work better when your enemy thought he had you completely in his power. So Ki unbuckled his gun rig, tossed gun and all aside on the dry grass, and asked, "Could I have that coffee now?"

Meanwhile, well out of sight if not out of mind to the north, the hatchet-faced hand called Gash was riding Lone Star's pony and leading the pack brutes Chief had brought in. Rafe Grayson had paid Gash off to the end of the month with orders to ride out and just forget where he'd last been employed. Gash didn't know what Rafe intended to do with the bodies of Chief, Snotty, or that blamed blond bitch if she ever came back up. He didn't want to know. As far as he and the Texas Rangers were concerned, he'd never heard of the Grayson outfit. He'd likely been shacked up somewheres since he'd ridden for the Jingle Bob, over New Mexico way, last fall.

As he walked Lone Star's pony up a rise toward the rocky live-oaked ridge, Gash helped himself to more vinegar-laced water from the lady's canteen. Gash had used the trick himself in hot dry country. He was glad the otherwise useless she-devil had topped fair well water with maybe a couple of spoonfuls of wine vinegar. For while the day was still young, the Texas sun had glared the canteen water lukewarm and the slight tang helped a heap.

He didn't drink much. It wouldn't have been smart, and his throat still smarted from where that crazy little cunt had tried to split his Adam's apple with her dainty bare hand. It had felt more like a dull ax. He'd had to take a lot of what had happened after that on faith. The boys had stretched him out alongside Chief and Snotty, but he'd had the good fortune to moan before his pals had decided to get rid of the three inconvenient cadavers.

Near the crest Gash turned in the saddle to gaze back the way he'd come. He'd ridden over more than one similar rise as well as across the intervening draws. So while he still knew where his old outfit was, he marveled as ever on how easy it was to hide most anything out in the open on this innocently rolling range.

He ducked under some low live-oak limbs as he topped the rise, then reined in to enjoy the sudden coolness where ridge breezes blew through sweet-smelling tree shade. Then a mountain lion, at least, landed smack on top of him to twist him off his mount like the lid of a mason jar, and the completely confounded Gash lay flat on his face in dry grass and fresh horseshit with all the breath knocked out of him and Lone Star perched atop him like a witch aboard a broom before he knew what in blue blazes was happening.

The smaller but astoundingly strong girl had both of his arms twisted painfully behind him, as if she intended to tie them in a

128

pretzel knot as soon as his poor bones gave way. Gash sobbed, "Jesus H. Christ, I was only funning when I mentioned ass-fucking, ma'am!"

Lone Star answered, coldly, "I know exactly what you had in mind for me, Gash. But let us not dwell on the past. What are you doing this far from camp with my pony and pack stock?"

Gash groaned. "Rafe told me to get rid of myself and all the other evidence. He knew you had lots of friends in high places, and he thought you'd kilt your fool self to avoid a fate worse than death. How come you ain't dead, ma'am? We all thought you drownded in that spring water back yonder."

Lone Star smiled thinly down at the nape of his neck. "I thought I had too. I doubt I could have hauled myself another fifty yards when I suddenly came to a little air above a lot of mighty cold water. As I'd hoped, that tank was fed by an elaborate cave system. I still didn't owe you boys much. Such air as there was tasted like bat dung, and you haven't seen dark until you've been down in unmapped limestone caverns after midnight."

"I see you got out, though," Gash sighed.

To which she replied dryly, "It wasn't easy. I swam and waded, waded and swam, to where I could mostly walk on wet sand and use every one of the waterproof matches I had on me, one at a time mayhaps every million years. I mostly groped my way in the dark, choosing forks in the passages that seemed to lead up instead of the other way. I was all right once I came to a larger chamber the bats were using as a sort of nursery. I heard all this mousy chittering, and when I struck a light I was under a domed roof covered with Lord knows how many thousand head of tiny freetail kittens, pups, or whatever in thunder you call a baby bat. I knew their mommas had left them tucked in their cave to go out hunting bugs. That didn't help much at first. Then sure enough, the momma bats commenced to flutter home to their babies, along towards morning, and all I had to do was grope the other way, listening to 'em flutter overhead and sometimes lower. I got brushed by their little leathery wings a time or more. But nobody got hurt."

Gash groaned. "Speak for yourself and the bats, ma'am. I'm hurting awful, and you said yourself you didn't want to dwell on the past."

Lone Star tightened her death grip on his wrists, as if he'd reminded her. "I don't care about your friends, unless they know something about a friend of mine. I crawled up out of a sort

129

of badger hole in a clump of scrub cedar just about five in the morning if I still know my Texas sky. The sun came up to finish drying out my boots and duds about the time I spied you and my stock topping that rise to yonder south. I'm glad we met like so. I've a change of socks and unmentionables in my saddlebags."

She glanced up at her recaptured mount, quietly browsing feathery mesquite leaves while avoiding the thorns a few yards off. "I see they told you to get lost with my Winchester and birthday gun as well. So now all I'm missing is my fairly new hat and a very old friend. My *segundo,* a tall, dark, and handsome gent of Oriental mien, couldn't have been far away when you all captured me. He must have figured out I'd been captured by now. So where in thunder would you say he is right now?"

Gash answered, truthfully, "I can't say. There wasn't no strangers of any persuasion about as I rid out of camp. I do believe I might have spotted movement on a distant rise as I was riding out by the dawn's early light. You know how coyotes or Comanche sort of vanish into thin air just as you spy them out the corner of an eye?"

Lone Star did. She nodded. "That sounds like Ki. But if he was scouting you . . . Right. I'm fixing to let go and get off you now, Gash. If you've a lick of sense you'll just stay flat on your face till after I mount up and ride out, hear?"

Gash protested, "You can't strand me out in the middle of the Hill County without a gun or a pony!"

She let go of his wrists and sprang to her feet. "Sure I can. You'll find your gun where I threw it, over in that clump of jimson near yonder cedar stump. Those ponies were mine to begin with. What more do you expect from me, an egg in your beer?"

Gash started to rise. She warned, "Don't. I mean it." She turned toward her saddle bronc, noting the pack brutes had steadied to graze further along the ridge.

As Gash watched her trim rear view receding, eyes narrowed and teeth bared, he marveled that he'd ever wanted to rut with such a spitfire. He still knew that once she'd ridden off he faced a mighty uncertain future afoot, a long ways from anywhere they served food and drink.

He knew she was as dangerous to grab on to as a whirling buzz saw, but if she got to her damned guns before he could stop her the results could be worse. Gash figured she'd written him off as licked, that she couldn't have eyes in the back of that blond head, and that once he landed on her back, far heavier than she'd landed on his . . .

But of course Lone Star heard him spring to his feet and commence his rush. So as Gash caught up with her in six or eight bounds and grabbed for the back of her neck with both hands, Lone Star didn't seem to be there anymore.

Gash gasped, "Oh, shit!" as his questing hands closed on thorny mesquite branches a full fathom beyond their intended target, and Lone Star threw a vicious side kick at him from where she'd replanted her own center of balance. Then her high boot heel broke his right floating rib to drive bone splinter up into his lung.

Gash landed on his face again, gibbering with fear and pain as his chest filled with fire and his schoolmarm-sized opponent seemed to loom above him like an elephant intent on stomping ants.

Gash sobbed, "Don't stomp me! Have mercy on a poor sinner, ma'am!"

Lone Star shrugged. "I already tried that twice with you." Then she simply killed him with a well-aimed kick where his spinal column joined his skull—or where it *had*.

Muttering unkind things about her own softhearted streak, the lady known as Lone Star caught up with her cow pony, mounted up, and went after the pack brutes.

She naturally had a throw-rope lashed to her saddle swells just overlapping the upthrust stock of her saddle gun. But she didn't have to rope anybody. The two pack brutes were tethered to the same dragging line, and only played tag with her along the ridge to where the shade ran out. Then foolishly assuming they had a choice of sunbathing or going along with human design, they stood staring sheepishly at her as she swung down off her saddle without dismounting to grap a rope end draped over some prickly pear.

Straightening back up, Lone Star muttered, "That's better. Now where's my damned hat and that *segundo* of mine?"

Her only reply was the wistful tweet of a distant horned lark. So she dug her gun rig out of a saddlebag, strapped it back on, and headed back the way she'd just come, toward the east, clinging to the cover along the ridge. None of the stock spooked as they passed the fresh body of Gash. As cool as it was atop the rise, he'd likely keep a day or more before his demise got obvious.

She didn't know where Ki could be, but she knew the way he thought because Ki had trained her to think the same way.

She figured he'd either ridden for help, a most unlikely but possible move, or much more likely, Ki, like she, was scouting that Grayson outfit Comanche-style, clinging to such cover as there was on higher ground.

She failed to see how Ki could know she'd gotten away on her own. So he was likely some damned place closer to that line camp. She knew Ki would want to see as much as possible, which was more than one could do from this far out. So she followed the one ridge to where it wasn't too far from a wooded spur that would lead her back toward that hidden herd and remote camp. Then she simply loped down and across the open shortgrass there was no other way to avoid.

Once under cover again, she cut west, hoping to stay more or less north of the Grayson outfit as she picked her dainty way back among big limestone fangs and runty trees. By now the sun was higher and brighter, casting blacker shadows even as it made it impossible to miss grasshoppers moving in the open.

A lot of them seemed to be, considering the time of the year and the stillness of the air. As any country kid west of the Mississippi knew, the big gray grasshoppers infesting the sea of grass as if they thought they were fool shrimp liked to wait until you were almost on top of them. Then they'd startle you with flashing fake butterfly wings and a rattlesnake buzz that carried them about five yards off before they turned back into invisible dirt-colored surprises again. Kids walking a country road or a rider following the edge of sun and shade could wind up following the same series of sudden flashes for miles, and Lone Star thought little of it, until she noticed puffs of hoppers way out ahead of her headed *her* way, and reined in to move deeper into the shadows and study on that.

When she heard a distant harness jingle she quietly hauled her Winchester from its boot, dismounted, and levered a round of .44–40 in the chamber as soon as she'd tethered her stock safely out of the way—she hoped. She'd been following a sort of game trail along the ridge. She assumed that the other rider, or riders, had been stirring up hoppers the same way.

It took forever. For a time she feared they'd spotted the hoppers *she'd* spooked as well. But as she finally heard low voices, cautious but not too proddy, she realized that, as usual, time had slowed down on her because she was thinking so hard and fast.

There were two of them, dressed Texas cowhand and Mex vaquero, the Texican aboard a paint and the Mexican riding a cordovan. She was sure she'd seen neither in the Grayson camp. Rafe Grayson had said something about his two brothers. These boys were coming from an odd direction if she had her own location right, and she failed to see how either Jake or Alvin Grayson could have been born a Mex.

They were sure to spot her anytime now. So she took a deep breath and stepped out into view, both her guns pointed politely enough as she called out, "Morning. Before you ask, I'd be Jessie Starbuck of the Circle Star and I'm searching for my *segundo,* a tall, dark, and handsome cuss on a buckskin gelding. You gents would tell me if you knew where he was, wouldn't you?"

The Texican and Mexican exchanged off-glances. Then the Anglo ticked the brim of his ten-gallon to her and said, "He's riding with us agin cow thieves, ma'am, if we're talking about that Ki from Japan Land. I'd be Jeff Bushmill and this here's Concho Valdez. We've been out scouting for the Lazy S. We're headed back to report in, and that's likely where you'll find your friend, if you'd like to tag along."

She naturally said she would. So Jeff felt no call to disarm the lady he knew to be Lone Star this early in the game.

★

Chapter 12

As Ki was considering ways to escape from the Grayson outfit, and Lone Star was riding blithely into the trap Jeff and Concho were planning to spring on her when they met up with Billie Sanford, Longarm was getting off at Austin feeling grim. He'd caught a few winks of fitful sleep, sitting up half the night. Then a shitty little kid had commenced running up and down the aisle at dawn, and the breakfast they'd served him up forward had been shitty as well.

He picked up some peppermints in the Austin depot, once he'd made certain his saddle and possibles had gotten off at the same stop. Then, leaving his gear in the custody of the railroad for now, he went first to Western Union, found neither a message from Billy Vail nor anyone pretty as Kathy Turnbolt waiting for him, and headed on over to the Austin office of Starbuck Enterprises.

The lady known as Lone Star knew how tough it was for her sisters in a man's world. So it wasn't as surprising as it might have been at, say, McCoy Meat Packing Incorporated to find the office manager a female of thirty or so and not bad-looking, if sort of severe. She invited Longarm to sit, and even offered him a cigar from the humidor atop her imposing desk once he'd flashed his badge and identification.

She didn't say so, and it would have been dumb of him to ask, but Longarm got the distinct impression she knew he was on better than average terms with her own boss lady. It was hard to hide some things from all the help, and the help always shared such secrets. So, severe or not, she hung on every word as Longarm brought her up to date on the misadventures of that missing crate. Once he'd finished, it got tougher. She sighed and said, "I wish they had those new Bell telephones out here in Austin and we could call back and forth all around. For I don't know where to send you first, Deputy Long."

He said he was willing to go anywhere that fool crate had wound up. She sighed some more and said, "That's just it. This is the first I've heard of anyone being dumb enough to dispatch any of Miss Jessie's property all the way from her main ranch by buckboard, and I mean to wire that fool *tercero* what-for for doing it!"

She slid a fancy metal matchbox across the desk at him, likely thinking he couldn't light the fool cigar with his own matches. He shook his head. "I mean to smoke this swell Havana later, ma'am. You were saying there's more than one place them old boys with the missing crate on their buckboard might be headed, right?"

She nodded. "I don't see how they could have made it a quarter of the way to Austin that way yet. You say you've been hoping they'd wise up and consider more modern ideas such as telegraph and railroad lines, and I tend to agree. Any wires they'd sent, asking for help or further instructions, would have reached this desk by now. As you can see, none have, so I simply can't say where the fools and that mysterious crate might be right now."

Longarm grimaced. "What if a semi-literate but willing worker who didn't speak much English got the not-too-fantastic notion railroad trains moved faster? Most railroad freight agents in Texas know Miss Jessie and how important Starbuck Enterprises might be to the local economy. They'd take that crate to forward by rail C.O.D., wouldn't they?"

Lone Star's local manager nodded. "They would if they knew what was good for them. But in that case I'd have surely gotten a wire from the railroad by now. The wires run anywhere one could put that crate aboard a railroad car."

Longarm nodded. "My job would be way easier if nobody ever did anything wrong, or simply dumb, ma'am. Say one of them not-too-sharp vaqueros told a not-too-sharp railroader that crate was meant personal to be delivered to Miss Jessie at her private quarters here in Austin."

The manager frowned thoughtfully. He admired nice-looking gals who thought before they babbled. She finally said, "The hotel

135

across town would have surely told me if anything bigger than a candy box had been delivered for Miss Jessie. They've told me, for example, about her and Mister Ki riding off somewhere and leaving some other stock in the hotel stable. I have to approve such expenses as even a few ponies may incur for this Austin branch of Starbuck Enterprises, you see."

Longarm nodded and gallantly lied, "Miss Jessie has often bragged on how well things are run for her here in Austin, ma'am. But that don't mean every last cog in the machinery is oiled and meshed to perfection."

She nodded curtly. "The amazing travels of that mysterious crate so far prove you right on that point, Deputy Long. But I'm still certain any literate employeee of Starbuck Enterprises here in Austin would have informed me about a massive crate addressed to Miss Jessie or anyone else, once they'd signed for it."

Longarm was starting to feel sorry he hadn't accepted her invite to light up. His poor innards were growling. But since duty came before lunch he went on. "Sensible gents, Anglo or Mex, never would have occasioned all this confusion to begin with, ma'am. For all we know that poor crate's still baking under the Texas sun out in the middle of nothing much. You surely grow a heap of that in Texas. But suppose them vaqueros got weary of poking along so tediously and that crate *did* get sent on. Then suppose the baggage handlers delivering it were too dumb, or too lazy, to ask anyone to sign for it. Then suppose the Starbuck hand they delivered it to was just filling in for someone smarter, and just shoved it in some corner and forgot about it."

She didn't look as if that notion pleased her. "If anyone on our payroll's been that stupid, he, she, or it won't be on our payroll long! I hope you're wrong, but we can start right here!"

She banged on a desk bell, hard. When a skinny young gent who reminded Longarm of Henry, their clerk back in Denver, came in to ask what she wanted, she snapped, "We're searching for a big shipping crate, a little larger than this desk. I want you to look in the basement, and then I want you to check the storerooms upstairs. By now the crate should be looking at least a little weathered, and it might or might not be addressed to Miss Starbuck. Suffice it to say, I want to hear about anything at all like it, addressed or not addressed to anyone."

Her Boy Friday protested there wasn't any such crate anywhere about, since it was his chore to notice. She told him to check

136

anyway, adding, "I want you to ask all the shopkeepers we rent to on the ground floor. There's an outside chance some idiot simply hauled it here, and some other idiot accepted it as a shipment of tobacco, ladies notions, or whatever, see?"

He didn't seem to, but he left to carry out her orders, grumbling but willing. Longarm suspected he wouldn't have been working there if he hadn't been.

Turning back to the pretty but imposing female Longarm said, "I can nose about Miss Jessie's top-floor suite and the storage rooms of your hotel, once I get there, ma'am. I have to mosey over in any case. Some chambermaid or stable hand might have a better notion than you as to where your boss lady and Ki might have been heading, no offense."

She didn't seem to take any. So he went on. "Does that hotel and this location here cover all Miss Jessie's company property in Austin, ma'am?"

She sniffed sort of proudly, allowed Starbuck Enterprises was one of the biggest agricultural trading outfits in these United States, and started writing neatly but quickly on a legal pad with one of those patent pens you didn't have to dip between words.

As she wrote she explained, "Our reason for being in business here is that Austin sits astride the line that separates the cattle country of West Texas from the croplands and timber reserves of East Texas. I can't see even a drunken Indian delivering that crate to any cotton gin, tannery, cannery, or such because nobody working for us in such a facility would accept it. We do have more than one warehouse, however, and good help being hard to find . . ."

He said he followed her drift. She tore off the sheet of yellow foolscap and handed it to him. He noticed she hadn't signed it. As he was folding the list to stick it in a vest pocket, he asked if she had any business cards with her very own handle on them. She looked surprised but not displeased when he explained, "We like to keep track of folks going out of their way for the federal government, ma'am."

She dimpled mighty girlishly for such a severe-looking gal and got a card out of a drawer for him, observing as she presented it, "To tell the truth, my father and four uncles rode for the South with Hood's Texas Brigade. But I suppose we're all on the same side now."

Longarm chuckled and made no reference to his own military history as he put her card away—to show Jessie, not Billy Vail, when and if he ever caught up with this sweetly grim little thing's boss lady. It was the least he could do. He'd have been a total asshole to make a play for anyone on Jessie Starbuck's payroll.

They jawed just a bit more, and then that skinny kid returned to deny that crate they were looking for could be anywhere about. So Longarm got to his feet, shook hands with both of them, and said he'd start with the Starbuck hotel.

He'd lied a bit. He'd been through Austin a time or two before. So he knew of a chili joint between hither and yon that served molten lava just the way he liked it.

It was odd how often places that served fine food at fair prices tended to be rundown and small, while prissy folks with rotten grub and high-toned manners got to charge as high as seventy-five cents for a sissy lunch in a gussied-up joint. The Mex place he so fondly recalled from earlier visits was a hole-in-the-wall on Sixth Street, reeking of peppers and corn meal and, at this hour, filled with flies and the sort of gents that lunched on Sixth Street.

Most were dressed cow, Texican or Mexican, with a sprinkling of poor souls whose jobs, like Longarm's, forced them to dress a bit less casually. He could see in the big mirror on the wall behind the lunch counter that their hearts just weren't into starched shirts and seersucker jackets on a summer's day in Texas. When the pleasantly plump *muchacha* working the counter asked Longarm what she could do for to make him *mas feliz,* he winked at her, allowed they'd better settle for her serving him some grub, and ordered chili con carne over three or four Texas tamales. She agreed that would make him break into a sweat if anything would, and waddled off to fill his order.

The Anglo cowhand seated next to him observed, "It sure beats all how hot Mex grub makes the air all about feel cooler. Do you reckon that's how come greasers admire pepper so?"

Longarm made a noncommittal noise as he shot a thoughtful glance at the mirror. There was no way you could tell an asshole what an asshole he was acting like by using that word on Sixth Street without being an asshole yourself. It was likely safer to sound off about niggers on a Saturday night over on Basin Street, further east. Tex-Mex vaqueros were more apt to be packing a gun as well as a blade, and gentlemen of color tended to warn you that you were annoying them before they blew up in your face.

But none of the others there seemed to be staring sleepy-eyed with that tight little smile you had to worry about in Spanish-speaking circles. The place was really crowded, and the cowhand's dumb remark had likely been lost in the shuffle. There were even a few standees now. One morose-looking cuss who likely worked in a nearby undertaking establishment was leaning against the pressed-tin wall directly behind Longarm's stool, avoiding Longarm's eyes in the mirror but still looking anxious. Longarm knew the feeling. But what the hell, he hadn't been served yet himself.

The fat *muchacha* came back with Longarm's order. He told her she was *una angela de merced* and dug in. He liked her even better once he had. For they'd seasoned the grub just right, neither show-off hot nor sissy mild. As he dredged up shards of tamale through pungent chili con carne, Longarm reflected on the similar meals, good and bad, he'd had in similar joints all over the West. He was pretty sure the saddest excuse for chili he'd ever been served had been cooked by a total greenhorn up Idaho way, while the few times it had been just too spicy to finish had been smack on the border, Juarez one time and Nogales the other. It was funny, until one studied on it, how Mex food got milder as one rode deeper into Mexico. It was likely more accurate to call such grub Chihuahua than Mex. Once you got south of, say, Monterrey, the grub got more surprising than hot. Fried bananas and chocolate-covered chicken weren't peppered worth mentioning.

A couple of Mexicans who'd been eating together got up to leave. Two others slipped into their places, leaving the one cuss in the undertaker's suit and black Stetson. Longarm didn't care. He'd had to wait in line a time or more, and nobody had seen *him* glaring at other customers' backs like that.

He was still mildly relieved when the dumb kid who'd mentioned greasers burped, dropped a two-cent tip by his empty plate, and got up to go pester someone else. That is, Longarm was relieved until he noticed the somber cuss behind him didn't seem to want to sit by his side after all.

Longarm had long since taught himself to keep tabs on others without staring directly at them. So as he went on stuffing his own face he was able to determine, for certain, that whatever the sullen bastard wanted in there, it couldn't be a seat at the counter. Others got up. Others came in and took their places at the busy counter. When Longarm finished the tamales and chili con carne, he allowed that *muchacha* could bring him some coffee and pie. She said they had pecan, raisin, or beach-plum pie. When he ordered the pecan, she noticed the black-suited cuss hovering behind Longarm, and told him there was a seat down closer to the kitchen. But the morose cuss just shook his head, turned on one heel, and strode out the front door, then out of sight, without a word.

The counter gal looked at Longarm and demanded, "Did I say something wrong?"

Longarm shrugged. "You only offered to *feed* the loco cuss. He must have mistook this place for a barbershop or railroad depot."

They both laughed. She went to fetch his dessert. The coffee was strong as an ox and bitter as bile. The pecan pie was sweet as they could get the fool nuts with honey and brown sugar. He wondered what their other pies might taste like. He decided he might be overdoing it, and settled for one more cup of their swell coffee before he paid her outfit the thirty-odd cents he owe'd them, tipping her a whole dime lest she suspect he thought her too fat.

Crossing the street out front, he dodged a beer dray, and got out that list of dumb places Queen Victoria's present to President Hayes could have wound up instead. One of Jessie's warehouses seemed closer than anything else. As he reached the far side he put the list away and shot a casual glance at a plate-glass shop window. He wasn't out to admire his own sun-baked shirt and vest. That mysterious cuss in the buzzard-black frock coat and wide sombrero was still hovering behind him, although at a more discreet distance now. Longarm rounded a corner and cut across the side street, lining up on the bay-window panes of a hat shop as he strode on to confirm that there the cuss was, watching from the corner as if he was having a conversation with that cigar-store Indian under the awning.

Longarm paused to light a cheroot and study reflections some more. "Well, Kathy told you that limping man back in Alpine had wired Austin in a mighty simple code, and she sure was truthful about other things."

Then he shook out his wax match and went on. A greener lawman might have simply flattened out against a wall around a corner to confront the silly son of a bitch trailing him. Longarm had done that often enough to know how tough it would be to convince any judge he wasn't a nervous nelly worried about possible queer admirers. There was no law saying a grown man couldn't walk the downtown streets of Austin by broad-ass day, provided he had at least two dollars and any identification at all on him.

There was no federal vagrancy code in any case, and it was up to the Austin P.D. to worry about any weapons that gloomy cuss might or might not be packing under that frock coat. So Longarm kept going, not looking back but keeping tabs just the same as he softly hummed the tune of "Farther Along."

Not wanting to make it easy on the cuss, but not wanting to give anything away, Longarm made a few of the easier moves as he worked his way the six or eight city blocks to that warehouse. After entering a corner saloon by one door, taking the leak he needed to, and exiting via a side door without ordering a drink, he thought he might have lost his semi-skilled shadow. He failed to spot anyone on his tail after that. If he hadn't thrown the cuss, he'd taught him to be more careful.

The big redbrick warehouse stood near a railroad siding in a less built-up part of Austin. Longarm took a shortcut across a vacant lot overgrown with tumbleweed, still rooted and green but starting to sprout kitten-claws that brushed his tweed pants better than any whisk broom could have. So it wouldn't be long now before the big fuzz balls went straw-dry, busted off at ground level, and commenced to imitate jackrabbits hither and yon.

It was funny. There hadn't been any tumbleweeds when he'd first come West back around '66 or '67. Sodbusters had imported the species all the way from the Russian steppes with some of that otherwise grand Russian seed. The original intent had been to grow the sorts of wheat the Russians grew on similar high plains. Nobody had ever ordered any tumbleweeds, or great thistles, as Russian farmers called them.

In either land they could be a bother or a boon, depending on how one managed one's range. Stock could graze fresh-sprouted tumbleweed and it never seemed to get out of hand, unless you overgrazed down to bare patches, as in the case of this lot. For as the dead but loaded tumbleweed balls rolled about, they shed seeds in their wake that took root best where the ground was bare. Tumbleweed seeds hung up in dry grass were more apt to feed some hungry bird.

As he approached the gaping door of Jessie's warehouse, he saw an older man in faded denim overalls regarding him from just inside. So he waved, and when the gent waved back, Longarm flashed his badge on the way in, and that inspired the older ware-houseman to step out into the sunlight to greet him.

They shook as Longarm introduced himself and explained what he was there for. The older man said to call him Sal. "I don't recall any such delivery, Deputy. But as my kids would be proud to tell you, I don't know everything. Come on in and we'll both have us a look about."

They did. The cavernous interior was big enough to hold hundreds of desks from Queen Victoria, if not the old steamship all that oak had come from. But fortunately for Longarm's patience, if not his quest, the place was filled from brick flooring to trussed rafters with bales, not boxes. There were cotton bales to one side of the wide central aisle and lower piles of baled hides to the other. The warhousemen had wisely left fire gaps by the side walls as well. So they wasted a few minutes peering into such natural hiding places, although with no luck. The older man led Longarm to the corner office partitioned off from the rest of the layout, and opened a ledger atop his battered desk, saying, "We keep a tally of everything coming in and everything going out. I'm fixing to get surprised as hell if there's anything about a crate a mite bigger than this here desk, addressed to Miss Jessie or anyone else."

As he turned pages, muttering, Longarm asked, "Where might I be sent from here if I was a crate delivered casual and shipped with more important stuff from out back?"

The warehouseman scowled. "I wish you hadn't asked that. Some cotton and hides go east by rail. Most leave here for Corpus Christi or Galveston if Miss Jessie means to service clients by sea. She sends a heap of raw cotton and cowhide to Nagasaki, mostly by way of Galveston. But I don't see how we'd ever ship a bale-sized crate to Nagasaki or even Galveston without even one peep inside!"

Longarm agreed he'd never do a thing like that either. "I've seen the Starbuck steam clippers tied up in Galveston. Knew about all that cotton the Japanese take off your hands. Thought Miss Jessie sent most of her cows to market alive, to get skinned after slaughter back East."

The old-timer, who might have known Jessie Starbuck better in the business sense at least, said, "We don't have much to do with Miss Jessie's main cattle operation. You'd have to ask her or that Ki cuss how they deal with that beef, dead or alive. Them hides out back are part of a sort of charitable notion Miss Jessie's daddy, the late Alex Starbuck, started just after the war to help small holders druv to the wall by the Damnyankee Reconstruction."

He sighed and added, "You'd have had to have been there. There were hardly any railroads. Nigger soldiers or them even nastier state police appointed by carpetbaggers stopped you every time you loped your pony after a damned old cow."

"I know about the Reconstruction," Longarm told him, without going in to his mixed feelings about an era few on either side seemed able to recall with any accuracy. He said, "You were explaining about all them hides, seeing Jessie Starbuck ships stock to market from way further west."

The warehouseman nodded. "Small holders with just a few cows and a heap of debts can be hard put to get a square deal on their beef. A Texas cow sold on the hoof in Texas don't go for half as much as it'd be worth up to Dodge or Ogallala, but do a poor debt-ridden ranchero head up the long trail with only a few head of scrawny stock . . ."

"So Miss Jessie pays a fair price closer to home," Longarm said. "But why slaughter and skin 'em out here? Even if you all had some of that fancy cold-storage gear invented by Mister Linde, there can't be that many folks in Austin who eat that much beef morning, noon, and night. We're talking a heap of hides out yonder, you know."

The old-timer grimaced. "Who did you think got to pile 'em up so neat? We don't deal in cold-stored beef here yet. Half them hides come off dead and dying critters Miss Jessie takes off otherwise desperate *rancheros* at a loss. The salvaged hides sell well enough in Japan Land, but she'd go broke on the deal if she didn't buy other critters, more fit for human consumption, to be skint for the same hide market and canned for the British Empire."

"Would you say that again slower?" Longarm demanded.

So the older man explained, "Bully beef, in cans. Queen Victoria feeds it to her army and navy, and she's sure got big ones. Starbuck Enterprises sells canned beef to the Czar of All the Russians too. The Jap Mikado and Empress of China would rather eat the swell long-grain rice Miss Jessie grows over by the Sabine. We don't ship no rice from these parts."

Longarm said he should think not, muttering, "Cans of bully beef would be more likely than hides or cotton to wind up in crates. Is it safe to assume there's a warehouse like this full of canned cow?"

The older man disappointed him by saying, "Not hardly. Like I said, all that cotton and cowhide winds up in the Far East, by occasional ship. Queen Victoria and the Czar of All the Russians have their own freight lines and purchasing offices smack in Galveston. So the Starbuck cannery here in Austin ships fast as they can can the fool beef. When you get over yonder you'll find freight cars parked on cannery sidings. The mostly Mex help loads the bully beef off the labeling and boxing line direct in the railcars. As the cars fill they get hauled over to the main yards and from there . . ."

"Aw, shit!" Longarm said. "If some asshole delivered that fucking crate to a loading dock where nobody speaks English . . . It's been nice talking to you, pard."

They shook on it and Longarm left, puffing furiously on his cheroot as he consulted the list of possible addresses. The ferocious Texas sun glared blindingly on the canary-yellow paper. He still read off the cannery's address, near a railroad trestle crossing Shoal Creek, an easy enough walk away, and shoved the list back in his vest pocket to get over there.

He was cutting back across that same weed-grown lot when a voice behind him yelled, "Longarm! Hit the dirt!"

So he did, and not too soon, judging from all the gunshots he could hear as he rolled sideways, crushing green tumbleweeds as he got out his own gun and put some space between where he'd landed and where he wanted to be when and if someone tried to send a bullet up his ass through the hardly bullet-proof screen of knee-high greenery.

Then the same voice that had warned him called out, "I got him. Where might you be, Longarm?"

Longarm waited before he answered. It hardly seemed likely the same gent who'd warned him to duck would be out to shoot him on the rise. So he called back, cautiously, "I'm just about where I want to be for now. Who might the him you got be, and do you have any identity of your own, you helpful cuss?"

His apparent benefactor called back, "I don't know who I just backshot. It seemed like a good idea when he rose from those same weeds to backshoot you. I'd be Agent MacIntosh, Ed MacIntosh, of the U.S. Secret Service."

Longarm started to ask why in thunder anyone from Washington would be interested in him. Then suspecting he knew, he raised his head and six-gun high enough to make out the Secret Service agent who'd just saved his bacon.

It was that black-clad cuss from the chili joint. He was standing over something or somebody else in the knee-high tumbleweeds, reloading his own Smith & Wesson. So seeing the gun was aimed politely, Longarm rose to full height and headed over to join him, his own gun muzzle trained downright rudely as he said, "Howdy, pard. I suppose you have some means of backing your brag."

The other federal agent holstered his reloaded weapon and told Longarm he was an asshole as he flashed his own identification and somewhat smaller badge. Longarm muttered, "I could have nailed you by mistake, speaking of assholes."

Then he spied the Mex in a checked shirt and white duck pants, spread out in the weeds between them, faceup and smiling, as his big brown eyes stared unwinkingly right into the overhead sun. "Funny, that just wasn't my picture of Aunt Felicia—save for her complexion, I mean."

That inspired MacIntosh to ask what in blue blazes they were talking about. So Longarm brought him up to date in a few terse words as that old-timer from the warehouse cautiously approached from one direction and a blue-uniformed copper badge and some railroad hands came wading through the weeds from another.

The old warehouseman had never seen the dead Mex before, but backed up the Secret Service man's story. He'd seen the whole affair from just inside the gaping doorway yonder. The Mex had obviously followed Longarm from somewhere—a chili joint sounded as possible as anywhere else—and dropped into the weeds to lay for his intended victim when Longarm offered him the chance. The copper badge said *he'd* have hung back farther had he been keeping an eye on Longarm but hadn't wanted to crawl about in vacant lots. Longarm said he was sure glad MacIntosh had done that, hanging back farther when he'd seen Longarm taking such a sudden interest in window glass. The copper badge said he'd go get the meat wagon and more law. So Longarm and MacIntosh went over to the warehouse to take in the shade with the old-timer as they waited.

★

Chapter 13

Arbuckle Coffee was the brand of choice in most cow camps because the folks who roasted and packed it in Frisco and Chicago gave premium stamps and knew how their product was likely to be brewed in the wilder parts of the West. Arbuckle was drinkable, though barely, brewed in an old tin can or milk bucket. When it was perked halfway civilized in a patent pot, just the hearty smell could wake one up all bright-eyed and ready to ride.

It had still taken Billie Sanford two extra cups, brewed strong and black, to clear her head once she'd popped her eyes open in broad day to find she had an odd bruise on her neck, a still twitchy twat, and nobody else in her bedroll to do anything about that with.

For a time she'd hoped her amazingly hung new friend was just out in the mesquite enjoying a good crap. By the time she'd learned he'd recovered his guns and his buckskin barb before slipping away like a dirty dog, she was feeling as vexed as a she-wolverine with a toothache. But she never let on as Jeff and Concho rode in with that other gal around noontime.

Billie knew who Jessica Starbuck was at first sight, thanks to Ki having told her that the infernally rich bitch was somewhere in these hills. Billie greeted her fellow Southwestern belle as if butter wouldn't melt in her mouth. Lone Star dismounted and hugged her back. Southwestern belles tended to act sweetest while sparring for each other's weak spots.

146

Billie Sanford wanted information more than she wanted Lone Star's sixgun. Concho was already leading their guest's livestock and saddle gun away. As Billie led Lone Star to the cook fire she knew she had the other woman outgunned as well as surrounded on all sides. If push came to shove, Billie was packing her own Schofield .45, and she knew she was as quick on the draw as she needed to be. Sitting Lone Star on a live-oak log near the small cook fire, Billie told Gimp Laydon to give them both some coffee and rustle up some flapjacks for their guest before she sat down beside that guest, or victim, and said she was waiting to hear her sad story.

Lone Star told her the simple truth as she knew it. Southwestern belles as a species were capable of talking more and saying less, without actually lying, than most human beings. So Billie was taking all Lone Star said with plenty of salt, even as she kept nodding her head and encouraging her to go on.

By the time they were serving her those flapjacks Lone Star had brought Billie Sanford and the men around the fire up to her escape from the enemy camp, leaving out that last grim adventure with Gash, or trying to. Billie Sanford proved she'd been paying attention by innocently asking, "How did you ever get your guns, gear, and three whole horses back after leaping into that tank and crawling through a bat cave, dearie?"

Lone Star dimpled back at her and confided, "I stole 'em back of course, dearie. One of the Grayson hands had 'em up on a rise to graze or whatever. So I simply took 'em back and lit out."

Jeff Bushmill, who'd just returned from tethering Lone Star's brutes with the Lazy S remuda in time to hear the last of that, hunkered down nearby to light a smoke before he shook out the match and told his boss lady, "She's leaving some of the best parts out, Miss Billie. Me and Concho met her out yonder like she just said. Riding back with her we passed what might have been somebody else, lying in some jimson off to one side. This little lady here didn't see fit to mention it. So neither did we. I just now sent Concho back, with Gordo and Caddo Bill, to have another look."

Billie Sanford looked at Lone Star, thoutfully as well as sweetly. Lone Star smiled back, sheepishly, and said, "I never said that Grayson hand gave up my property willingly."

Turning to Jeff she added, "I could have saved you boys the trouble had you simply asked, you sharp-eyed thing."

Jeff shrugged and said, "Ain't no trouble, for *me*, ma'am. Them two greasers and the breed could use the exercise."

A hand dressed Anglo but a bit dark of feature spoke up, across the way. "Is most curious you mention grease, my unwashed patron of Mamma Rosita and her *muchachas* of many colors."

Jeff blinked, recovered, and said, "Oh, sorry, Robles, I didn't see you ride in."

Billie Sanford said soothingly, "Nobody here rode in to fuss with one another, durn it. We're all in the same boat as far as those poison-mean Graysons go."

Turning back to Lone Star she said, "You and that Ki are in it too, if half you've told us about your own missing stock is true."

Indicating the sullen young Mex and some other hardcases hovering at that end of the fire, she explained, "These boys from the Matanza outfit just caught up with us as well, dear Jessie. We're waiting on some more Anglo riders as should have got here already. It don't seem Rafe Grayson's brothers mean to join him over at that line camp. It seems more likely they've already found a buyer for that purloined herd and don't mean to hold it yonder all that long. Either way, we're fixing to hit 'em good smack at sundown."

As Lone Star stared in disbelief, Jeff nodded and said, "From their west, with the setting sun at our backs to dazzle their gunsights. If they know we've trailed 'em this far, they'll be expecting us to attack from this direction, and that'd be dumb."

Lone Star dryly replied, "It certainly would. Can't anyone here see the advantages of waiting out that buyer you just mentioned? You know where your stock is. You know who ran it over into that secluded draw. Wouldn't it be smarter to put them out of business for good than to simply grab your cows back and hope for the best?"

Billie Sanford smiled sweetly but uncertainly. "I just said we mean to end their raiding once and for all, dear Jessie."

To which Lone Star responded, "How? By recovering a few cows and at most gunning one out of three known cow thieves?"

She saw she had their attention now. "Please don't anyone spout nonsense about wiping out Rafe and his crew, then riding on to the main Grayson spread to make a clean sweep of it. I know a thing or two about range wars and so do the Texas Rangers. They'll never stand back and let you all fight it out to total victory. I wasn't there, but I was following the recent Lincoln County War

148

in both the Republican and Democrat papers. So I can tell you the territorial government sent in troops to break it up just as the shootings were getting interesting."

The sullen young hand called Robles grumbled, "The New Mexico Guard was paid off. It sided with the Murphy Faction against El Chivito."

Lone Star shrugged. "Billy the Kid wasn't in command of the McSween Faction. Whether the troops were paid off or not, they did make it impossible to go on with that private war, and the last I heard both sides had been ruined by the uneasy peace. El Chivito's employers, Tunstall and McSween, died in the fighting. Major Murphy on the other side died natural and his business partners, Dolan and District Attorney Catron, were put out of business by the new governor, Lew Wallace, sent to Santa Fe to tidy things up."

Robles grinned softly. "That's what we're going to do to the Graysons. Gun the *cabrones,* the way El Chivito gunned that crooked Sheriff Brady!"

Lone Star grimaced. "It doesn't work that simply. I know Billy the Kid backshot Bill Brady. He never quits bragging about it, and now the new sheriff, Pat Garrett, has The Kid running for his very life instead of punching cows through the week and riding in to town for the Saturday dancing. Is that what you boys want, a half-baked range war ending in nobody at all ever daring to show his fool face in these parts again?"

There was a grumble that could have been taken as agreement. But Billie Sanford insisted, "We can't let the Graysons get away with our damned cows, damn it!"

Lone Star nodded. "I feel the same way about cow thieves, and I get to call some Ranger captains uncle, Billie dear. You said yourself those high-handed lowlifes likely planned to sell that herd off sudden. My plan is that we simply wait and see who's buying and where he's driving 'em after. I've told you all about my own missing stock. I was with the Graysons long enough to know they had already gotten rid of them, if they ever had 'em at all."

A roughly dressed but educated-sounding rider of around forty who didn't look at all Mex called out, "How do you know they ever had any Circle Star stock to begin with, Miss Starbuck? Seems a far piece for the Graysons to ride, considering how much closer our own herds were and how free those Graysons can get with a throw-rope."

There was a murmur of agreement. Billie muttered, "Who said a thing about *her* planning squat in these here hills of *mine*?"

Lone Star let that go to explain, "I don't know the Graysons stole any cows of mine. Somebody surely did. My point is that there'll ever be sneak thieves. They spawn like flies fast as you can swat 'em, anywhere conditions are right for cow stealing. You have to get rid of the dealers in stolen property, just as you have to clean the dung out of the stable, before you can hope to cut down on either sort of pest."

Billie Sanford pouted, "I say we've already spent time enough on this chore. We know who stole our stock. We haven't even a hint as to your mysterious buyers, dearie. What gives you the right to ride in here and act like you're in charge anyways? You're as bad as that infernal *segundo* of your'n, for land's sake!"

Lone Star cocked a brow. "You know Ki, dear Billie?"

The other woman looked away, cheeks flushing, to reply, "Maybe I do and maybe I don't. You didn't mention that old boy you killed out yonder until somebody asked either, did you?"

Lone Star said, quietly, that she was asking now. So Billie shrugged and said, "He did pass through, last night. Never said where he was headed as he left unexpected."

Jeff volunteered, "He told us you was in the Grayson camp. He might have headed yonder to uncapture you." Then Billie shot him a warning look and he clammed up.

Lone Star nodded and got back to her feet, saying, "It's been grand meeting up with you all, dear Billie. But if Ki's out yonder looking for me, I'd best go catch up with him lest *he* wind up in that Grayson camp, hear?"

By this time Billie Sanford had risen as well, softly observing, "I don't want you to do that, dearie. You know too much. You talk too much and they've already proven they can capture you."

"Not this time," Lone Star said. "They surprised me before by striking first with less reason than I could see. Now I know they've something to hide from one and all, not you folks alone. Just let me gather in my *segundo* before *they* gather him and we may rejoin you here. I'm sure Ki will agree our best bet would be to scout the rascals till we know once and for all where they mean to unload all that beef."

She started to turn away. Billie snapped, "No! I mean it!" in a tone Southwestern belles reserve for stubborn mounts and pups that piss on the rug.

Lone Star swung around to face the slightly larger and older woman squarely, softly asking, "Are we having a disagreement, dear Billie?"

"Not if you'd be good enough to hand that gun over now," the other woman replied pleasantly enough. "They've told us you West Texas ladies are inclined to take the bits in your pearly teeth and act independent. I don't *want* you acting independent. I want you to stick tight as a tick with me and mine till I'm ready to make my own damned moves. I told our mutual amigo, Ki, the same thing. I made the mistake of being nice to *him* and look where it got me. So now I'll take that gun, and if you promise to behave we may not have to tie you to a tree."

"I can't do that, Billie," Lone Star said, her own voice dead on the level. "I'd sure like to leave here like a lady. So why don't we keep this nice?"

Billie spread her boot heels wider, and her right hand rose to hover near the grips of her bigger six-gun as she gasped, "Have you gone *loco en la cabeza,* girl! There's one of you, a dozen of us by this fire alone, and I could holler for more!"

Lone Star knew a thing or two about Texican manhood, and not only in the Biblical sense. She shook her head soberly. "I can't see any Texas rider of the old school slapping leather on a woman when she's offering to fight another fair and square, can you?"

The older man answering to Matanza cleared his throat nervously and said, "I wish you little ladies would cut this out, Miss Billie. You know I'm with you against the Graysons, but us Matanzas had dealings with this other lady's daddy when he was still alive and he was all right."

Billie snapped, "This ain't betwixt me and her daddy, Roy. It's betwixt me and her, and it's gone too far for me to back down now!"

Lone Star said nothing. She'd seen that wild-eyed expression before, although usually on a less feminine face, so she knew Billie Sanford was as apt to go either way. Lone Star knew it was best sometimes to wait a proddy gunhand out, and sometimes to draw first.

As Lone Star waited, heart pounding but outwardly calm, Billie demanded, "Jeff Bushmill, stand up in the presence of a lady and back my play, hear?"

Jeff muttered, "Aw, gee whizz, Miss Billie . . ." But he rose to stand beside her, staring thoughtfully at Lone Star as he told her,

"I'd sure hate to have to, ma'am. You're right about us Texas riders, but on the other hand I promised Miss Billie's daddy I'd look after her and, well, you do have a mighty scary rep, Miss Lone Star."

So it was two against one, Lord willing and the creeks didn't rise. Then another Lazy S hand swore softly under his breath and rose to make it three against one, morosely observing, "You'd best give it up, Miss Lone Star. I just don't know how I'd ever explain this either way, but if push comes to shove, I ride for this other lady's dad too."

Then the youth called Robles got up, wearing a sleepy smile, to nod at Lone Star and say, "I'm coming around this fire to join you, not jump you, ma'am."

Billie snapped, "Stay out of this, Robles!" But the sullenly handsome Mex still moved around to stand beside Lone Star, muttering, "Me and you, Jeff. Any time you're ready."

Then Roy Matanza sighed wearily and called out, "*Basta!* I thought we all rode out after the Grayson bunch! This is really getting stupid! Miss Starbuck, you just go on your own way and consider your pretty little back covered by old Roy Matanza, hear?"

Beside her, Robles nodded and softly murmured, "*Si, quitar* while we see how brave these big gringos are, eh?"

"This ain't fair!" Billie protested, "You boys are all supposed to be with *me*, not *her!*"

Lone Star didn't hang about to hear how the obviously more sensible menfolk dealt with that complaint. She was on her way to the pony line. She was pretty sure the worldly Roy Matanza could calm the proud and proddy Billie down. She knew she owed his backing more to who she was than how pretty he found her. She'd meant what she'd told them about casual killings in even the wilder parts of Texas, and old Roy had doubtless known the Rangers would never just drop it if the daughter of Alex Starbuck turned up missing or worse in these parts.

The young colored wrangler didn't dispute her right to saddle one of her own, and even helped her cinch the pack saddles on the other two. She thanked him graciously and lit out at a trot, hauling the pack ponies after her whether they felt like moving that quickly or not.

She knew now she'd never find Ki on that timber-dotted ridge she'd already explored. So seeing she was a safer distance from the Grayson camp at the moment, she cut south over hill and dale to crest a ridge she felt ought to be related to the rock-fanged rise just to the south of that line camp. If they knew anything at all about the underground sources of that tank, they'd suspect she'd crawled north. If they didn't, she still had to approach from one damned direction or the other, and both she and Ki had in fact been even further south when she'd been captured by that cross-grained Grayson outfit.

By this time the sun was over the ridgepole of the sky and rolling a tad to the west. That didn't help worth spit on a sunny summer day in the Texas Hill Country. It would be even hotter by, say, three that afternoon. Heat trailed the sun by about three hours or three months, depending on whether one was discussing the day or the year. She found she could shade her hatless head about a third of the time by choosing her route along the ridge with some care. Neither mesquite nor scrub cedar offered enough shade to matter, but the gnarled old oaks made up for it, if only there'd been more of them.

She had to weave through or around the outcrops of weathered limestone, and at this hour the sun-dazzle off the chalk-white rock was blinding.

That was doubtless why Lone Star spied Concho Valdez and his two companions before they'd spotted her. She was cooling her head a bit under a wind-tortured oak, which hid her inside its ink-black outline, as they rounded a hogback to be spotlighted against the rocks' white backing. She saw one of the men was leading a riderless buckskin. That appeared to be Ki's saddle as well. Eyes narrowed thoughtfully, Lone Star drew her saddle gun from its boot as she eased her own three ponies down the far side, dismounted, and retraced her way, afoot, to that same dark puddle of oak shade, levering a Winchester round into the chamber as she did so.

The three Lazy S riders might have passed on the far side of a house-sized boulder had she let them. As Concho, in the lead, got close enough to speak with, or shoot with ease, Lone Star softly called, "Rein in and we'll talk, Concho. Try anything silly and we won't."

The Mex-dressed Concho reined in with his left hand even as he raised his empty right hand to halt his diminutive cavalry column, saying, "Howdy, Miss Jessie. Why are you pointing that gun at us? We were just on our way back to assure Miss Billie you were on our side."

The obvious breed just behind him called out, "You got that mean one. Gash, I think they calt him. Seen him in town many a time with other Grayson riders."

Concho silenced the part-Caddo kid with a gesture and told Lone Star, "He was over on that ridge we met before, as Jeff said. There was nothing we could do for him, even if we'd wanted to, so we thought as long as we were out this way we'd give the Graysons another look-see."

Lone Star pointed at Ki's barb with her gun muzzle, saying, "That's the pony my *segundo* was riding the last time I saw him. Your turn, Concho."

The young Mex met her eyes innocently enough and explained, "We found him tethered in some mesquite south of them cow thieves and our cows. He'd been there a good spell, judging by the sorry condition of all the mesquite in easy reach. We didn't know who he belonged to till just now. But we couldn't just leave him there. So we watered him—he needed it—and now we're taking him back to our own camp, see?"

Lone Star shook her head. "No, you're not. I just told you that's a Circle Star pony, and if you think those Graysons are in trouble over cows, just you wait till I report you to the Rangers for stealing a *horse* in *Texas*!"

Concho must not have wanted her to do that. He twisted in his saddle and called out in Spanish. The other vaquero, who'd been leading Ki's mount, swung out of line to lead it over to them.

Lone Star took the reins with a nod of thanks and then, keeping the big barb between herself and the three men, she tucked the action of her Winchester under her left arm long enough to get at the saddlebag on her side. The odds were against Ki having found her Stetson at all, and only fifty-fifty he'd have stuffed it in his left saddlebag. But for once she won, and while her good old Stetson was all bent out of shape, it still had its throwing star pinned to the crown. Once she'd slapped the hat against her right leg a few times and put it back on her head, she felt a lot friendlier.

So she kept the Winchester aimed at the ground as she swung up in Ki's saddle, saying, "*Muchas gracias, señores.* That sun was really commencing to bake my fool face. Now that I've everything back but my *segundo*, I only have to find *him*. You say this barb was tethered an easy foot patrol from that Grayson line camp?"

Concho nodded. "*Si,* perhaps a little over a mile. Your friend should have returned for to water that poor *caballo* at least before we found him."

Lone Star nodded soberly. "I know. Ki has always been kind to animals. It's been nice talking to you, señores . But now I'd best get over yonder and find out why Ki couldn't get back to his mount."

★

Chapter 14

The early afternoon sun was glaring down just as hard back in Austin, and thanks to the lower elevation and breeze-blocking sun-baked walls, the results were even more unbearable. By the time Longarm and Agent MacIntosh had satisfied themselves nobody had tried to can President Hayes's new desk, they'd brought one another up to date to the point of fatigue. Or so Longarm felt. The infernal Secret Service man was still on the subject as they crossed the dusty railroad siding to get to a nearby cantina they'd been told about in Jessie's beef cannery.

Longarm said, "You've told me how they sent you up from Galveston to cover all bets when they intercepted my wired reports to my own office. Well, they ought to be ashamed of themselves. We have a tougher time getting Western Union to cooperate. Watch out for that cow pat. It looks fresh."

As they went on, heels dry as before, Longarm continued. "I've told you a dozen times I've no idea why some asshole called King Kellog wants me dead. This fool chore they've put us both to would be as interesting as slopping the hogs or making sure the henhouse was locked for the night if only someone didn't seem to be making so much noise. Yonder cantina looks pretty Chihuahua. I hope you know barkeeps of the Mex persuasion don't really like to be called greasers."

MacIntosh assured Longarm he'd been stationed out this way a spell, and they ducked inside to find the dark interior smelled like a pepper-picker's armpits, but it was at least ten degrees cooler, so what the hell.

The moon-faced Mex behind the bar did look sort of greasy in such stuffy surroundings. Longarm was feeling sort of greasy himself. He wondered how MacIntosh could stand that frock coat on a day like today. He didn't ask. He ordered them a pitcher of *cerveza* and some *tostadas* to munch at a corner table.

The table was naturally rickety pine, painted robin's-egg blue to scare off flies or evil spirits, depending on whether one heeded one's Spanish or Indian granny. Longarm put down the glassware and suds. MacIntosh had been good enough to carry the big earthenware bowl of deep-fried tortilla chips. It sure beat all how he managed to look so cool despite his dark wool undertaking outfit. Longarm didn't think it polite to ask folks whether or not they had consumption or the ague. But MacIntosh reminded him of that dangerous dentist from Baltimore who'd been making a nasy name for himself after coming out West to get over consumption. Longarm had met up with the fool out Arizona way a spell back, and had nearly had to cure him for keeps with some .44–40 pills, the sullen son of a bitch.

As he poured both their clay mugs Longarm idly asked, "Have you Secret Service boys anything on your yellow sheets about a Baltimore shootist called Holliday, John a.k.a. Doc Holliday?"

MacIntosh shook his head. "No. What's he been up to?"

Longarm said, "Nothing federal yet. He drinks and gambles too free for a man with no visible means of support. So I'd say it was only a question of time, and he's a real mankiller. I can't say from personal experience whether he beats his victims to the draw by drawing quick as a flash, or whether like The Kid and other harmless-looking pests, old Doc gets the jump on overconfident bullies by simply being alive and awake."

He sipped some *cerveza* and continued. "Like I said, he's a pasty-faced consumptive and a hopeless drunk besides. Last time I saw him he'd got skinny as a rail and Big Nose Kate, his true love or nursemaid, depending, could likely lick him in a fistfight. But he's man enough, and mean enough, with a shooting iron handy. He's taken out a couple of old boys with a sawed-off twelve-gauge. Lucky for both of us, most likely, me and Doc managed to get on friendly terms. Say, this is mighty fine *cerveza*!"

He turned on his stool to ask the barkeep across the cantina how in thunder they'd managed iced suds on a day like today.

The Mex, no doubt pleased someone had noticed, called back, "We got lots of ice. We get it at a fair price from a member of La Raza who makes ice, even in the summertime, with a steam engine."

Longarm turned back to the other lawman, observing, "He must mean a steam-powered ice machine. I was just reading about how good they've started making 'em of late, and you know, *that's* an angle I'd like to explore with Jessie Starbuck, once I catch up with the wandersome little thing."

MacIntosh sipped at his own mug, nodded his own approval of the iced *cerveza*, and demanded to know what on earth artificial ice might have to do with Queen Victoria's missing present to President Hayes.

Longarm explained, "Jessie and old Ki are missing, unable to help us *find* the fool desk, only because somebody stole a heap of beef from her earlier."

MacIntosh snorted in disgust. "You told me about that already. That's not our job. The Texas Rangers have jurisdiction on Texican stock stolen in Texas and, as far as we know, never transported across any state borders."

Longarm washed down the mouthful of *tostada* he'd been munching. "I've gone after rascals stealing army or Indian beef within state limits, and we don't know them Circle Star cows are still in the same state. If we had any notion at all of their present whereabouts, we might have a better line on their owner. Jessie Starbuck's one hell of a tracker."

MacIntosh shrugged. "So I've heard. Why should we care? We were sent to recover that Presidential furniture, not Jessica Starbuck's beef on the hoof!"

Longarm finished his first mug, started to pour another, and lit a cheroot instead before he said, quietly, "How do we know? How do we know some slicker didn't slaughter and butcher that Circle Star herd close to home, getting rid of their brands along with their hides, to ship 'em openly anywhere as refrigerated sides of wholesale beef?"

The Secret Service man laughed incredulously. "From West Texas, in high summer? To where, for Pete's sake?"

Longarm blew a thoughtful smoke ring. "Most anywhere they figured on getting the best price. Ain't modern science wonderful? Like I said, I was just reading about it in the *Scientific American*. With them new ammonia compressors invented by Linde—"

"Deputy Long," MacIntosh said. "We're supposed to be looking for an oakwood desk, kept at room temperature, preferably in that oval office at the White House, once we *get* it there. I don't give a fart in the bathtub about cows lost, strayed, stolen, or frozen with ammonia, for Pete's sake!"

Longarm poured them both some more cold suds. "I ain't lost sight of our main mission. I just suspect we're more apt to sight that damned desk with Jessie Starbuck's help, and you know what they say about one hand washing the other."

MacIntosh nodded. "I'd be proud to find the little lady's lost handkerchief for her as well, if I thought that lost desk was anywhere near her or her lost cows. But they told us at her hotel she and that Oriental cuss had left town without leaving any word as to their intended destination."

Longarm smiled sheepishly and said he was working on that.

MacIntosh grimaced and said, "They told me she was a real beauty, and we've some interesting if unconfirmed gossip about the two of you that time you both got into a war with Mexico. Meanwhile, since she's ridden off for parts unknown, I fail to see how even really stupid help could be trailing her with that heavy crate aboard a buckboard!"

Longarm took the cheroot from between his teeth, sipped some suds, and said half to himself, "If those vaqueros are still hauling that furniture the hard way, I'd put 'em somewheres betwixt the Pecos and Devils Run about now. They should have forded the Pecos somewheres betwixt Langtry and Pandale, only they never did. I've wired to have them stopped by Val Verde County, and that crusty old Judge Bean would have wired me back he was holding that crate for us."

The other lawman asked, "What if they haven't made it as far as the Pecos yet?"

Longarm smiled thinly. "Then our troubles should soon be over, one way or another. If they wised up and put the crate aboard a train at, say, Sanderson, it ought to show up at Jessie Starbuck's branch office or hotel at any moment. If they're still trudging on across all that desert range, they'll be stopped near the river by the Rangers or Val Verde deputies."

MacIntosh looked dubious. "In that case, why do you want us riding out after Jessie Starbuck, or would you rather go alone?"

Longarm cocked an eyebrow at his fellow lawman and growled, "Watch it, Secrets boy. You're talking about a friend of mine as well as a lady, and it's a hot day for skating on such thin ice."

The older lawman assured him it had been meant as an innocent question. "I only meant I wasn't about to ride out after a lady searching for stolen stock when that damned fool desk can't be anywheres near her! I'm going to pester both the railroad and that crazy old bird who thinks he's the only law west of the Pecos some more. Would you like to walk me over to Western Union?"

Longarm shook his head. "Nope. You go on and hunt furniture your way. It's a free country. If you need me some more I'll likely be somewheres near the capitol grounds this afternoon. One of the stable hands over to the hotel said he overheard Jessie and old Ki jawing about a call she'd paid on the brand inspector. They might be able to tell me there just which brands aside from her own she might have been interested in."

MacIntosh drained his mug, muttered something about it being too hot for romance, and got up to leave before Longarm could ask him what he'd meant by that.

The consumptive cuss didn't look healthy enough to recall romance at any temperature. But Longarm had heard such unfortunates could get horny as hell in point of fact. It was something the lung-eater bugs did to the sex glands as well. Consumptives enjoyed such a rep as passionate lovers that even gals who'd never caught the white plague powdered their faces pale and rouged their cheeks feverish to hint at the back-busting passions they were capable of.

Longarm finished his second mug, but left plenty of *cerveza* in the pitcher, the afternoon not being half over yet. He then left the smelly but cool cantina to ankle on over to the capitol grounds in the sterile ovenlike atmosphere. As he did so he wondered idly whether MacIntosh had transferred out this way for his lungs. A lot of Western folks seemed to be lungers. Those shitty little bugs that rotted out a body's lungs and made them screw like mink didn't like the hot dry summers out this way any more than other creatures great or small.

At the same office Lone Star had visited earlier, Longarm found the old brand inspector gone for the day, likely inspecting some brands according to the plain-faced but nicely built gal he'd left to hold the fort and answer questions.

Longarm had no way of knowing she was smiling far more at him than she had at Miss Jessica Starbuck, whom she recalled for him willingly enough, although with a singular lack of enthusiasm.

160

She didn't have to explain that part. He'd noticed in the past how homely gals stared at Jessie's back, even after she'd been nice to them. This one told Longarm what she recalled of the conversation "that dear sweet thing" had had with her boss about local cattle operations. She seemed to have trouble recalling any details. She frowned thoughtfully, not a pretty sight, and declared, "It was something to do with trail-branding. Somebody marking cows with a big old triangle?"

He nodded. "I know about the vaquero spotting Circle Star beef heading for points unknown with fresh trail brands. After that I've yet to hear of anyone else spotting 'em. I suspect they weren't trail-branded to trail all that far. Cows moving through slaughterhouse yards might look odd to the casual eye without some indication they'd been resold to somebody."

He started to grope for a fresh smoke, recalled his manners, and added, "Aside from that, it's the most recent-looking brand the meat packers record, if they record any at all. If Miss Jessica was pestering your boss about trail brands, she must have been thinking along lines I just covered. So who do you have on file that fits?"

She pursed her lips, not quite as unsettling a sight as her frown if a man had a wicked imagination, and declared, "I'm trying to remember. It wasn't as if I was included in the learned discussion, and that flashy blonde wasn't the last person who's ever paid this office a call, you know."

Longarm nodded sympathetically, knowing better than to chide an already unfriendly witness on her mean-mouthing. When he insisted a smart-looking little thing like her must have heard something, she dimpled and decided, "Something about a registered trail brand that *wasn't* a triangle but could be run to one easy enough."

He studied on that with a thoughtful frown, then he objected. "I fail to see much sense in trail-marking stolen beef with a real brand and then running it to something that's not registered. It'd make more sense to make up a whole new fake brand."

She looked so confused he explained, "Jessie Starbuck must have wanted to start with at least a possible lead. My way don't lead to nowheres. I'd likely never get caught if I was a cow thief."

She said she still didn't know what he was talking about. So he said, "Sometimes I confuse me too. Let's stick with what your boss

161

and Miss Jessica might have worked out. Are you certain there's no registered triangle brand?"

She said, "Good heavens, I don't have every brand in this county, let alone West Texas, committed to memory! I simply remember the two of them agreeing there wasn't any. Not any that simple, at any rate. There could be any number of brands with a triangle, a chevron, or a V as a part of it."

He held his impatience in check—it wasn't easy—and suggested, "Let's try it this way. Would you recall any outfit the two of 'em might have found interesting enough to mention if you was to read its brand off aloud your ownself?"

She said, "Maybe. But if I knew which brands to look up . . . Oh, I see what you mean. But we've got so many brand books and most of 'em are down in the basement and . . ."

"It's early yet, and likely much cooler in the basement on a day like today."

She glanced at their wall clock. "Well, it's not that long before our regular closing time, and I suppose if I were to leave a note on the door . . ."

He whipped out his notebook and tore loose a page. She laughed and said she had her own pencil, drawing it from the mousy bun atop her plain but friendly head. It only took her a few moments to describe what they were about as "research out of the office." Then they were on their way to the lower depths.

It really was much cooler at the bottom of the steel spiral stairway she led him to. It was dark and cobwebby as well. He struck a match to see they were in a long dank corridor floored with cement and walled in with clammy brick. She said they'd been talking and talking about putting in those new Edison bulbs, oil lamps making folks feel proddy, burning untended under ancient wooden floor joists, but as he started to strike another light she assured him she knew the way in the dark. So he let the matchlight go out as she coyly grabbed him by the other hand to drag him somewhere she likely wanted him better.

He managed not to trip over her or anything else by brushing his free fingertips against the brick wall to one side. The bricks felt cool as well as damp. That part was all right on a Texas summer afternoon, but he had to wonder whose grand notion it had been to store important papers down there.

After some turns and door openings she asked him to strike another match for her. When he did she was holding a coal-oil

162

lantern out to him, so he lit it. As she placed it atop a row of shellacked oak filing cabinets, he saw they were in a brick-walled chamber of medium size and surprisingly plush appointments. The cabinets formed a sort of L along two walls. There was a rolltop desk and a tufted leather chesterfield sofa against another wall. As she shut the door after them the helpful mouse-brown thing in slate gray and ivory calico—whatever in thunder her name was—told him to take a seat, pointing at the chesterfield.

Longarm placed his hat atop the rolltop before doing as she demanded, observing he'd seldom met up with a more comfortable file room.

She said, "I don't know who fixed it up like this. But I've been eternally grateful, working overtime some evenings. You wouldn't know it to look at me, I hope, but there are times I just get tired on my feet and, well, let me show you something nice about this setup."

She hauled a big file drawer completely out of its cabinet and sank down beside him on the cushioned morocco leather with the soapbox-sized drawer in her lap, explaining, "This one's cross-indexed T for Triangle. As I told you upstairs, lots of outfits use such a design as a part of their brand. It's harder to steal stock when the brand's more intricate, right?"

He nodded, not wanting to get into old John Chisum's stupendously simple Long Rail brand and Jingle Bob earmarks.

Had Longarm seen any sense in contradicting a lady who considered herself an authority on brands, he could have mentioned the way Chisum cows were branded with one simple straight line from shoulder to rump. Big John had once explained he depended on the sheer size of his Long Rail brand to discourage artistic endeavors. There was hardly anything you could run the long rail to that wouldn't look like one of them wall murals, and Chisum's Jingle-Bob earmarks, making his cows look as if they each had four ears, must have discouraged a certain amount of temptation as well.

Musing half to himself as the mousy gal beside him pawed on, he said, "Big John Chisum's almost as big a boo to cow thieves as Miss Jessica Starbuck. They both keep more gunhands on their payrolls than the U.S. Army has west of the Mississippi betwixt Indian risings. Yet the Chisum herd did get hit, back around '78, as the Lincoln County War was starting."

She looked up from her tabbed manila folders. "Oh, are you

talking about all those cows stolen by that dreadful Billy the Kid in New Mexico Territory about the time I first went to work here?"

Longarm grimaced. "A heap of people mix poor little Henry McCarthy, alias Billy Bonney, alias Kid Antrim, and so forth, with the cow thieves he was hired to go after. He's on the run right now for a heap of transgressions, but stealing beef from John Chisum ain't one of 'em. It was Chisum, the late John Tunstall, and Lawyer McSween who first deputized the kid and his young sidekicks to go after wholesale cow thieves backed by U.S. Attorney Catron and the Santa Fe Ring."

She seemed interested, but he said, "Let's not go into Billy the Kid and the Lincoln County War. Suffice it to say, it *does* seem possible to run off whole herds of beef bearing famous brands, provided one has a mighty tricky way of moving them to market, or friends in high places. There was nothing all that ingenious about the way cows kept vanishing from the Lincoln County range. Major L.G. Murphy kept selling them to all comers without even bothering to run the brands. He doubtless found it cheaper to just pay off the local law from territorial judges down. Miss Jessica and me could be playing chess when the name of the game is checkers. I still don't see why she figured her missing cows could be over this way, and now that I study on it, that magazine never said they have any refrigerator cars in actual operation."

She said, "Nothing here that would account for her tale of a great big triangle alone next to a circle star. What on earth was that about refrigeration?"

He explained. "To preserve stolen cows, without their brands or other distinguishing features. Fish will keep a good spell spread out atop crushed ice, as any Yankee fisherman would bet you. But you can't do that to meat. It discolors. They call the disgusting marks ice burns. That's what makes the Western beef industry so colorful. Long cattle drives to packing plants or rail transportation there were invented simply to avoid ice-burnt beefsteak back East."

She said she knew that, and got up to swap drawers as she added she still didn't know what they were talking about.

He said, "Nonsense, most likely. I recalled an optimistic article about this meat packer named Swift who'd applied for a patent. They never said he'd gone and built any of his new-fangled refrigeration cars yet. It'd take a whole mess of such cars to sneak more than a thousand head of stolen beef out of Texas. I do that all the time. Dream up fiendishly clever ways for crooks to operate, when in point of fact your average crook is dumber than your average field hand."

She sat back down beside him, closer, as she patted the second file drawer and said, "I just remembered. That blonde you admire so much said something about running a fake trail brand into a triangle."

He started to say something dumb. On reflection he saw right away that crooks slapping a hasty trail brand by the original to account for their driving it far from home would hardly use their *own* known brand.

She said, "I think they were talking about a chevron or a lazy V, and I believe we did have something on file that fit, if only I could even remember which files we dug through for her."

He asked, "How many filing cabinets might we be talking about, and wouldn't you remember whether your boss sent you down here to fetch anything, Miss . . . ah?"

"Call me Violet, or better yet Vile. And yes, I was sent down here more than once the other day. It's just that I'm not sure whether your beautiful cattle queen found what she was looking for from the files upstairs or the files down here. I'm not dead certain she found anything. Nobody ever seems to include me in the conversation when they're gushing at a bleach-blond cowgirl in a thin silk shirt!"

Longarm said soothingly, "She's a natural blonde, but I know how proddy she makes some of you other gals without even trying. Could you try to recall her with less distaste and make at least an educated guess as to why she lit out of town in some infernal direction, Miss Vile?"

The jealous mouse didn't answer. He could see she was thinking a mile a minute. The question now was about what. He tried, "She must have had *some* destination in mind. She and her *segundo* lit out dressed and outfitted for serious riding."

Violet said she was trying. Longarm hauled out his pocket watch, consulted it morosely, and said, "Well, the little hand pointed at the six and the big hand pointed almost straight up means there ain't that much light left for me to work with if I have to cut their trail the hard way, starting Lord knows where."

She nodded. "I had no idea it was getting so late. It's after office hours upstairs now. It's a good thing I've a key ring under this bodice, or who knows how you'd ever get out of the building now?"

He said in that case he'd be obliged if she'd come along and let him out. But as he started to rise she told him in no uncertain terms to stay put. "I'm sure it'll come to me if only you'll give a girl time to gather her wits."

He put his watch away and leaned back as she sprang up to carry the second drawer back where it belonged, murmuring something about a lazy V or chevron if only she could recall the fool conversation between her boss and that brazen blonde.

He let the unkind remark about poor Jessie go. He felt a mite two-faced, but he was sure Jessie would have condoned it seeing it could be in a good cause.

She put the second drawer away and opened another to produce a big brown jug of cider and a pint-sized bottle of clear glass, filled with something the same tempting shade as Maryland rye. Turning back to the chesterfield, she confided she kept medicinal supplies down there for female complaints. He didn't ask if she was suffering cramps as she sat back down beside him, gently uncorking the bottle with her teeth. He said he could see she'd made this particular file room a mighty comfortable retreat.

She handed him the uncorked bottle as she drew the corncob stopper out of the cider jar, confiding, "I spend my lunch hours down here, alas. There's no better place an unescorted spinster can eat alone within walking distance."

He agreed some men had no sense about unescorted ladies in working-class bean parlors. Then he tasted the hundred-proof bourbon, blinked his eyes to keep from crying, and gasped, "Might this be what you call *eating*, Miss Vile?"

She handed him the cider. "I fear I consumed all the ham sandwiches I came to work with this morning. But I'm not ready for supper yet. I just hate to dine on pot roast and steamed onions in a steamy boardinghouse dining room, even when it's cooler outside of an evening."

Pot roast and steamed onions sounded pretty good right now to Longarm. But a man worked with what he had to work with, and the cider was hard, cuss her thirsty soul.

It still helped. He handed both containers back to her and let her swill some as he gently reminded her they'd been trying to come up with the outfit Lone Star and Ki might have headed for.

She drank deep, from both bottle and jug, before she handed them back with a sigh and confided, "Sometimes I bring books down here to read. Sometimes I while away a whole evening down here, after closing time, before I have to go home to that lonely old boardinghouse."

Longarm set the jug and bottle aside, near one leg of the sofa, as he nodded knowingly. "It sure beats all how a house filled with strangers in a strange town can seem more lonely than, well, a place like this where one has more control of the stillness all around."

She swung her mousy head to stare big-eyed at him, saying, "Oh, I knew you were a man of sensitive notions! I noticed when first you come in, upstairs, how you reminded me of that soulful young master of *Wuthering Heights*! Have you ever read that thrilling romance by Miss Emily Bronte?"

He had. He'd found it more depressing than thrilling, and it was easy to see it had been written by some daydreaming spinster who'd thought moaning across the Yorkshire moors, fully dressed, was more fun than down-to-earth slap-and-tickle in a hayloft with someone less soulful than that brooding asshole in the made-up story.

He didn't think she wanted to hear that, though, so he declared, "It sure was sad, how they all wound up so horny, dead, or both. You said your boss and Miss Jessie were jawing about a fake brand that could have been mistaken, or run, for a triangle?"

She nodded. "Where have you put our refreshments? Oh, I see them." She reached for the bottle or jug—her aim was uncertain— by sort of flopping tits-down across his lap. Her tits sure felt grand between his thighs like so, as she seemed to be having trouble groping for the refreshments on the floor. He could only hope she'd assume he was packing a concealed weapon in addition to his six-gun, if she felt what was prodding her fool armpit at all. He bent forward at the waist to see if he could pick up the damned booze, or at least get his hard-on out of her damned armpit. This meant he had to press his upper body down against hers. Her calico bodice buttoned up the back. So damned if a couple of buttons didn't pop undone by the time he had both the bottle and jug. She'd felt her bodice being unbuttoned, whether she knew what else she was feeling or not, and purred, "Oh, Deputy Long, whatever gave you the notion I was that kind of a girl?"

He chuckled dryly and said, "A little Bronte named Emily told me. But could we stick to trail brands just the same? No offense, but I got to catch up with Jessie Starbuck."

She propped herself up on one elbow, that elbow in his crotch, to

167

sip some cider and snap, "Oh, screw Jessie Starbuck, the stuck-up thing."

Then she fluttered her lashes and gasped, "Oh, Lord have mercy! I must be drunk and I haven't had that much! I'm mortified I said such a thing, but as long as we're on the subject, have *you*? Screwed that blonde, I mean."

He said, "I know what you mean. That's for me to know and the rest of the world to guess. How would you like it if I was to do you that way and then tell everyone in Texas."

She slurped some bourbon, giggled, and declared, "I wouldn't mind at all. Lord knows, a girl don't get many offers working in this durned old office building."

He said he was sorry to hear that and tried, "If you was to recall anything I could use to track down my others pals, I'd be proud to walk you home first, Miss Vile."

She shook her head so hard her mousy hair began to come undone. "You've got to stay here with me past sundown now. What would others suspect if they saw us leaving the building so late, after everyone else had gone home for the evening?"

He said they'd likely assume the two of them had been looking up brand registrations late, unless they possessed mighty suspicious minds. He added, "I pass folks coming out of schoolhouses, libraries, and such long after closing hours. I can't recall all that many dirty thoughts about innocent-acting strangers, though."

She looked so hurt he said, "All right, we can wait till eight or so if you'd like to haul out some more files now."

She rose, he thought, to see if she could refresh her memory with some other dusty records. But as he watched, bemused, she moved over to trim the wick of the oil lantern down to a ruby glow she must have found more romantic. There was just enough light to see she seemed to be shucking her calico dress over her head, and that she'd put nothing on under it to face the Texican heat of her warmer office upstairs.

As she strode boldly back to the sofa in just her high-button shoes and thigh-high black cotton stockings, her hair falling down to frame her plain love-starved face in what now seemed a warmer shade of brown, Longarm gulped and declared, "No offense, ma'am, but I fail to read any brand on your otherwise interesting hide!"

She smiled down lewdly, arms akimbo, hands on hips, her nicely formed lower limbs slightly spread to afford him a clear view of all her charms, as she demurely replied, "It's starting to come back to me. Maybe if we both came together at least once . . ."

So he rose to reel her in, swap some spit with her, and lower her bare body to the soft smooth leather, telling himself it was the least he could do for Lone Star, Queen Victoria, et al. She helped him shuck his own duds, and then he was in her, on the bottom, for she sure had worked herself up, reading all those romantic novels down there with just her poor personal fingers for company.

The sacrifice he was making in the line of duty would have hurt more if she hadn't had a perfectly proportioned body and lovely love-slit to go with her homely little face. It felt more piquant than disgusting to kiss her as things heated up where she was prettier. That last helpful gal he'd helped out back in Alpine had been possessed of a kissy face and sort of grotesque figure. The way old Violet reversed things was sort of inspiring. One he got her on her back so he could stare down between their bare forms as they bumped and ground, she was downright lovely, from the chin down, and it felt more romantic to close your eyes when you were kissing a gal in any case. She liked to kiss French, doubtless from reading all those English romance novels. She enjoyed repeated shuddering orgasms on his willing but hardly as enthusiastic shaft, and when she felt him finally letting fly inside her, she suggested they switch to a position he'd never encountered in anything Emily Bronte—or for that matter either of her love-starved sisters, Charlotte or Annie—had ever even whispered about as far as he knew.

He wasn't sure he wanted to get that personal with a strange gal who got personal so free and easy with strangers passing through her basement hidey-hole. She seemed to like the position he invented for them, halfway between dog-style and a head-stand, with her bare spine against the back of the chesterfield and her homely face staring up at his crotch as he entered her own, with his knees planted to either side of her head and her knees tucked under either of his arms.

She said she'd never in her born days witnessed a sight half so inspiring, and confessed that included candlesticks and hand mirrors.

He chuckled, told her he'd heard those big smooth-skinned Polish or German sausages were next best to the real thing, and asked how she might be coming with those trail brands Jessie Starbuck had asked about.

She groaned, "Faster, faster, speaking of coming! I'll tell you in a minute. Who told you she'd done it with a sausage? That other young snip you're so anxious to catch up with?"

He humped her harder. "Now, honey, you know I'm after Miss Jessie to question her for the government, and you've my word I don't mean to stuff any sausages in her."

"Have you ever done *this* to her?" Violet demanded. "It feels too teasy and I'm right on the very edge if only you'd . . . Harder! Faster! Make me come, you teasy thing!"

He pulled her bare behind toward him to take his deeper but even slower thrusts as he growled, "Never mind how that other lady might or might not screw. Which way might she have *gone*, God damn it?"

Violet moaned, "Over to the Hill Country. The Grayson spread, I think. I can show you their claim on the land management map later. But I swear I'll kill you if you stop now and leave me in this awful fix!"

He begged her for mercy with a wicked grin, rolled her into an even more awkward position, for her, and pounded her to glory with his socks planted on the cement and her bent over one arm of the big chesterfield in a sort of reversed jackknife dive, assuming anyone ever dove with their thighs spread that wide apart.

She screamed like a jackrabbit caught on bob-wire when he made her come again, hard, and sobbed she'd never dreamt it could feel so swell, just doing it to herself with the help of the Bronte sisters.

He found the notion of her being even a technical virgin a hard row to hoe. But he knew women didn't like to be accused of bullshitting about their love lives, anymore than men liked to be accused of drawing the long bow about their military careers. So he just said he'd been told one time by an English lady visiting the American West that the poor Bronte sisters had been housebound preacher's daughters, trapped in a cold stone parsonage on the Yorkshire moors, which likely accounted for their odd notions of romance, running all about with wet feet and catching agues. He said, "Poor Charlotte was the only one as ever got herself a man instead of just brooding shadows, and in the end she died the same year she was married. Getting some for the first time at the age of thirty-eight or nine must have jarred her some. That Mister Rochester she wrote about in *Jane Eyre* strikes me as a man who'd go see a doctor if he ever woke up with it hard."

She laughed and agreed that, once you thought about it, nobody the Bronte sisters ever mentioned seemed to know what all that heavy panting and tear-assing across moors was supposed to lead to. She slid her bare rump from the armrest down into a more comfortable position, hanging on to his half-sated shaft as she asked if he supposed that could have been what made all those Yorkshire folks act so mean to one another.

He said he'd never been to Yorkshire as he bent over to grope a cheroot, some matches, and his pocket watch from the duds piled on the floor. He politely lit them a smoke to share before he glanced at the watch. He offered her a drag on the cheroot as he quietly observed it was almost dark out now, and that she'd said something about a land management map.

She started to object, gave his soft organ-grinder a last wistful squeeze, and allowed the map was upstairs in the office. He was too polite to ask why she'd brought him down there if the papers he really wanted to look at were up yonder. They both knew why, and the sacrifices he'd just made in the line of duty hadn't done him any permanent harm. As long as Lone Star never found out.

★

Chapter 15

.

Farther to the west, as the same sun was setting, the man called Ki still hunkered on his haunches with his back to that same free-stone wall, idly watching the Grayson hands rekindle the camp fire they'd lost interest in during the heat of a Texas afternoon. Ki had been trying to get them to lose interest in him as well, by keeping still and hardly moving a muscle since they'd grudgingly given him some tepid unsweetened coffee and a nearly tasteless gob of grits wrapped in a tortilla at noon. They were waiting for someone else to show up before they started supper. It was tougher to follow conversations in the middle distance when one pretended not to be listening. But he thought the one called Rafe was anxious for his brothers to bring some buyer called Kellog out from town to look over the herd.

Meanwhile the herd the Graysons had apparently gathered to sell cheap to this Kellog was just beginning to come back to life as the shadows lengthened and the evening breezes began to stir. The longhorn beef critter, like its Hispano-Moorish ancestors, knew the survival value of *la siesta*. Neither Spanish-speaking herders nor the tough dry-country livestock they herded were less active than Anglo folk or, say, whiteface cattle. They simply preferred to move after dark when their distant cousins from more northern climes were asleep. Ki knew Indians of the American Southwest were night crawlers too. He'd yet to figure out why some army manuals said Indians seldom attacked after dark. Ki glanced at the sky without moving his lowered head. It would soon be dark enough for Apache, Kiowa, or Comanche to close in, if Indians had been the main worry this evening. Ki knew Billie Sanford and her posse of pissed-off rival rancheros would be coming after sundown if they came at all. There was an outside chance they'd assume he'd told these Grayson riders, in which case they might hold back. Ki hoped they would, at least until he could get out of this dumb bind himself. The Grayson riders had taken his saddle gun and side arm. They'd even thought to look in his boots, the bastards. So all he had left was the well-balanced but modest throwing knife down the back of his shirt. That was another good reason to keep the back of his shirt to the otherwise uncomfortable freestones of the wall behind him.

Neither a *samurai* nor a professional *ninja* was trained to consider anything as unimportant as his comfort in a situation like this one. Ki was half-American and in point of fact, despite their reputations, neither Orientals nor American Indians felt discomfort less than others. Ki repressed a sardonic smile as he recalled the time at the Circle Star when Jessie's guest, her "Uncle Eskishay" of the Kiowa-Apache, had burnt himself lighting a smoke with a hot poker. That old war chief had let out an anguished scream they'd heard all the way to the bunkhouse before he'd recalled who he was, and where he was, and calmly scratched an itch, or pretended to, with the red-hot iron. It was all in being prepared to feel discomfort, or rather, in being prepared not to let it bother you. At the moment Ki's legs were painfully cramped from squatting this still all afternoon. His left armpit itched, and it wouldn't have killed him to heed the call to nature either, had there been any way to stand up and move around the corner of the building without someone noticing and asking why.

He knew they'd probably let him if he simply said he needed to take a leak. But he was saving that excuse to move until he had more important movement in mind. Meanwhile, his will was stronger than his bladder, and the trick of remaining an uninteresting lump was in letting one's mind instead of one's body pace like a caged tiger. Ki was out of interesting things to do to both groups of riders as he considered their mutual pigheadedness. Getting himself out of this dumb situation before he was killed in the cross fire was more important than considerations of revenge. He wasn't even certain they'd killed Jessie yet, although she was surely taking her time if she'd actually broken free from these triple-thumbed spawn of a dung-eating she-fox and a leper's ghost. It wasn't as if the daughter of Alex Starbuck didn't have friends in high places, and she'd had close to twenty hours to ride for Austin. A pony could go farther than that in one day if pushed at full gallop even half the time.

Ki spotted movement in the distance. So did the Grayson riders piling dried cow chips on their twig and dry grass kindling. One said, "Looks like old Alvin and Jake, loping in with old Amarillo. Didn't Rafe say his brothers were bringing a buyer for all them cows?"

The other hand muttered, "Not in front of the Chink." So Ki knew his imitation of a wooden Indian, or maybe a wooden Asian-American, had been wasted effort, damn their attention to duty.

As the three newcomers swung around the herd to approach the line camp by way of the south rise, Rafe Grayson came out from the tumbledown shelter in response to the chatter around the smoldering cow shit. Ki was hoping Rafe might not remember him there. Rafe did, growling, "You just keep your mouth shut and your eyes open whilst my brothers help me decide about you, Squint-eyes."

Ki didn't answer. The short stocky Amarillo and the two Grayson brothers, trying to outdo one another in looking as mean as Rafe, dismounted a few yards off and headed on over. The one called Alvin spotted Ki, scowled, and demanded, "Where did we get that ugly Chinee, Rafe?"

The brother who'd been holding Ki all day said, "Never mind him. How come you failed to bring that fucking Kellog?"

Jake Grayson shrugged. "His gal said old Kellog's afraid we've got on the wrong side of somebody with them cows. Then she made the sign of the cross."

Rafe snorted in disgust. "God damn it, we told King Kellog when we set up the deal that the stock we meant to maverick was Mex. If he'd get his scared ass out here he'd see there ain't a Texas brand on any cow, yonder! What do you suppose got into the fool?"

Jake said, "Don't ask us. All we know is the little we could get outten Kellog's play-pretty. She said her man said, just afore he lit out for parts unknown, there were just too many others interested in yonder stock."

Alvin frowned. "Didn't she say something about some hardcase lawman as well as a mean Mex who'd be pissed off about that there herd?"

Jake shrugged. "She did, and you heard me tell her what I thought of her man's *cojones*. We all knew to begin with them cows were born and raised in Chihuahua. So of *course* some fool Mexicans are pissed about other Mexicans running 'em up this way for us to maverick."

He thumbed a match head aflame to light a stogie before he went on. "No Anglo lawman, state or federal, has any call to pester us about rightfully mavericked stock. We told Kellog when he told us the Lazy S had set the deal up how safe it would be for all concerned, as far as the fool law went."

Amarillo nodded. "But there's something else you ought to know, Rafe. I met your brothers over to the east as I was fixing to report back to you on the other side. I suspect I got Billie Sanford's main camp located. It ain't all that far, and from the little I could make out at a safe distance, she's gathered quite a bunch of small holders yonder."

Rafe snorted proudly. "Shoot, let her gather all the pool sharks and crap shooters in these parts if she's of a mind to. We got all the real red-blooded Texas rebs riding with *us*!"

Amarillo insisted, "They still got us way outnumbered, Boss."

Rafe shrugged. "Numbers don't count when nobody stands up to be counted. Miss Billie herself is more likely to piss standing up than the pathetic trash she's gathered in vain hopes of bluffing us outten that herd we mavericked fair and square. Neither she nor her sissy squatters have enough hair on their chests to swap lead with real men!"

Then he belied his own optimism by pointing at the sunset with his chin. "If they do attack, they'll have three good reasons to hit us from the west. Number one, they'll have the sun-dazzle at their backs as they ride down the draw at us. Number two, the noise will stampede the cows along the draw to the east if it stampedes them anywhere. And number three, they'll figure we won't be expecting 'em to circle all the way round to the west. So that's how they'll try to outsmart us, and ain't it a good thing I'm smarter?"

Some of the others chuckled, while still others went on looking worried. Rafe glanced at the sunset again, consulted his pocket watch, and went on. "Collins and Manheim, grab some cold grub, fill your canteens with coffee, and git yourselves and your cutting horses down the far side of that herd. If they start to run, mill

175

'em. If we wanted them cows moved towards the Lazy S range, we'd have moved 'em that way our ownselves!"

The two young riders he'd indicated exchanged injured looks. One said he'd see to their grub if the other would fetch their ponies. Ki watched that one move around the north corner of the freestone wall with interest. They had their damned remuda tethered out of sight on the far side, save for those three who'd just loped in, standing about fifty feet to the south with their reins grounded. Ki was pretty sure he could make it to them before anyone else came unstuck, but then what? It was a good hundred yards to the nearest cover to the south, and that was skimpy mesquite, barely saddlehorn high. The big paint Alvin Grayson had been riding looked like a fast runner, but nothing on two legs or four could outrun a bullet, and there were a lot of damned guns all about.

Rafe was instructing two others to grub up and take lookout positions around to the back. Then he suddenly glanced Ki's way. "We'd best move their pal here around to the back and stake him against the wall so's they can see from a distance what a fix he'll be in do they attack."

Ki didn't think he ought to let them do that to him. But he kept the thought to himself as he slowly rose to his considerable height, raising his empty hands even with his own ears, as if to show he had no intention of resisting. Meanwhile, he got set to go for the hilt of that throwing knife nestled between his shoulder blades.

Then someone else gasped, "Look yonder! What the hell is that?"

Ki was the only one there who knew as they all turned to stare thunderstruck at the first *shuriken* Lone Star had sent pinwheeling across the purple eastern sky, golden sunset light reflected back their way from the polished spinning steel. As it spun down into the mavericked herd, inspiring a loud protest from the longhorn it thunked into at the end of its flight, Rafe yelled, "I don't know, but the cows sure hate it! To your ponies *poco tiempo*, boys! All but Amarillo! Stay and guard this Chinee whilst we keep the stock in one place, hear?"

Amarillo did. He drew his sixgun, threw down on Ki, and said, "One fart I can smell and you're dead, Ching Chong. My daddy kilt a dozen of your kind out in the Nevada gold fields, and I've always felt left out."

Then Lone Star must have started throwing with more malice aforethought. Ki couldn't see the wicked steel stars as she sent

176

the ample supply from her recovered saddlebags into bawling beef on the hoof from her meager cover just up the slope. Ki knew she'd thrown that first one higher and slower to give him a line on where she might be throwing from. Now she was out to stampede that herd, and it only took half a dozen dreadful injuries to well-selected bovine victims to set the whole frightened herd in motion, come hell, high water, or the vain efforts of the whole Grayson outfit to turn 'em!

"Oh, shit!" gasped Amarillo as he stood pointing his gun at Ki but staring the other way—just long enough for Ki to whip out his *kogatana* and throw. Ki threw hard as well as accurately. It was still a near thing as the pudgy Amarillo, stabbed to the hilt through the heart, managed a goggle-eyed but accurate shot through the very space Ki had thrown from. But Ki had expected that and crabbed sideways as he'd thrown. Then, even though it was a simple fact that a man with his heart stopped by cold steel could admire such a beautiful sunset a full minute or more, Amarillo was down on his hands and knees and Ki was running, just in time, it would seem, as all hell proceeded to break loose around him.

For over to the west, waiting for the sun to sink just a degree or two more, Billie Sanford had seen the stampede brewing and, not even guessing as to why, shouted, "Let's git 'em, boys! They're busy with their stock and we'll never get us a better chance!"

Nobody gave her an argument. Despite Rafe Grayson's lofty dismissal, Billie and her crew were all well-versed in the way of a man with a cow, and old Roy Matanza backed her play by firing his sixgun at the sky and yelling, "*Vamanos, muchachos*! Ride through them shooting, and when we come to the *vacas*, keep *them* running the same way!"

He didn't have to explain to experienced stockmen how the herd would slow to a manageable pace after running a spell in the very direction everyone but the Graysons wanted. The whole long ragged line of riders was moving down the draw toward the enemy line camp, whooping and hollering with only old Roy Matanza shooting, until he ran out of sixgun rounds, called himself an old fool, and whipped out his saddle gun to ride on more seriously.

Meanwhile, Ki had made it aboard Alvin Grayson's prize paint, and he'd been right about the pony's ability to move. Ki still hung down the off side of his purloined pony Comanche-style, to offer no more than his left foot and rein hand to the bulk of the Grayson outfit. Nobody seemed to notice. With stock bawling and tear-assing in most every direction, what was one spooked pony that didn't seem to have anyone riding it?

By this time the whole draw was hazed with stirred-up dust, rusty red and gunsmoke blue in the tricky sunset light, so Ki took a chance and swung upright in the saddle to ride more directly at the clump of mesquite he felt most sure of.

As he approached at a dead run, spine tingling in anticipation of a bullet overtaking him, he heard Lone Star shout, "*Iie, koko, Ki san*! So he swerved toward the lower but thicker clump of nearby jimson, and then Lone Star sprang up into the open, and then he'd locked wrists with the strong young woman to swing her back up behind him to ride for their lives, as a rifle round tocked the very brim of her star-spangled Stetson.

A lesser woman would have been clinging to Ki's waist for dear life as he loped her up such a slope with no stirrups to call her own. But Jessica Starbuck had learned to ride Indian-style with the help of Indian playmates before she'd ever tackled her ABCs. So in point of fact she was pegging shots back at the world in general as they rode up out of that red dust. She couldn't see to aim at anyone in particular. When nobody got either one of *them*, she decided she'd almost been killed by a stray round. Then they were tearing through taller cover further up the slope. Ki asked where they wanted to go now, and she told him, "Over the top and east through the high chaparral. I hid my own pony in some poison oak there, knowing that loco Billie Sanford was planning to come in from the west!"

Ki didn't ask why she'd chosen poison oak to hide a horse in. He knew. He found it more interesting that she knew the same Billie Sanford he did, although not likely as well. So by the time they'd followed the ridge about half a mile, they'd brought each other up to date on the excitement they'd been having since last they'd ridden together.

She said, "That Kellog who thinks he's a cattle king thinks big as well as cautious. My gelding's just beyond that big skull-shaped boulder."

Ki reined in, observing, "Neither of us saw one head of Circle Star stock back there, though." He swung his right leg forward, over the saddlehorn, to dismount. It was awkward for him but easier for her. She simply had to leapfrog herself over the cantle to take Ki's place in the saddle.

Still standing nearby, he began to adjust the stirrup strap lengths, but she shook her head and said, "No thanks. I'll be getting back in my own saddle, Lord willing and the creeks don't rise."

Then, because they were used to working together, they split up to move in, even though it seemed an unlikely precaution.

It wasn't. As Lone Star rounded the big white boulder aboard the paint, the Lazy S hand she recalled as Jeff Bushmill stepped into the open, on foot, with his Henry repeater aimed casually although not entirely politely, to say, "Howdy, Miss Starbuck. You sure do git around, and I *thought* that was your bay barb some idjet tethered back yonder in that poison oak."

She smiled down at him and said, "I cannot tell a lie. I left him there in hopes of fooling at least some of you, Jeff."

The Lazy S rider chuckled. "I've been out this way long enough to savvy lots of Comanche tricks, ma'am. What were you figuring on using later, jewelweed?"

She said, "Only on myself, if I spied any rash. I'm at least partly immune to poison oak, and as you likely know, it hardly bothers critters with hairy hides at all."

He nodded. "That's why I like to scout heavy growth of poison oak, ma'am. We'd best carry you back to Miss Billie now. I don't hear much gunfire to the north now, and—" Then Ki chopped him from behind, not quite hard enough to break his neck, but enough to require Ki to catch him on the way down. They only wanted the nosey hand out of the way for a spell, and he'd been fixing to land facedown on some jagged rock.

Ki deposited his unconscious victim on grass, in the shade, and straightened up to fasten Jeff's gunbelt around his own hips, muttering, "Thanks, I needed this. I'll get your bay, Jessie."

He did and they rode on, with Ki in the lead now, to recover his own bay barb. He'd left it further out, amid mesquite it could brouse in, but it was still dangerously thirsty after so many hours untended. They gave it some cracked corn along with the canteen water in its nosebag, to show it they still cared. Then Ki said, "Well, that was fun, Jessie, but since neither crazy outfit had any Circle Star stock to begin with—"

"How do you know?" she asked. "All either of us ever saw was that herd they admitted mavericking off the Sanfords and those other newcomers. They admitted right in front of you that they had a dealer in stolen stock bidding on the beef we both saw. Who's to say this King Kellog hasn't already bought my poor Circle Star stock off self-confessed cow thieves?"

Ki sighed. "Jessie, some of your best friends are self-confessed cow thieves, and we're a long way from home. I told you way back when that these hills seemed too far to drive West Texas cows."

She insisted, "The danged cows were driven somewhere. I want a word with that King Kellog cuss before we give up on these parts."

Ki said, "He's hiding out. As I just told you, he told his *mujer* this game was getting too rich for his blood. I doubt he'll surface until he's sure we've lost interest in those Grayson boys. They said something about Anglo lawmen and Mexican outlaws taking an unhealthy interest in that mavericked herd too. So I don't see where we'd even begin to look for him."

She said, "Let's start with the Grayson home spread. That was where we were headed for when they captured us, right?"

★

Chapter 16

By this time the first evening stars were winking down on Austin as well. Longarm was glad it was getting dark as he reined in near the Western Union and dismounted to report in before riding out. The otherwise helpful hostlers at Jessie's hotel stable had refused to lend him any Starbuck riding stock. He'd written their names in his notebook, in hopes of bluffing at least one pony out of them, and to cite them to their boss lady later as loyal employees. So meanwhile, he was riding a horse-sized but silly-looking Spanish saddle mule.

Cinching his own McClellan saddle to the rabbit-eared jackass hadn't made it look any fancier. The only thing to be said for such a mount in hot dry weather was that mules could carry a body farther on rougher fare and less water. So what the hell.

By now the Western Union clerks in Austin were starting to know him almost as well as that Miss Kathy back in Alpine, although none of the ugly mutts acted like they wanted to kiss him. So Longarm wasn't surprised when the tall drink of water he handed his night letter to said, "Your office should get this by nine or ten in the morning, Deputy Long. That Secret Service man was looking for you earlier here. He said to tell you, if and when we saw you, he'd be over to Pandora's Billiard Parlor betwixt suppertime and bedtime."

Longarm nodded, broke out two cheroots, and offered the clerk one as he asked whether MacIntosh had said what he wanted to talk about with a man in a hurry to ride.

The telegrapher shook his head and said, "Nope. He did seem excited about a wire he got all the way from Washington, though."

Longarm naturally asked what Washington had wired his fellow federal agent. The clerk as naturally said Western Union didn't allow them to divulge such matters. They both knew Longarm could win that argument if he really put his back into it. But as the clerk had hoped, the tall deputy decided, "MacIntosh can likely tell me his fool self if it was any of my beeswax. You said the Pandora Billiard Parlor, near here, pard?"

The clerk nodded. "They shoot pool out front, play cards in the back, and you can order cheap whiskey or expensive women anywhere on the premises. Turn left as you leave and watch for a plain stove-blacked door with a red railroad lantern hung just to one side, two streets down and around the corner to the east."

Longarm agreed that seemed a sneaky enough place to scout for Secret Service agents as he lit both their smokes. Then he went back out to the tethered mule, mounted up, and found the oddly named house of ill repute in next to no time.

Pandora turned out to be a fat former beauty who still thought she looked grand under lots of rice powder and rouge as well as a purple sateen dress, cut indecently low for a gal with such monstrous tits. He'd asked for the madam and flashed his badge at her the moment he'd strode in to find no trace of old Ed MacIntosh in the not-too-crowded poolroom/taproom. Madam Pandora led him into her private office, broke out some good stuff for the two of them, and sat him down on a red plush sofa as she poured, confiding, "I know the soberly dressed gent you mean. He never said he was the law, though. He ought to be back down directly. I sent him up to the cribs with French Fran when he described his heart's desire. She could blow a dead man to his heart's desire in about three minutes."

Longarm accepted the thick-walled tumbler of bourbon and branch water she offered, without commenting on the sexual preferences of a somewhat older and stuffier-looking gent. Such services as Madam Pandora intimated were a violation of Texas statute law, but MacIntosh no doubt felt federal employees were excused. There were, in fact, no federal laws covering so-called crimes against nature, praise the Lord and common sense of Congress. Longarm could take or leave his own crimes against nature. The fact that MacIntosh had specified such services might have indicated a warm nature coupled with lack of energy. MacIntosh was almost surely a lunger, it would seem.

As he sipped more sedately with the old bawd who catered to all tastes, Longarm decided he might as well gossip with her about a cow town she had to know better. He asked if she bought any artificial ice, and when she snorted, "Lord, no, why should I?" he explained. "I heard tell earlier of some local boy who makes it good. A Mex who served me some swell *cerveza* said some member of La Raza—meaning *his* race, I'd guess—brews ice right in town with a steam-powered compressor."

She started to deny any fool Mex could work such wonders. Then she brightened and said, "Oh, he must have meant Roy Matanza. Runs a few cows over to the Hill Country and has his fingers in many a pie here in town. He's only part Mex, like that cattle baron from New Mexico, Pete Maxwell. In old Roy's case it was on his daddy's side instead of his mammy's he has greaser blood. How much depends on who you ask. Like most such gents he tends to act Anglo or Mex as his company calls for. Lives Texas-rich with a pretty little *mestiza* I'd just love to have on my own payroll. A ten-dollar ride if ever I saw one."

"We were talking about the gent's ice business," Longarm said politely but firmly. "What another man's *mujer* might look like is no beeswax of mine."

She smiled sheepishly, sipped at her own tumbler, and said, "It's still a crying shame she's wasting all that talent on one old man. I do recall he peddles ice, now that you've brung it to mind. I don't know how he or anyone else makes the stuff. Does it matter?"

Longarm got out his notebook and pencil stub. "Likely not. Worth a look-see, though. You say this Roy Matanza and his ice machinery should be easy enough to find?"

She said, "Over near the rail yards. You'll have to ask your way from there. But everyone knows old Roy Matanza. Doubt he'd be there at this hour, though."

Longarm said he doubted it too. She didn't seem to know much more about the ambitious Tex-Mexican, and when she offered to refill his tumbler he respectfully declined, and said he'd like to see if old MacIntosh had come back down from his French lesson yet.

MacIntosh had. Longarm found him in the main room, shooting rotation pool with more rustic-looking patrons. MacIntosh had hung his hat and coat on a wall hook handy to the cue rack, and

Longarm was mildly surprised to note his fellow lawman packed a Webley Bulldog in a shoulder rig as well as the .45 on his right hip, slung low and *buscadero* style. Their eyes met and they both nodded, but neither said anything just yet. MacIntosh was on a run.

Rotation was a game for suckers or pool sharks, depending. Longarm was good at rotation because he liked to cannonball and hope for the best when he didn't have to worry about sinking the wrong ball out of turn—as one did in, say, eight ball. But while most gents shooting rotation followed the same strategy, lucky accidents counting when you sent the ball you were supposed to aim at every which way, MacIntosh played as sober as he dressed, running the table in a slow methodical manner his friendly rivals clearly found unfriendly.

Sinking all the numbered balls on it in turn, without smiling or even frowning once, he strode over to the rack, saying, "If you gents will excuse me, this other gent and me have more important matters to discuss."

They didn't argue. They were likely glad to see him drop out so *they* could get to play. As MacIntosh put his hat and coat back on, Longarm observed it was a good thing nobody had been playing for money, explaining, "It's tougher to quit when you're ahead, should the cuss you're ahead of be a poor loser."

MacIntosh nodded. "That's why I never play for money. I had to shoot a poor loser in El Paso back in '73, and it really threw me off my feed. But that's not what I wanted to talk to you about. I just got word on those foolish Mexicans and that fool desk everyone's been stewing about. Shall we wander over to the bar?"

Longarm shook his head. "No, thanks. I just had a stiff drink and I got me some night riding ahead of me. What's the story on Queen Victoria's present? Last I heard it was aboard a damned buckboard in the middle of nowheres much."

MacIntosh nodded. "It's aboard an express car bound for Washington by now. Washington just wired me. Seems those vaqueros hauling it the hard way across open range thought to wire in a progress report once they got to Girvin, on the Pecos."

Longarm squinted his eyes half shut to picture his mental map of West Texas. "That's a railroad town. Panhandle and Santa Fe, I'd guess."

MacIntosh nodded. "No guess. P&SF to San Angelo and then on east via Lord knows how many connections. The point is that the moment the idiot Miss Starbuck had left in charge figured out where that damned desk was, he started acting less like an idiot. He wired his vaqueros to address the damned crate right and get it the hell where it belonged *poco tiempo*."

Longarm smiled thinly. "That ought to mean four or five days, Lord willing. Billy Vail will be pleased as punch. He misses me when I stay out in the field running around in circles."

MacIntosh came as close to smiling back as his cold fish features allowed. "I'll be on my way back to Galveston come midnight. How do you get back to Denver from here?"

Longarm grimaced. "The hard way. Back to El Paso and the D&RG, unless I'd like to make even more transfers. But I ain't heading back just yet. Long as I'm here I thought I'd help Jessie Starbuck recover her missing cows."

MacIntosh frowned and declared rather primly, for a man who'd just had a French lesson and run a pool table, "I didn't think stock stealing was a federal crime."

Longarm shrugged. "It ain't, unless government beef or the crossing of jurisdictional borders enters into the complaint. But who's to say the rascals who ran off with Miss Jessie's cows never run 'em out of the state or, hell, the country?"

MacIntosh insisted, "I heard Jessica Starbuck was a looker too. I'd still get my ass back to Denver if I was you, now that the case you were sent out on seems to be closed."

Longarm smiled sheepishly. "I'd get my ass back to Denver too if I had a lick of sense. But old Billy Vail's one of Miss Jessie's godfathers, and I'd have never met her if old Billy hadn't sent me far and wide to investigate her father's murder, Texican jurisdiction or not. I'll wire him what you just told me about that desk, and like I said, he'll be pleased as punch. That'll still give me a few days' leeway. I'm sure he'll agree I should have hung around down this way long enough to make sure President Hayes got that old desk, just in case he never does."

MacIntosh demanded, "How the hell could it get lost again? It's been put aboard an eastbound train with the correct destination written on it in indelible crayon, according to my latest information."

Longarm said soothingly, "Hell, I ain't saying it figures to get lost again. I'm only saying it's possible, seeing how many times it's already happened. Meanwhile, keeping my eye on Texas till we're sure gives me those three or four days do something *useful* down this way."

He glanced at his pocket watch and confided, "I got time to sneak into an ice factory before I ride out after Miss Jessie and her *segundo*. Would you like to tag along?"

The older man said he'd walk Longarm to the door at least, if only someone would tell him what ice factories could possibly have to do with Jessica Starbuck or even her missing cows.

As they moved together through the smoke-filled pool room Longarm explained. "Miss Jessie and Ki headed out to a cattle spread of ill repute in the Hill Country across the river. I'll ask when I catch up with 'em whether they've caught up with any of her cows. Meanwhile, it's occurred to me a butchered cow hung in cold storage would be even tougher to catch up with, and there's an enterprising cattle man called Matanza, here in Austin, as deals in both beef and ice. So add it up."

MacIntosh tried to, shrugged, and said, "Lots of folk in the beef business have ice machines or even cold-storage plants. It's the wave of the future. So what? You can't possibly investigate every such lead in even half of Texas on your own!"

They'd paused near the one discreet exit now, as Longarm explained, "I was hoping for at least a little help. Do you recall the doubtless phoney name that hired gun gave us, pard?"

MacIntosh thought, then nodded and said, "Kellog, King Kellog. What about it? You just said yourself the mastermind who'd hired them doubtless used a phoney name."

Longarm said, "Kellog is what you call an occupational name, like Miller or Smith. In old English it means a slaughterhouse hand. The Spanish name, Matanza, has the exact same meaning, and of course Roy is just another spelling of the Norman French Roi, or King."

MacIntosh whistled softly and said, "Kee-rist! Do I get to watch when you sweat this Tex-Mexican ice maker in a back room?"

To which Longarm modestly replied, "I'd rather have the goods on a suspect before I pick him up. Some judges and juries can be so mule-headed about a few minor cuts and bruises. I thought I'd go poke around Roy Matanza's warehouses and such before I accused him of anything. I'll be surprised to find him there at this hour. Would you care to come along and cover my back anyways?"

MacIntosh said his train didn't leave before midnight, and allowed breaking and entering without a search warrant had to be more exciting than rotation pool.

As they were leaving, MacIntosh asked whether they shouldn't wire in this latest angle, just in case anything went wrong with Longarm's grand notion. He pointed out, "Your office and mine would follow up on this Tex-Mexican ice monger if we never returned from visiting him, right?"

Longarm shook his head. "We ought to be safe enough, doing it sissy with one of us going in for a look-see whilst the other pulls lookout at a safe distance. It wouldn't be fair to old Roy Matanza if he was to wind up innocent with both my office and your'n holding yellow sheets on him."

MacIntosh replied, "I suppose not. I know how tough it can be to apply for government handouts once you've been listed as a possible crook. But what if Matanza *is* a crook, and laying for someone just as pretty as you, Longarm?"

The taller and younger Longarm snorted and said, "I'd never sniff his ass or footprints if I didn't think it possible he could be a crook. But like I just said, I don't see how he could get the two of us, or even be laying for one of us. I only just now found out about Matanza and his wondrous ice machine. As you just pointed out, cold-storing facilities alone do not a stolen herd of sparrow birds make."

As they ducked outside MacIntosh said that the mare tethered across the way was his livery nag. So it only took them a few moments to mount up and get over to the railroad yards.

Once there, they tethered their mounts near the freight dispatcher's shack and asked the old geezer inside about Matanza.

The sleepy-eyed railroader muttered, "How should I know? I ain't his mother. What's that you're smoking, young feller?"

Longarm gave him a couple of cheroots. One for now and another for later. As he lit the ornery old fart's smoke for him, the dispatcher thawed enough to say, "Hold on, seems to me I did hear the boys jawing about old Roy this morning. I think they said Roy and some of his hands rode out to join forces with the Lazy S in the Hill Country to the west. Something about mavericking pushed to impolite extremes. That's as much as I know. Do I look like a cowboy?"

Longarm chuckled, refrained from declaring what the ugly old fart reminded him of, and got directions to the Matanza railroad siding as well.

MacIntosh agreed it made sense to leave their steel-shod ponies where they were and ease their way along the yard tracks afoot. The shadows grew ever longer and darker as they left the lantern light around the depot ever farther behind. They'd have had a tougher time finding the cluster of tin-roofed buildings along a private siding if they hadn't been told exactly where to look.

There was one faint light coming from a corner window. As MacIntosh covered him, Longarm eased up to it for a peek through the grimy glass. A big fat Mex was enjoying a good doze in a tiny office, a shotgun across his thighs and both feet up on the desk. Longarm eased back, softly smiling, to tell his fellow pussyfooter, "Watchman. Drunk or mighty lethargic by nature. Seems a mite subtle for a planned ambush. I'll start with the locks farthest from the sleeping beauty and work towards him, saving the best for last. Why don't you take up your own position by yonder tool shack? I doubt it's Matanza property, being it's on the other side of his siding rails."

MacIntosh peered into the darkness in that direction until he made out the apparently formless black mass the younger deputy had to mean. He muttered, "You have good eyesight. Remind me never to get into it with you in a dark cellar."

Longarm said, "You should see this one Mexican cat-eye I know. Don't try to mix into it if I wind up in trouble. You're so right about the grim mistakes a firefight in the dark can lead to. I'm counting on you to report in, for the both of us, should I walk into anything I can't get my fool self out of."

★

Chapter 17

Over in the Hill Country, Lone Star and Ki had naturally tried to follow the progress of the big showdown from a safe distance. It hadn't been easy. A safe distance after sundown but before moonrise involved a heap of guesswork, with the undisciplined gun waddies on both sides making a heap of pointless noise as they peppered away at nothing much in passing.

As far as Lone Star and Ki could tell, the Grayson bunch was trying to hold a roundup by starlight, with Billie Sanford and her bunch just as determined to drift the scattered herd eastward to be regathered and redealt on range more to their liking. Since half-wild longhorns could be tough enough to round up in broad day without anyone sniping at you, Ki predicted and Lone Star agreed that both sides figured to be mighty busy for a spell.

Ki had to agree this offered them a golden opportunity to pay a call on the Grayson home spread. The ornery Grayson boys would have likely left lesser lights in charge of their property, but anything beat having to cope with the three of them en masse. Lone Star didn't want to gun anyone she didn't have to, and she'd cross that bridge when and if she found they'd stolen one head of her own damned stock. She declared, and Ki sheepishly agreed, that Billie Sanford could look after her own danged interests in these danged parts.

Knowing their way, and riding faster once the moon came up,

they still took half the night to reach the original claim of the Grayson clan, closer to the Pedernales. The willow-lined and moonlit stream that wound past the cluster of 'dobe walls and cottonwood rails in a secluded side-draw was far too modest to call a river. But it still offered plenty of water as it wound through grassy flats toward the more imposing Pedernales to the north. As they scouted the layout from a rocky ridge to the south, they didn't take the small dark dots spattered across the moonlit meadows down below for ants. Lone Star tallied the stock bedded down on just one five-acre patch, multiplied in her head, and decided, "Over five hundred head, and any number could be wearing my brand and that stupid trail brand of their own."

Sitting his well-ridden bay beside her, Ki said, "I doubt we'd find any stock within sight of their kitchen windows that they might not want to discuss with the Rangers, Jessie. We know they were holding those other cows more privately for that mysterious Kellog."

She nodded. "Speaking of kitchen windows, I don't see any lights down there at all."

Ki shrugged. "It's after midnight and most country folk don't read in bed the way you do, Jessie."

She sniffed. "Never you mind what I might or might not do in bed at midnight. We'd better leave our ponies up here and move on down Kiowa-style."

Ki agreed but suggested, "Let me cinch our saddles aboard fresher mounts first. I wouldn't let you creep closer if I thought we might creep into anything serious. But just on the outside chance we have to *saru* without taking time to say *sayonara*, we'd better have the ways and means waiting up here, *iie*?"

She agreed, and together they switched their saddles and bridles to less-jaded horseflesh. Ki wanted her to take the big paint he'd helped himself to escaping from the Grayson line camp. He'd found it moved well, even packing his heavier weight, and being led about in the cool shades of evening under a light packsaddle should have restored the paint's powerful haunches. But Lone Star told him not to be silly, explaining, "I was holding this husky roan in reserve with my own trim figure in mind, you moose. The idea is to ride together if we have to ride out fast."

Ki didn't argue. Little Jessie had gotten hard to argue with since the first lessons in the martial arts her father had requested for his cute little girl-child. She still bowed and addressed him as Ki-San, with the formal sucking hiss of the *samurai* caste, whenever they worked out on the training *mushiro* back at the main spread. But she'd been in command, and known everyone *knew* she was in command, from the moment her father had been murdered by those poor unfortunate bastards who'd thought that was all it took to take over Starbuck Enterprises.

Ki didn't say that reminded him of their first adventures with U.S. Deputy Custis Long, as the two of them left their tethered ponies atop the ridge to ease downslope through the sparse cover of scattered trees. Ki knew they both owed their lives to Longarm, and vice versa. The big, less gracefully moving deputy was a good man to have by one's side in a fight. He could move well enough in his own lethal way. But Ki was as content to back this latest play of the lady known as Lone Star without any help from the one man Ki was just a little jealous of. Ki knew Longarm was hardly the only less platonic pal she'd ever had. Thanks to the more pragmatic sexual attitudes of his mother's people, Ki was devoid of prudish Victorian ideas about virginity or even ladylike conduct in the privacy of that lady's bedding. Having literally watched Jessica Starbuck grow up, Ki could picture her shapely young body indulging any guest of her choice in various positions of pleasure. He had, in fact, walked in on her in the act now and then. Neither, naturally, had ever mentioned it later. Such events simply took place in a less than perfect world when a mistress and her devoted servant and protector happened to be of opposite genders. Ki had his own feelings toward her lush blond body under almost perfect control. His reservations toward Longarm weren't based on a conscious desire to take his place in Jessie's arms and more intimate places. Ki was afraid of Longarm hurting her, where it really counted, in the inner reserves of her sometimes too generous heart.

He put such morose thoughts to one side as a dark form in the grass ahead turned into an obviously suspicious steer, rising to full height even as it lowered its long horns and raised its tufted tail like a battle pennant, cussing at them softly in cow.

Lone Star talked back to it, as if it reminded her of a lost pup. Her soothing words didn't work. As it snorted and charged, she twirled out of its path with a grace that would have won her some cheers in a Plaza del Toros. Then Ki had jumped the cantankerous brute by the horns from the far side, and using its own momentum against it, wrestled it to the ground with its horn tips embedded in the overgrazed but tangle-rooted sod.

Lone Star dimpled and dropped one knee beside them as she said, "Nice *sumo* throw. Let's see whose critter this might be, as long as it's being so cooperative."

Running her bare fingers lightly over the big brute's steaming hide she decided, "Same trail marking the Graysons used on that other herd. Hair's grown back over its original . . . One hundred and one? That's a big California outfit, isn't it?"

Ki nodded. "Biggest cattle operation on the West Coast. This cow's a long way from home, and remember your chum Longarm and that Laredo Loop he worked on one time?"

She said, "Custis never worked on the Laredo Loop. He arrested those stock thieves who moved Texas cows to Arizona and Arizona cows to Texas by way of Old Mexico. He put the Laredo Loop out of business while he was at it."

Ki insisted, "The Reno brothers were put out of business years ago and people still rob trains. That herd the Graysons mavericked off their new neighbors originated down Mexico way, remember?"

She said, "All too well. But they were wearing typical Mexican brands. Let's chew this apple a bite at a time. I suspect this critter has had enough fun for now if you'd like to let it up so's we can find out what spooked it to begin with."

Ki didn't ask what she meant. Everyone who worked with cows knew longhorns grazing far from human habitation tended to charge anyone they saw afoot as a novel and hence threatening sight, while at the same time beef grazing within the sights and smells of a home spread tended to accept humans afoot as harmless little critters.

Ki waited till Lone Star had risen and moved well clear before he let go of the steer's horns and leaped up and away before it could figure what it might want to do next. As its human tormentors moved on down the slope, the longhorn rolled to its own four hooves, bawling for its momma and lighting out up the other way.

Knowing the stock around the Grayson spread had been spooked by something, or someone, Lone Star and Ki took the time and extra steps required to avoid further misunderstandings as they eased in on the brooding dark windows of the rambling ranch house and scattered outbuildings. Ki put a hand on Lone Star's silk sleeve to stop her in the inky shade of a moonlit oak, saying,

"Chui suru! Why are there no ponies in that corral behind the house?"

She started to say something thoughtless. Then she nodded. *"Hai,* they'd have surely left at least a few hands, and enough riding stock, to manage that fair-sized household herd. Maybe that long low outbuilding on the far side could be a stable?"

Ki shook his head. "It's hard to make out by this light, but I'm pretty sure the corral poles block easy access from this side. It's as likely to be a bunkhouse."

She stared thoughtfully for a moment or more before she said, "I think you're right. They have an otherwise oddly placed outhouse serving the needs of anyone bunking there. That open-sided shed on the north side of the corral is probably where their ponies shelter when the blue northers blow."

Ki said, *"Toshite mo,* it's empty at the moment. No ponies in sight. No yard dogs asking what we might be doing here this close. Don't you find this *myo na?"*

She frowned thoughtfully and replied, "Weird was the word you were groping for. Why would the Grayson boys leave their property completely deserted like so?"

Ki warned, "It might not be completely deserted. Why don't you stay here and cover me while I play *ninja?"*

She said she played *ninja* pretty good too. But he got her to agree anyone chasing one shadow would be more confused by another opening up on him from another direction. So she drew her birthday gun with one hand, tapped the muzzle against the star pinned to her hat to make sure she was loaded for bear, and murmured, *"Ki o tsukete!"* Ki was on his way without a word.

Ki wasn't being rude. A cloud was moving across the moon, casting a shifting shadow on the otherwise silvery shortgrass. By the time it had swept on, Ki had made other cover. Not even Lone Star could be certain now whether he was hunkered in that scrub cedar straight down the slope or a tad to her left amid that cow-filled mesquite. She knew anyone staring up their way from that deserted-looking ranch house would have even less reason to guess.

Ki had, in fact, dropped into the mesquite as he'd run out of shifting shade. By the time another cloud swung across the moon from the southeast, Ki had picked his next cover and was running at the same speed, in the same direction, a good deal farther, although now much closer to the windows at one end of the main house. He watched them for any sign of movement from his new vantage point amid knee-high tumbleweeds still rooted where the grass had been really overgrazed. He detected no signs of life from the house as he waited for another cloud. The wind, such as it was, was from the distant but steamy Gulf of Mexico, promising more cloud cover than it appeared to want to deliver. Ki swore softly up at the too bright moon and then, since there was always a way in the ways of the *ninja*, he twisted a ripe but not yet dried-out tumbleweed off at the roots to see what it would do about that.

The tumbleweed did nothing. The breeze sweeping down the slope from the southeast simply wasn't strong enough to roll an only half-dried-out tumbleweed. But how was anyone at any distance to know this?

Ki twisted off two more, slowly easing the three of them into one big bundle he could grip from the middle with his left hand. He got them to gently stirring in the silvery moonlight, as if they were one outsized fuzz ball getting set to travel. Nobody else seemed at all interested. Ki took a deep breath, commended his own hide to gods he wasn't too sure about, and began to bounce on his heels and haunches across the last bad open stretch, trying to pass for a big tumbleweed, doubting he would, and then, a million heart-stopping miles on, letting go of the sticker brush with his hip and shoulder against the 'dobe wall just under the gaping windows at that end of the ranch house.

Ki let another million years pass slowly by before he did another thing. The secret of *ninja* night-crawling, aside from dark clothing and soft soles, was in working with the familiar sights and sounds of the night. People tended to cock an ear and listen, then decide they'd only heard the wind, as long as they heard nothing else for a time.

What Ki heard, after your average intruder might have concluded there was nobody home, was the soft creak of a cane-seated chair, followed by a sleepy voice muttering, *"Ojala, es muy tarde y muy estupido, muchachos!"*

It was just as well Ki spoke pretty fair Spanish as well as the tongues of his Japanese and American relations. Had he not, he'd have had a tougher time following their drift as yet another voice told the one who'd grown weary of their game to quit his bitching and carry out their patron's damned orders.

Ki doubted their patron could be named Grayson. Now that he had at least some of them located in the main house, Ki slid silently along the wall to the back. A convenient cloud shadow gave Ki the chance to flit across the modest backyard and roll under the rails of the empty corral. He followed the black shadows of the poles along the moonlit dust, spine tingling, until he made the deep shade of the bunkhouse roof's verandalike overhang. He still worked his way around to the far side, hoping anyone inside would expect visitors by way of the usual doorways. He found the first body between one end of the bunkhouse and the outdoor crapper. The cowboy lay on his face with his pants half down and a big dark patch of half-dried blood staining the back of his white shirt. Ki whistled softly and murmured, "I've heard of being caught with one's pants down, but that was really sneaky!"

He found two more bodies inside, once he'd slithered over a bunkhouse windowsill on his belly, the fresh *kogatana* from his saddlebags gripped by the blade between his teeth.

Both the dead Grayson hands appeared to be only cowboys, probably left to keep an eye on things while the bigger boys rode off to war. Ki knew any womenfolk that had lived here would have been in the main house when those Mexican killers hit. That they were killers was self-evident. Whether they'd killed any women on the property right out or had some fun with them first was academic by now. They'd had time to deal with all the riding stock and any watchdogs as well. So they'd been there awhile. Their reasons for laying in wait after silencing everyone and everything that belonged there was plain to see. The only question left was what Jessie might want to do about it. So Ki made his way back, the same slow way, to ask her.

By this time Lone Star had squatted to pee nervously more than once, and would have gnawed her nails to the quick if she'd been a nail-biter. But Ki's exciting tale seemed to have a calming effect on her. She said, "Billie Sanford had a few vaqueros riding with her, and that Roy Matanza had even more. But I can't see either outfit as the Spanish-speaking killers laying for the Grayson boys down yonder."

Ki nodded. "*Hai*, the last we saw of that bunch, they were shooting it out with the Graysons at shorter range. You and I rode almost directly here from that other confusion. To beat us here by the time they needed to work with, the ones in the house must have started much earlier, from other parts. The one giving the orders mentioned a boss they were working for. Remember what I told you about that mysterious cattle buyer, King Kellog, Jessie?"

Lone Star nodded soberly. "It works if we assume a nervous mastermind with a gang of his own and worries about the Grayson boys talking."

Ki said, "*Hai*, they said he'd backed out of a deal he'd made with them because too many others were interested in that mavericked herd. That would still leave the Graysons to tattle on him, if they got picked up by the law."

She nodded but pointed out, "Or Mexicans with their own ax to grind. What was that about Mexicans being sore about those disputed cows as well? They were branded Mex, and the bunch just down the slope weren't planning to ambush the Graysons in Gaelic!"

Ki smiled thinly and pointed out, "I didn't tangle with them. They're still there, all set up to welcome the Graysons warmly the moment they get home."

Ki glanced at the sky before he added, "That's apt to take them a while. Even if the Grayson bunch wins the running gunfight with Billie Sanford and her boys, they're going to need some daylight on the subject to round those scattered mavericks up."

He saw she was still undecided. He said, "Jessie, this is getting to be just too big a boo! It's very sweet of you to want to hang around and warn the Grayson brothers. But how might we do that without getting shot up ourselves?"

She sighed. "Yes, both of us sort of parted company with the grumpy Graysons on unfriendly terms. What if we were to just go back down yonder and do some housecleaning for them in their absence?"

Ki refrained, out of respect, from saying she seemed *baku* bent on *jisatsu*. He settled for, "If we find suicide a desirable goal, there is still a problem. We don't know who those Mexicans lying in wait for known wildmen might be. What if we were to find out, after killing them, they were on *our* side?"

Lone Star wanted to say that sounded silly, till she thought about it. "You're right. Cows branded Mex must have started out with Mex owners. The patron they mentioned could have been a big Mex ranchero as easily as that mysterious King Kellog. But whoever they may be, they do play rough. So what do you suggest we do now?"

Ki said, flatly, "Let them play as rough as they like. It's not our fight. So far we don't have a shred of evidence that anyone over in these central hills has ever seen a Circle Star cow, Jessie.

Why don't we quit while we're ahead and get back to West Texas where you and your cows belong?"

Lone Star shook her head stubbornly. "If my cows were still in West Texas we wouldn't be here having this dumb conversation about 'em. That mysterious King Kellog deals in stolen beef. Until I'm sure he hasn't been buying and selling any beef of mine, I've still got a beef with him, and those Graysons know the rascal on sight. So come hell or high water, we can't let anyone kill those otherwise useless rascals until I've had my own way with 'em. You say those Mexicans have to be holding Grayson ponies as well as their own somewhere further out? Might not their camp in more open country be a safer place for a parley?"

Ki said, "Jessie, those boys have killed, and they'll know we know they've killed, Anglo Texicans in the dead heart of Texas."

She nodded soberly. "One of the first things they might like to hear is that we're not out to lynch anybody over a little old private fight. They'll probably have their riding stock atop some timbered ridge, like us. Once we find it, to discuss their feud with the Graysons just outside of easy shooting range . . ."

"They're not going to tell you the truth even if it's in their favor!" Ki said, "Whoever they may be, they knew it was war to the death before they backshot that poor boy on his way to the outhouse, and God only knows what they've done to the Grayson women."

She started to ask how he knew there'd been women in that ranch house. Then she nodded and said, "Right. It's a long ride to town, and none of the Graysons looked like sissy-lovers. But whether those mysterious Mexicans have killed woman or even children is not the question before the house. The question before the house is how we're to save those hot-tempered and hair-triggered Grayson brothers without getting into an all-out gunfight with anybody!"

To which Ki could only answer, "Jessie, I just don't think there *is* any way."

★

Chapter 18

As old mission bells tolled midnight in Austin, Longarm was more concerned about Agent MacIntosh than sore at him. The warrantless and apparently unwarranted sweep of the Matanza property had taken longer than expected, but just the same, it had given Longarm an uneasy turn to find MacIntosh missing when he'd returned to that railroad toolshed.

MacIntosh had said his night train to Galveston was leaving around midnight. But it had already left when Longarm made it over to the depot around eleven-forty-five. Nobody there could say whether an undertaker packing two guns had left aboard her or not.

The tall worried deputy found his hired mule, but not the livery nag MacIntosh had said he was riding back near Pandora's Billiard Parlor. In a town the size of Austin there were liveries enough to keep a man busy longer than Longarm wanted to be. He rode back to the Western Union instead. An older gent wearing a ten-gallon hat and high-heeled Justins under his cheap seersucker business suit was jawing with the same night clerk. As Longarm entered the clerk brightened and said, "Here he is now, Mister Sanford."

The older man turned from the counter to tell Longarm, "I'd be Kentucky Bob Sanford, and I rode for the Union in the Wilderness Campaign."

Longarm shook friendly, but replied with some reserve, "Then I'd be Custis Long from West-by-God-Virginia, and I disremember which side I was on when me and the world were so young and foolish. I take it you had something more important to discuss with the law, seeing you already know who I ride for these days?"

Sanford nodded. "Tim here tells me you aim to ride out into the Hill Country this evening. I got to get on home myself, and if you're really headed for the Grayson spread, my spread is on your way."

Longarm said, "Well, I could use some guidance as well as your fine company, Kentucky Bob. Just let me get off some wires first. I seem to be missing another lawman, and I'd best inform his own office he's either on his way home or mayhaps being held for ransom by French gals."

He picked up a Western Union pencil and tore off a telegram blank as the clerk informed him, "That Agent MacIntosh was just in here, wiring Galveston on his way to the railroad depot, if that's who you're worried about."

Longarm nodded and started writing anyway as he said, "I'm only pissed at him now. Remind me never to call on the Secret Service for serious backing. No thanks to him, I didn't need any after all, but he still backed me casual as hell, considering."

He wired an update to Billy Vail in Denver while he was at it, sending the message collect but at night-letter rates lest they fuss at him for being wasteful with the taxpayers' *dinero*. Then he offered Kentucky Bob a smoke, lit two of them, and said, "I'm ready to ride anytime you are. I hired a Spanish mule, and I got him sort of heavy laden as well because they couldn't spare me a pack mule. I'd appreciate it if you'd keep the humorous remarks to yourself."

Stanford said he'd never found mules all that amusing in his army days. So Longarm allowed they'd likely get along.

As they stepped outside, where the older man had a jug-headed sorrel waiting for his own ass, Sanford confided, "I don't get to laugh much about anything lately. Are you a married man, Custis?"

The younger deputy shook his head. "Nope, knock wood, and my pals call me Longarm. It was my mother's odd notion to call me Custis. I never got a straight answer on that either."

Sanford said, "My old woman died on me a few years back, and you're so right about knocking wood if ever you bust free. But I'm still stuck with a grown daughter, twice as stubborn as her mother ever was, and that's why I got to get on out yonder, despite the threat of thunder in the air and the other dangers of night travel in them infernal hills!"

Longarm gripped his cheroot between his teeth and forked himself aboard the Spanish mule before he felt up to coping with all that grim information.

As the older man mounted his buckskin and rode over to fall in beside him, Longarm glanced up. "Yep, the stars are fuzzy enough now for rain this side of sunrise. You say your spread and your willful daughter are about halfway to where I got to get?"

They started moving out, Sanford pointing the way as he replied, "My Lazy S is just an overnight ride if we don't pause to piss too often. You'll want to breakfast with us at least, and mayhaps rest a spell afore you ride on to arrest them pesky Grayson boys. We can offer you that pack pony you said you'd like, along with some hands to back your play, no offense. Lord only knows where my Billie is right now. That's how come I'm in such a hurry to get home. We want to swing right at the next cross street."

Longarm didn't want to argue about that, but observed, "You're dealing words faster than I can pick 'em up, Kentucky Bob. Lots of us do that when we get our heads overstuffed with worries. Suppose you slow down and start with why you expect me to arrest anyone."

The older man said, "Hell, everyone knows you're the law, just as everyone knows the Grayson boys are thieving trash! I came into town to swear out a warrant accusing 'em of stock stealing. Only my damn-fool lawyer says he don't want to write one up for me because of some fool technicality. Compounding a felony, he calls it. Have you ever run across that fool term?"

Longarm nodded and explained, "Lawyers don't like to press charges for a client that could get that client in as much trouble as the other side. For example, if a crook was to steal something one didn't have clear title to oneself, things could get sort of complicated in court."

They were coming to the covered bridge across the Texas Colorado now. Sanford sighed and said, "That's what my Billie said as I was fixing to ride in. You see, them Grayson brothers grabbed some maverick beef just as we and some of our neighbors were fixing to maverick it. But if that wasn't enough on a poor man's plate, one of Roy Matanza's vaqueros just rid back to town, flesh-wounded, to tell me my Billie went out after them cows, and them Graysons, without my parental consent. And

200

worse yet, the Mex says shots have been fired in anger by both sides!"

Longarm whistled, but didn't answer as they crossed the river. It would have been impossible to make himself heard as they clomped through the reverberating boxed-in timbers of the thundering bridge.

Riding out the far side, where one got to hear oneself far better, Longarm said, "Your daughter must take after a willful mother, and how come other men seem willing to follow her into battle?"

Old Sanford said, "She's prettier than her late mother. Not that she ain't an innocent maid, you understand. Sometimes I do wish she'd pay more mind to gentlemen callers and less time to shooting bottles off fence posts. Be that as it may, I got to get on home before she kills somebody, or vice versa. I told her, leaving, no beef born of mortal cow was worth a shootout! That's why I headed for town and the law courts to begin with!"

Longarm didn't point out the obvious fact that serious shootouts tended to be over long before the two of them could possibly get there. He said, quietly, "I'm only looking for the Grayson boys, and any cows they might have on them as a sort of side issue. I'd be playing you false if I didn't inform you this dispute about cows is a side issue to my superior, Marshal Billy Vail of the Denver District Federal Court."

Stanford frowned and said he didn't savvy how any Denver districts, state or federal, could have any jurisdiction over livestock stolen in the Sovereign State of Texas.

Longarm replied, "That's what I just said, albeit them cows the Graysons mavericked off you all might have been, ah, mavericked on the far side of a federal border. Never mind all that. My point is that I'm really looking for Miss Jessica Starbuck of West Texas and Starbuck Enterprises."

Sanford said, "I've heard of her. She's got holdings back yonder in Austin. So how come you're looking for her in the Hill Country, and what do you want with her when you find her, if it ain't cows?"

Longarm hesitated, preferring not to fib to his elders. For if what MacIntosh had said about that Presidential desk being recovered was true, he really *had* no valid excuse to track old Jessie down, bless her sweet little derriere. He'd just wired Billy Vail he only meant to verify that fool crate had been sent on to Washington right. He knew Vail would have kittens if ever he even suspected a paid-up deputy was trying to help a lady recover lost, strayed, or stolen property on Uncle Sam's time. So he thought it best to tell old Sanford, "I want to question Miss Jessica about some state secrets I am not at liberty to divulge."

Sanford gulped and said, "Mum's the word then. You're riding with an old soldier loyal to the Union!"

In point of fact they were riding along a darker cinder-paved lane now. Kentucky Bob had swung them off the main east-west wagon trace, and there were no street lamps at all this far from the center of town. But the general gloom all around wasn't what had Longarm a tad concerned. He reined in. The older man naturally did the same, asking why. Longarm said, "I just heard someone loping across that covered bridge back yonder."

Sanford shrugged. "So did I. What of it? It's a free country, and some old boy's likely as anxious as me to git on home."

Longarm said, "That only works when a rider loping his own free way pays less attention to the hoofbeats of others. I slowed without really thinking as I heard him thunder across that bridge. So did you, the same unthinking way."

The older man cocked his head. "I don't hear nothing back yonder right now."

To which Longarm softly replied, "Neither do I. He reined in, just as we did. You still think we're talking about an innocent cuss on his way home at this hour?"

Kentucky Bob repressed a shudder. "Not hardly. Some son of a bitch must be following us home in the dark!"

After they'd silently sat their mounts a spell Longarm decided, "He ain't going to follow us unless we go somewheres. What say we ride on?"

Sanford protested, "Ride on, out into the hills, where he'll have us at his mercy?"

Longarm ginned wolfishly and replied, "That's an interesting question. I make it one of him, and anyone can see there's two of us. That is a Henry you're packing as a saddle gun, ain't it?"

The older man nodded, and said he had a Walker Conversion under his seersucker coat as well. Then he brightened and said, "Oh, I follow your drift. It'll be easier to spy other riders in the moonlight once we're out in open country. But what if he just hangs back, stopping when we stop, never giving us a crack at him?"

Longarm said soothingly, "Nobody will get hurt. Let's hope he only wants to know where we're headed."

Sanford protested, "Hell, everyone in town knows where my place is, and where else might I be going at this hour?"

Longarm started to say their mysterious shadow could be trailing *him* instead. But the poor old cuss seemed worried enough about his willful daughter and all. So he settled for saying, "It's hard to say what might inspire anyone to behave so sneaky. Have you ever heard of a jasper called King Kellog, said to deal big in beef on the hoof or mayhaps frozen?"

Sanford thought. "Might have heard the name. I know there's a King *Fisher* in the beef business. Mean son of a bitch, the way I hear it. King Kellog don't match up with any hands I've ever shook, though. Why would he be after us, Longarm?"

The tall deputy explained, "Such jaspers generally hire others to go after folks. I don't see why a man you've never met would be after you either. How do you get along with that other budding beef baron, Roy Matanza?"

The older man blinked in surprise. "Swell, the last I'd heard. It was one of his riders, like I said, who told me tonight about my willful daughter's latest scrape. Old Roy wouldn't have anyone following me. He *knows* where I live. He lives right down the road, and for all I know he's with my Billie, even as we ride to catch up with the fool girl."

Longarm lit a fresh cheroot as they rode on. He wasn't required by the code he followed to offer all around every damned time. As he'd hoped, the older man was inspired to break out his own chaw, and after they'd ridden on a spell Kentucky Bob asked, "What was that you said about frozen beef before? Roy Matanza peddles ice from a patent ice machine in town. But I've never heard tell of anyone dealing in iced beef. You can ice fish. But beef turns black and blue if you lay it in crushed ice."

Longarm nodded. "I know. I was in Roy Matanza's plant this evening. That ice machine he's got must be a thumping wonder when it's running. But near as I could judge, he's only set up to make big blocks of ice-wagon ice. He had eight ice wagons lined up in this one carriage house."

"I just said old Roy peddles ice in town," Sanford reminded him. "Lots of folk in Austin have ice boxes these days. We like to keep up to date as anyone else out our way. Roy don't sell no beef outten them buildings, though. Come roundup time he ships his beef on the hoof, same as us, from the auction pens on the south side of the rail yards. You got to have cows where the buyers are bidding if you expect to have anyone bidding on 'em, you know."

Longarm nodded. "I just said I saw no evidence of meat packing, canning, or whatever on the premises. It's likely just a coincidence that Kellog and Matanza mean the same in different tongues. Hold on, let's rein in and see if we can catch that mystery rider by surprise."

They did, but apparently they couldn't. Longarm muttered, "If he's still following us, he's good."

Old Sanford said, "I wish you wouldn't talk like that. We got a long ways to ride, and look how dark the moon is getting now!"

Longarm glanced up. "Hell, the moon's not getting any darker. It's just them storm clouds rolling in full of summer lightning that's making the sky so dark this evening."

★

Chapter 19

It got even darker within the hour as ever more cloud cover swept up out of the southeast. Over to the west, Ki was insisting, "It's going to rain fire and salt any minute, and these ridges are hardly the place to be in a real Texican thunderstorm, Jessie!"

Lone Star kept legging it up the slope ahead of him. "We'll follow the contour lines a third of the way down as we scout for those Mex ponies, Ki. We're fixing to get wet no matter where we may be, once those clouds up yonder rip open, so we may as well be doing something useful as we move about to keep warm, hear?"

He grumbled something about rain slickers and waterproof tarps as he followed her trim form in the tricky light. He knew why she wouldn't want to scout in her crinkle-crackle rain slicker. Back home in Dai Nippon, where they'd made tolerable rain capes of water-repellent rice straw, no *ninja* out for blood on a rainy night had ever worn one. Nothing at all waterproof moved as quietly in the dark as miserable human flesh covered with goose bumps and soggy soft clothing.

Near the crest where they'd tethered their ponies they both hunkered down, every hair atingle, as their world lit up brighter than broad day for the split second it took a tremendous lightning bolt to shatter a nearby limestone crag.

Lone Star gasped, "*Hayaku!* We have to get our poor ponies to lower ground before they wind up fried on the hoof!"

Ki didn't argue as he hurried after her. He still felt mighty *baku* as they tore into the thick cover they'd left their mounts hidden in, only to find themselves surrounded by over a dozen gun muzzles, each aimed their way by a dark figure under a big Mexican sombrero. As Ki froze in place, trying to come up with something, anything, that didn't seem sheer suicide, Lone Star nodded pleasantly at the mysterious Mexicans to say, "*Buenos noches, señores. A 'onde esta nuestros caballos?*"

One of them purred back, in pretty fair English, "We did not know they belonged to anyone lovely as yourself, señorita. Perhaps you will get them back. Anything is possible as long as I, El Temperamento, am your friend."

Then he added, with a dry chuckle, "Alas, for some reason I do not make friends easy."

She hadn't needed that warning as to their probable future relationship. She'd already known what *temperamento* meant, and to rate it as a nickname he had to be a real joy to be around.

Neither Lone Star nor Ki resisted as less vocal members of the sinister band disarmed them, or in point of fact took their side arms away from them. Lone Star still had her *shuriken* decorating her Stetson, while Ki still had various blades hidden on his person in some of the oddest places.

El Temperamento said, "*Bueno.* Now that I see we may be friends after all, why do we not join my comrades in that *rancho* down below?"

Pointing at the moody sky with his gun muzzle, he added, "Is going to get most unpleasant out tonight. We were on our way for to shelter in the *casa de los ladrones* when we noticed the *caballos* someone had left up here and thought it best to wait for you, eh?"

Ki knew anything he might say might only get him pistol-whipped.

Lone Star laughed lightly and said, "Anyone can see you know a thing or two about scouting. Would it help if we assured you we are not on good terms with the Grayson brothers either?"

El Temperamento replied, "*Quien sabe?* Tell me about it as we all seek shelter from the coming storm, eh?"

So she did as they marched her and Ki back the way they'd just come. Out in the open El Temperamento turned out younger and nicer-looking than she'd pictured from his sinister tone and casually pointing six-gun. She'd have felt better about him and

206

his followers if they'd been clad in the white cotton shirts and gunbarrel chaps honest vaqueros found comfortable in the heat of summer. She knew from having met El Gato and other such adventurous Mexican lads that Mexicans who took the trouble to wear dark from head to toe, in hot weather, had less innocent riding in mind.

By the time they got down to the ranch house she'd filled the young Mex leader in on her reasons for being there. She'd told him the terse truth because there'd been simply no lies she could think of that might improve his uncertain disposition. She was glad she hadn't elaborated on her modest part in stampeding that mavericked herd when the mysterious Mexican glanced up at the glowering sky to growl, "*Cojones del Diablo,* is impossible to even search for scattered *vacas* on a night like this one!"

Then he slipped a casual arm around Lone Star's trim waist to add, "More better we ride out after them *mañana,* after a good night's rest, or at least a good *night,* no?"

She felt like stiffening up, but forced herself to fall in step with him and simper when he drew her closer. Ki had taught her, long before she'd known why boys and girls were different, how to use an opponent's own sudden moves against him. A girl less skilled in the martial arts might have wound up bruised already, feeling this much disgust and allowing it to show.

They'd just reached the Grayson house when lightning flashed again nearby, and what felt like big soggy frogs began to war-dance around the brim of Lone Star's Stetson. They all ran inside without concern for procedure. Ki skipped over one body on the dirt floor of the dimly lit main room, and almost dived out an open window on the far side. As he recovered, holding on to the rain-splattered sill, another lightning flash revealed slicker-clad figures herding ponies, a lot of ponies, into the corral out back. Ki said so casually, in Japanese, as he turned around to see Lone Star staring stricken at the dead woman he'd just jumped over.

The facedown cadaver was that of a breed or Mexican girl in her teens. Her face was half hidden by her messed-up mop of ebony hair. One could best judge her youth by the way she'd been left exposed from her trim waist down. Her print Mother Hubbard had been shoved up around her rib cage. So it was hard to say where she'd been shot, but shot she'd been, more than once, for few folks crapped that much blood when stabbed somewhere above the waist.

207

El Temperamento still had his left arm around Lone Star's waist as he grimaced and snarled, in Spanish, "I told you *cabrones* to tidy this place up, damn the vomit your mothers give for milk with their purple tits!"

Then, in English, he demanded to know what Ki had just said and in what language. So Lone Star answered, "He forgets his English when he is afraid. He only said you and your *muchachos* were being wise about your riding stock with such a storm brewing up."

El Temperamento relaxed, although not in his firm grip on her, and said, "*Si*, I have always been most wise as well as most ferocious. Tell your frightened Chino nobody will hurt him, just yet, as long as he behaves himself."

Then he spoiled it all by pointing at the dead girl at their feet with a boot tip, adding, "This one did not behave herself. Me and my *muchachos* had ridden far and only wanted for to have a little fun. She said no, the stupid little Caddo, and as you see, she got to take care of us anyway."

Lone Star forced herself to smile instead of retch as she softly asked, "All of you, after she was dead?"

He hugged her hip to his own, reassuringly, and said, "*Pero* no. I am fastidious as well as wise and ferocious. Only a couple of poor *cabrones* too ugly for to get a pig to kiss them, willingly, bothered with that one after someone else, I forget who, shot her in a fit of pique. But why are we still out here in the front *sala* in this ridiculous vertical position?"

She coyly asked whatever he might be suggesting. He laughed smugly and announced, "We shall be in that one nice *recámara* I chose for my own repose if anything most important should develop. If any of you value your lives, you will not disturb us regarding anything less important than the second coming of El Cristo!"

Everyone in the crowded room but Ki, and of course the dead woman, laughed. Ki murmured, "*Watasi mo ikitai desu!*" Only to hear Lone Star laugh and trill, "*Nandemo nai koto desu,*" before casually adding in Spanish that she'd be all right as long as he behaved himself too.

She'd wanted El Temperamento to follow her drift, or think he was following her drift. She explained, "He's afraid you might hurt me. I assured him I felt sure you were a gentle lover."

The rough-looking Mexican had her in the bedroom doorway by this time. He shoved her toward the four-poster across the room,

208

slammed the door shut, and bolted it after them as he declared, "*Si*, I am a great lover as well as fastidious, wise, and ferocious. Take off your clothes and let us see if you are blond all over, eh?"

She dimpled at him and said, "Ooh, you're so masterful! But what about your own things, *querido mio*?"

It worked. He hung his gunbelt on a wall hook before he took off his big sombrero. As he began to unbutton his elaborately buttoned *charro* outfit, she began by tossing her own hat aside and shucking her thin silk shirt to inspire him with her proud bare breasts, hoping that would allow her to stall a bit with the waistband of her heavier cover from the waist down. She sat on the edge of the bed in her split skirt to cross a booted ankle over an exposed knee, making a pretense of really removing it as she casually asked, "Will we have the time to really know one another before you must ride on, *querido mio*? You said something before about rounding up that herd when this stormy but romantic night dies with the dawn."

The young and healthy border ruffian looked as if he was about to start drooling as he tore at his own leather outfit, assuring her, "We got plenty time for to fuck, if ever I get out of these fucking *chaparajos*! Don't worry about those *vacas* and our troubles down in Chihuahua. Just think about *nosotros y nuestro noche del gusto*, eh?"

She said, "Oh, you're so *romantico*. But I *do* worry about you, now that we've become so close. What kind of trouble are you in down Mexico way?"

He'd already shucked his own boots, jacket, and shirt. As he dropped his pants and gunbarrel chaps together, she saw how much trouble *she* might be in as he turned to face her, hairy of belly, stiff as a poker, and badly in need of a bath. She licked her lips and said, "Ooh, is all that meant for little old me? Be a good boy and help me get these damned boots off, won't you?"

He moved closer, smelling like sweaty goatskins, growling, "Just take off that damned *falda* and give me what I got to have! I got to have some hot *succion* for to start, and then I got to come in you right!"

"I can't get this heavy skirt off over my spurs, can I?" she pleaded, adding in an imploring tone, "*Prisa!* I'm even hotter than you are."

He laughed. "No, you are not. Is impossible." He reached down for one booted ankle. Then, since there was only one sensible way to help any pal out of a high-heeled riding boot, he turned his hairy bare behind to her, and bent over with her boot held in both hands between his bare knees as he muttered, "Be careful with that boot heel, *gringa linda!*"

She was. It would have seemed rude to shove a boot heel up his rectum as they worked together to remove her boot, with her other boot shoving him from behind.

That is, it seemed to *him* they were working together. Her boot would have slipped off easily had she not bunched her toes under so hard. He grunted, growling, "*Caramba!* How did you ever get into such tight boots?"

She said, "They're damp and my feet must be swollen from walking so much earlier. Who's after you in Chihuahua, *los rurales*? We heard those cows had been stolen down yonder."

He grunted, "*Los rurales?* I spit on *los rurales* and your *estupidos* Texas Rangers as well. Was deal gone wrong. A, how you say, Indian giver who made *estupido* mistake and now we got to put things right or fight *muchachos* tougher than any Rangers or *rurales*. What is going on here? For why won't this boot come off? Are you trying for to be funny with El Temperamento, *gringa*?"

She told him to try harder, then let him get the boot off. He still seemed sore. He really did have a quick and nasty temper. So she let him get the other boot off. Then she rose to stand close to his naked flesh, her own bare breasts heaving as she smiled brazenly and slowly, deliberately, slithered her split skirt down and then down some more, allowing him to feast his eyes on her firm but softly rounded belly and lamplight-gilded body hair.

Then she killed him with a single *genkotsu* thrust to the vulnerable pressure point where most men parted their mustaches. It was dangerous to both parties in that a strong man who wasn't hit there just right could wind up more enraged than dazed. But of course she hit him just right, to spread-eagle him across the bed with his shattered nasal septum driven up into his brain like the bony spike her blow had been intended to make of it.

As she quickly put her boots and shirt back on, Lone Star called out, "Oh, no! It's too big! I can't take it back *there*! Not *all* of it back there, you brute!"

She couldn't tell how her act was being received until she yelled louder, with her own ear closer to the door still barred on her side, "Oh, my God, you *did* get it in, that way, and I *love* it! Do it deeper! Harder! If you don't treat me right I'm just going to *mado kara tobidasu!*"

Outside, someone else marveled, "Oh, that *muchacho travieso*! He's got her going out of her blond head with that *palo furioso* of his, eh?"

Everyone but Ki laughed, and Ki was grinning like a Cheshire cat. For what Lone Star had moaned in her mock passion had been that she was about to depart the premises by way of the nearest window. Ki hadn't needed further explanation. He'd assumed that poor Mexican chump was in a whole heap of trouble from the moment she'd gone into that Southwestern belle act. In telling him she was ready for the next phase, she'd naturally meant *he* was supposed to get cracking as well. So Ki stepped away from the corner he'd been lounging upright in to announce he had to take a piss. When nobody seemed to be listening, Ki shrugged, unbuttoned his fly to haul out his pisser, and really would have pissed right there had not one of the Mexicans gasped, "Not in here with us, you disgusting Chino! Pablo, go with him to the back door. Make sure he clears the steps and shoot him if he tries anything else, eh?"

A scrawny, somewhat older Mex with a parrot nose and a nice silver-mounted Remington .44-40 got to his own feet, drawing the side arm as he nodded at Ki and said, "*Vamanos*, Chino. Listening to El Temperamento in there with that *puta* has me thinking about my own *vejiga* too. Maybe we hold one another's *tubos* for to aim right, no?"

Ki said, "*Prisa!* My back teeth are starting to float!" He turned away to head for the kitchen at an undignified pace.

The older Mex went after him, demanding, "Not so fast! I mean it!"

Ki made it to the back door on the far side of the dark kitchen, and threw it wide open to the rain as Pablo caught up with him and kept going, end-over-end, to land flat on his back, too stunned to scream, five yards out in the darkness. Then Ki sprang silently from the back steps to land with one foot in the rain-lashed mud and the other planted in Pablo's throat, which gave with an explosive pop just a tad too soft to be heard inside the house.

The hip throw alone had sent Pablo and hence Ki too far from the back door to be easily seen from inside. Still, Ki dragged the corpse to one side by its heels before he helped himself to Pablo's gunbelt. It took a few seconds longer to locate that nice .44-40 in the mud. Then Ki was on his way through the rain, armed and dangerous again. He caught up with Lone Star on the far side of the corral, where she already had their own four ponies ready to go, although sheltered under that shed roof while they waited. She was armed and dangerous too. El Temperamento had taken her birthday gun as well as her to bed with him, or so he'd planned. As Ki joined her she asked, "What kept you?"

He turned his back to her as he finished that delayed urination, saying, "I don't enjoy your advantages when it comes to luring men to their doom. I take it El Temperamento was lured to his doom?"

She answered simply, "*Hai*, it was the least I could do for that poor Caddo girl. If you're about finished, could we get the blazes out of here now?"

As they both heard shouting from the direction of the house Ki hastily rebuttoned his fly, saying, "We'd better. I don't know which of those poor *yaban na* bastards they're yelling about, but they sound sore as hell."

★

Chapter 20

The same summer gullywasher had caught Longarm and Kentucky Bob on open range a long way from anywhere. They'd donned their oilcloth slickers, of course, but they'd still gotten mighty soggy by the time they made it to the older man's Lazy S spread around four in the morning.

Someone inside the sprawling main house lit a lantern as they rode in, old Bob bawling like a milk cow with a teat caught on glidden-wire. But as a Mex kid in cotton pants and rope sandals took the reins of their mounts, the two of them stomped into the kitchen and were greeted by an enormous colored mammy. She declared she'd be proud to rustle up some coffee and grub for them but that, no, Miss Billie and the boys hadn't come back yet.

As they peeled out of their soggy slickers, old Bob sounding mighty anguished, their cook said soothingly, "She's all safe and sound, Marse Bob. Jesus Garcia came in hours ago, nursing his buckshot left leg, to say Miss Billie and the others meant to shelter with Marse Roy at the Matanza spread."

As she bustled at the stove, shoving fresh-split cedar in the fire box, her boss demanded, "How bad was Soos hurt, and how come that fool girl's spending the night with Roy Matanza? He's old enough to be *my* father, and half-greaser besides!"

The black mammy, as if oblivious to the racial slur, said, "Now, Marse Bob, the girl-child has plenty of Lazy S hands nearby lest any of them fool Mexicans trifle with her. Jesus Garcia's got a tetch of fever, but we got the pellets out and poulticed him good with wasp-nest paper and vinegar. So his leg will doubtless heal in the Lord's own good time."

They hung up their slickers, hats, and while they were at it, damp frock coats. As the cook warmed a monstrous speckleware coffeepot and greased a big skillet, she explained how Miss Billie and the others meant to round up the scattered cows after things got brighter and drier. She said, "Jesus Garcia said the herd those trashy Graysons mavericked on you all stampeded just as Miss Billie and the boys was fixing to maverick 'em back. A couple of other boys on our side got winged, but nobody got hit bad as that Rafe Grayson, I'll warrant."

Kentucky Bob grinned and sat down at the table, saying, "Hot damn. Rafe would be my first choice if I was allowed to smoke up smoke-up artists. Who winged him and how bad, Mammy?"

The cook said, "One of Marse Roy Matanza's vaqueros shot him dead, right off his pony, with a Winchester bullet betwixt his mean eyes. Jesus Garcia said Alvin Grayson might have been hit too. Rafe is the only one kilt dead for certain. Come morning, if this rain's blown over, Miss Billie and the other decent folk mean to bunch and cut the herd the way you and Marse Roy Matanza intended in the beginning."

By this time Longarm had quietly taken a seat at the same unpainted kitchen table. He felt like another smoke, but didn't think he'd better, this low on cheroots this far from town. Kentucky Bob seemed to savvy what had inspired that curious look when Roy Matanza's name had come up yet again. He explained, "Like I told you before, old Roy's more a mover and shaker than a cattle cuss like me. He's got a fairly fancy townhouse, with a rose garden, in Austin. The cattle spread that fool girl of mine is at right now is little more than a damned old Tex-Mex *jacale*, and it'll serve Billie right if she gets et alive by bedbugs and rained on through the brush roof."

Longarm didn't seem to care about that part. So Kentucky Bob said, "Be that as it may. Old Roy keeps a few head grazing out here in these hills with a few poor relations watching over 'em. Me, my own hands, and some other more serious neighbors keep an eye on old Roy's stock as it grazes mixed with our own. He hires extra help at roundup time to pull his fair share as the increase is tallied, docked, and branded. But to tell the truth, his beef operation was marginal until recent, and I feel sort of guilty for talking him into . . . well, what I talked him into, damn those thieving Graysons!"

The big black woman started busting blue eggs into her big greased skillet. Longarm knew she hadn't robbed a mighty big robin. Spanish hens from Majorca laid eggs just as blue, for some fool reason. He asked Kentucky Bob to go on about their Spanish-speaking neighbors, and the older Anglo confessed, "I talked him into investing money, real money, in that Mex beef the Grayson boys run off on us."

Longarm smiled thinly and asked, "Don't you mean after some-one run 'em off some *rancho grande* down Mexico way?"

The older man glowered and pouted, "There you go sounding like my infernal lawyer in Austin again! Like I tried to tell him in vain, the sissy bastard, there was more to the deal than sim-ply paying some fool greasers to steal greaser cows and sort of lose 'em in a Texas draw. Maybe nobody paid no import export duties as they sort of drifted up this way. Maybe nobody saw fit to pester Texas or the U.S. Agriculture boys to examine such furrin cows for hoof-and-mouth or blackwater. But they was nev-er *stole* down Chihuahua way. They was *swapped* for, fair and square and head for head, brand inspections being more casual down Chihuahua way."

What he'd said made no sense at face value. Longarm studied the big plate of scrambled eggs Mammy served him along with a steaming mug of bitter black coffee, strong enough to wake Abe Lincoln if only he'd been willing to try some.

Majorca eggs were as yellow inside as any other, and she'd salted them just right. As they dug into their pre-dawn breakfast, Longarm chewed on what the older man had just told him too. Since they'd both been country-bred, they polished off their grub without bullshitting. Then, over coffee and a swell peach cobbler Mammy had been saving as a surprise, Longarm decided, "I'm missing something. You say you and Roy Matanza went halves on a herd of beef with unclear title but not truly stolen goods?"

Kentucky Bob looked sheepish and said, "Me and mine sup-plied the, ah, expertise. Old Roy put up most of the *dinero* and did most of the talking, once I'd introduced him to some semi-domesticated vaqueros I'd bought a head here and a head there off in the past. The deal we made with 'em, this time, was for a really big herd, worth our time and trouble with the price of beef climbing back East."

"And Roy Matanza's ice machine's a part of the big deal?" Longarm demanded, one eyebrow raised.

The old stockman shook his head and answered, "Nope. Beef is beef and ice is ice, far as I've ever heard. We only meant to hold that scrawny desert-riz herd on good Texas grass and water long enough to get some increase or, hell, sell it in the fall in whatever condition, the usual way, at the Austin auction yards. I don't see what you and my fool lawyer find so complicated. Ain't you never heard of buying cheap and selling dear?"

Lonarm nodded soberly and replied, "It's the American way. Meanwhile, cows cost much less down Mexico way than in, say, Baltimore or Boston. But not *that* much less, unless you get 'em for next to nothing. It costs to drive cows, even on free grass, with cow hands that require a dollar a day and all the beans they can eat. So let's see now, the last Mex beef prices I heard quoted . . ."

"I told you the greasers herding them cows up our way got 'em for next to nothing, or to be exact, a head-for-head swap."

Longarm sipped some coffee to clear the damp cobwebs. "So you did. And the only way that works sounds like another way to run a crooked cattle operation I thought we'd cleaned up a spell back!"

He swallowed some more and explained, "The original Laredo Loop involved American beef being moved to distant range and brand inspection by way of the Chihuahua-Sonora dry country."

"Indian country too," observed the older man. "Yaqui as well as Apache, to hear tell."

Longarm frowned. "Forget the Laredo Loop. We busted it up. It sounds like the rascals you rascals were dealing with have a new angle. They run nice fat Texas cows down to the dry Mex range, swap 'em head for head with doubtless delighted Mexican *rancheros*, and drive scrawnier Mex cows north to be sold under shady but not downright criminal conditions! There'd be no profit, and in point of fact a net loss if anyone wanted to swap fat lawfully obtained longhorns for Mex scrub. But as soon as one considers the price thieves pay for *stolen* longhorns, it all falls neatly into place."

Kentucky Bob complained, "No, it don't. The infernal Grayson boys went and stole them cows from us afore we could claim title to 'em under the maverick laws."

"We're jawing in circles," Longarm said. "I told you on the way out here that I was never sent out after stolen cows. You and your own kith and kin seem to be licking that other outfit disputing your claim to those stray cows I doubt anyone's reported stolen. So all I got to do now is track down those *other* folks I told you about, tell 'em what I strongly suspicion happened to their own West Texas herd, and let them and the Rangers deal with it."

As he drained his cup he added ominously, half to himself, "I know one cat-eyed lying Mexican who'd best have some answers or a mighty fast pony. I'd hate to think he lied flat out to me. So let's hope it was some sort of mix-up."

Sanford asked who they were talking about. It wouldn't have been nice to talk about El Gato before he was certain he'd been lied to, so Longarm replied, "Nobody important. Like I said, the Rangers can worry about it and, no offense, I'd like to get an early start if the sun ever rises in these parts again."

So Kentucky Bob rose, told Longarm to tag along, and led the way to a spartan but clean and comfortable guest room at the far end of the rambling 'dobe.

As soon as he was alone behind a stout barred door, Longarm shucked his damp duds and trimmed the oil lamp to catch some shut-eye. He hadn't known how wary-eyed he'd been feeling till he got to shut both eyes behind a locked door with the rain drumming on the roof above, which knocked him out despite that black coffee.

Then a damned old rooster was bragging about something, likely blue eggs, and Longarm woke bright-eyed and coffee-jangled to see sunlight grinning through the shutters at him. So he propped himself up on one elbow and fumbled for the pocket watch he'd left chained to his derringer atop the bed table. When he saw he'd lain slugabed close to two whole hours, he swung his bare feet to the rug and proceeded to get dressed, cussing softly but sincerely.

He found nobody else up and about as he left the guest room and found his way back to that kitchen, gummy-eyed and flannel-mouthed. But cold black coffee and some stale but mighty sweet marble cake he rustled up restored him to more human feelings, and he was ready to ride on.

He couldn't ask for that extra pack pony with the owner of the spread still bedded down. But the sleepy young Caddo he found in the stable helped him saddle that livery mule, and offered detailed directions to the Grayson spread. They both agreed that with a full-scale range war in progress, his best bet would be a beeline for the Pedernales, followed by a discreet ride along the wooded riverbanks to where the draw the Graysons had claimed emptied into the main stream. The short but neighborly exchange cost Longarm one of his last cheroots. He knew some others of his kind held one didn't have to be that nice to Indians, but his folks had raised him by the Golden Rule, as modified by the facts of a hard country life. The Caddo kid had met him halfway. So he owed the Caddo a favor instead of a bullet in the head. It was as simple as that.

Anyway, he'd been telling himself he ought to cut down on his smoking.

He lit both their smokes on the same wax-stemmed Mexican match, mounted the Spanish mule, and headed north. The range smelled like a new straw hat drying out after a summer shower, and somewhere a horned lark was singing its bitty heart out. So all seemed right with the world for the first few miles. Then the sun was a tad higher, that damp straw smell was turning to dusty hayloft, and Longarm peeled off his frock coat to latigo to his bedroll, muttering, "I'm sorry as hell about this, mule. But we got us a long way to travel no matter how hot it gets."

The mule couldn't answer. But it didn't have to. He was glad it wasn't a real horse as the morning kept heating up. But infernal mules made up for their superior endurance by being stubborn as, well, mules. Longarm seldom wore spurs, for the same reasons that he favored low-heeled army boots a body could move faster in on his feet. So he could only kick with his heels and lash with the rein ends as, every time they passed through any shade at all, the damned mule just stopped and brayed for mercy.

A lesser man might have had to offer some. The white-hot sunlight made it feel like they were out to cremate themselves alive in a blast furnace every time they crossed an open windless draw. Longarm was just big enough, and his drumming heels hung down just far enough, to keep the poor sweaty critter going.

Then things got even less pleasant. The mule commenced to shy and roll its Spanish eyes as they started passing dead, dying, or mighty unhappy cows. Longarm tethered his mount to some mesquite and moved in afoot for a closer look the first time they met up with an already flyblown longhorn near the bottom of a rise. It only took him a few moments to determine the poor brute had been hit in its near hindquarter and the paunch, doubtless by stray rounds. Nobody would have slaughtered beef so slowly and painfully on

218

purpose. The cow had been hit by cross-fire and strayed out this way to lie down and die.

After he'd examined another couple of dead cows, and a cow pony sprawled atop a rise with saddle and bridle still in place, he just rode on past other widely scattered casualties, explaining to his own mount, "That late night shootout sure scattered that disputed herd to hell and gone. It's going to take the better part of a week to round 'em all back up no matter *who* won!"

Then, as they topped yet another timbered rise, a chongo-horned calico cow came charging at them out of some cedar, red of eye and out for blood. So Longarm shot it with his pistol, more than once, because he'd have never managed had he tried to get his Winchester out of its boot in the time the loco had given him to work with.

Three head shots had done it. As he circled the downed brute on his mule, he saw it had been gut-shot earlier. He sighed and said, "I'm sorry I said you were loco, ma'am. That earlier round must have really thrown you off your feed, and you had every right to feel grumpy this morning."

He rode on, reloading. It seemed he'd no sooner done so before they encountered another riderless as well as shot-up cow pony.

This one was still alive, if that was how one could define pure misery in motion. As if recognizing the human figure aboard another riding mount as a possible savior, the badly hurt little mare, a roan with a pretty white blaze, whinnied soulfully and tried to trot to meet them, holding its one shattered hoof up under it.

The rifle round that had mangled its near forehoof so untreatably was the least of the poor mare's problems. She'd taken two more rounds in her innards. Her lungs still seemed to be working, but she was dribbling blood and crud down both hind legs. As they met on an open grassy slope the shot-up pony seemed to plead for him to do something for her with her big soft eyes. So Longarm nodded, got a good grip on the reins of his own mount, and had the muzzle of his .44-40 almost touching the velvety depression just above the hurt pony's big sad eye before he pulled the trigger.

By the time he'd steadied his own mount enough to look back, he could see the one he'd gunned had already stopped twitching. So he rode on, reloading, as he muttered, "There ought to be a way to keep horses, women, and children out of gunfights. They all look so bewildered when they're hit by cross-fire, and they always are, no matter how careful the rest of us try to be."

It only got hotter as they forged northward toward the tree-lined Pedernales, if the son-of-a-bitching river was really up ahead amid these literally infernal hills. They stopped longer, more often, when they came to merciful patches of shade. They'd had to share many a clump of live oak with a panting cow, and in one case a jaded but otherwise unhurt cow pony. Longarm relieved it of its bridle and saddle, and from the way it nickered and nuzzled him, it wanted to offer a grateful screw in return. But he told it he was hung too modest, while his mule just wasn't meant for such pleasures. He added, "Our main reason for lingering here in the shade with you concerns our back trail, ma'am. Last night we seemed to have somebody tailing us. We may have lost him by taking some unexpected turns on him in the rainsome dark. He may have been discouraged by a lightning bolt. In any case, nobody seems to be tailing us now."

He still kept an eye on their back trail until, with the sun lashing down from just about the dead center of the cloudless cobalt sky, they topped yet another east-west rise to spy the pretty Pedernales running cool and muddy at high water from wooded bank to bank as it tried to rid the Hill Country of all that recent runoff. Longarm had to really haul back on the reins as his mount smelled all that sweet water and tried for a running dive into the wide but shallow river.

Once he'd stopped them amid some peach willow and choke-cherry growing out of ankle-deep water at this flood stage, he let the thirsty mule inhale as much of the Pedernales as it wanted, knowing that unlike hounds and horses, cat and mules had sense enough to stop before they'd made themselves sick. The swiftly running water tempted him to stick *his* head in it as well. But he contented himself with staring upstream and down as his mule drank, musing to them both, out loud, "Streams in dry country tend to get quicksandy at times like these. I reckon we'd best mosey west a ways and see if there's any signs to indicate a safe ford."

There was. Less than two furlongs up the south bank they came to what seemed a game trail or pony trace leading down the bank right into the swirling tawny water. Longarm heeled his mount that way, braced for as much sudden swimming as the Pedernales might surprise them with. But in point of fact the water never got much more than stirrup deep, and then they were up the far bank, trending on westward through willow, cherry, and cottonwood, the roots of live oak and cedar drowning in often-soggy soil.

But by now it felt too hot and sultry to go on, shade or no shade, so Longarm reined in near a fallen cottonwood and declared, "Siesta time, Señor Mulo. I'll stuff my face and clean my gun whilst you browse yummy cottonwood leaves and that son-of-a-bitching sun works its way down the sky a ways, hear?"

The mule was in no position to argue. Longarm dismounted, watered it again at the river's edge, then tethered it amid cottonwood saplings before he broke out some baked beans and tomato preserves for his own noon meal, seated low but comfortable on that fallen cottonwood.

Canned pork and beans went down just as well cold from the can. The tomato preserves he swilled from that second can served to clean the pork grease off his teeth, and would hopefully keep him from farting too much later. Then he lit his last cheroot, and spread a pocket kerchief on the dirt between his boots to keep the innards of his .44-40 from getting lost or gritty as he proceeded to strip it, bent over at the waist with his elbows resting on his knees.

Taking one's gun apart and cleaning it was a tedious chore. A lot of old boys, including army regulars and train robbers, tended to put it off a day or more after shooting up livestock or anything else. But a lot of old boys wound up with fouled weapons at embarrassing times. The black powder of his .44-40 rounds left a disgusting amount of soot in the barrel, and if one gave it time, it could set like stove blacking. So seeing that he had the time and nothing more amusing to do without unbuttoning his fly, he removed the Colt's cylinder and set it on the kerchief with all six chambers empty. Then he popped open the little leather cleaning kit from his saddlebag, and broke out a small container of naptha and a clean linen patch already strung on a length of stout fishing line with a common brass furniture brad tied to the other end.

He used a brass brad because he knew brass couldn't scratch the steel lining of his gun barrel. Once he'd dropped the brad-weighted line through the barrel, it was a simple matter to haul the tight-fitting naptha-soaked patch through. It came out the other end dirty as hell.

He repeated the procedure till he was able to draw a fresh patch through without picking up the least bit of gunpowder grime. He

221

put that patch aside to use another time, brass brad and all. For he had yet another length of weighted line prepared for oiling the cleaned but now vulnerable barrel. Spermaceti whale oil, the kind one got from whales like Moby Dick in that swell book, was the very best gun oil one could buy. That was why Longarm bought it. A man could get by on modestly priced tobacco, and it wouldn't kill you if you wore socks till they wore out, but a man who depended on his gun to keep him alive treated his gun decently if he had any sense worth mentioning.

Putting the cleaned and oiled main frame aside, Longarm picked up the cylinder to clean as well. It was easier to run the patches through the shorter chambers with a pencil, eraser end first. He had his .44-40 cleaned and oiled, but still disassembled, when someone else with a gun cocked its hammer with an ominous click behind him and close.

Longarm tried to ignore the way the hairs on the back of his neck were acting as, staring soberly the other way, he quietly called out, "Let me guess. You asked at the Sanford place, and that Caddo kid told you I'd be beelining for the Pedernales with a view to following it upstream along this far bank. So you rode wider but faster, not having to study your own back trail, to spot me from this side as I forded in broad-ass day like a big-ass bird, right?"

An all-too-familiar male voice replied, "That's about the size of it. What else have you guessed, seeing you're so all-fired smart?"

Hoping the gun for hire wouldn't want to gun anyone before he'd learned all he could for the other side, Longarm left his disassembled gun at his feet and slowly turned on the fallen cottonwood to smile sheepishly at the black-suited cuss he'd been calling Ed MacIntosh. He said, "You must have intercepted that wire I sent the Secret Service about you. No offense, but when old Allan Pinkerton started the U.S. Secret Service during the war, he mostly recruited healthy clean-living college boys and, well, you just didn't strike me as a college boy. What did you do to the real Ed MacIntosh? We both know there had to have been a real Ed MacIntosh, right?"

The fake MacIntosh, covering Longarm from just too close to miss and just too far to jump, chuckled fondly down at his victim. "I didn't pick up his badge and identification in any pawnshop, and Washington might not have been so anxious to keep me posted by wire if I'd been using my real name."

"What name might that be, pard?" asked Longarm, as pleasantly.

The mock MacIntosh shook his head, politely enough, and said, "We haven't time to talk about me. As you've likely figured already, you've been a dead man since you let me get the drop on you. But I do like to wind things neatly up, and to tell the pure truth, the boss finds you mighty confusing, old son."

Longarm said, dryly, "That makes us even. Your Mister King Kellog sure moves in mysterious ways, but let's see if we can sort some of it out for the both of us. I told you true, back in town, neither the real Ed MacIntosh nor myself were after anything more sinister than some missing furniture and—oh, shit, were you telling me the truth about that desk being on its way to the President at last?"

The paid assassin who'd been reading Secret Service dispatches shrugged. "Why would I lie? My boss ain't interested in furniture. As you've doubtless guessed, we took Ed MacIntosh out before we had the least notion what he might be up to. Mister, ah, Kellog liked to shit when we learned *you* were on your way here as well. It was my own grand notion to postpone your execution and see if you had any answers to some otherwise mighty unfathomable wires addressed to your fellow federal agent from Galveston."

Longarm nodded knowingly and said, "That's how come you backshot one of your own, ah, subcontractors before he could backshoot me near that warehouse that time. What did your King Kellog say when you got to tell him we were only after misdirected furniture, not him?"

The mock MacIntosh chuckled. "He was greatly relieved. I reckon it's safe to allow you've guessed right on a few things, seeing how unlikely it is you'll ever tell the Rangers on us."

His gun muzzle was rising even as he spoke. Longarm said, "Hold on, let's see what else I can guess. It ain't as if you ain't got time to kill, as well as me. It's too blamed hot to ride and, well, *I* ain't in no hurry neither."

The gun for hire chuckled in a surprisingly boyish way. "I admire a man who can keep his eyes and pants dry as he pays his respects to the last sunshine he'll ever see. They say the great Davy Crockett wept and begged for mercy when the greasers stood him agin that wall down San Antone way, and I'll bet Custer just bawled like a girl-child at Little Bighorn."

Longarm shrugged. "I wasn't at either place to witness either dolorous death. You're figuring on gut-shooting me, ain't you?"

The killer with the drop on him nodded soberly and said, "It's more fun that way when there's time, and speaking of time . . ."

"Just one more thing I'd like to clear up." Longarm said, adding, "It can't hurt you or your King Kellog if I die knowing just a few bitty answers, can it?"

The mock MacIntosh said, "You're trying to buy more time. But go ahead, for all the good it'll do you, and someday I'll get to tell some admiring cunt how I made the great Longarm beg for just a few more minutes."

Longarm said, "You're just too softhearted for your own good. Call this begging if you like and try her this way. Your King Kellog made a kingly business deal he thought me and poor Ed MacIntosh had been sent to look into. You killed the Secret Service man before you discovered your error. When you found out what I was really doing in these parts, your mastermind decided it made more sense to let me live at first."

He shifted his seat on the fallen cottonwood to face the killer more squarely as he continued. "He figured, correctly, there'd be enough of a fuss when Uncle Sam noticed he was missing a Secret Service agent. I seemed to be barking up a whole forest of wrong trees so . . . When did I change someone's mind by sniffing right? It couldn't have been my snipe hunt through Roy Matanza's plant by the rail siding. Three reasons. I found nothing incriminating anyone there. You could have gunned my unsuspecting back, going in or out, if there had been anything there your King Kellog wanted nobody to know about. And lastly, you told your lesser gun waddies they were working for a King Kellog, knowing that should any of 'em talk to somebody half as smart as me, King Kellog could be translated from old English to modern Spanish as Roy, or Rey, Matanza."

The professional training a sixgun his way smiled thinly down at him. "They warned us you were good. I'm glad you've lived up to your rep. It ain't every day a man in my line of work gets to murder a real man."

He meant it. Longarm knew just how he meant it. So he rolled sideways as he fired his palmed derringer, and even so, it was close. For the killer fired, thrice, smack through the space Longarm had been just a split second earlier. Then as Longarm watched from flat on his gut behind the fallen cottonwood, the mock MacIntosh buckled at the knees, jackknifed at the waist, and wound up facedown in the dappled shade with his face buried in the crown of his black hat and what looked like a silver sheriff's badge imbedded edgeways in the back of his skull.

Longarm regarded the familiar steel *shuriken* for a long unwinking moment. Then he called out, "He's dead as he means to get now, Jessie. Come out, come out, wherever you are, honey."

Then he sprang to his own feet as, sure enough, Lone Star busted out of some chokecherry to come running, arms spread and eyes brimming, to crash into him and bear-hug him breathless as he hugged her back as hard, sighing, "I wish you'd let me do things *my* way, doll face. I aimed a tad low deliberate, hoping for some last words, and now look what you've done with your Japan Land toys!"

She gripped his buttocks, grinding her pelvis hard against his as she replied, "Pooh, you damned near got your fool self gut-shot. Weren't you paying any attention to that sadistic rascal as he set out to ruin my day completely?"

Longarm laughed and let her go so he could reload his little belly gun, observing, "Aw, I was covering him with this peashooter, palmed. I usually get my derringer out and set it near to hand, unsnapped from my watch chain, whenever I take my more serious shooting irons apart."

He slipped the derringer back in his vest for now as they both moved closer to the victim of their combined marksmanship. She naturally asked, "Who was he and what on earth are you doing down our way? I only heard a part of what the two of you were saying, once I recognized your voice from afar and moved in for a discreet peek at the proceedings."

He hunkered down to go through the dead man's pockets as he told her, "I've been looking for *you*. I'm still working on what this jasper's boss suspected I was looking for. My own tale is tangled, so you'd best go first, starting with where Ki might be."

She called out *"Anata wa doko ni imasu ka?"* in a louder tone, and then explained, "Just upstream, with our ponies. We'd stopped for a trail break and I was, you know, in the bushes, when I heard you and this animal in the distance. Ki speaks Comanche birdsong as well as Japanese, so I tweeted for him to stay put and . . . Is that a federal badge you've found on that killer, dear?"

Longarm put the real Secret Service agent's badge in a hip pocket for safe keeping as he growled, "Yep. The bastards killed a poor cuss called MacIntosh for no good reason at all. You were right about this one enjoying his work, the two-faced son of a . . . Howdy, Ki."

The tall Asian-American, moving Comanche-style to join them, put his own sixgun away as he took in the scene at a glance. Ki said, "Howdy yourself, and life sure seems filled with surprises. The ponies are tethered within easy reach, Jessie. I heard the gunshots. He needed that *shuriken* too?"

Lone Star dropped to one knee to take back her throwing star, twisting just enough to free the two points imbedded in bone and brain tissue, and wiping them fastidiously with the tail of the dead man's frock coat before she removed her hat to pin the *shuriken* back in place.

Longarm explained to Ki, "She thought he had the drop on me. He was a hired gun. They called him off when it looked like I was getting cold. Then they sent him after me some more when it looked as if I might be getting warm. But I'll be switched with snakes if I can make out what they were worried about. I was looking for the two of you. Now that I've found you, I still can't see what they were afraid any of us knew about 'em."

When Lone Star rose, putting her dangerous hat back on, Longarm got to his own feet, deciding, "We've got time to sort things a heap betwixt now and the cooler riding after, say, three or four. Why don't you go first, Jessie? Like I said, my own tale's a mite confusing as well as silly."

Ki said he knew their own story already, and headed back to get their stock. Longarm sat Lone Star on that same cottonwood, between his tethered mule and the dead man, telling her to commence at the beginning, She did, and sticking to plain facts she knew for certain, had him about caught up by the time Ki returned, leading their saddle broncs and pack ponies. As Ki tethered them near Longarm's mule to browse the same cottonwood saplings he called out, "There's a nice-looking but long-in-the-tooth bay tied up farther off. Looks as if it could be a livery mount."

Longarm said it doubtless was and added, "It's only right that mysterious cuss should ride back to town aboard his own horse. He was only packing another dead man's identification, but mayhaps the Rangers have someone as ugly on file. I'm pretty sure he wasn't wanted federal. I suspect he and his mysterious King Kellog dealt the federal government in just because someone had a guilty conscience about something, damn 'em."

Lone Star and her *segundo* exchanged startled glances. She told Longarm, "We heard mention of some big cattle buyer called King Kellog, Custis!"

Ki nodded. "He was supposed to take some mavericked beef off the mavericking Grayson brothers, only something went wrong and he backed out."

Lone Star said, "I just told you about those Mexican riders who made even less sense. We really had to do some riding, and Lord knows how we'd have shaken them in that awful storm if that storm hadn't been so awful. We failed to find one Circle Star cow in anyone's possession around here. But that disputed herd did seem to be grazed and branded Chihuahua-style, and if your mysterious King Kellog thought Mexicans as well as federal lawmen were interested in that same herd . . ."

"A picture may be emerging from the mists," Longarm concluded. Then he said, "Both you kiddies pay close attention and try not to laugh as I approach it from my own angles."

Neither actually laughed, but both Lone Star and Ki got to grin a heap as Longarm covered the inane adventures of Queen Victoria's gracious gift to the colonies. Lone Star turned thumbs down on Ki's suggestions about their *tercero* back at the ranch. She said, "Pooh, the poor *tonto* could never support his family doing *that*, and as long as they finally got it all straightened out, let's worry about more serious problems, beginning with my own missing property!"

Longarm bent over and began to put his sixgun back together as she insisted, "We've all been on some sort of wild-goose chase here in this infernal Hill Country. You thought we knew something about that dumb missing desk, and we thought one side or the other knew something about my dumb missing cows. But all we've gotten for all our trouble is . . . well, trouble!"

Ki grumbled to Longarm, "At least you don't have to worry about that misdirected office furniture. Jessie and me don't even have an educated guess as to who might have taken all that Circle Star beef, or *where*!"

Longarm reholstered his reassembled .44-40 and got out the derringer to break open in turn as Lone Star said, "It's the where part I find most vexing. Saddle tramps are always running off cows, and with any luck they soon get run to earth. Someone always seems to notice, no matter which way you want to drive a herd that size. But since none of the good old boys I know have

227

spotted my cows going east, west, north, or south . . ."

"They went south," said Longarm flatly as he poked a naptha-soaked patch through the top barrel of the double derringer with his pencil.

The owner of the stock he'd just mentioned blinked at him and objected, "I don't see how they could have, Custis. Our mutual pal, El Gato, assured me nobody he knew had run any stolen Texican stock across the border, and El Gato knows most everyone in that line of work down Mexico way."

Longarm began to oil his ferocious little ace in the hole as he insisted, "El Gato lied or, seeing he's never lied to either of us before, somebody lied to *him*. The deal was supposed to work more subtle than that old Laredo Loop I must have told you about one time. The Texas Rangers are interested in stolen Texas stock. *Los rurales* further south are more interested in stolen Mex stock and even meaner than the Rangers when they catch some old boy running a Mex brand."

He snapped the bitty butt of his derringer back on his watch chain and made himself look innocent as ever across the vest as he continued. "Your stolen longhorns, prime beef critters one and all, were run south of the border and swapped, more or less head for head, or who cares when one's paid nothing, for that herd the Graysons mavericked and you stampeded all over creation, you noisy child."

Ki snapped his fingers and said, "I see it! *Los rurales*, as paid-up gringo haters, couldn't care less about Texas cows rebranded by a Chihuahua ranchero who no doubt votes faithfully for El Presidente Diaz."

Lone Star grimaced. "Campaign contributions count for more in a country where the elections are rigged well in advance. Suffice it to say, I see it too. A smaller, skinnier herd, still worth a good deal with beef prices so high this year, was supposed to be picked up at a nice profit to the original thieves and . . . Why all that nonsense about leaving such a big herd to be mavericked, Custis? Seems to me, if I wanted to unload that many head for a quick profit . . ."

"El Gato," Longarm answered, fumbling for another smoke but noting he was out of cheroots, damn it. "Thanks to past services to La Causa Libre by both you and your late dad, Jessie, old boys like El Gato disapprove of raiding Starbuck stock, and I'd sure hate to feel El Gato and his private army were sore at *me* if I was

Mex *ladrone* with a need for drinking money and little else to
ck my play. When your cows were stolen, El Gato naturally
ead the word. Just as naturally, the word he got back was that
body in Mexico with a lick of sense had even seen any cows
nded Circle Star. El Gato has pals of the Hispanic persuasion
both sides of the border. So the rascals delivering that herd all
vered with Mex brands couldn't deliver 'em personal, lest some
quero riding for, say, old Roy Matanza recognize 'em and—"

"Wait, where do those mean Grayson brothers fit in?" Lone
ar asked with a sincerely puzzled frown.

Longarm said, "As loose cannons on the deck, to the *original*
oks, of course. They hadn't made any deal with the crooks
o'd swapped your stolen herd for Mex cows they could sell
a tidy informal profit to Sanford, Matanza, and other smaller
ckmen. The mysterious mastermind we may as well go on call-
; Kellog found out about it. There were just too many in on it to
ep it secret. So he put the Grayson brothers up to mavericking
herd ahead of everyone else, with a view to selling all that
ef, cheap, to guess who."

Ki frowned. "But then this King Kellog backed out of the
al and . . . Oh, right, El Gato found out, the same way, and
ng Kellog crawfished before that gang of Mexicans showed up
. . . ?"

"El Temperamento couldn't have been any friend of that nice
Gato!" Lone Star interjected, firmly enough to all but stamp
r foot.

Longarm made a mental note to tell El Gato how nice he was,
owing it would piss the deliberately sinister young *maligno*,
d informed them both, "We had a border raider called El
mperamento on our yellow sheets as a plain old bandit. Try
r this way. Say El Gato and his less indecent bunch found out
ere your Circle Star stock really wound up. Say he informed
rtain rancheros, in that purry way he has, that they'd better get
ery damned one of those cows right back where they belonged,
co tiempo on pain of, well, some pain."

She nodded. "The big rancheros involved would threaten the
iginal cow thieves with as much or more pain, and they'd either
me north after stock to replace my stock or, failing that, send
even nastier gang, like the one we tangled with last night."

Ki glanced skyward through the flickering green leaves, mut-
ring, "This is all very interesting. But isn't all such speculation

a waste of time until we get some solid facts to build on?"

Longarm nodded, rose to put his gun-cleaning kit back abo[ut] his hired mule, and said, "Half a dozen telegrams hither and y[on] ought to do her. I got an old signal corps kit amongst my possib[les] as lets me splice into cross-country wires in a pinch. But West[ern] Union sure sends mean wires about me to Billy Vail wheneve[r] do that. So we may as well wait till we get back to Austin."

Lone Star's expression reminded him of a pretty tomboy fix[in'] to swipe some apples as she said, "Oh, goody. I can hardly w[ait] to get back to my hotel and, ah, a nice hot tub."

Ki looked away and said something about going to fetch [the] dead man's livery mount. For everyone there but the dead m[an] knew exactly what she'd be wanting, the moment she had Longa[rm] alone in her private suite at her very own hotel.

★

Chapter 21

was well after moonrise, and the sidewalks were being rolled
 for the night, by the time they made it back to Austin. But
e Ranger station near the railroad depot stayed open around
e clock, and Longarm felt the Rangers might prefer to regard
e corpse lashed across its own livery saddle before the county
orgue got it.

He'd guessed right. Their captain had gone home to his pretty
lex bride by now, but the desk sergeant in command had some
 his own boys haul the rascal right in and lay him out on the
le floor of their fancy new latrine. They said it was all right with
em if Lone Star wanted to come on back there too, seeing not
ven the dead man was leaking at this hour.

By the time Longarm had told the Rangers all he knew about the
adaver in the black wool suit, they were ahead of him. The desk
ergeant checked a manila folder an underling had gone out for
e moment Longarm had mentioned the real Agent MacIntosh.
anding the yellow sheets to Longarm, the sergeant said, "This
ne's previous alias was likely Meeker, Silas Meeker, also known
s One Lung. I say this because up until just now we had him
own as dead. I mean dead as of a few days ago. Bastrop County
shed his danged body out of the shallows this very morn. That
ig storm likely moved it from the original place of deposit. At
ny rate, Bastrop County identified the remains as those of this
ther One Lung Meeker, likely on account of it was wearing a

prison-release suit of soggy shoddy and packing the cheap billfo
and prison release of this other son of a . . . Sorry, ma'am."

Lone Star dimpled at the fatherly Ranger, and sweetly assur
him she'd thought Meeker was *acting* like a son of a bitch wh
she'd wound up with her throwing star.

When they got done laughing, Longarm said, "I'm glad the re
Ed MacIntosh will get a proper burial with a flag-draped box a
all, no thanks to this hired killer who killed him for little or
good reason."

By now Lone Star was fidgeting like a little kid in church wh
needed to take a pee but was afraid to ask. Longarm was as anxio
as she, and likely then some. He hadn't had a smoke for some tin
either. But duty was duty. So having sorted out the fake Secr
Service man and the real one sent on such a fool's errand, Longar
tersely told the Rangers about that range war they'd only witness
around the edges, and again the Rangers were ahead of him.

The sergeant explained, "We got all the survivors locked u
over to the county jail, where there was more room. I just to
you the captain has gone home for some well-earned rest. We g
early reports of stampeding cows and gunshot cowboys tearing a
over creation last night. So whilst you folk were having all that fu
up along the Pedernales, us Rangers were rounding up boistero
buckaroos, and some on both sides seem to be in serious troubl
Two of the Grayson brothers were killed, along with lesser ligh
on both sides, and both Jake Grayson and Miss Billie Sanfor
are in County General clinging to life by spiderwebs. Jake wa
hulled through the liver and spleen. If Miss Billie lives, it seen
highly unlikely she'll ever bear children or dance without limpir
again."

As the three newcomers exchanged thoughtful glances the Rang
er sergeant added, "Whether they live or die, they're both bein
held in high bail as the leaders who inspired so much bloodshe
for such a dumb cause. I'm still mighty puzzled as to how th
dead cuss at our feet fits in. If neither the Justice Department no
Secret Service was taking sides in that dumb dispute over Mexica
cows, why was Meeker here after either of you, and who was h
working for?"

Longarm sighed and said, "We've been working on that all th
way back to town. First we'd best get some Mex raiders out of th
way. These friends of mine found 'em out at the Grayson sprea
and—"

"We found 'em too." The Ranger sergeant said, smiling wolfish-. "To be more precise, we found some dead ones on or about the rayson property, along with the Grayson help they'd butchered. he ones who'd ridden after Miss Jessica here then veered off head on south. Never made it to the border as they'd likely lanned. We wired ahead and Comal County headed 'em off this fternoon south of San Marcos. They sure were dumb to resist rest like that. County posses don't have half the discipline of s Rangers, and we'd mentioned the women they'd murdered in ur all-points bulletin."

Longarm agreed it had been dumb of those border raiders to ver come north of the border. Then he nudged the body at their eet with a toe. "Be that as it may, I reckon all that confusion over ne final disposition of that Mexican herd inspired the mastermind nat this cuss and his underlings were working for to pull in his orns. The surviving Grayson brother may or may not know the ue identity of the mystery man who inspired the Graysons to naverick all that unclaimed beef before Kentucky Bob Sanford nd *his* faction could claim it. Meanwhile, knowing Miss Jessica nd Ki here were mighty interested in any disputes over cows, and nowing I was a pal who'd worked with them both before . . ."

"It's all too wheels-within-wheels to abide," Lone Star declared, rabbing Longarm's left elbow possessively as she added, "There's othing more to be said for certain before we have more facts to o on. Meanwhile, it's getting mighty late, and I surely wish omeone around here felt up to escorting a lady home for the ight!"

Hoping that wouldn't sound as forward to anyone else, Longarm atted the back of her hand and said he'd be proud to take her back her hotel on his way to Western Union.

They both knew he had no intention of wiring Billy Vail just et. But he'd had to say *something*. Ki followed them outside, urmuring to Lone Star in that dumb lingo he and Lone Star used talk sneaky. But before Longarm could get pissed, Lone Star miled at her *segundo* and murmured, "*Arigato. Asi wa aruku tame i arimasu.*" She quickly assured Longarm, "Ki's taking care of ne riding stock while we just get on over to the hotel afoot with o further care or delay, dear."

Longarm felt no call to argue. The hotel was only a pleasant troll from the Austin depot, and putting ponies away for the night ook time. He knew without asking that old Ki would store his

McClellan and possibles safely in the tack room of the hotel st. ble. There were times old Ki reminded him of that genius in t whale-oil lamp young Allan Dean had found over in Araby. I could look about as spooky, if he put his mind to it.

One of the nice things about owning a whole hotel was th nobody pestered you in the lobby and you got to just go on upstai without explaining anybody you might have tagging after yo Longarm still felt his ears blushing by the time they'd made t stairwell with nobody saying a word. But then they were windir on up through more romantic darkness, and Lone Star laughed ar called him a fool tomcat when he pinched her firm bottom to her her higher, faster.

Then they were up in her plush private suite, and someho across her four-poster with all their duds as well as the Ediso ceiling fixture still on. That situation didn't last long. The mo willing woman was impossible to screw in split skirts. They didn care about the bright lights beaming down on their naked flesh a they stripped for action. But even as he rolled her on her bac stark naked save for one sock, to settle into her sweet flesh so of sidesaddle, she asked if it might not be even nicer if they to a bath together first.

He proved it could be pretty damned nice all stinky from ha riding through thunderstorms and heat waves by simply shovir it where they both wanted it, hard as it could get. As their ba bellies met, with the turgid tip of his erection probing her inne most being, their pubic bones ground clock-and counterclockwis depending. Lone Star dug her nails into his bare buttocks ar pleaded, "Get both your legs between mine and quit teasing both, you brute!"

So he did, and once she had her ankles hooked over h collarbone, that one sort of lived-in sock brushing his right ea she quietly complained, "I've really been learning disgusting habi from you, Custis Long! Who was it taught you how exciting could be to rut all barnyard stinky like this?"

He tongued one shell-like ear, noting how salty it tasted, as l replied, "Napoleon. The first one, not that sissy who just lost tl war with Prussia. That Empress Josephine kept lots of letters tl first Napoleon wrote her, and he likely never figured they'd l read by anyone else."

Lone Star giggled, bit down harder on his no-doubt salty sha with her sweat-slicked vaginal opening, and marveled, "My Lor must smell like a codfish schooner becalmed in the tropics! What on earth could Napoleon and Josephine have to do with the way we're stinking up this hitherto fresh bedding?"

He said, "He wrote her from some battlefield, in high summer, he'd be back in Paris in three or four days, so she shouldn't bathe. I reckon *they* had fancy bedding too, and Lord knows the Empress of France could afford all the fancy soap and perfume she wanted. But that horny little Napoleon wanted to enjoy her natural, the way Eve must have stunk in the Garden before humankind got to feeling ashamed of their natural feelings. Have you ever noticed how stud horses sniff at pretty mares before they mount 'em, Jessie?"

She closed her eyes, firm naked breasts heaving in time with his thrusts, but protested, "You are not about to shove your fool nose in me down there, Custis Long! Not before I've enjoyed a good bath and a vinegar *kancho* first. Could you, ah, move a little faster, darling?"

He could and did, bringing them both to climax and resisting the temptation to just let go and die all over her as he gasped, "Kee-rist, that was swell, Jessie. What's a *kancho*?"

She giggled, tickling them both with her sweat-slicked nipples, and said, "I might have known you'd care. I was taught how to, ah, take care of myself by that motherly retired *geisha* Father brought back to care for me when I was little."

He cocked a brow and demanded, "She taught you to wash your sweet little love box out when you were little? What did she do for your daddy once she'd put *you* away for the night, you innocent child?"

She began to move her hips under him, experimentally, even as she demurely replied, "You might be right. Father was a widower with natural feelings, and he'd have felt even sillier jerking off. But for the record, the word *geisha* means an artist, not a whore. Japanese say *geijutsu* when referring to the fine arts."

Then she moved her strong horsewoman's limbs down to get them between his and grip his half-sated shaft in an almost painfully tight grip as she began to literally milk it with her amazingly skilled love-maw, murmuring, "My governess called this the *ingyo* position. Do you find it as exciting as I do?"

He laughed, and spread his knees wider to reply in kind as he responded, "Sure beats pissing, like they say back home. Them Jap notions you picked up from the household help have a whole

lot going for 'em, once you get over the odd notion that fuckin,
is a fine art."

She sniffed. "Don't be vulgar just 'cause I'm fucking you. Th
Japanese are not the only people in this world who find Quee
Victoria's current views on the subject bewildering. Nine tenths o
the human race, including many of our own, if only they'd admi
it, *do* consider fucking a fine art worth learning to do right."

He groaned, "You're sure doing it right, Lord love you! I'n
fixing to come in you some more and, damn it, I was lookin;
forward to keeping it in you all night!"

She clenched her own teeth, bit down harder with her toothles
parts, and moaned, "Me too. But who said anything about lettin;
you take it out, you adorable moose!"

★

Chapter 22

It was well after midnight when the man called Ki strolled into the dimly lit lobby of Travis County General. It had taken him some time to attend to his earlier chores at the hotel stable and Western Union. Unlike Longarm and Lone Star, the naturally fastidious Ki had taken a hot shower and changed his shirt in his own suite at the hotel, trying not to think about anyone doing anything else in the rooms above. But the ash-blond nursing sister on duty behind the admitting desk still shot Ki a wary look as he stepped into her circle of light, murmuring, "Good evening. They told me over at the Ranger station that Miss Billie Sanford was brought to this hospital earlier today suffering gunshot wounds."

Reassured by the tall dark stranger's reference to the Texas Rangers, the Texican blonde nodded soberly and replied, "She may be beyond further suffering anytime now. The surgeons have done all they can for her. She was gunshot indeed. So I fear it's in the hands of the Lord now. Her father is up there with her. Are you a friend of the family, sir?"

Ki said, "You might say Miss Billie and me are well-acquainted. I can't say I've ever met her father. They told me, over at the Ranger station, everyone involved in that big shootout had been arrested."

The nursing sister nodded. "Mister Sanford, the poor girl's father, was never involved. It's not for us here at County General to judge. But as we were given to understand it, the shooting began out on the range last night whilst he was here in town."

Ki nodded. "That's probably just as well for Miss Billie. *Someone* has to be free to bail her out, should she live. They said you had casualties on the other side here as well?"

The nursing sister nodded and confided, "Jake Grayson, not hurt as badly as Billie Sanford, but still in a bad way. May I ask which one you came to ask about in particular?"

Ki said he'd come to have a word with both, should that be possible. The pretty but sort of frosty blonde shook her starched cap primly and told him, "I fear that's out of the question. Visiting hours were over hours ago, sir."

Ki tried, "You said her father is with Miss Billie, even as we speak?"

The nursing sister sighed. "That's not quite the same. Doctor Miller left orders to let close kin up to her room, subject to quiet behavior, because to tell the sad truth, she may not be with us during the next regular visiting hours."

Ki nodded soberly. "I understand. In that case I'd best just have a few words with Miss Billie then."

"You don't know her father, yet you claim to be close kin?" the nursing sister demanded, dubiously.

Ki smiled sheepishly. "I'm not sure how I ought to put it. I can see you're a sophisticated young lady who knows more of life than your average schoolmarm."

The ash-blonde must have. She lowered her lashes and turned a most becoming shade of pink as she half-whispered, "Oh, I'd rather not know the details, if we're jawing about knowing a lady in the Biblical sense."

Ki purred, "I didn't come to gossip about her. I only wanted to see her before she breathes her last, ma'am."

So the understanding nursing sister dinged a desk bell, and told the younger but uglier young lady who responded to show Ki up to the dying girl's room.

Ki could see the once-imperious Bille Sanford was dying the moment he entered her room. The whole hospital reeked of pine oil and lye water, but he could still detect the stale cesspool odor of abdominal wounds. The brunette, now oddly shrunken, was alone in the room, propped up in bed with her eyes open but already glassy-looking. The nurse who'd brought Ki up the stairs and down the hall quickly moved over to the bed to feel Billie's throat. She sighed with relief and said, "She's still with us after all. I thought her father was supposed to be on death watch up here."

Ki said, "He's probably just stepped out for a smoke or a . . . you know. I'll keep her company till he gets back."

The ugly but otherwise pleasant little gal nodded, said to give a holler down the hallway if anyone died around there, and left Ki alone with the glassy-eyed Billie.

She tried to focus on him as he dragged the bentwood chair he found against the wall over by her bed. As he sat down beside her Billie croaked, "Lord, I'm so thirsty and they won't let me drink nothing, Daddy. Not even water, the sons of bitches! Please get me something to drink, Daddy. I'm so thirsty I could die!"

Ki softly replied, "That's what they're afraid you'd do if they let you have liquids right now, Billie."

He placed a gentle hand on her belly, feeling the drum-tight bandages through her top sheet and flannel night dress as he nodded more to himself than her, adding, "That Doctor Miller they mentioned seems to know his business. They'll doubtless let you have a sip at a time as they monitor your condition, Billie. You've got to go along with them and let them try to save you as best they can."

She complained, "I don't care if they save me. I want a drink of cool sweet lemonade. I could die content right now if only they'd let me have a glass or more of good old lemonade!"

Ki didn't think she needed to hear how painfully someone shot in the guts, more than once, could die with anything as acrid as lemonade adding to the confusion of their ruptured plumbing. He took one of her limp hands in his. Her flesh felt cold and clammy despite the warm night air. "Billie," he said, "they had to open you up and patch your, ah, innards with catgut after they'd cleaned things up in there as best they could. You won't be able to eat at all, and you're going to have to get by on a few sips of sugar water a day until some raw edges heal a mite, hear?"

The Asian-American's attempt at common sense, despite his pretty fair Texas twang, failed to sooth her as intended. She stared owl-eyed at him, protesting, "Gawd damn it, I'm just persishing for some lemonade and . . . Say, you ain't my daddy. You're that long-donging Chinee who run out on me just as I was commencing to enjoy it!"

Ki patted the back of her limp hand and said, "I'm glad you're starting to feel peppy again. I was starting to enjoy it too. But I had to get away, and it's a good thing I did. When you're all better we'll have a good laugh on those Grayson boys and some even meaner raiders I met up with, after leaving you. But that's not what I came to see you about."

She moved his hand to her lap, murmuring, "Is *this* what you come to see some more, you sweet screwing devil?"

Ki left his hand where it was, counting on the sheet and heavy hospital gown to prove innocent intent should anyone come in on them just now. He said, "We've time for that later, after you're really up to it, Billie. I wanted to ask you about those Mexican cows all of you seemed to take so seriously. Since last we spoke I've learned a hired gun called Meeker, or maybe he told you to call him MacIntosh, was mixed up some way with the rascal who masterminded that grab for those cows."

"Neither Meeker nor that other name means shit, and Jesus H. Christ, I'm so *thirsty*!" she said, trying to sit up.

Ki gently forced her back down. "Easy does it, honey. I'll get the nurse for you if you promise to lie still."

Then he heard something rip, and as the room filled with a ghastly sulfurous stench the gut-shot girl gasped, "No! Please, God, I wasn't ready for this yet!"

Then she fell back, limp as a discarded rag doll with some of its stuffing missing, a soft puzzled smile on her ashen face. Ki waved his free hand back and forth between the lamplight and her wide innocent stare. Then he muttered, "*Sayonara*," which can mean good-bye but literally translates as, "Since it must be so," before he turned away from the bed to fetch the nurse.

As he did so, a smaller, much older man, dressed cow and looking mighty worried, came in from the hallway with his side arm out and trained on Ki as he demanded, "What are you doing in my child's room at this hour, stranger?"

Ki kept his own hands polite as he soberly replied, "Call me Ki. She may have mentioned me. Either way, we were . . . friends. I'm sorry to say she seems to have died just now, Mister Sanford. I was on my way to fetch some help, just in case I'm wrong."

The older man gasped and let his gun drop to his side as he moved over to his daughter, sobbing, "Oh, no! She can't be dead! She was my only child! Everything I did was done for her and . . ."

Ki didn't hear the rest as he hurried out to scout up someone who might be able to prove him wrong. Like most men who'd taken part in more than one life-and-death struggle, Ki knew how tricky life and death could both get. He spied that ugly little nursing sister coming out of another room way down the hall. As he hurried her way she came running his way, even faster, and seemed less concerned about the rest of the patients as she bawled, "Somebody call the law! Mister Grayson in 208 is dead!"

As she reached him and might have run past him, Ki grabbed her and said soothingly, "Easy does it, ma'am. Lots of folks die late at night in hospitals. I think Miss Sanford just cashed in her own chips as I was talking to her. Her father's with her and—"

"You don't understand!" she insisted, trying to break free from Ki, as if she could. "I didn't mean Jake Grayson just died of his *wounds*. I meant somebody's gone and *killed* him! With a Bowie knife! It's still stuck in the poor boy's heart!"

It sure was, Ki saw after letting the nurse run on to spread the alarm and dashing smoothly down the dark hall to the doorway he'd seen the nurse coming from.

He knew Jake Grayson on sight as well as he'd known Billie Sanford, although hardly in the exact same ways. Overwrought or not, the ugly nurse had described Jake's ugly condition to a T. The erstwhile mavericker lay even flatter in his own bed, mouth as well as both eyes gaping wide as they could gape. The knife someone had driven through his sternum to split his heart was probably imbedded in the mattress below as well, if it was a genuine full-length Bowie. The true Bowie knife, as designed by the late Rezin Bowie rather than his more notorious brother Colonel James, simply wasn't made with a blade less than fourteen inches in lethal length.

Staring soberly down at the murdered man, Ki muttered, "If you'd like an educated guess, I'd say the mastermind who sent those other killers after Longarm sent one after you. For had you lived, Longarm as well as the Rangers would have had a lot to talk over with you."

Then Ki stepped back out in the hall. He wasn't surprised to see lights flickering and all sort of folks coming up the stairwell. He'd have sent out for the Austin P.D. too had he been either of those nursing sisters. As the ugly one reached the top of the stairs with two uniformed copper badges, she pointed Ki's way but said, "He didn't do it. He was in Miss Sanford's room when I found Mister Grayson stabbed to death!"

Ki smiled at them and stood to one side as they dashed by him. He rejoined the disconsolate Sanford in Billie's room. They'd been

241

joined by that pretty blonde from downstairs. As their eyes met over the bowed head of the seated Sanford, she nodded and silently mouthed, "She's dead" before murmuring in a more audible tone, "We've sent for the resident. He's getting dressed."

As if to prove her point, a youthful but mighty-filled-with-himself young man with a white smock over his summer suit came in to demand, "What's going on up here, Sister Ann? Can't I turn my back on things a second without you girls losing two whole patients, count 'em, *two*—"

"Neither lady lost spit!" Ki cut in, adding in a voice of authority, "This one's surgical sutures failed in the absence of any attending physician. The one down the hall was stabbed by a ward prowler. Why did you leave no more than two unarmed women in charge of patients being slated for court hearings on serious charges?"

Sister Ann shot Ki a grateful look. The resident shut up. The dead girl's father protested, "My poor Billie never done nothing to deserve no court hearings. She may have been excitable, but she never set out to crook nobody, dang it!"

Ki said soothingly, "You're right about that. She couldn't have known anything about the crook known as King Kellog putting the Grayson brothers up to mavericking that herd before you and your business partner, Matanza, could slap your own brands on it. She'd have never gone to war with anyone she was in league with."

Sandford sobbed, "That's what I just said."

The other nursing sister came in with only one of the copper badges, who blinked at the sight of Sister Ann covering Billie's dead face with the sheet and announced, "My pard's gone to fetch the Rangers, seeing it's their case. We got us a genuine murder down the way. Has that poor little gal been murdered as well?"

Ki shook his head and said, "Most likely an internal hemorrhage. The killer had no call to murder her. She didn't know anything. The dead man with the Bowie in him knew the identity of a dealer in stolen goods who preferred to be called King Kellog. The Graysons had made a deal with the sneak. He crawfished out of it, and even ordered federal lawmen killed to cover his tracks. Just now he rid himself of the last of the Grayson brothers."

The copper badge whistled and said, "He sure sounds nervous. Smart as well. How'll we ever figure out who King Kellog is with the only folks we could question about it silenced forever?"

Before Ki could answer, the intern and both nursing sisters left so the young sawbones could feel Jake Grayson's pulse or whatever.

The copper badge shot a sympathetic look at the older man seated by his dead daughter's bed, and suggested he and Ki wait for the Rangers out in the hall. Ki nodded, but settled for lounging against the doorjamb as he politely turned down the copper badge's offer of a slightly used Havana claro. The roundsman lit a perfecto he'd salvaged at the courthouse that afternoon for himself. Ki was tempted, but it just wasn't for him to say whether smoking was allowed up there or not.

Ki wasn't surprised when, sure enough, the pretty Sister Ann came their way holding a water glass to sniff disdainfully and exclaim, "I fear you'll have to put that out, sir. You did set that length of rope on fire on purpose, didn't you?"

As the copper badge was sheepishly putting his cigar out, his sidekick came up the stairs with one of the Rangers Ki recalled from his recent visit to their nearby station.

The Ranger recalled Ki as well and nodded, observing, "You surely get around. Where's your sidekicks, Longarm and Lone Star?"

Ki stood straighter as he quietly replied, "I work for Miss Starbuck. Deputy Long is with her, not me. They've both called it a day. I can't say where or with whom. I told them both I'd tidy up any last details before I called it a day myself."

The Ranger stepped past him, nodded not unkindly to Kentucky Bob, and bent to remove the sheet from Billie Sanford's dead features. Sister Ann snapped, "Don't! She died of gunshot wounds she received last night. The one who was murdered here at County General lies down the hall."

The Ranger lifted the sheet anyway. The dead girl's father glanced at her face, gagged, and ran out of the room with both hands to his mouth. The Ranger dropped the sheet back in place and muttered, "I don't see why he had to take it that hard. He must have already known the poor little thing was dead, and them funny faces we makes when we die are only natural."

Sister Ann muttered something venomous under her breath, glanced down at the glass in her hand, and added, "I was hoping this sedative would help the poor old man. You really helped him a lot. We prefer to let a fresh cadaver's features compose themselves before we offer them to public view. I'd better go after the poor girl's poor father with this."

She did. As she vanished from view as well a copper badge asked Ki, "Is she allowed in the men's shithouse?"

To which Ki replied with a thin smile, "I imagine she's allowed to go anywhere in this hospital she wants." Then he motioned to the Ranger, closer to the dead girl's bed, and added, "Come on. We'd best all join them."

The Ranger shook his ten-gallon hat and said, "I don't need to shit and I ain't viewed the late Jake Grayson yet."

Ki said, "He's dead. Take my word for it. Wouldn't you rather take his killer back to the Ranger station with you?"

By this time Ki was already in motion. The three lawmen exchanged puzzled glances and fell in on either side of the tall Asian-American. That same self-important young resident was coming out of the other corpse's room as the four of them strode in step down the hall at him. As he stared back, uncertainly, Ki asked where the men's room was. The resident pointed and said, "Just around the bend at the far end." Sure enough, that was where they found old Kentucky Bob, bent over a white sink with Sister Ann standing by, trying to get him to sip more soothings from the glass she'd tracked him down with.

The Ranger said, "I'm sorry I upset you so, Mister Sanford. I forgot some folks just ain't used to being around dead folks." Then he turned to Ki and added, "You said something about us catching the mysterious King Kellog as just killed Jake Grayson, didn't you?"

Ki nodded, pointed his chin at the older man bent over the sink, and quietly said, "There he is. Anytime you'd like to take him."

Later, Ki would chide himself for placing too much confidence in gray hair and Sister Ann's sedative. Before the Ranger could even say that Ki was full of it, the wiry old man slapped leather.

Kentucky Bob Sanford was surprisingly quick on the draw, but Texas Rangers were paid to be surprisingly better. So things might have wound up really nasty had not Ki, more concerned for the ash-blond Sister Ann than a mean old man, dropped low to sweep both off their feet with his long left leg.

Sister Ann landed on her shapely rump without losing her grip on the glass in her hand. Kentucky Bob cracked the back of his head on the tiles, and didn't do his gun much good there either, as the Ranger shot two tiles on the wall above and behind them to shattered tinkling shards.

As Sister Ann rolled to her white-clad knees to skim the downed man's gun across the tile floor, the Ranger stared down thunderstruck to demand, "Why did we just do that?"

Ki got gracefully back to his considerable full stature, saying,
My fault. I expected at least a few denials. He'd been acting
wfully cool and calculating up until just now. I suppose his daugh-
r's death really did a job on his conscience, and that sedative he
st swallowed might have muddied his thinking as well."

The nursing sister looked up to say, accusingly, "He's comatose
s a plank. I'm sure he's suffered a concussion."

The Ranger began to reload as he decided, dryly, "He's likely
o suffer rope burns as well, now that he's as good as confessed
y his own actions."

Then the Ranger looked at Ki to ask, "What was he confessing
vhen he commenced to resist arrest so dumbly just now?"

Ki said, "Deputy Long could no doubt explain things more
learly, since I'm only going by what he related, a good many
mes, riding in from the Hill Country. To begin with, Sanford
as to be the killer of that other crook around the corner because
obody else will work half as well. It wasn't either nursing sister,
nless we assume one or more to be homicidal lunatics. The
esident was asleep in his room. I can't see any other wounded
nembers of either faction wandering the halls after midnight."

"Nobody else who survived that range war has been quartered
n this floor," Sister Ann declared. "Both those private rooms cost
xtra. Wounded poor boys are kept in the open wards on the main
oor."

"With pretty good alibis then," said Ki, turning back to the
Ranger. "That leaves nobody at all up here within the time that
vorks save for this old goat and me. I'll admit I had the opportunity
f you'll allow he had the better motive."

The Ranger growled, "I just agreed his slapping leather was as
ood as a signed confession, but what in tarnation was his infernal
notive?"

"He was a crook," Ki answered simply, as Sister Ann got up
o go fetch that doctor. Ki explained, "He told Longarm he and
he more successful Roy Matanza were business partners, with
Matanza putting up the money and him setting up the purchase
f some casually recorded Mexican beef."

The Ranger looked impatient and said, "Yeah, yeah, we cov-
red all that stuff about mavericking greaser cows over to the sta-
ion."

Ki smiled thinly and said, "You ought to ride hour after hour
vith Longarm on an already tedious afternoon. Matanza would

245

have been a fool to put up all the money if all he was suppose
to get out of the deal was half the herd or less."

The Ranger nodded and said, "He'll be lucky if he don't g
some time to repent the deal for quite a spell in State Prison. B
I see what you mean about the partner putting up the most mone
expecting to take the lion's share of the profits."

Ki said, "Sanford didn't want Matanza to reap *any* profits. H
approached his old rivals, the Graysons, with yet another dea
Am I talking too fast for you?"

The Ranger shook his head. "We arrest lots of two-face
businessmen. He meant to have the beef he was helping Matanz
get at a bargain as mavericks mavericked by others so's he coul
buy it all even cheaper on the sly and ... Hold on now. .
he had the money to pay off them hired guns and still hav
enough to bid anything at all on that Mex beef, how com
he had to get Matanza to put up the seed money to begi
with?"

Ki shrugged. "He was a crook. By definition crooks would rathe
diddle others out of money than put it up themselves. By lettin
Matanza and no doubt some other small holders pay the Mexica
crooks off in full, *his* profit as King Kellog, a cattle buyer biddin
on them for even less—"

"Right. Longarm mentioned how the two-faced sneak made u
the Kellog alias to throw suspicion on old Roy Matanza. But ho
come he even got the Graysons to call him Kellog in public and—

"You just explained that when you mentioned the public," K
answered. "They called Sanford Kellog in front of me, among oth
ers. What were they supposed to call their secret partner, Sanford
Nobody but they and they alone were supposed to know just wha
was going on."

The Ranger nodded. "Longarm's already told us why the ol
rose who'd stink by either name had that Secret Service man kille
and went after *him* as well them times."

Sister Ann came back in with the resident. As they hunkere
over him the old crook opened his eyes to say, "That stuff you'r
stuffing up my poor nose smells awesome! What am I doing dow
here?"

The Ranger said, not unkindly, "To begin with you are unde
arrest. The charges are grand theft, cow, murder, several, an
resisting arrest. So what have you got to say to that?"

Sanford said he meant to sue the state of Texas, and declare 'd have nothing more to say until he'd seen his lawyer.

The Ranger opined, "You'd best hire yourself a good one. For e got you dead to rights on most everything but mopery in the rst degree."

Thus it came to pass that a little over an hour later, as Longarm as enjoying a bubble bath with Lone Star, there came a gentle apping on Lone Star's bath chamber door.

She was on top at the time. She stiffened atop Longarm's well->aped stiffness and softly shouted, "*To o akenaide kudasai!*"

Longarm didn't have to ask how she figured that was Ki instead f a raven gently rapping. Nobody else could have gotten through e two locked doors between them and the hotel hallway without aking much more noise.

As if to prove him right, Ki called back, as softly, "I had no atention of opening the door, Jessie. Your guest should be neater 'bout hanging up hats, and I assume you both carried your gunbelts a there with you?"

Lone Star called back, "Never mind what we're doing in here. What are you doing out there and can't it wait until morning?"

Ki decided, "*Hai*, I just thought you might find it desirable a know the Rangers have the mysterious King Kellog. He was .entucky Bob Sanford. Everyone else who could do us any ossible harm in this part of Texas is dead or under lock and ey as well. Now could anyone tell me what mopery might be? 'he Rangers keep threatening to add it to their list of charges very time old Sanford mentions their mothers."

Longarm laughed out loud. Then seeing how indiscreet he'd lready been, he called out, "That's a joshing term for padding ae felony counts against a crook so's there'll be plenty left after is lawyer manages to get some dismissed."

Lone Star murmured, "For land's sake, is this any time to lecture ay *segundo* on the law?"

He thrust up into her, soothingly, as he called out, "The classic efinition of a mopery charge reads "indecent exposure in front f a blind person." I'd be proud to tell you more about mopery ver breakfast in the morning, Ki."

Ki agreed it had been nice talking to them. Before he could eave, Lone Star called out, "Thanks for telling us the mastermind as been caught, Ki. Who caught him, by the way?"

To which Ki could only modestly reply, "Me. Just doing my job."

★

Chapter 23

The nicest thing about the fancy imported soap Lone Star bough as the sophisticated Jessica Starbuck, aside from its lavender sme was the way you could lather your most delicate parts without burning. She said you could get it in your eyes without a lick discomfort, if you wanted. He found it far more fun to scrub h insides clean as a whistle with a soaped-slick erection. But sh insisted on them both rinsing every bit of soap off before they g back in bed so she could serve him some breakfast.

She even rustled up some real ham and eggs afterwards, chidin him gently for chaffing her so indelicately with his unshaven jav He said it was her own fault for leaving his saddlebags in th possession of an infernal Oriental who likely didn't know as muc about shaving. When she said Ki had a pretty rough beard as wel Longarm dug into his breakfast, trying not to think of ways sh might know. He'd never insisted on knowing all about everything But she'd implied, more than once, she and Ki were more lik brother and sister than things might appear. Longarm had neve argued, or brought up the simple fact that incest was at least twic as common as murder.

By now it was broad day outside, and Longarm was dying t learn all the details of Kellog's/Sanford's arrest. But Lone Sta pensively insisted it was early yet, and when he asked her wha was really making her so broody, as they finished off dog-style tha time, she pouted, "It's over. My missing beef's been accounte

248

r, and I reckon I can sustain the financial costs, seeing the guilty
rties know better than to mess with my herd by now."

He gripped her trim hipbone in either palm to rotate her rump
e way as he ground the other. "I might be able to steal at least
day or so more with you, honey. We both got to get back to
'est Texas before even Billy Vail could expect me to hop the
&RG north from El Paso."

She arched her spine to take it deeper even as she complained,
"hat's still not long enough. It seems every time we just get
arted we crack the damned case and . . . Damn it, Custis, why
e we both acting so silly about this? You know there's no lover
d rather have in me than you, and I know I must do something
r you most others can't."

He started pounding harder as he grunted, "The word you're
oping for is magic, you sweet screwing little love witch! It has
be magic when a man can come this often in a gal without it
er feeling the least bit like work!"

She closed her eyes and moaned, "Oh, yesss, I never have to
ake any effort either with you. So tell me something, damn it,
it my fault I was born to wealth and power beyond that of most
en?"

He didn't answer. He knew where this was leading because
one Star wasn't the first or only rich gal he'd ever had this dumb
scussion with. He withdrew, and when she complained he rolled
er on her back, half on and half off the mattress, to part her thighs
ide as they could spread, then enter her face-to-face in a mighty
ominant position.

She sobbed in ecstasy, and responded with submissive but bone-
rring bumps and grinds. So they never got around to his yearly
lary plus six cents a mile traveling expenses, or the simple fact
liked his job, hard and dangerous as it could get at times.

He'd never asked what he paid Ki, let alone what she'd pay *him*
ever he took her up on that standing offer to be her play-pretty.
e knew he'd feel guilty enough by the time they parted in a day
so at the most. For it would have been dumb as well as ornery to
eny a woman of quality the simple luxuries she was used to, and
ere was simply no way to travel with her in style without letting
er pay their way. She was inclined to tip more handsomely than
e damned old Justice Department was inclined to pay him.

Later, smoking one of the really expensive cheroots she'd
sisted on sending down for, he agreed with her plan to have

249

that special private railroad car sent up from Galveston so the
could enjoy that much privacy while rolling westward with enoug
of a staff to keep her from burning herself frying eggs bare-a
aboard a moving train. She said they could easily make up th
time lost waiting for it there in Austin. He said he hoped so, sin
by now that Presidential desk should be much closer to that ov
office and he wanted to get back to Denver before the desk g
to Washington.

She complained that it sounded to her as if he was in a hurry
get rid of her again. He was proving he wasn't when they hea
that same gentle tapping, this time on her bedroom chamber doc
and when Longarm paused in mid-stroke Lone Star called ou
waspishly, "Damn it, Ki, I thought we'd agreed to jaw about tho
trash whites and mavericked Mex cows later!"

Ki called back, "That's not why I disturbed you, Jessie. I ju
came from Western Union. You'll never guess what some of yo
line riders stumbled over, a day's ride out from your home spread

Longarm nodded and told her, "Them Circle Star cows someor
unwisely run south of the border without asking El Gato's perm
I was expecting him to see you got 'em back, but I didn't wa
to get your hopes up."

Ki had been listening through the door panels. He said, "
you want, I could go on ahead to oversee the roundup and tall
Jessie. The boys say some of your cows seem a little the wors
for wear, although some of the surprise beef from Mexico nee
to be branded our way, if you mean to keep it."

She laughed and said she'd always thought El Gato was a swe
young man. When Ki repeated his suggestion she trilled, "Ha
Itu dekakemasu ka?"

When Ki replied, "Chodo ima," and lit out, Longarm figured
was safe to torture the bedsprings some more. So they did.

Thus, by the time Longarm finally made it over to Wester
Union that morning, it wasn't morning anymore and it was sa
to assume Ki was long gone. So Longarm was cussing fit to bu
by the time he got back to the hotel and found Lone Star seate
at her dressing table in no more than some fancy body powd
while she rearranged her hair.

Waving the wire he'd just received from his home offic
Longarm explained, "Washington's on Billy Vail's back abo
that fool oak desk from Queen Victoria, and now he's all ov
mine! Seems some State Department jaspers tried to intercept

along the way with orders to guard it with their lives the rest of the way and . . . Damn it, Jessie, them damn fool vaqueros working for you never put it on the train. Not the *right* train leastways. State's wired tracers out to every damned dumb railroad dispatcher they can find betwixt the Pecos and the Big Muddy. So far to no avail."

Lone Star rose in all her nude glory to move toward her wardrobe, saying, "That's impossible. I know both the boys who wired home that they'd personally slid that big packing crate from my buckboard to a railroad baggage car. Even if I couldn't vouch for them, why would they have lied? Who on earth would want to steal a heavy oak desk with the Presidential seal carved all over it? Where on earth would any thief unload such awkward loot?"

As she started to slip into fresh duds, more suited to the streets of the city than a range war, Longarm told her, "Somebody must have, if you're right about your hired help. Anytime you're ready, I'd be much obliged if you'd traipse over to Western Union with me and help me question your help by wire."

As she slipped into riding boots despite the summer frock and fancy straw boater she'd elected to face Austin with that afternoon, Longarm explained, "I reckon I could wire in Spanish or English, if I knew which was more likely to please 'em. It's odd how some Spanish-speakers feel you're trying to be nice whilst others think you're teasing when you come at 'em in their own lingo."

She pinned the boater atop her upswept blond hair at just the angle she fancied before she said, "Let's go then. Since the poor confused *tercero* as well as both vaqueros speak Spanish as their first tongue, I'll wire them in that. I wish Ki was already there, but since he can't be far as San Antone yet, we'll just have to make do without him."

As they left her suite she dimpled and added, "I'm glad. Sometimes it's awkward to ravage a friend with another friend watching, and since we won't be needing any backing, just sending telegrams, let's hope it takes ages to get this all straightened out."

Giving her his arm on the stairs, Longarm said, "Billy Vail hasn't given me ages. He says I told him that fool desk was on its way, that he told Washington the same thing, and that I'd best commend my soul to Jesus if I don't locate it *poco tiempo*, because if I don't, my ass will belong to *him*, whether they fire him or not!"

251

★

Chapter 24

Until such time as Professor Bell worked all the kinks out of his marvelous talking telegraph, people would just have to wait while they communicated the old-fashioned way with dots and dashes. It was still far faster than anything anyone had come up with in all the years since humankind had first discovered reading and writing. The Morse telegraph had been in limited use before either Longarm or Lone Star was born, however, and they were both getting mighty tired of waiting for the Bell Telephone outfit to string those long-distance lines they kept talking about without really getting around to doing it.

Meanwhile, there were other chores to attend to, such as returning that hired mule and the pony the late One Lung Meeker had hired there in Austin to their proper owners. Lone Star wanted to go over to the county jail and visit the dolorous results of their recent adventures in the Hill Country, but Longarm warned her they'd best quit while they were ahead. The Texas Rangers didn't seem to need their testimony, seeing there were only so many times, and ways, one could hang anyone for backshooting, and even those who'd fought fair were likely to catch some hard time one way or the other. But both old Kentucky Bob and the doubtless enraged Roy Matanza could afford slick lawyers, and Longarm had been summoned by slick lawyers in the past. He explained it worked sort of like mopery. Slickers liked to blow as much smoke in a courtroom as possible, and even testimony that got

252

rown out tended to confuse the judge and jury.

So they went out to Barton Springs, Austin's famous swimming hole, where crystal mineral waters bubbled up just a tad cooler than body temperature and bathers dressed in scandalous knee-length outfits splashed each other's bodies all the live-long day, laughing like drowning jackasses.

Lone Star said she'd rather eat tamales and sip *cerveza* at one of the picnic tables under the shady old oak trees of the surrounding Zilker Park. So he bought them both at a Mex-run refreshment stand, and the tamales were so good they had seconds as they watched less sedate lovers try to drown each other in the springs.

She opined you could tell which couples had been to bed together by how silly they acted in public. She declared no girl who'd done all the way with a boy was inclined to blush beet-red every time their wet wool brushed a tad suggestively. But he said he wasn't so sure about that. Then he clammed up before she could ask how he knew how really bawdy young gals liked to act in public. He settled for, "I keep saying, if only someone would listen, that things are seldom just as they seem. My job would be much easier if you could really separate the sinner from the pure just by looking at 'em."

By now Western Union had surely had time enough to offer some answers to their earlier questions. Western Union had. The Spanish-speaking *tercero* Lone Star had wired had wired back, in Spanish, how he'd wired that buckboard crew to address that damned crate right and send it C.O.D., direct, to the plain-as-day resident in the plain-as-day capital of these United States. Some Western Union operator along the line, less fluent in Spanish, had messed up a verb ending here and there, but the answer to Lone Star's earlier simple message was just as simple. So she said, and Longarm had to agree, it looked as if the railroad, not her boys, had somehow messed up.

As they left the telegraph office he reached absently for one of those swell but expensive cheroots, musing, "Well, the fool crate was put aboard a ship on the far side, addressed plain enough, only to wind up at your Circle Star by way of Washington on the Brazos. I don't suppose there's any way your vaqueros could have inspired the railroad crew they must have said *something* to to send it to the Czar of All the Russians."

She handed him the telegram, saying, "See for yourself. You

253

read Spanish almost as well as I do. They put it aboard rollin
stock of the Panhandle & Santa Fe. You don't suppose Quee
Victoria's present wound up in Santa Fe, mayhaps delivered
that new territorial governor—what's his name?"

Longarm frowned thoughtfully and said, "Wallace. Lev
Wallace. Good man, and smart enough to write books abo
ancient Romans too. I can see a mighty stupid railroad dispatch
mistaking a federal governor for a President but . . . No, I can'
Governor, in Spanish, is almost the same word. So's Presiden
and there's just no way to mix up Washington, D.C., with San
Fe, New Mexico Territory."

She murmured, "I think you'll find they simply addressed th
crate to the capital of the United States, American geography n
being their strong point. But I don't see how anyone could mistak
Santa Fe for the capital of the whole country."

Longarm opened the telegram to read it over, scowling dow
at the yellow paper in the bright Texas sunlight as Lone Star cor
tinued, "I've been thinking about that private car from Galveston

He shook his head and said, "This is more serious. Old Bil
sounds really worried. Lord knows it looks as if I got some trai
riding ahead of me, but old Billy's fixing to have a fit if I can
tell him soon I'm on my way to some damned where!"

She said, "Well, we don't need quite the privacy I intended, wit
Ki out of the picture and mayhaps cold meals in our compartme
with the summer nights so warm now. I've more than one com
pany car already on hand here in the Austin yards, if you'd lik
to tell me where we want to go, by way of which line out."

He sighed and said, "Lord love you, Pullmans or even boxca
sure beat horseflesh from here to wherever, and that infernal des
has one hell of a lead on us by rail by now. Let's start by loadin
our saddles and such aboard, and by then, with luck, my otherwis
useless head will get struck by inspiration!"

But by sundown, over on a rail siding, as they ate the suppe
she'd rustled up for them aboard a Starbuck Enterprises Pullma
they were still stuck for answers, as the yard dispatcher was fo
any destination to chalk on the outside of their car, still parked o
the same weed-grown siding with other Starbuck rolling stock.

Women who liked men always seemed to cook better than eve
a cow-camp Chinee, as if to chide him for his wandering chi
parlor ways. Seeing she'd had an apron on while fully dresse
she'd chanced deep-fried chicken parts and collard greens, know

254

ıg how Longarm felt about that prissy omelet she'd once tried to all a *pomme soufflé*.

They ate it out back on the observation platform, along with ɔme fancy white wine he agreed went well with chicken. The big ɪd stars of Texas were coming out as the cloudless sky above went ɔm crimson to royal purple, and somewhere in the gathering dusk p to commence their nightlong serenade. Washing down some ied chicken breast with chablis, he said he was glad they'd be edded down so intimately amongst cricket weeds. He didn't have ɔ explain further to a lady raised in Indian country. She said, "I ɪish we could just stop time's cruel march in its tracks and just ort of sit out here like this forever, or at least until we've had ur fill. Have you ever noticed how hours feel like seconds when ɔu're even halfway content, Custis?"

He downed some collard greens—she cooked everything just ght—and decided, "I ain't sure how long one would feel conɛnted the moment one was told he or she *had* to stay put in this ne time and place for the whole future. Many a man in jail, along bout this hour, may be comfortable enough, relaxing after supper ith enough tobacco and even a good book to read. I doubt it ɪakes him feel a lick better about being in prison, though. It's ɪe freedom to change whatever you may be doing that makes the ɔing of it seem so swell."

He polished off a perfectly browned morsel of chicken, sipped ɪe just about perfect wine, and added, "I'd be enjoying this supper ɛss, for example, if you'd told me I wasn't to have any more of ɔu later this evening."

She dimpled sweetly at him and replied, "Just you try to get ut of it, now that we have a whole railroad car to run up and ɔwn in like naughty children. But damn it, that's what I mean bout time's cruel march. I know we're going to make mad sweet ɔve to the love songs of horny bugs in the weeds all around, and very thrust will be divine and . . . Then it'll be the cold gray awn and you'll want to go searching for that dumb old desk some ɪore!"

He said soothingly, "I don't want to, honey. I *have* to. Billy ˈail told me to make sure President Hayes gets it no matter how feel about it."

He drained his glass, and she poured him another as he groused n. "If only I had the least notion where to start! I doubt it's been stolen. It's likely just been sent the wrong way again, and it woul[d] be fun chasing it all over creation with you in this swell Pullma[n] car if only I knew which way to *go*! We got to go *somewhere*. Billy Vail will give birth to clawing wolverine cubs if he catche[s] me simply shacked up here not even trying."

She purred, dangerously, "Thank you. How often does yo[ur] office catch you shacked up, as you so delicately put it?"

"So far they ain't," he fibbed, adding, "I never meant to sa[y] my boss would find the two of us all that crude. He just don['t] approve of me visiting art museums, even, when I'm supposed [to] be tracking someone, or in this case something down. So I got [to] get going, Jessie, with or without your swell company."

She asked if that meant right now. He reached out to plac[e] a fond hand in her lap, assuring her, "*Mañana* will do, damn [it] to hell, and would you like to tag along at least as far as San[ta] Fe?"

She said she could get home from there as easily as from her[e]. She was too big a girl to point out Santa Fe would put him well o[ut] his way back to Denver, no matter what they found there. She ros[e] to gather up the remains of their light supper, muttering somethin[g] about time's cruel march. When he offered to help she shook he[r] head and said, "I'd like to have my hands and my thoughts [to] myself for just a few moments, Custis. Don't worry, we'll be i[n] bed together before you know it."

Then she added, turning from him lest he see the tears in he[r] eyes and ask about them, "Then, before you know it, we'll be o[ut] of bed again, and then we'll be back in bed, and then we'll b[e] up again, and then . . . Aw, hell, let's talk about something les[s] scary, such as how high is up or who created the Lord before th[e] Lord created us."

Longarm snorted. "Stewing over things we'll just never kno[w] and couldn't do a thing about if we did know, is a stew best serve[d] to women, children, and men with no serious chores to stew over."

She said, "Thanks." Longarm said, "Aw, you ain't a woma[n] you're a pal. I was talking about sissy folks who've never ha[d] any real worries and feel the call to worry anyways."

He reached for that wire confirming her vaqueros had forwarde[d] that infernal crate to the President back East as he added, "Bil[l] Vail never sent me out to determine the extent of the universe o[r] the beginning and end of eternity. He gave me a far easier puzz[le] to solve if only I had any notion where to begin!"

He unfolded the yellow form, now somewhat wilted. He could see at a glance there wasn't enough light out there to read by. But that was all right, he decided. He'd already read the fool wire so many times he could picture every word, as transcribed by a telegrapher not as familiar with Spanish. And so, half closing his eyes, he willed the block letters to appear on the dusky blob he held up in the starlight. They still read the same way. The Panhandle & Santa Fe had been directed to deliver the damned crate C.O.D. to the damned President in the damned capital of the damned United States, and all that had been written on the crate in red crayon on both sides.

In Spanish?

"Jesus H. Christ!" Longarm gasped, tossing the telegram aside as he sprang to his feet, telling Lone Star, "I got to get on over to the telegraph office as of days ago! I'll explain later! If you'd like to help a heap, see about attaching this car to anything southbound for Ciudad Mejico, *poco* damn *tiempo*!"

As he vaulted over the observation platform's railing to hit the yard ballast running, Lone Star wailed after him, "How soon might you be back, and why do we want to go to Mexico?"

He ran on, not looking back as he shouted, "Read that wire, and this time don't translate it into English!"

And then he was out of sight, although thudding along that cinder path through the cottonwoods and sunflowers mighty intent on something.

Lone Star took the telegram from the tea table inside the Pullman, and turned up a wall fixture to illuminate the simple-enough message. Custis had said not to translate from the Spanish. That was easy enough, but so what? "El Presidente" meant "The President," and there was no more difference between "El Capital" and "The Capital."

"Los Estados Unidos," of course, simply meant "The United States." Or did it, to your average Mexican or even Anglo railroad worker moving freight this close to the border?

Lone Star laughed girlishly and exclaimed, "Goody! Mexico City is over eight hundred miles from here, and with any luck at all we'll wind up stuck for days on some siding in the Chihuahua Desert!"

Then she went to her compartment to change into her range riding outfit, not to scout up the yardmaster but to trail after Longarm. For she could see the poor dear hadn't been thinking clearly in his first flush of excitement, or relief. Perhaps more accustomed to traveling by private rail car, the mistress of Starbuck Enterprises knew the Austin yard switchers could have this car on its way to couple up with a southbound combination of the Laredo y Mejico most any time she wanted. But she wasn't about to leave without Custis Long, and she knew it was going to take more than a single telegram to sort out all this confusion if she was sorting things the same way.

As she strapped on her six-gun, she failed to see any other way it worked. Americans might forget, but few Mexicans ever forgot the formal name of their country was "Los Estados Unidos De Mejico," or "United States Of Mexico," and of course the current dictator, General Porfirio Diaz, preferred to be called "El Presidente"!

So where else would a railroad dispatcher who knew Spanish send a crate addressed to him at his capital, Mexico City?

★

Chapter 25

Longarm was just as glad Lone Star wasn't there to look over his shoulder as he composed a simply coded message to another lady best known to both the revolutionary movement and the dictatorship it was out to overthrow as La Mariposa. He had no way of contacting the even more wandersome El Gato by wire, and even if there had been a way, La Mariposa and her particular gang had to be far closer to the railroad yards of Mexico City. When she wasn't dancing in flamenco skirts, pretty and flirty as her butterfly namesake, La Mariposa sort of ran the Mexico City railroad yards from her secret lookout atop a signal tower the official managers of the national railroad thought they'd decomissioned when the dictatorship had combined various privately owned rail lines at gunpoint.

He didn't think it wise to inform a gang leader who supported herself and her gang as well as La Revolucion by pilferage just what he wanted them to pilfer. He described the Presidential desk, knowing they'd peek, as his own personal property, dispatched by mistake to the wrong address. It would have been really stupid to mention which wrong address over wires *los rurales* regularly tapped. He simply told La Mariposa he'd be forever in her debt if she'd just have her "fellow railroad workers" keep an eye peeled for that red crayon lettering, then tossed in that the original mistake had been made at the Panhandle & Santa Fe depot.

He'd just finished and paid the telegraph clerk behind the counter in cash from his own pocket when Lone Star caught up with him. He took charge of a silk sleeve and got her over to a nearby open-air beer garden of the German persuasion before they both perished of thirst on such a sultry Texican night.

Lone Star was a good sport about swilling lager with him while some fool sporting an accordion and short pants sang wistful songs about Miss Laura Lee. But then she had to go and spoil it all by asking who he'd contacted down Mexico way in hopes of heading off that desk before El Presidente Diaz sat down at it to write Queen Victoria a polite thank-you for such a swell surprise.

Longarm didn't like to lie to anyone. He and Lone Star were good friends as well as great lovers because they lied even less to one another. He sipped some suds to give himself time to choose his words. Then he said, "I don't think I ever told you about the swell time I had down yonder during their Day of the Dead. That odd fiesta wasn't what Billy sent me down there for, but . . ."

"Were you supposed to be south of the border at all?" she demanded with a knowing look. "I thought we had standing orders on that from both the Justice and War Departments. That's why I thought we'd best be sure before I took you for a train ride through Chihuahua."

He smiled sheepishly and said, "In point of fact, Billy sent me to pick up a federal want in Nuevo Laredo, and after that things just sort of got out of hand. The rascal made a run for Mexico City, and we got to chase each other all over while everyone else, innocent or guilty, wore spooky ghost costumes, as they're prone to do down yonder during the Day of the Dead."

She sweetly said, "You're being evasive, Custis. Who do we have heading off that damned crate and is she good-looking?"

Longarm chuckled fondly. "Pretty enough to be known to friend and foe as La Mariposa. But that ain't why I wired her, care of a less romantic cantina keeper selling *mescal* and *pulque* near the railroad yards. I met up with what I suppose you'd call the butterfly gang as I was chasing more serious crooks for Billy Vail. It's too long and tedious to go into. Suffice it to say they owe me, since all right-thinking folk share the same feelings toward El Presidente Diaz and his bloody-handed followers. If that desk meant for President Hayes hasn't already been delivered to El Presidente Diaz, La Mariposa and her *ladrones* ought to be able to salvage the situation for us. But your point about your Uncle Billy fussing at us about our last trip to Mexico is well taken. Mayhaps I'd best just hop a freight and make my way down yonder alone and more discreet.

'ou could wait for me at, say, Laredo with that swell Pullman if
ou'd like."

"And miss my chance to compare notes with La Mariposa?"
he said with just a hint of steel in her voice. Then she laughed
nd added, "I'll behave, and you're going to need my railroad car
› smuggle that crate back across the border whether La Mariposa
nd I snatch each other bald-headed or not, dear."

★

Chapter 26

Both the federal troops and rural police of Los Estados Unido
de Mejico were mighty pissed at the two rude gringos they ha
down as Brazo Largo and Estrella Solitario, but since El President
Diaz prided himself on his relationships with Americano busines
interests, La Señorita Jessica Starbuck of Starbuck Enterprises wa
not only welcome, but her private railroad car was chalked "*Arrib.
Sospecha!*" at the border and free to roll on anywhere, immune t
inspection by the usually snoopy minions of a police state.

The next few days on the high dry deserts were unbearable, eve
with the train in motion and roof vents open. But the deliciously dr
and cool summer nights of the Mexican high plains made up fo
that as they alternated between feasting and fornication with th
entire car, attached to the rear of a passenger-freight combination
all to themselves.

But as Lone Star was prone to bitch every time he had to take i
out, all good things had to end some damned time, and so there the
were, parked on a railroad siding near the Mexico City terminal
when all at once they felt an unexpected jolt and Lone Star sat u
in bed to peer out under the drawn curtain, saying, "We seem t
be backing up, dear. Didn't you say our best bet, once we got here
would be to simply sit tight and let your pretty butterfly flutter i
in her own good time?"

He grumbled that he hadn't put it just that way as he swun
his bare feet to the rug and proceeded to get armed and dressed

Once he had, he ambled back to the rear platform, to see right off why they were moving the other way, uncoupled from that combination. A stubby pufferbilly switch engine was backing them into yet another siding screened by unpainted and likely long-abandoned boxcars of another age. The revolutions they kept having down this way were hell on railroad traffic. Then he saw who'd climbed up on the platform to sort of lurk beside the sliding door. He slid it open anyway and stepped out to join La Mariposa, pretty as ever as long as one liked gals with Aztec eyes and casually held ten-gauges. Save for her shotgun she was trying to look like any other pretty peon dwelling amid the shanties along the wrong side of the tracks.

Longarm ticked his hat brim to her and said, "Morning, ah, *querida*. I see you got my message."

The lovely young *mestiza*, who'd once confided his *brazo* wasn't the only *largo* thing about him she admired, licked her lush lips and almost whispered, "*Si*, we got your *caja grande*. Was no problem. We only had for to take out one *guarda*. We got it ready for you up the track, and we can couple you pronto to a northbound, crewed by friends of La Revolucion, if you are in a hurry. You *are* in a hurry, are you not, Custis?"

He said he surely was, and then, old times being old times, he might have come up with some excuse not to haul her right in and heist her cotton skirts in front of another gal, had not she looked nervously around, as if afraid they'd be overheard, and confided, "I do not know how else for to put it. I shall ever be most fond of you and I do not wish for to hurt your feelings, Custis, but since last we, ah, you know, this one hombre and me, a hero of La Revolucion who may die for La Causa anytime . . ."

Then Lone Star stepped out on the platform to join them, hatless but otherwise looking armed and dangerous as she sweetly asked whether Longarm meant to introduce her to la señorita.

So Longarm nodded pleasantly and said, "Jessie Starbuck, allow me to present La Mariposa, the brave little rebel gal I've already told you about. She and her rebels have that crate we come all this way for, and we were just talking about her wedding plans."

"La señorita is getting married?" Lone Star asked as they shook hands while Longarm, for some fool reason, felt his ears burning up.

The pretty Mariposa fluttered her lashes and replied, "Maybe I will only get to be his *adalita* as I follow him from battle to

263

battle. Is so difficult to make permanent plans when there is so much noise all about. *Pero* if we live to see the restoration of Libertad . . ."

"We're going to have to keep in touch so you and your hombre get some wedding presents whether you get to have a wedding or not," the American girl declared, as if she meant it.

She must have, Longarm decided, as she screwed like a mink that night while they rolled northward with the now-battered crate stowed forward, its contents, however, still pristine. When Longarm said it might be best to sand off all those conflicting instructions on the battered packing crate, Lone Star hugged him tighter, in every way, and pleaded, "Don't stop. I've an import-export plant in Laredo that can repack the fool desk in a spanking new crate if you like. Just don't stop doing what I like until we get there, darling!"

But of course, in time they had to, and he didn't ask why she was crying in the dark all over his bare chest as they rolled northward toward tomorrow and tomorrow. He patted her naked shoulder soothingly and said, "Delivering that gift from Queen Victoria in a fresh crate will doubtless save the diplomatic corps and the writers of future history books some bother. I was wondering, though, now that we've gone to so much trouble recovering that furniture and getting it aimed the right way, whether Billy Vail wouldn't want me to make dead certain it wound up in that there oval office forever instead of, say, the U.S. Mint or Patent Office."

He hesitated and suggested, "I'm sure my office would approve if Starbuck Enterprises was to offer me a lift all the way to Washington Town and back aboard this safe and secure Pullman car."

Lone Star gasped with delight and rolled back atop him to get down and dirty. When he complimented her on how swell that felt, she demurely replied it was only her patriotic duty.

Watch for

LONGARM AND THE GOLD HUNTERS

153rd novel in the bold LONGARM series

and

**LONE STAR AND
THE YUMA PRISON BREAK**

109th novel in the exciting LONE STAR series

Both Coming in September!

At supper Norris, my middle brother, said, "I think we got some trouble on that five thousand acres down on the border near Laredo."

He said it serious, which is the way Norris generally says everything. I quit wrestling with the steak Buttercup, our cook, had turned into rawhide and said, "What are you talking about? How could we have trouble on land lying idle?"

He said, "I got word from town this afternoon that a telegram had come in from a friend of ours down there. He says we got some kind of squatters taking up residence on the place."

My youngest brother, Ben, put his fork down and said, incredulously, "*That* five thousand acres? Hell, it ain't nothing but rocks and cactus and sand. Why in hell would anyone want to squat on that worthless piece of nothing?"

Norris just shook his head. "I don't know. But that's what the telegram said. Came from Jack Cole. And if anyone ought to know what's going on down there it would be him."

I thought about it and it didn't make a bit of sense. I was Justa Williams, and my family, my two brothers and myself and our father, Howard, occupied a considerable ranch called the Half-Moon down along the Gulf of Mexico in Matagorda County, Texas. It was some of the best grazing land in the state and we had one of the best herds of purebred and crossbred cattle in that part of the country. In short we were pretty well-to-do.

But that didn't make us any the less ready to be stolen from, if indeed that was the case. The five thousand acres Norris had been talking about had come to us through a trade our father had made some years before. We'd never made any use of it mainly because, as Ben had said, it was pretty worthless, because it was a good two hundred miles from our ranch headquarters. On a few occasions we'd bought cattle in Mexico and then used the acreage to hold small groups on while we made up a herd. But other than that, it lay mainly forgotten.

I frowned. "Norris, this doesn't make a damn bit of sense. Right after supper send a man into Blessing with a return wire for Jack asking him if he's certain. What the hell kind of squatting could anybody be doing on that land?"

Ben said, "Maybe they're raisin' watermelons." He laughed.

I said, "They could raise melons, but there damn sure wouldn't be no water in them."

Norris said, "Well, it bears looking into." He got up, throwing his napkin on the table. "I'll go write out that telegram."

I watched him go, dressed, as always, in his town clothes. Norris was the businessman in the family. He'd been sent down to the University at Austin and had got considerable learning about the ins and outs of banking and land deals and all the other parts of our business that didn't directly involve the ranch. At the age of twenty-nine I'd been the boss of the operation a good deal longer than I cared to think about. It had been thrust upon me by our father when I wasn't much more than twenty. He'd said he'd wanted me to take over while he was still strong enough to help me out of my mistakes and I reckoned that was partly true. But it had just seemed that after our mother had died the life had sort of gone out of him. He'd been one of the earliest settlers, taking up the land not long after Texas had become a republic in 1845. I figured all the years of fighting Indians and then Yankees and scalawags and carpetbaggers and cattle thieves had taken their toll on him. Then a few years back he'd been nicked in the lungs by a bullet that should never have been allowed to head his way and it had thrown an extra strain on his heart. He was pushing seventy and he still had plenty of head on his shoulders, but mostly all he did now was sit around in his rocking chair and stare out over the cattle and land business he'd built. Not to say that I didn't go to him for advice when the occasion demanded. I did, and mostly I took it.

Buttercup came in just then and sat down at the end of the table with a cup of coffee. He was near as old as Dad and almost completely worthless. But he'd been one of the first hands that Dad had hired and he'd been kept on even after he couldn't sit a horse anymore. The problem was he'd elected himself cook, and that was the sorriest day our family had ever seen. There were two Mexican women hired to cook for the twelve riders we kept full time, but Buttercup insisted on cooking for the family.

Mainly, I think, because he thought he was one of the family. A notion we could never completely dissuade him from.

So he sat there, about two days of stubble on his face, looking as scrawny as a pecked-out rooster, sweat running down his face, his apron a mess. He said, wiping his forearm across his forehead, "Boy, it shore be hot in there. You boys shore better be glad you ain't got no business takes you in that kitchen."

Ben said, in a loud mutter, "I wish you didn't either."

Ben, at twenty-five, was easily the best man with a horse or a gun that I had ever seen. His only drawback was that he was hotheaded and he tended to act first and think later. That ain't a real good combination for someone that could go on the prod as fast as Ben. When I had argued with Dad about taking over as boss, suggesting instead that Norris, with his education, was a much better choice, Dad had simply said, "Yes, in some ways. But he can't handle Ben. You can. You can handle Norris, too. But none of them can handle you."

Well, that hadn't been exactly true. If Dad had wished it I would have taken orders from Norris even though he was two years younger than me. But the logic in Dad's line of thinking had been that the Half-Moon and our cattle business was the lodestone of all our businesses and only I could run that. He had been right. In the past I'd imported purebred Whiteface and Hereford cattle from up North, bred them to our native Longhorns and produced cattle that would bring twice as much at market as the horse-killing, all-bone, all-wild Longhorns. My neighbors had laughed at me at first, claiming those square little purebreds would never make it in our Texas heat. But they'd been wrong and, one by one, they'd followed the example of the Half-Moon.

Buttercup was setting up to take off on another one of his long-winded harangues about how it had been in the "old days" so I quickly got up, excusing myself, and went into the big office we

271

used for sitting around in as well as a place of business. Norris was at the desk composing his telegram so I poured myself out a whiskey and sat down. I didn't want to hear about any trouble over some worthless five thousand acres of borderland. In fact I didn't want to hear about any troubles of any kind. I was just two weeks short of getting married, married to a lady I'd been courting off and on for five years, and I was mighty anxious that nothing come up to interfere with our plans. Her name was Nora Parker and her daddy owned and run the general mercantile in our nearest town, Blessing. I'd almost lost her once before to a Kansas City drummer. She'd finally gotten tired of waiting on me, waiting until the ranch didn't occupy all my time, and almost run off with a smooth-talking Kansas City drummer that called on her daddy in the harness trade. But she'd come to her senses in time and got off the train in Texarkana and returned home.

But even then it had been a close thing. I, along with my men and brothers and help from some of our neighbors, had been involved with stopping a huge herd of illegal cattle being driven up from Mexico from crossing our range and infecting our cattle with tick fever which could have wiped us all out. I tell you it had been a bloody business. We'd lost four good men and had to kill at least a half dozen on the other side. Fact of the business was I'd come about as close as I ever had to getting killed myself, and that was going some for the sort of rough-and-tumble life I'd led.

Nora had almost quit me over it, saying she just couldn't take the uncertainty. But in the end, she'd stuck by me. That had been the year before, 1896, and I'd convinced her that civilized law was coming to the country, but until it did, we that had been there before might have to take things into our own hands from time to time.

She'd seen that and had understood. I loved her and she loved me and that was enough to overcome any of the troubles we were still likely to encounter from day to day.

So I was giving Norris a pretty sour look as he finished his telegram and sent for a hired hand to ride it into Blessing, seven miles away. I said, "Norris, let's don't make a big fuss about this. That land ain't even crossed my mind in at least a couple of years. Likely we got a few Mexican families squatting down there and trying to scratch out a few acres of corn."

Norris gave me his businessman's look. He said, "It's our land,

Justa. And if we allow anyone to squat on it for long enough or put up a fence they can lay claim. That's the law. My job is to see that we protect what we have, not give it away."

I sipped at my whiskey and studied Norris. In his town clothes he didn't look very impressive. He'd inherited more from our mother than from Dad so he was not as wide shouldered and slim-hipped as Ben and me. But I knew him to be a good, strong, dependable man in any kind of fight. Of course he wasn't that good with a gun, but then Ben and I weren't all that good with books like he was. But I said, just to jolly him a bit, "Norris, I do believe you are running to suet. I may have to put you out with Ben working the horse herd and work a little of that fat off you."

Naturally it got his goat. Norris had always envied Ben and me a little. I was just over six foot and weighed right around one hundred ninety. I had inherited my daddy's big hands and big shoulders. Ben was almost a copy of me except he was about a size smaller. Norris said, "I weigh the same as I have for the last five years. If it's any of your business."

I said, as if I was being serious, "Must be them sack suits you wear. What they do, pad them around the middle?"

He said, "Why don't you just go to hell."

After he'd stomped out of the room I got the bottle of whiskey and an extra glass and went down to Dad's room. It had been one of his bad days and he'd taken to bed right after lunch. Strictly speaking he wasn't supposed to have no whiskey, but I watered him down a shot every now and then and it didn't seem to do him no harm.

He was sitting up when I came in the room. I took a moment to fix him a little drink, using some water out of his pitcher, then handed him the glass and sat down in the easy chair by the bed. I told him what Norris had reported and asked what he thought.

He took a sip of his drink and shook his head. "Beats all I ever heard," he said. "I took that land in trade for a bad debt some fifteen, twenty years ago. I reckon I'd of been money ahead if I'd of hung on to the bad debt. That land won't even raise weeds, well as I remember, and Noah was in on the last rain that fell on the place."

We had considerable amounts of land spotted around the state as a result of this kind of trade or that. It was Norris's business to keep up with their management. I was just bringing this to Dad's attention more out of boredom and impatience for my wedding day to arrive than anything else.

I said, "Well, it's a mystery to me. How you feeling?"

He half smiled. "Old." Then he looked into his glass. "And I never liked watered whiskey. Pour me a dollop of the straight stuff in here."

I said, "Now, Howard. You know—"

He cut me off. "If I wanted somebody to argue with I'd send for Buttercup. Now do like I told you."

I did, but I felt guilty about it. He took the slug of whiskey down in one pull. Then he leaned his head back on the pillow and said, "Aaaaah. I don't give a damn what that horse doctor says, ain't nothing makes a man feel as good inside as a shot of the best."

I felt sorry for him laying there. He'd always led just the kind of life he wanted—going where he wanted, doing what he wanted, having what he set out to get. And now he was reduced to being a semi-invalid. But one thing that showed the strength that was still in him was that you *never* heard him complain. He said, "How's the cattle?"

I said, "They're doing all right, but I tell you we could do with a little of Noah's flood right now. All this heat and no rain is curing the grass off way ahead of time. If it doesn't let up we'll be feeding hay by late September, early October. And that will play hell on our supply. Could be we won't have enough to last through the winter. Norris thinks we ought to sell off five hundred head or so, but the market is doing poorly right now. I'd rather chance the weather than take a sure beating by selling off."

He sort of shrugged and closed his eyes. The whiskey was relaxing him. He said, "You're the boss."

"Yeah," I said. "Damn my luck."

I wandered out of the back of the house. Even though it was nearing seven o'clock of the evening it was still good and hot. Off in the distance, about a half a mile away, I could see the outline of the house I was building for Nora and myself. It was going to be a close thing to get it finished by our wedding day. Not having any riders to spare for the project, I'd imported a building contractor from Galveston, sixty miles away. He'd arrived with a half a dozen Mexican laborers and a few skilled masons and they'd set up a little tent city around the place. The contractor had gone back to Galveston to fetch more materials, leaving his

Mexicans behind. I walked along idly, hoping he wouldn't forget that the job wasn't done. He had some of my money, but not near what he'd get when he finished the job.

Just then Ray Hays came hurrying across the back lot toward me. Ray was kind of a special case for me. The only problem with that was that he knew it and wasn't a bit above taking advantage of the situation. Once, a few years past, he'd saved my life by going against an evil man that he was working for at the time, an evil man who meant to have my life. In gratitude I'd given Ray a good job at the Half-Moon, letting him work directly under Ben, who was responsible for the horse herd. He was a good, steady man and a good man with a gun. He was also fair company. When he wasn't talking.

He came churning up to me, mopping his brow. He said, "Lordy, boss, it is—"

I said, "Hays, if you say it's hot I'm going to knock you down."

He gave me a look that was a mixture of astonishment and hurt. He said, "Why, whatever for?"

I said, "*Everybody* knows it's hot. Does every son of a bitch you run into have to make mention of the fact?"

His brow furrowed. "Well, I never thought of it that way. I 'spect you are right. Goin' down to look at yore house?"

I shook my head. "No. It makes me nervous to see how far they've got to go. I can't see any way it'll be ready on time."

He said, "Miss Nora ain't gonna like that."

I gave him a look. "I guess you felt forced to say that."

He looked down. "Well, maybe she won't mind."

I said, grimly, "The hell she won't. She'll think I did it a-purpose."

"Aw, she wouldn't."

"Naturally you know so much about it, Hays. Why don't you tell me a few other things about her."

"I was jest tryin' to lift your spirits, boss."

I said, "You keep trying to lift my spirits and I'll put you on the haying crew."

He looked horrified. No real cowhand wanted any work he couldn't do from the back of his horse. Haying was a hot, hard, sweaty job done either afoot or from a wagon seat. We generally brought in contract Mexican labor to handle ours. But I'd been known in the past to discipline a cowhand by giving him a few days on the hay gang. Hays said, "Boss, now I never meant nothin'.

275

I swear. You know me, my mouth gets to runnin' sometimes. I swear I'm gonna watch it."

I smiled. Hays always made me smile. He was so easily buffaloed. He had it soft at the Half-Moon and he knew it and didn't want to take any chances on losing a good thing.

I lit up a cigarillo and watched dusk settle in over the coastal plains. It wasn't but three miles to Matagorda Bay and it was quiet enough I felt like I could almost hear the waves breaking on the shore. Somewhere in the distance a mama cow bawled for her calf. The spring crop was near about weaned by now, but there were still a few mamas that wouldn't cut the apron strings. I stood there reflecting on how peaceful things had been of late. It suited me just fine. All I wanted was to get my house finished, marry Nora and never handle another gun so long as I lived.

The peace and quiet were short-lived. Within twenty-four hours we'd had a return telegram from Jack Cole. It said:

YOUR LAND OCCUPIED BY TEN TO TWELVE MEN STOP CAN'T BE SURE WHAT THEY'RE DOING BECAUSE THEY RUN STRANGERS OFF STOP APPEAR TO HAVE A GOOD MANY CATTLE GATHERED STOP APPEAR TO BE FENCING STOP ALL I KNOW STOP.

I read the telegram twice and then I said, "Why this is crazy as hell! That land wouldn't support fifty head of cattle."

We were all gathered in the big office. Even Dad was there, sitting in his rocking chair. I looked up at him. "What do you make of this, Howard?"

He shook his big, old head of white hair. "Beats the hell out of me, Justa. I can't figure it."

Ben said, "Well, I don't see where it has to be figured. I'll take five men and go down there and run them off. I don't care what they're doing. They ain't got no business on our land."

I said, "Take it easy, Ben. Aside from the fact you don't need to be getting into any more fights this year, I can't spare you or five men. The way this grass is drying up we've got to keep drifting those cattle."

Norris said, "No, Ben is right. We can't have such affairs going on with our property. But we'll handle it within the law. I'll simply take the train down there, hire a good lawyer and have the matter settled by the sheriff. Shouldn't take but a few days."

Well, there wasn't much I could say to that. We couldn't very well let people take advantage of us, but I still hated to be without Norris's services even for a few days. On matters other than the ranch he was the expert, and it didn't seem like there was a day went by that some financial question didn't come up that only he could answer. I said, "Are you sure you can spare yourself for a few days?"

He thought for a moment and then nodded. "I don't see why not. I've just moved most of our available cash into short-term municipal bonds in Galveston. The market is looking all right and everything appears fine at the bank. I can't think of anything that might come up."

I said, "All right. But you just keep this in mind. You are not a gun hand. You are not a fighter. I do not want you going anywhere near those people, whoever they are. You do it legal and let the sheriff handle the eviction. Is that understood?"

He kind of swelled up, resenting the implication that he couldn't handle himself. The biggest trouble I'd had through the years when trouble had come up had been keeping Norris out of it. Why he couldn't just be content to be a wagon load of brains was more than I could understand. He said, "Didn't you just hear me say I intended to go through a lawyer and the sheriff? Didn't I just say that?"

I said, "I wanted to be sure you heard yourself."

He said, "Nothing wrong with my hearing. Nor my approach to this matter. You seem to constantly be taken with the idea that I'm always looking for a fight. I think you've got the wrong brother. I use logic."

"Yeah?" I said. "You remember when that guy kicked you in the balls when they were holding guns on us? And then we chased them twenty miles and finally caught them?"

He looked away. "That has nothing to do with this."

"Yeah?" I said, enjoying myself. "And here's this guy, shot all to hell. And what was it you insisted on doing?"

Ben laughed, but Norris wouldn't say anything.

I said, "Didn't you insist on us standing him up so you could kick him in the balls? Didn't you?"

He sort of growled, "Oh, go to hell."

I said, "I just want to know where the logic was in that."

He said, "Right is right. I was simply paying him back in kind. It was the only thing his kind could understand."

I said, "That's my point. You just don't go down there and go to paying back a bunch of rough hombres in kind. Or any other currency for that matter."

That made him look over at Dad. He said, "Dad, will you make him quit treating me like I was ten years old? He does it on purpose."

But he'd appealed to the wrong man. Dad just threw his hands in the air and said, "Don't come to me with your troubles. I'm just a boarder around here. You get your orders from Justa. You know that."

Of course he didn't like that. Norris had always been a strong hand for the right and wrong of a matter. In fact, he may have been one of the most stubborn men I'd ever met. But he didn't say anything, just gave me a look and muttered something about hoping a mess came up at the bank while he was gone and then see how much boss I was.

But he didn't mean nothing by it. Like most families, we fought amongst ourselves and, like most families, God help the outsider who tried to interfere with one of us.

Norris got away on the noon train the next day. I took him in myself as a good excuse to go by and see Nora. The last thing I told him was not to spend much time or money on the matter. I'd said, "Just put it in the hands of a good lawyer and then get on back here. Your time is too valuable to waste fooling around with that worthless land."

He'd said, "I'll wire you my plans."

I'd said, "You just wire me what train to meet in the next couple or three days."

I'd come into town in the buckboard because I intended on bringing home a few supplies. So before I went to hunt up Miss Nora I took the wagon and team over to the livery stable to see to their watering and feeding. Besides, it was the noon hour and I didn't want to just drop in at the Parker's unannounced.

For lack of something better to do I went into Crooks Saloon & Cafe and had a beer and a bowl of stew. I never passed up a chance to eat in town when I could. It meant just one less meal I'd have to endure at Buttercup's hands.

Lew Vara, the sheriff, was at the bar. When he seen I'd finished my stew he ambled over. Lew and I were pretty near the same age. Before he'd got to be sheriff he and I had had just about the roughest fist fight I'd ever been involved in. I'd finally won it, but I'd done so unfairly. He'd had me nearly finished and I'd grabbed a revolver off the floor and split his head open with it. It had been understood that he was going to come for me when he got able, but that hadn't been the case. Instead of holding what I'd done against me, he said he reckoned he'd of done the same himself if he could have reached anything. Then, after that, he'd been a big help to us in some trouble we were having at the time. The upshot had been that we'd stood him for sheriff against the then sheriff, a man we felt had gone wrong. He'd won and it had been the making of him.

Lew had a good bit of Mexican in him, but you'd have never known it to look at him. We weighed about the same, but he was a couple of inches shorter than I was, with heavy shoulders and big, muscled-up arms. The man could hit like the kick of a mule.

We talked a while about nothing and I sent for another round of beer. After a time, I told him about the business down along the border and he was as surprised as I was. He said, "Hell, I know that country like the back of my hand. They ain't nothing worth stealing down there if you threw in Laredo and Nuevo Laredo in the bargain."

I told him I knew but that we had to look into it. I said, "I just put Norris on the train there."

He raised his eyebrows. "Norris? Padnuh, that's pretty rough country down there. Bunch of bad hombres. You sure you should have sent Norris?"

I told him how we were going to play it. I said, "I can't see how he could get into any trouble that way."

But he shook his head. "I don't know about that. Laredo is one town you can get into trouble just being on the wrong side of the street. Maybe you should have sent Ben with him."

I said, "Huh! Now *that* would have been looking for trouble. Naw, it'll be all right. Norris will get a lawyer and the sheriff will run the squatters off. It won't come to nothing."

When it was good after one o'clock I went and got the buckboard and stopped it in front of Parker's Mercantile. The interior was cool and dark and felt mighty pleasant after the heat of the day. Lonnie Parker, Nora's dad, was behind the main counter. His face lit up when I came in. "Why dog my cats," he said. "Here's the bridegroom."

"Unless Nora's come to her senses."

"I wouldn't count on that," he said. "You never saw such a

power of sewing as has been going on at the house in all your life. How come ever' time a woman goes to get married they got to take to needle and thread? I tell you, a man is lucky to get a meal around my place these days."

I told him he looked to be holding his own and gave him my list of supplies. He let out a yell—"Harvey! You, Harvey!"—and about a seventeen-year-old rawboned kid came skidding out of the back and reported for duty at the counter. Lonnie gave him the list and told him to load it in my buckboard.

I said, "Reckon Nora's home?"

"Yeah, but you'll play hell finding her amidst all the material and cloth goods and thread."

I said I thought I'd stroll down and make a short visit while Harvey was getting my order up. Lonnie said he'd send the kid down with the wagon and have him park it under the shade tree. He gave me a wink and said, "You might be surprised how short yore visit is. Right now you is the least part of this wedding. Women set a great deal of store by weddings and they don't much take to men gettin' in the way."

Lonnie hadn't exaggerated over much. Both Nora and her mother were rushing around like chickens with their heads cut off. Nora answered the door with an oh-it's-just-you look on her face, but she bade me come in. "But stay out of the way," she said.

So I went in and watched them, taking a seat on the divan. They had a huge cedar chest in the middle of the room and they were busy filling it up and then taking sheets and pillow cases and comforters and I don't know what all out and then putting them back in again. And when they weren't doing that they were having hurried conversations about swatches of cloth and hemlines and other things I didn't know a great deal about.

I just sat there watching Nora. As hot as it was and as hurried as she was she still looked as cool and collected as a cold beer. Her light brown hair bore a deep sheen, like she'd just finished brushing it, and the square-cut opening in the top of her bodice was big enough to reveal a span of clear, cool, cream-colored skin. Just below that bodice was the swell of her breasts against the thin gingham of her dress. I'd touched those breasts bare in the moonlight one night when we'd both got carried away. I'd even kissed one. But that had been as far as it went. But just the thought, just looking at her and remembering, made my neck get thick like a rutting bull and put the taste of copper in my mouth. I could only guess at what the silken feel of the inside of her thighs would do to me. Just thinking about it was doing enough and I forced myself to wrench my mind around in another direction before it became obvious what I was thinking about.

After about a half an hour of watching two women scurrying and scattering I figured I'd been ignored long enough. I got up and said, "Well, I reckon I'll be getting on back. Y'all appear to be pretty busy."

Nora turned around and looked at me like I was a truant trying to slip out of the schoolroom. She said, "Justa Williams, you sit right back down there. I want to talk to you."

I said, "When?"

She had several pins in her mouth so it come out kind of mumbled, but she said, "Here in a minute. Besides, you ought to stay for supper."

Of course the idea of eating hers or her mother's cooking was always bribe enough for me. But I couldn't see when they were going to have time to fix it. I said, doubtfully, "Y'all are plannin' on cooking, are you?"

"Well, of course," she said. "Did you think we couldn't hem up a few sheets and cook too? Now you go on down to Crooks and drink a beer. But don't you dare drink too many. You come back in about an hour."

So I went down to Crooks and had a beer. Since she'd told me not to have too many I didn't. But since she hadn't said nothing about whiskey I did have several tumblers of that. I also played a little poker and managed to win about forty dollars. I arrived back at the house at about five, just in time for supper, and got a good eye-scolding from Nora.

Later, when it had cooled down a little, we sat in the swing on the front porch. I was feeling pretty mellow after a supper of fried chicken and mashed potatoes and gravy. Or at least I was until Nora wanted to know when the furniture was going to arrive. We'd picked it out in Galveston better than a month before and some of it had to come from New Orleans and other points. I said, a little uncomfortably, "It'll be here right about the time the house is finished."

She asked, "And when will that be? You keep saying we'll go see it when it's finished. And I keep expecting you every day."

I said, reluctantly, "Well, there's been a small delay."

"Oh, no," she said, and put her hand to her cheek.

281

"Don't worry," I said hastily. "It'll be all right. Fact is we run short of those red Mexican roof tiles you wanted. Said they went with the house. Well, the contractor has gone back to Galveston to get more. Said a boat ought to be in from Vera Cruz right away with another shipment."

She genuinely looked distressed. She said, "Oh, Justa, don't tell me it's not going to be ready in time."

I said, "I'm not telling you it's not going to be ready in time. Did I say it wouldn't? Listen, if I have to I'll stand over that building crew with a whip in my hand."

She said, "Justa, it just has to be. The invitations have gone out. Mother and I are working ourself to death to finish my trousseau."

Well, I didn't know what that was, but I figured it had something to do with all the sewing and flaying around. I said, "Hell, Nora, even if it's not finished on the exact date we can always stay in the big house until it's done."

I might as well have slapped her across the face the way she jumped back. She said, with plenty of gumption, "Justa Williams, I am not going to be staying in someone else's house. I'll stay in my own house or I won't get married at all."

I said, "But we're going on a honeymoon. That's two weeks."

"I want it ready before we leave. And that's that."

There wasn't a hell of a lot I could say to that. I just stood up and put on my hat and said I'd better be getting back to the ranch. She gave me her cheek to kiss, which was not a good sign. As I left I said I'd have the house ready if I had to go to Mexico myself and fetch the tiles back single-handedly. It didn't warm her up over much.

A special offer for people who enjoy reading the best Westerns published today. If you enjoyed this book, subscribe now and get . . .

TWO FREE WESTERNS!
A $5.90 VALUE—NO OBLIGATION

If you enjoyed this book and would like to read more of the very best Westerns being published today, you'll want to subscribe to True Value's Western Home Subscription Service. If you enjoyed the book you just read and want more of the most exciting, adventurous, action packed Westerns, subscribe now.

TWO FREE BOOKS

When you subscribe, we'll send you your first month's shipment of the newest and best 6 Westerns for you to preview. With your first shipment, two of these books will be yours as our introductory gift to you absolutely **FREE**, regardless of what you decide to do.

Special Subscriber Savings

As a True Value subscriber all regular monthly selections will be billed at the low subscriber price of just $2.45 each. That's at least a savings of $3.00 each month below the publishers price. There is never any shipping, handling or other hidden charges. What's more there is no minimum number of books you must buy, you may return any selection for full credit and you can cancel your subscription at any time. A TRUE VALUE!

Mail the coupon below

To start your subscription and receive 2 FREE WESTERNS, fill out the coupon below and mail it today. We'll send you first shipment which includes 2 FREE BOOKS as soon as we receive it.